SHILOH

The Civil War Battles Series
by James Reasoner

Manassas

SHILOH

James Reasoner

CUMBERLAND HOUSE
NASHVILLE, TENNESSEE

Published by Cumberland House Publishing, Inc., 431 Harding Industrial Drive, Nashville, Tennessee 37211.

Cover design by Bob Bubkis, Nashville, Tennessee.

Library of Congress Cataloging-in-Publication Data is available

ISBN 1-58182-048-8

99-046301

Printed in the United States of America.

1 2 3 4 5 6 7 8—03 02 01 00 99

For Livia, of course,
because I couldn't have done it without her

Chapter One

G ET UP, BRANNON." A moment of silence followed the command, then the harsh voice directed, "Blast it, on your feet, Reb!" A hard jab of a booted toe accompanied the words.

Coriolanus Troilus Brannon groaned and rolled over. He wasn't really seeking to escape from the voice or the threat of a harder kick. He knew he couldn't escape. But if he could just snatch one more moment of rest, a few more heartbeats of blessed oblivion . . .

This time the thud of the boot was harder and made pain shoot through Cory's body.

"I'm gettin' up, Mr. Vickery," he mumbled. "I swear I am . . ."

"Then do it. We ain't got all day, and them crates won't load themselves."

Cory pushed himself to a sitting position and pried his eyes open. All day? The sun wasn't even up yet. He looked across the broad, ceaselessly moving waters of the Mississippi and saw a lighter half-circle, like the band at the bottom of a fingernail, extending into the sky over the eastern horizon. The sun wouldn't be up for an hour yet.

He supposed he should be grateful that Mr. Vickery had roused him early so he could get his work done before the steamy heat came down over the land like a wool blanket. The only problem with that was that it was already hot, even though the sun wasn't up.

If it was this bad now, what would it be like by midafternoon? And when was fall going to arrive? Cory asked himself. Late September it was and still as hot as it had been in the dog days of August.

"Well?" Mr. Vickery demanded.

Cory pushed himself to his feet. "Yes sir," he managed to say fairly clearly, even though his throat was thick with tiredness

9

and thirst. He saw that the other men who had been sleeping under the shed were already trudging out onto the dock, gray figures moving in a gray landscape. Cory stumbled after them.

He was a tall young man in his early twenties, and at one time he had been pretty sturdily built. The past few months had honed that off of him like a sharp knife so now he supposed he looked more like a scarecrow than anything human. Even after all the hardship, however, his face still had a hint of fullness. His sister Cordelia had always said that he had a baby's face, even though she was the youngest one in the family, and Cory supposed that was true. He had tightly curled brown hair that lay close to his head like a skullcap, and his beard was thin and wispy. The whipcord trousers, linsey-woolsey shirt, and boots that were run down at the heels were the only clothes he owned. He guessed he would wear them until they rotted and fell off him. He surely couldn't afford to buy any new ones. When these clothes were worn out and he was naked, he thought, he would run through the streets of New Madrid, Missouri, and flap his arms and screech like some sort of crazed giant bird until finally somebody shot him and put him out of his misery.

That was just the weariness talking, he told himself. He wasn't really crazy. He was just tired, a tiredness that had settled down deep in the bone, and hungry. There'd be food after the crates were loaded on the wagons. Mr. Vickery would give all his dock workers something to eat, a handful of grits, a scrap of salt pork.

Cory followed the other men onto the dock, went to the big stack of crates they had unloaded from a riverboat the day before, and put his arms around one of them. The raw wood was rough and splintery on his hands. He didn't feel the pain, not much anyway. Fire rippled across his back and shoulders as he lifted the crate and turned back toward the waiting wagons.

An hour, he thought. It wouldn't take much longer than that to load all the crates. Work for an hour, and then there would be food, and a few minutes of blessed rest . . .

"'MR. VICKERY says that in a fortnight, he will make me the assistant superintendent of the docks, with an appropriate increase in my wages,'" Cordelia Brannon read from the letter in her hand. "'I expect that within the year I shall be in charge of all the daily operations of the port of New Madrid.'" Cordelia looked up, her green eyes shining. "My, doesn't it sound like Cory's doing well for himself."

On the other side of the parlor, her mother, Abigail, continued rocking slowly in the rocking chair. Back and forth, back and forth. Without looking up at Cordelia, without taking her eyes from the needlework in her lap, Abigail asked, "When did your brother write that letter?"

"Back in July." Cordelia looked again at the date at the top of the single sheet of paper. "July 12, 1861, it says."

"I wonder why it took more than two months to get here," Abigail mused.

"Yankees probably held it up for some reason," Titus pronounced sourly.

Abigail nodded. "More than likely." She didn't have any more use for Yankees than her son did. "I hear tell they've invaded Saint Louis and taken over just about all of Missouri." She sighed. "I wish Cory hadn't taken it into his head to go west."

It was a lament that all the members of the Brannon family had heard more than once. Cory the wandering son. Cory the restless one, the one who hadn't been able to live within the boundaries of the family farm, who had set out to make his fortune on his own.

Still, thought Cordelia, from the sound of the letter he had written from New Madrid, he was well on his way to doing that. Assistant superintendent—that was a mighty fine job, wasn't it?

Evening had fallen over Culpeper County, Virginia, the Confederate States of America. Chores were over for the day on the Brannon farm, several miles from the county seat of Culpeper. A lamp burned in the parlor, casting enough light for Cordelia to read her brother Cory's letter for the dozenth time and for Abigail to work on her needlework. Across the room, Titus Andronicus Brannon sat on a ladderback chair and whittled, leaning forward so that his long dark hair fell around his face and masked his expression. Henry, the youngest of the Brannon brothers, sat cross-legged on the floor and hummed softly to himself. Mac, the oldest of the brothers still at home, was out in the barn with the horses. He usually stayed out there pretty late, and often Cordelia had wondered what he was doing. Probably talking to them, she had decided after pondering the question. MacBeth Richard Brannon had always felt more comfortable around horses than people. He wasn't likely to change.

Abigail tied off a stitch and set her handwork aside. "I believe I'll turn in," she announced. She stood up, her movements slow and stiff with late middle age. Her fingers were still as deft and nimble as ever—the elaborate pattern on the sampler she was producing was proof of that—but the rest of her was slowing down. She said to her children, "Don't forget to say your prayers before you go to bed."

"We won't, Mama," Cordelia said, replying for Titus and Henry as well as for herself. She tried not to feel resentment toward her mother. Here she was, eighteen years old—well, nearly eighteen—and Abigail still talked to her like she was a little girl. But Abigail talked to Cordelia's brothers like that, too, even Mac, who was nearly thirty years old. And she had talked to Will like that when he was still at home, too, Cordelia recalled, and Will was the eldest. Children were always children, and parents were always parents, no matter how many years they'd spent here on God's green earth.

Cordelia wished she hadn't thought about Will. She missed him so much it was like a physical pain, a cramp in her insides. She wondered where he was tonight. Probably sitting around a campfire in front of a tent in some Confederate army camp, maybe laughing and singing with the other soldiers.

Cordelia hoped Will was all right, wherever he was.

OVER THE objections of his mother, his father had named him William Shakespeare Brannon after the man John Brannon admired most in all the world, living or dead. No one even came close to the Bard of Avon as far as the elder Brannon was concerned. Growing up, Will had heard probably thousands of lines from the plays and the sonnets being quoted by his father, the eloquent words coming easily and dramatically from the tongue of John Brannon. Sometimes when he was listening to his father, anything had seemed possible to Will, no matter how grand or glorious.

Right now, as he crouched in a ditch in a driving rain and felt the water rising, his ambition was to live through the night without either drowning or getting shot by a Yankee.

"Dang it, Cap'n," Sgt. Darcy Bennett hissed beside Will, "I didn't sign up to be no frog!"

Will made a quieting motion, even though he wasn't sure if Darcy could see him or not in the darkness. He didn't think anybody could have heard the sergeant's whisper over the steady sloshing sound of the rain, but he didn't want to take chances. There was a Union patrol in this area of northern Virginia; Will was certain of that. Confederate scouts had seen them earlier in the evening, just before night fell and the rain began. It was entirely possible the Yankees knew that Will and his men were out here, too. And so they all blundered around blindly in the wet darkness, hoping part of the time that they would encounter the enemy—and praying fervently the rest of the time that they wouldn't.

Finally, Will had had enough and ordered his men into the ditch beside the narrow, crooked road. The road was what they were supposed to be defending in the first place. If the Yankees came marching along it—and only a damn Yankee would try to march in weather like this, Will thought—he and his boys would be ready to turn them back.

Darcy flexed his right shoulder and muttered, "Sure does stiffen up in wet weather like this."

Will didn't try to silence his sergeant this time. After all, it was indirectly Will's fault that Darcy had been wounded during the battle of Manassas a couple of months earlier. It hadn't even been a Union minié ball that had plowed through Darcy's upper chest, luckily missing his right lung and any bones. The shot had been fired by Ransom Fogarty, an old enemy of Will's from back home in Culpeper County, where Will had been the sheriff and the Fogartys a family of no-account thieves and murderers. Not even war had been enough to stop the feud between Will and the Fogartys; Ransom and George, the surviving brothers, had enlisted in the army at the same time as Will, just so they could follow him and bide their time until they could take their revenge on him for killing their younger brother, Joe.

George and Ranse were both dead now. The feud was over, or at least Will hoped so. There had been no mention of trouble in the letters he'd received from his sister, Cordelia.

Darcy Bennett had recovered from his wound, since he'd been fortunate enough not to get blood poisoning. His big, burly frame had shrunk a bit during his recuperation in a Richmond hospital, but he was pretty much back to normal now and had been happy to reclaim his place as top sergeant in the company Will commanded. Tonight, however, the two-month-old injury was hurting again, as it probably would for the rest of Darcy's life under certain conditions.

Will was about to offer a word of sympathy when a faint noise caught his attention. He waited, listening intently, to see if it was repeated. After a moment, he heard it again: a soggy, slapping sound. It was followed a minute later by several more.

A humorless grin stretched Will's mouth. Bless the Yankees and their inflexible ways. A group of men couldn't march on even a muddy road without making *some* noise. The Union patrol should have been stealing through the woods. That was what Will would have been doing if the tables had been turned and he'd been searching for the camp of Stonewall Jackson's Thirty-third Virginia.

But then, he was an old country boy, Will told himself. Couldn't expect those Yankees, most of whom he figured came from big cities, to know how to do much of anything.

He tapped Darcy on the shoulder and pointed down the road. It was too dark to see anything, but Will could hear, and the sounds of marching men grew louder. Even over the continuing rustle of the rain, he could now detect metal gear clinking. The Yankee commander, whoever he was, was doing a mighty poor job of keeping his men quiet.

Will sensed as much as saw or heard his men tensing and preparing to meet the enemy. In a downpour such as this, it was extremely difficult to get a rifle to work. A man sure couldn't bet his life that his powder would be dry enough to fire. That meant the coming clash would be work for bayonets and sabers. Bloody work. The sort where you looked into the enemy soldier's dying eyes from a distance of a few inches—or he watched the life go out of yours.

Will swallowed hard. The Yankees were here now, only a few yards down the road. They came out of the shadows and the curtain of rain, and there they were, dark shapeless figures moving through the night.

With a long, shrill yell, Will came up out of the ditch, his saber clutched tightly in his hand. He swung it as hard as he could at the figure in the lead. The Yankee tried to twist out of the way, but he was too late. Will felt his steel slice through flesh and then crunch against bone as the saber cleaved through the Union officer's shoulder all the way down to his collarbone.

Rebel yells filled the night, the ululating cries that were designed to strike terror into Yankee hearts. Will didn't know if they did or not, but if he heard somebody coming after him and hollering like that, he would be scared. With a grunt, he wrenched his saber loose from the body of the man he had just either killed or badly wounded. The man toppled to the side.

Guns popped, so somebody had dry enough powder to fire. Orange muzzle flashes split the darkness. Will whirled around, still yelling at the top of his lungs. That was another trick the Yankees hadn't tumbled to: in a fight such as this, where it was too dark to tell friend from foe, the Rebel yell was one way for the Confederate soldiers to recognize each other.

Of course, the sound provided something for the Yankees to aim their guns at, but no system was perfect.

Will saw one of the blue-uniformed Yankee troopers stumbling toward him, rifle held low so that the soldier could bring his bayonet up in a disemboweling stroke. Will didn't give the man time enough to do that. He slashed from left to right with the saber and then darted backward to avoid the clumsy attack. The trooper dropped his rifle and fell to his knees. He made a horrible gurgling sound as his hands went to his throat, which the tip of Will's blade had sliced open cleanly. After a couple of seconds, he pitched forward and died, his blood pumping out to mingle with the mud.

Boots slipping on the slick road, Will made another half-turn, looking for someone else to fight. No one was within arm's length of him. He heard the sounds of men struggling and dying nearby in the darkness. No more guns were being fired. A few rounds were all the Yankees had been able to manage. Will stopped yelling, but he didn't lower his sword.

Gradually, all the sounds except for the rain faded away. After a moment of silence, Darcy Bennett called, "Cap'n?"

"Over here, Sergeant," Will replied.

"Looks like all the Yanks are dead, Cap'n."

"Someone strike a light."

A slicker was tented over a small pile of tinder from a man's pouch. The troops didn't have any matches, so a spark had to be struck from flint and steel. A moment passed, and then a tiny flame curled from the tinder, and someone used a splinter to transfer the flame from the tinder to the wick of a lantern. It was a delicate operation under such wet conditions, but eventually the lantern was burning, and it cast a yellow circle of light over the road and the bodies of the six Yankees sprawled there.

Darcy held the lantern while another man checked the bodies. He looked up at Darcy and nodded curtly. The sergeant turned to Will and noted, "All dead, Cap'n."

Will was looking at the insignia on the uniforms of the Union soldiers. The first man he had struck down, the man who had been leading the enemy patrol, was only a corporal. No wonder he hadn't been very good at his job. The other five were all privates . . .

"Damn it!" Will exclaimed involuntarily as a thought flashed through his mind. Not even the Yankees would trust a patrol to a corporal. Not unless that patrol was really bait.

Will's hand shot out and knocked the lantern from Darcy's hand. The glass chimney shattered when it hit the road, and the flame sputtered out. Too late. Already more muzzle flashes winked from the trees on both sides of the road. A trap, Will thought bitterly as he shouted, "Down! Get down!"

And he had walked right into it, yelling blithely at the top of his lungs.

CORY'S HAND clenched tightly around the coin he held. He walked into the tavern, squinting a little at the sting of the thick haze of smoke floating in the air. Raucous laughter, both male and female, filled the room along with the smoke. Cory moved through the crowd toward the bar, being careful not to jostle anyone. The last thing he wanted tonight was trouble.

His body ached all over from the day's work on the docks. He had heard talk about how the war was going to shut down the riverboat trade on the Mississippi, but Cory hadn't seen any evidence of that so far. His throbbing muscles bore mute witness to the amount of cargo he had loaded and unloaded from the sidewheelers and sternwheelers.

He had gotten his pay today, such as it was, and he wanted to buy a hot meal and a bucket of beer. If he could just have those two things, he might feel human again, he thought. A real bed might have been nice, too, but his wages wouldn't stretch that far. He would have to settle for continuing to sleep under the dockside shed with several of the other workers.

Farther south, in Memphis and New Orleans, they would have slaves doing the work on the docks, he thought. Up here in Missouri, folks couldn't decide if they wanted to be a slave state or free. It was the same way across the river in Kentucky. The Confederacy claimed both states, but that didn't mean the majority of the people in Missouri and Kentucky went along with that claim. There had been skirmishes all over between Unionists and Confederates, and when Cory thought about it—which wasn't all that often, really—he didn't have any idea which side in the struggle was going to emerge triumphant.

As a matter of fact, he didn't care, either. His only real concern was making it from one day to the next.

This waterfront dive was called Red Mike's, and the man who gave it its name was standing behind the bar. Mike had a thatch of fiery red hair and a sweeping mustache of the same shade. He sported thick muttonchop whiskers, too, which only partially concealed the deep pits of smallpox scars across his cheeks. The apron he wore over his rough clothes might have been white once; now it was a filthy gray. Since fights were common in the place, he kept a bungstarter handy underneath the bar. Rumor had it there was a sawed-off shotgun down there, too, in case things got really dicey.

When Cory finally worked his way to the bar, Mike barely glanced at him. "What'll it be?" the bartender asked over the rumble of the crowd.

Cory leaned over the bar so he could make himself heard. "Bucket of beer. And could I get something to eat?"

"Somethin' to eat?" Mike repeated. "Ha! You must be really hungry, boy, if you're willin' to sample the swill we got in here!"

Cory placed the coin on the bar but kept his hand on it. Mike could see the edges of it poking out from under Cory's fingers. "A bucket of beer and something hot to eat, if I could." Cory felt as if it were taking most of his meager supply of energy just to speak.

"Sure, sure," Mike muttered. He turned away and yelled something through the small window that led into the tavern's back room. The kitchen was in a separate building out back, but Mike's orders would be relayed to the cook by the small boy who served as a runner. Mike turned back toward Cory and took a small wooden bucket from under the bar. He started filling it from a keg.

"I tell ye, I've heard that the damn Yankees are planning to take hold of the river all the way down to New Orleans, even as we speak." The loud voice came from farther along the bar. "Mark my words."

"And what's wrong with that?" another voice challenged. "It's about time somebody taught those stinking Rebs a lesson."

Cory paid little attention to the words. *Damn Yankees. Stinking Rebs.* They were just meaningless sounds to his ears, like the babbling of a baby. His eyes avidly followed Mike's movements as the bartender set the bucket of beer in front of him.

"Food'll be here in a few minutes," Mike said. "I'll take that money now."

Reluctantly, Cory lifted his hand from the coin. Mike raked it off the smudged, dirty surface of the bar and caught it deftly in his other hand. He bit it to make sure it was the real thing then dropped it in a pocket of his apron.

Cory wrapped his hands around the bucket, lifted it, and sipped the beer. It was weak, bitter stuff, but his sip turned into a healthy swallow. Maybe he would sleep better tonight, he hoped.

He lowered the bucket, licked foam from his lips, lifted it again. Before he could take another drink, however, someone jostled him heavily from behind. Cory was knocked forward, and the bucket slipped from his hands. Most of the beer dumped down the front of his shirt and trousers before he was able to grab the bucket and right it.

"Watch what you're doing, damn it," someone growled at him.

Cory was never completely sure what happened next. Something ruptured inside of him, a festering sore comprised of the high hopes he'd had when he left home and the dismal reality he'd found once he was on his own. Bit by bit, the hardships and indignities of the past few months had built up, and his hopes now had the taste of bile and corruption. That was what came flooding up his throat. It tore out of him in a high-pitched yell as he swung the nearly empty bucket at the head of the man who had just bumped into him.

The man saw the bucket coming, let out a desperate curse, and tried to duck out of the way. The bucket cracked against the side of his head, but it was only a glancing blow. Still, the impact was enough to send the man staggering against the bar. He caught himself, shook his head groggily, and then pushed upright. He was almost as wide as he was tall, a Kaintuck riverman in a homespun shirt and a broad-brimmed hat that had been knocked off by the blow from the bucket. His beard bristled as he glared at Cory. The Kaintuck's hand went to the hilt of the knife tucked behind his belt as he roared, "I'll gut you for that, you damned pup!"

The rage that had filled Cory a moment earlier now ran out of him like water. He glanced down at the bucket in his hand as if he had never seen such a thing before. His eyes went back to the furious Kaintuck, who was snarling in his beard.

Cory dropped the bucket and turned to run.

Even as he did so, he felt a flash of shame. Brannons didn't run from a fight. His brother Will had been a lawman back in Culpeper County, Virginia, first a deputy and then the sheriff of the whole county. Will had faced down thieves and killers and never flinched. None of his other brothers had ever backed down from trouble, either, not even his little brother Henry.

But none of them had ever bragged about how they were going to take the world by the tail, as he had done when he left home. None of them had ever set out to make their fortune only to have everything come crashing down around them.

Damned right he was running, Cory thought. He wasn't going to stay here and let some stupid Kaintuck carve on him.

Hands grabbed him, flung him back. "Let me through! Let me through!" he barked, and his voice broke in a sob. Laughs and shouts answered him.

"Get him, Strunk!" "Carve him a new one!" "Don't let him out!"

Cory didn't have any friends here, he realized. Most of the patrons in Red Mike's were rivermen, and the few dock workers didn't give a damn what happened to Cory. He was one of them, but none of them would risk standing up for him. He was on his own.

And he was going to get killed. He knew it. He just knew it.

"Come on, boy," the Kaintuck called Strunk said in his gravelly voice. "Put up a fight, anyway, you whelp."

Cory turned slowly. The crowd had congealed into a solid half-circle around the bar, leaving an open area in which he and Strunk stood. The Kaintuck was grinning at him and weaving the knife slowly back and forth. Lamplight struck yellow glints from the blade as it moved.

From behind the bar, Red Mike said, "I don't want a lot of blood in here, Strunk. Don't make a mess of it."

"Sure, Mike. Quick and clean, if that's the way you want it."

Strunk took a step forward, and Cory felt a warm wetness seeping through the crotch of his trousers and running down his legs. He burned with shame as more laughter welled up from the onlookers.

Strunk laughed. "Sorry, Mike," he called over his shoulder to the callous bartender. "At least it ain't blood makin' a mess on the floor."

Maybe it would be better, Cory thought, if Strunk went ahead and killed him after all.

That was when the gun went off with a loud, cracking report, and a voice said commandingly into the stunned silence that followed the shot, "Leave the boy alone, Strunk, or I'll put the next ball right through that thick skull of yours."

Chapter Two

CORY DIDN'T RECOGNIZE THE voice, and his brain was still so filled with fear that it was a moment before he even comprehended the meaning of the words. But Strunk understood them, and even though the Kaintuck didn't lower the knife, he looked a bit less sure of himself than he had a moment earlier.

"This ain't your fight, Farrell," he growled, "not a bit of it."

"I'm making it my fight. Now, I won't tell you again to put that knife away and leave the boy alone."

Cory managed to turn his head and look toward the corner of the tavern where the voice came from. The crowd had parted at the sound of the shot, so Cory could see the man who stood there holding a long-barreled Colt Dragoon revolver. A wisp of powder smoke still drifted from the muzzle of the weapon.

The man was medium height and stockily built, with graying dark hair and a neatly trimmed mustache. He wore a dark suit and a string tie, and a cream-colored planter's hat sat on the table beside him. Those details impressed themselves on Cory's mind, but the main thing he noticed about the man was his eyes—dark, deep-set, intelligent eyes. Eyes with no fear in them.

"Damn it, Farrell—"

The man's thumb was hooked over the hammer of the Colt. He eared it back with a metallic ratcheting that sounded loud in the anticipatory silence that had replaced the usual hubbub in the tavern.

With a snarled curse, Strunk turned suddenly and drove the point of the knife into the bar. "There!" he snapped. "Are you satisfied now, blast it?"

"Step away from it," the man called Farrell ordered. As Strunk did so, Farrell continued, "You, boy, get out of here. Now."

25

Cory realized Farrell was talking to him. He started to edge toward the door, then stopped. He'd paid for a hot meal, and Red Mike still had the coin. But Cory hadn't gotten anything to eat.

"I was supposed to get some supper—" Cory began.

Farrell's intense gaze darted toward him. "Out, I said!"

Cory started moving again. He cast a glance at Red Mike, who was glowering at him. Mike probably wasn't too happy about having that knife stuck in his bar, even though the wooden surface was far from pristine. In fact, it was already scarred and pitted all over from hard use. Still, Cory didn't think Mike would be in any mood to give him his money back, so he didn't ask.

Men stood aside to let him through. He heard several muttered comments and derisive chuckles. Cory kept his eyes on the floor. His face was warm with shame.

Another thought occurred to him as he pushed the door open and stumbled out into the night. Strunk had friends in there; from the look and sound of things, Farrell didn't. Even armed as he was, how was Farrell going to make it out of the place unharmed? If several men jumped him, someone was bound to bring him down. Then Strunk and his cronies could do whatever they wanted to him.

Cory knew what Will would do if he were here. Will would march right back in there and make sure that Farrell made it out all right.

But he wasn't Will, Cory realized. He tried to make his feet turn back toward the door, but they wouldn't go.

The door suddenly opened again, and Cory jumped, turning around in the air so that he'd at least be facing whatever came at him. Instead of an attack, he saw a man in a planter's hat backing out of the tavern toward him. Farrell still held the revolver in his hand, though it was partially lowered now. He shut the door firmly behind him.

"Mr. Farrell?" Cory questioned.

Farrell turned quickly, the gun coming up again, and for a second Cory thought he had made a terrible mistake. It would be just his luck to be accidentally shot by the man who had just saved his life. But Farrell was able to hold off on the trigger, and he snapped, "Blast it, boy, I told you to get out of here! I thought you'd still be running. Don't you have any sense?"

The words stung. Cory explained, "I was worried about you. I thought maybe I ought to come back in and help you—"

Farrell snorted. "Fine lot of help you'd have been, pissing your britches that way. And don't think I was any too worried about that bunch in there. The word 'motley' was coined to describe them." He made a shooing motion with his free hand. "Now go on. Go crawl back into whatever hole you came out of."

"Why?" Cory's voice cracked as he asked the question.

"Why?" Farrell repeated. "So Strunk won't come after you when I'm not around to save you."

"That's what I mean," Cory followed up. "Why did you do it, Mr. Farrell? If you think I'm so no-account, why'd you step in and risk your life?" For some reason that he couldn't fathom, the answer to that question was suddenly very important to Cory, so important that he was wasting time standing here to ask it when he should have been putting distance between himself and Red Mike's.

Farrell didn't reply right away. After a moment, he muttered something under his breath and reached out to clamp his free hand around Cory's upper arm. "Come on," he commanded. "By now Strunk's getting liquored up enough so he won't care if I'm waiting out here to take a potshot at him. He'll come anyway."

Farrell began marching Cory along the boardwalk that flanked the muddy street, and the older man's grip was so strong that Cory had no choice but to go along with him. After a few moments of going past darkened businesses, Cory realized they were heading toward the waterfront. How did Farrell know that he lived and worked down at the docks? he wondered.

They followed a narrow plank walk from the main street over to the dock area. Half a dozen riverboats loomed darkly against the night sky, their Texas decks and smokestacks rearing high above the water. Farrell steered Cory toward one of the vessels.

"Strunk and his friends won't dare follow us onto the *Zephyr*," Farrell declared. "They know they would run into a much hotter reception than they'd like."

"Mr. Farrell, I . . . I can't impose on you . . ." Cory began as they reached the foot of a gangplank.

"It's Captain Farrell. This is my boat. And I'll bring anyone aboard her that I choose." Farrell tugged on Cory's arm. "Come along."

"You never did tell me why."

Farrell sighed in exasperation. "Because I see something in you, boy, that tells me you might not be as totally worthless as you appear to be. In all likelihood, I'm wrong. I have been before, on occasion." He paused, then added, "Besides, I don't like Strunk. I thought that denying him the pleasure of slitting you open from gullet to gizzard would be worthwhile."

A shudder went through Cory as he saw that grisly image in his mind. That was exactly what would have happened to him if Farrell hadn't stepped in, he knew. Out of sheer instinct, he would have put up a fight, but he would have been no match for Strunk.

"Thank you," he said quietly.

Farrell tugged on his arm again. "Come along," he ordered brusquely.

Cory let Farrell lead him up the gangplank and onto the main deck of the riverboat. Farrell had referred to the boat as the *Zephyr*, and Cory recalled seeing it dock here at New Madrid earlier in the day. The full name of the boat was the *Missouri Zephyr*, he remembered.

Something else about it nagged at him, some reason he ought to remember this particular riverboat, but for the life of him, he couldn't figure out what it was.

A tall man in the dark jacket of a crewman approached along the dimly lit deck. He asked in a deep voice, "Who's this, Cap'n? Found you a stray?"

Farrell let go of Cory's arm and turned to look directly at him. "As a matter of fact, Mr. Judson, I don't know who he is. What's your name, lad?"

Cory swallowed. "Cory Brannon, sir." He left it at that, not going into the way his father had named him after two of Shakespeare's plays.

"Looks like a water rat," Judson observed. He sniffed and then grimaced. "Smells even worse'n one."

"Indeed," agreed Farrell. "But Lydell Strunk was about to attack him with a knife in Red Mike's, and I took it upon myself to intervene."

Judson let out a low whistle. "What did Strunk do?"

"Listened to reason."

"Only after you showed him the muzzle end of that old Dragoon you carry around, I'll wager." Judson looked at Cory and shook his head disgustedly. "If it'd been anybody but Strunk about to carve you up, boy, I'd say the cap'n should've let well enough alone. But I reckon I can see why he took it on himself to step in. Want me to feed this feller and send him on his way, Cap'n?"

Farrell nodded. "Thank you, Mr. Judson. I believe I'll retire to my cabin for the evening, if I can leave matters in your capable hands."

"You sure can," Judson told him. "Miss Lucille's waitin' up for you."

"There was no need for her to do that."

"You can argue with her all you want, Cap'n. I ain't goin' to."

"Point taken, Mr. Judson." Farrell turned back to Cory. "As for you, Mr. Brannon, if I were you, I'd stay well away from Red Mike's place for the next few days. The *Prometheus* will be departing tomorrow, so if you keep your head down you shouldn't have to worry about running into Strunk, but Mike himself may bear a grudge and take it out on the handiest target."

Cory nodded, knowing that Farrell was referring to him. "Yes sir," he agreed humbly. "And . . . and thank you, sir."

"Next time you swing a bucket at someone's head . . . aim a bit better." With a chuckle, Farrell moved off down the deck, heading for the door of one of the cabins.

"Is that what you did?" Judson asked. "Busted a bucket over Strunk's head?"

"Well, I . . . tried to," Cory admitted.

Judson grunted. "Even if you'd hit him dead center, it probably wouldn't have hurt him. Strunk's got a skull like an anvil." A grin stretched across Judson's weatherbeaten face. "I ought to know, I've bruised my own knuckles on it enough times, brawlin' in taverns from N'Orleans to Pittsburgh with him."

Farrell had reached the door of the cabin. He opened it and stepped inside, and as he did, Cory looked past him and saw the young woman standing up from a chair to greet him with a worried expression on her face. The sight of her, even at this distance, was like a fist slugging Cory in the belly, and he knew now why the *Missouri Zephyr* had seemed so familiar to him . . .

IT WAS a fine June morning, with streamers of fog lingering over the surface of the river, and Cory still felt strong, still had hopes that his job on the docks would turn into something better. He saw the riverboat dock, an old, stately, fine-looking vessel. A couple of deckhands hopped off onto the dock and started winding the thick hawsers around the pilings. Cory saw the cargo piled on the forward part of the deck and knew he was likely to be unloading it later in the day. He stayed where he was, in the shade under the shed, unwilling to move out into the early morning sunlight until he had to.

Then she stepped out onto the deck from one of the cabins and strolled to the railing to look out at the docks, and Cory's breath stuck in his throat as he gazed at her. Young, probably no more than eighteen, she was, with long straight hair the color of fresh honey that swept down loose around her shoulders and framed a face so lovely that Cory thought his heart would stop dead in his chest as he stared at her. Her lips were full and red, and her chin had an almost defiant tilt to it. She was rather short, but she wasn't slight. The simple traveling gown she wore was modest, yet it revealed lush curves at breast and hip. Cory breathed, "Lord!" and it was a prayer, a prayer of thanksgiving that he had been allowed to feast his eyes on such a lovely creature.

Then she looked at him, and what he felt grew even stronger as he experienced the power of those warm brown eyes. He wished that he could crawl right into those eyes, that he was worthy enough for her to even acknowledge his existence . . .

Which, evidently, he wasn't, because her gaze didn't pause as it swept over him. Instead of her eyes locking with his so that he could wordlessly communicate what he was feeling, they moved on, ignoring him.

And Cory felt like one of the crates that he loaded and unloaded had just come smashing down on top of him, crushing him completely. If he wasn't worthy of being noticed by this beautiful young woman, then what was the point of even living? He wanted to hate her for not seeing him, for not realizing what had just happened. What could have happened.

But he couldn't hate her, and he couldn't forget her. Sometimes, over the past few months since that misty June morning, the hardships of his life had pushed his memory of her far into the back of his mind, but it had never gone away entirely. Her image was always there, ready to be called up like the memory of a breathtaking landscape or a poignant strain of music or the smell of honeysuckle with the morning dew on it.

Now, here she was again, not a memory but real and alive and less than fifty feet from him.

But the door closed, and once again she was gone.

"BRANNON? AIN'T that your name? Brannon, what the hell's wrong with you?"

Judson's harsh voice snapped Cory back to reality. He blinked and gave a little shake of his head. Had he really seen her either time, or had he just imagined her?

"That . . . that girl . . ." he managed to croak out.

"Who? Miss Lucille?" Judson's hand came down hard on Cory's shoulder and tightened painfully. He jerked Cory around to face him. "Listen to me, boy," he grated. "Riverfront scum like you ain't got no business even *thinkin'* about a fine gal like Miss Lucille, let alone lookin' at her. You steer clear, you understand?" He gave Cory a shake.

"I . . . I didn't mean anything," Cory gasped out. "I just . . . I just saw her when Captain Farrell opened the door into the cabin—"

"And where else would the cap'n's daughter be but in the cap'n's cabin?" Judson shoved Cory toward some stairs that led down to a lower deck. "Better be careful, or I'll toss you off'a this boat without givin' you something to eat first. You hungry?"

"I . . . Yes, I am," Cory answered honestly.

"Well, then, come on."

Judson was half a head taller than Cory, with wide, brawny shoulders, so Cory had little choice except to cooperate with him. As they went down to the lower deck, Judson sniffed again and said, "What the hell'd you do, wet yourself?"

Cory wished Judson would stop talking about how he smelled. "I spilled a bucket of beer on me," he confessed.

"That ain't all. Got any clean clothes, wherever it is you stay?"

"No," Cory admitted. "All I own is what I'm wearing."

"Better take care of that first, then. Come over here."

Judson led Cory over to an opening in the railing that bordered the lower deck. The river lapped gently at the hull a few feet below them. The *Missouri Zephyr* was a sidewheeler, and they were just aft of the huge paddlewheel on this side of the boat.

"What are you going to do?" Cory wanted to know.

"Fix it so you don't stink quite so bad," Judson decreed. Without any other warning, he planted a big hand in the middle of Cory's back and shoved hard, sending Cory plunging with a startled yell into the water between the boat and the dock.

The Mississippi closed over Cory's head, filling his mouth and cutting him off in mid-yell. He strangled and coughed and sank for a few feet before he started flailing desperately with his arms and kicking his feet. That brought him back up to the surface. He didn't stay up long. Once again the river swallowed him.

A strong hand reached into the water, closed on his shoulder, and hauled him up. As his head broke the surface he tried to gulp down some air, but instead he just coughed wrackingly. He felt himself being lifted, then he sprawled wetly on the deck like a beached fish. The water he had inadvertently swallowed came up, too, spewing out of his mouth sourly.

"Hell, be careful!" Judson snapped. "I'm tryin' to make you smell better, not worse."

"By . . . by drowning me?"

"By washin' those rags you got on. A dunkin' probably didn't do the rest of you too much harm, neither."

Cory pushed himself into a sitting position. "But you didn't know if I could swim!"

"Didn't figure it really mattered," Judson said with a shrug.

Cory didn't know what to say to that, so he just stumbled to his feet and leaned on the railing while he caught his breath. He wished he was bigger and stronger. He would have liked to plant a fist in Judson's ugly, smirking face.

In fact, that sounded like a pretty good idea. With a snarl, he turned and started to swing a punch.

Judson's hand closed easily around Cory's fist, stopping it short. "Don't try it, sonny," he said. "From what little I've heard 'bout your run-in with Strunk, you got a habit of lettin' your temper get away from you at the wrong time. Best you learn how to rein it in."

"You tried to kill me!" Cory accused between clenched teeth.

"Nope, just to clean you up a mite. And I reckon you don't smell *quite* as bad now." With a little push, Judson let go of Cory's fist.

Cory's arm dropped. Judson was right. He was soaked, but when the clothes dried, he probably would smell a little better. Still, his throat burned from the water he'd swallowed, and he was shaking slightly in reaction to the unexpected plunge into the river.

"Still want something to eat?" Judson asked.

Cory coughed, "Yeah. Yeah, I do."

"ME AN' the cap'n been travelin' up and down the Ohio and the Mississipp' for nigh on to ten years now," Judson announced a short while later as he sat opposite Cory at a small table in the riverboat's kitchen. Cory had a hunk of bread and a slab of roast beef in front of him, and he was tearing off pieces of both and stuffing them into his mouth greedily. The food tasted better than any he'd had in weeks.

Judson went on, "A riverman's life is the best life I've ever seen. I still thank my lucky stars I ran into the cap'n and he took me on."

Around a mouthful of bread and meat, Cory asked, "What did you do before?"

"Little bit of ever'thing," Judson replied with a shrug. "Did some blacksmithin' and some carpentry. Felled trees for a while up in Pennsylvania. Did just about any kind of honest work. River's the best, though."

"What do you do on the *Zephyr?*"

"Pilot," Judson proclaimed proudly. "The cap'n taught me. I reckon I know just about ever' foot of the Mississipp' like the back of my hand."

Cory nodded and reached for the cup of buttermilk he was using to wash down the food. After he'd taken a long swallow, he observed, "That sounds like a good life, all right. I wouldn't mind giving it a try myself."

"You?" Judson gave another contemptuous snort.

"I can do anything I set my mind to," Cory maintained stubbornly.

"Oh, sure. I can tell." Judson shook his head.

Cory felt himself growing angry again, but he remembered Judson's earlier advice. Based on the evidence of his own life, Cory knew the riverman was right: he needed to learn how to control his temper. It was the Irish in him, he supposed. He'd always believed it was only John Brannon's wanderlust he'd inherited, but Cory realized that his short fuse was probably part of his father's legacy, as well.

"All I need is a chance," he contended.

"Well, you won't get it here. The *Zephyr*'s got a full crew, if you're askin' for a job." Judson gestured toward the food. "Just be grateful you're gettin' something to eat."

"I am. I'm grateful for the food, and for everything else the captain's done for me." Cory sopped up the last of the juices from the beef with the final piece of bread and put it in his mouth. He chewed slowly, wanting to make it last.

Judson put his hands on the table and pushed himself to his feet. "All right, you've had your meal," he declared. "Time to get off the boat."

Cory wasn't ready to go. It had felt like heaven, sitting here in a real chair and eating good food. He swallowed and said quickly, "I'd like to hear more about life on the river."

"I reckon you would, but it's late and I'm all talked out." Judson came around the table and put a hand on Cory's shoulder. "Come on."

Reluctantly, Cory stood up. "Where's the captain from?" he asked, trying to draw things out just a little longer.

"He was born in England but raised in N'Orleans. That's why he talks a mite funny, that and all the book-larnin' he's had. I never met a feller who's read as much as the cap'n has." Judson pushed Cory toward the door of the kitchen. A short companionway outside led to a set of stairs. "Don't reckon you'd know anything about that."

"I can read," Cory added defensively.

"Can you now?"

"And cipher, too. All of us Brannons went to school whenever we could. Ma and Pa both insisted on it."

"Why's that?" Judson prompted as they started up the stairs.

"Well, Pa wanted us to be able to read Shakespeare, and Ma said we had to be able to read the Bible."

"Huh," Judson said. "Sounds like your folks had somethin' in common with the cap'n."

"So, you see," Cory added quickly, "maybe I would work out if somebody gave me a chance to work on a riverboat." He wasn't completely sure where the idea had come from. It was probably a mixture of things. Certainly, life here on the *Zephyr* would be easier than living and working on the docks. He had seen enough to know that already. And there was the matter of the girl, too. Miss Lucille, Judson had called her. Captain Farrell's daughter. Cory knew it was ridiculous for someone like him, gaunt and dressed in rags, to even be dreaming about a woman such as Miss Lucille Farrell.

But dreaming had always been something that came natural to him.

Judson hadn't said anything, so Cory prodded, "What about it, Mr. Judson? Do you think Captain Farrell would give me a chance?"

"He's already given you your life, boy, 'cause Strunk would've killed you, sure as hell. And he gave you the first good meal you've had in a while. I reckon that's enough."

They stepped out onto the main deck. The gangplank leading to the dock was only a few feet away. Cory hung back, not wanting to leave. He felt that if he got off this boat, he would regret it for the rest of his life.

"Please, Mr. Judson—" he began again.

"Listen," Judson warned, his voice quiet but as hard as flint. "I still ain't sure why the cap'n would risk his own hide for a water rat like you, boy, but he did, so that says somethin' good for you. That's the only reason I didn't leave you to drown in the river. But that's all it buys you. Get off this boat, and don't come back."

Cory felt the sting of tears in his eyes. They were tears of anger and frustration. His dreams of coming west and making his fame and fortune had died in the harsh, bitter light of reality. But tonight, chance had given him the opportunity for something better, only to have it denied by Judson's stubbornness.

"I'm a good worker—"

"You're no-account." Judson clenched his fists. "Get off, 'fore I bust your jaw for you."

Cory couldn't fight the man. He knew that. Judson would just thrash him, and then he'd be worse off than ever before. At least he'd gotten a good meal out of it, he told himself resignedly.

"I'm going," he whispered.

"And don't come back."

Cory turned toward the gangplank. His footsteps rang hollowly from it as he descended to the dock.

It was a long walk, each step an admission of another defeat. Halfway down, he thought about Lucille Farrell and started to stop and turn around . . . but then he kept going.

Dreams didn't come true. It was time he admitted that, no matter how bad it tasted going down.

Chapter Three

MAC BRANNON SAT BOLT upright in bed, not knowing what had woken him but instinctively sensing that something important was happening. His hand reached out to grasp his brother Will's shoulder and shake him awake.

Mac's hand closed on empty air, and he remembered that Will wasn't here anymore. Months had passed since Will had enlisted in the Confederate army and ridden off on the train to Richmond. But despite those months, Mac still sometimes forgot that his older brother was gone. He'd shared a bed with Will as far back as he could remember, and at times like this, deep in the middle of the night, it seemed that Will still ought to be there.

With a shake of his head, Mac swung his legs out of the bed and stood up. The bedroom was very dark; only a faint glow of starlight came through the curtains over the single window. Mac moved over to it and pushed the curtains aside to peer out into the night. A breeze brushed his face.

The distant whicker of a stallion came to him on the night wind.

Mac's muscles all went tense as he stood there, a tall, rangy man with a shock of brown hair that was rumpled from sleep at the moment. He leaned closer to the window as if that would allow him to see better in the darkness. He could make out the shape of the barn and the corrals beyond it, and beyond them the fields of the Brannon farm, where Mac and his brothers had been working to get some winter wheat planted. On past the fields, at the boundary of the farm, were the woods where Titus hunted deer and squirrels and raccoons.

The starlight, faint as it was, suddenly reflected on something out there at the edge of the woods. Not the sharp glint of light on metal, but rather a dull silver gleam.

41

The ghost was back, Mac thought. Back to taunt him.

He wasn't sure when he had first started thinking of the big silver gray stallion as a ghost horse, but there was no doubt in a part of his mind that was what it was. No real horse could be so smart, so fast, so elusive, so downright maddening. He remembered the night he and Will had first tried to catch the stallion, when it had tricked them and gotten past them in an attempt to break down the barn door and steal the mares inside. Then, on a later occasion, the barn had been set on fire by the Fogartys, and the stallion had shown up to warn Mac in time for him to save the horses, if not the barn itself. The barn had been rebuilt, and the Fogarty brothers were dead, but still the ghost horse came to the Brannon farm.

Mac spun away from the window and grabbed his trousers.

Two minutes later, he was hurrying down the stairs, carrying his boots so that he wouldn't make enough noise to rouse the rest of the household. He had done this before, so many times, venturing out into the night in a vain attempt to capture a phantom. Always he had failed, and he knew of no reason why tonight should be any different.

But it might be. There was always a chance . . .

He sat down on the porch steps to pull his boots on, then finished tucking his shirt into his trousers as he trotted toward the barn. He didn't go all the way in, just paused and reached inside the doorway to grab a rope that was coiled and hung on a peg. As he hurried around the barn, he started to shake out a loop in the rope.

Even if he got close enough, he probably couldn't catch the stallion, he thought. He could imagine casting his loop and seeing the rope pass right through the stallion's neck as if it weren't there. That horse was made of nothing more substantial than moonlight and mist and dreams.

Mac gave a little shake of his head. That sort of fanciful thinking was the way his father's mind had run. John Brannon should have been a poet himself, but as far as Mac knew, his father had never put pen to paper in order to write down anything more than a list for the clerk at the general store in Culpeper.

As Mac cut across the fields, his booted feet sinking into the recently plowed earth, he kept watching the edge of the woods, searching intently for another sign of the big silver gray horse. The gleam he had seen a few minutes earlier was gone now. The stallion probably was, too. Mac told himself that he would get out here only to find nothing. This was just another example of the way the ghost horse liked to mock him.

Off to his right, something moved.

Like a silver streak, like a beam of moonlight come alive, it emerged from the woods, running smoothly and easily as it curved around him in a great circle. Mac stopped short, his jaw dropping in awe. His eyes were more adjusted to the darkness now, and he could plainly see the effortless play of powerful muscles under the sleek hide. The stallion galloped as if it were running for sheer joy, and suddenly Mac was afraid. If the horse turned on him, he would have no chance against it. He would be trampled, smashed to pieces by those mighty hooves, before he even had a chance to get away.

But the horse just ran around and around him, and he turned to watch it until he was dizzy from the turning. He forced himself to close his eyes and wait for the dizziness to go away, thinking that when he opened them again, the stallion would surely be gone. He heard the rapid rhythm of the hoofbeats continue, though, until they abruptly stopped a few moments later.

Mac opened his eyes and saw the horse standing about thirty feet from him, facing him. He could hear it breathing. No ghost horse, no phantasm, but flesh and blood. Mac took a shuffling step toward the horse, then another and another. The rope hung forgotten in his hand.

Twenty feet, fifteen, ten. Mac had never been this close to the stallion before. It gave a toss of its head and let out a soft whinny. Mac lifted his hand, held it out toward the animal. Another step and another, and still the stallion didn't bolt.

"You've decided you trust me after all," Mac breathed. He hated to break the silence, but at the same time he felt compelled to speak to the horse. "You're not a ghost at all. You're real."

He reached up and out, his fear of a few moments earlier forgotten, and rested his hand on the muzzle of the huge silver gray stallion.

For a second only his hand lay there, and in that second his palm seemed aware of every strand of hair on the horse's muzzle. He felt its warm breath against his wrist as its nostrils flared.

Then, with a jerk, the stallion turned away and leaped toward the woods. Too late, Mac remembered the rope. He made a desperate cast with the loop, but it fell far short. The stallion was already gone, swallowed up by the deep shadows underneath the trees.

Mac went to his knees. A sob of loss was wrenched from him. He lifted his hand and looked at it in the starlight. He seemed to still feel the stallion's breath brushing against it.

"YOU LOOK like something the dogs dragged up, Mac," Henry said at breakfast as he looked across the table at his brother.

Mac shook his head tiredly. "I didn't sleep well last night."

"I slept just fine," Henry said. "Better'n Titus, anyway. He was tossing and turning all night. Dreaming of Polly Ebersole, I reckon."

"Don't let him hear you say that," Cordelia warned as she set a plate of biscuits on the table. "He doesn't like anyone even mentioning her name now that her father's sent her off to live in Richmond."

Henry shook his head as he dug into the pile of fried eggs on the plate in front of him. He couldn't understand how anybody could get so worked up over a girl that he would allow thoughts of her to dominate his every waking moment—and most of his sleeping ones, too, judging from how restless Titus had been at night lately. Sure, Polly was pretty. Really pretty with that blonde hair and fair skin and lovely features . . . and that slender body that curved just so in all the right places . . . and her mouth that probably tasted hot and sweet at the same time . . .

"You just got up," Cordelia said. "It's too early to be dozing off again, Henry."

He took a deep breath. "I was just . . . thinking about something."

More than thinking, he realized. He felt his face grow warm as he realized he had reacted physically to the image of Polly Ebersole that his mind had called up. He was glad he'd just started breakfast and wouldn't have to stand up for a while.

He supposed he could understand, at least a little, why Titus was so upset about Polly leaving Culpeper County. But no matter how pretty she was, there were other girls in the world every bit as pretty, and some who were considerably nicer than Polly, who had always struck Henry as more than a little uppity. Of course, that sort of attitude was to be expected, since she lived at Mountain Laurel, the biggest, fanciest plantation in the whole county. And her father was rich, too, the richest man in these parts. A colonel in the militia to boot.

"Where is Titus?" Mac asked. "I'd've thought he'd be down for breakfast before now."

As if he'd been waiting for that question, Titus's footsteps sounded heavily on the stairs leading down from the farmhouse's second floor. A moment later, he came into the dining room. His eyes had a hollow look about them, and his hair was tangled from sleep. "Mornin'," he muttered without looking at his brothers and sister.

"Good morning," Cordelia greeted him. "I'll fetch you some coffee and some food."

"I can get it myself," Titus snapped.

"No, really, I don't mind—" Cordelia began.

Mac spoke up. "Suit yourself, Titus. Cordelia, sit down and eat." His voice had the sharp tone of command to it.

That was Mac for you, Henry thought, trying to take charge of the family now that Will was gone. The mantle of leadership didn't sit easily on Mac's shoulders, though. All the Brannon boys had a bit of a dreamy side, inherited from their father, but it was stronger in Mac than in the others. He had always been content to quietly go his own way. The responsibilities he was feeling now had to be hard on him.

Titus glanced around the room and then asked, "Where's Ma?"

"She's not feeling very good this morning," Cordelia replied. "I told her I'd bring her up something to eat in a little while. She said not to hurry."

Titus shrugged and went on into the kitchen while Cordelia sat down to her own plate. A few minutes later, Titus came back carrying a plate of flapjacks and a cup of coffee. He sat down beside Henry.

As Titus did so, Henry caught a whiff of an odd scent coming from him. It was faint, but Henry recognized it: moonshine.

Henry's eyes widened in surprise. He looked down at the table in hopes of concealing his involuntary reaction. Titus hadn't been outside this morning. Smelling corn liquor on his breath like that could mean only one thing: Titus had a jug of the stuff hidden somewhere in the room he shared with Henry.

Titus had spent more time off the farm lately than usual, and on more than one occasion, Henry had seen him ride in late in the evening and stumble a bit as he was coming into the house. Titus was going off somewhere and drinking, Henry knew. He didn't know if Mac and Cordelia were aware of it or not, but he was certain his mother, Abigail, wasn't. If Abigail had known, everybody in the family would have heard her preaching to Titus about the evils of alcohol. "Wine is a mocker, strong drink is raging." That was one of the Bible verses that had been pounded into the heads of all the Brannon children as they were growing up.

Looked like it hadn't taken very well with Titus, Henry thought wryly. He was trying to drown his sorrows over Polly with moonshine. Duncan Ebersole had seen fit to send his only child off to Richmond to stay with relatives for the duration of the war, declaring that she would be safer there when the damn Yankees launched their inevitable invasion of Virginia. Henry wasn't sure if that was really Ebersole's motivation; it seemed to him that Ebersole was too busy gallivanting around the countryside playing soldier to have much time for anything else. That was probably why he had sent Polly away.

"You feel up to doing some more plowing today, Henry?" asked Mac as he finished up his breakfast.

"Sure," Henry nodded. "Why not?"

"Well, I just thought . . ."

"I've told you, Mac, I'm all healed up from that bullet wound. It's not bothering me at all anymore."

"Doc Yantis said it would be better for you to take it easy for a while."

"That's what I've been doing for months now, ever since I got back on my feet," Henry protested, a bit of anger coming into his voice. "You're always giving me the easiest jobs. It's time I pulled my weight around here again, Mac."

Mac was silent for a moment, then shrugged. "Maybe you're right."

"I know I'm right."

"Plow away, then. Do as much as you feel like."

"Thanks," Henry muttered. He supposed he shouldn't be bothered by the way everybody in the family was always looking out for him. He *had* come pretty close to dying. If whichever of the Fogartys that had fired the shot that hit him had aimed a little better, he'd be lying in his coffin now.

But he had recovered fully and felt like all his strength was back. It was time the others accepted that.

"I'll need someone to take me into town this afternoon," Cordelia remarked as she began to clear away the dishes. "We need some things from Mr. Davis's store."

That was usually the sort of job Mac would assign to him these days, Henry thought. Driving the wagon into Culpeper and back wasn't that strenuous. Today, though, it would be different. "I'll be plowing," he volunteered quickly before Mac could look at him.

"I'll take you, Cordelia," Titus offered. "Be glad to."

"Thank you, Titus."

"Glad to do it. Be good to get off this stinkin' farm for a while."

Henry and Mac exchanged a glance. Henry could tell that Mac was concerned about Titus, too. But there was no real reason to tell Titus that he *couldn't* take Cordelia into town.

There were just too blasted many things to worry about when you were the oldest one around, Henry told himself. For a change, he was glad right now he was almost the baby of the family.

THE BIG old draft horses pulled the wagon easily. It rocked along the road to Culpeper, swaying slightly on its worn springs. Titus clung tightly to the reins and clenched his teeth together as his head spun. Even the gentle motion of the wagon was enough to make him sick. But he was damned if he was going to allow himself to show it in front of Cordelia. No matter how bad he felt, he wasn't going to stop the wagon and make a dash into the woods so that he could throw up.

"My, it's still pretty," Cordelia noted. "Almost like summer doesn't want to end this year."

Titus grunted, "Yeah."

What he really needed, he thought, was a drink. A nice, healthy slug of corn liquor would calm his stomach and quiet his nerves, which were jumping around madly. Of course, it was moonshine that had made him feel like this in the first place, but Titus didn't care about that. All he knew was what he needed right now.

Damn Duncan Ebersole, anyway! The man had had no right to send Polly away, just when it looked like she and Titus were starting to get along better. It had been mighty bad when Polly had invited the Brannons to the party at Mountain Laurel, only to have her father humiliate them and order his men to give Titus a thrashing, but something good could have come out of it. Titus had stolen a kiss while he and Polly were dancing in the garden, before everything went to hell, and he had felt her respond to him. He was sure she had. And afterward, the few times he had seen her in town before Ebersole sent her away, she had smiled at him. Something could have grown up between them, Titus thought, something real and good.

But now they would never have that chance.

He took one hand off the reins and wiped the back of it across his mouth. "How long you reckon you'll be at Davis's?"

"Why, I don't know," Cordelia answered. "However long it takes Mr. Davis's clerks to get our order together and loaded, I suppose."

"I might walk over to Riley's."

"You mean the tavern?"

Titus could tell without looking at her that Cordelia's lips had tightened in disapproval as she asked the question. She was just like their mother sometimes, prissy and self-righteous. Women just never wanted a man to enjoy himself.

"I just want to go see if there's any news about the war," Titus said. "The folks at Riley's always know what's happening. They hear all the stories."

Cordelia shrugged. "Do what you want."

He intended to, Titus thought. By God, he was going to do just exactly what he wanted for a change.

MR. DAVIS was a naturally slender man, so thin that Cordelia always thought he looked like he hadn't had a decent meal in weeks. But he was a good friend to the Brannons, as he was to most of the people in Culpeper County. He had extended credit on more than one occasion when farmers had a bad year with their crops. He took the list of supplies that Cordelia handed him and passed it along to one of his white-aproned clerks. "We'll sure get this order filled for you, Miss Cordelia," he said with a smile. "It may take a while, though. We're mighty busy today."

Cordelia nodded. "That's all right, Mr. Davis. I don't mind waiting."

That was true. The delay would give her a chance to wander up and down the aisles of the cavernous general store and look at all the things on the shelves. Things that she didn't really need, like strands of brightly colored ribbon and equally brilliant beads. She wouldn't buy any of them, but she could get a little guilty pleasure from imagining herself decked out in such doodads.

Her mother would probably scold her for such vanity, Cordelia thought, but she couldn't help it. A girl liked to at least imagine herself looking pretty every now and then.

It took longer to buy supplies now because the clerks working in the store were no longer young and energetic, as they had been before the war. After news of the bombardment and capture of Fort Sumter by Confederate forces had reached Culpeper, most of the men under thirty had joined the army. Word of the Confederate victory at Manassas had prompted practically all the rest of the young men to enlist. That left only middle-aged men to fill the jobs such as clerking for Mr. Davis, and they just moved slower and more deliberately.

Cordelia moved slowly herself as she strolled along the aisles and studied the merchandise on the shelves. She picked up a thimble and thought about adding it to her order, then regretfully put it back. She didn't really need a new thimble, and Brannons didn't buy things they didn't need. That would be wasteful, and the Lord hated waste.

Titus hadn't wasted any time striding off down the street toward Riley's Tavern. He was probably in there drinking right now, Cordelia thought. He could talk all he wanted to about finding out the news of the war, but she knew the real reason he'd gone to Riley's. Mac and Henry might believe she didn't know anything about Titus's drinking, but they were wrong. She had seen the signs, subtle at first, but becoming more glaring all the time. She wasn't blind or ignorant, despite what her brothers thought.

But then, all brothers probably believed that their sisters were sweet and innocent and never had the least little bit of an impure thought in their heads . . .

Cordelia turned the corner of one of the shelves and bumped into the man standing there. "Oh, I'm sorry!" she exclaimed as she stepped back hurriedly.

"No need to be, Cordelia," he told her with a smile. "No harm done."

She recognized him as Nathan Hatcher, a young man who worked as a clerk in Judge Darden's law office. He attended the Baptist Church, just like Cordelia and her family, and she had heard it said of him that he was reading for the law, intending to become an attorney like the judge. Cordelia knew him fairly well from church socials, and she had always thought he was a fine young man.

He was slightly built and only a little taller than she, with shoulders that were stooped a bit, probably from all the book work he did. His hair was brown, and he wore a brown suit and hat. The only spot of color about him was the pair of gold-framed spectacles he wore.

She saw that he was holding a book in his hand, a thick volume that he had half tucked under his arm. "What's that?" she asked, nodding toward it.

"This?" He lifted the book. "I had Mr. Davis order it for me from a publisher in Atlanta. It's a new translation of Plutarch."

Cordelia didn't want to admit that she'd never heard of that particular writer, so she just said, "Oh. Is it good?"

"Well, I hope so." Nathan hesitated, then offered, "I could let you borrow it when I'm through, if you'd like."

"Oh, no, that's all right. Thank you, though. We don't have much time to read these days."

"No one does," Nathan agreed with a sigh. "It's been a struggle for everyone here at home with so many of the men gone off to war, and I'm afraid it's only going to get worse."

He had brought up the war himself, so Cordelia commented, "I'm a little surprised you haven't enlisted, Nathan."

"Me?" He gave a rueful laugh. "Look at me, Cordelia. Do you honestly think that the sight of me in uniform charging would strike fear in the heart of any Union soldier?"

To be honest, Nathan Hatcher looked like a good stiff breeze would blow him right over, Cordelia thought. But she didn't say that, since she didn't want to hurt his feelings. She said, "I'm sure you'd make a fine soldier, a smart man like you."

Nathan shook his head. "Intelligence has nothing to do with winning a war. All that matters there is brute force and a willingness to die."

"To die for what you believe in," Cordelia shot back. She felt herself growing a little angry. Nathan had no right to take that mocking tone when so many of the South's young men were risking their lives in the fight against the North's tyranny.

"Yes, of course you're right," he conceded quickly. He must have seen that he had come close to offending her, she thought. "I still say I don't have much of a soldier in me."

"You might be surprised what you can do," she told him.

"Well, I doubt if we'll find out. By the time the Confederacy would even consider taking such a physical specimen as myself, the war will be over and the Yankees will be sent scurrying back where they came from. Don't you think so?"

"I hope so. About the war being over, I mean."

A moment of silence passed between them, and then Nathan cleared his throat and said, "Well, I'd best be getting on back to the office. No telling when Judge Darden will have some chore for me. It was nice seeing you, Cordelia."

"It was good to see you, too, Nathan," she replied, but she wasn't sure whether she meant it or not. Something about this encounter disturbed her.

It must have bothered Nathan, too, because after he had walked off toward the front of the store, Cordelia felt someone watching her. She glanced back over her shoulder and saw that he had paused in the doorway and was casting a peculiar, intense gaze toward her. When she looked at him, he turned away quickly and went on outside.

Now why in the world had he been watching her like that? she asked herself.

"ANOTHER?"

"Damn right," Titus replied as he held out his tin cup and let Albie Riley fill it with corn squeezings. Riley tilted the jug and let the blessed stuff gurgle into the cup. One of the sweetest sounds on earth, Titus thought.

He lifted the cup, drained it in one swift swallow, and placed it back on the scarred bar top. Heat from the liquor blossomed inside him, filling his belly. He already felt a hell of a lot better than he had while he and Cordelia were riding on the wagon into Culpeper. Now each slug of moonshine just added to the glow that was engulfing him.

"What do you hear from your brother these days?" Riley asked from behind the bar. "When are he and old Stonewall Jackson goin' to march on Washington and rid us of that damned Illinois ape?"

"Will never was much of one for writing," Titus replied. "We've only gotten a couple of letters from him since Manassas. Last one said there was talk General Jackson was going to be placed in command of all the Confederate forces in the Shenandoah Valley."

"Damned well about time," interjected one of the other men in the tavern. Several of them were gathered around Titus. "Jackson will give those Yankees what-for, just like he did at Manassas."

Another man spoke up, "I still don't see why Beauregard didn't just push on to Washington whilst we had 'em on the run. Could've had this war over with by now if he had."

Titus didn't care one way or the other, although he wanted to see the Yankees defeated, too. But the war didn't matter nearly as much to him as his loss of Polly Ebersole—and the next drink.

He shoved his cup toward Riley.

The tavernkeeper said, "Ah, now, it's hating to be doubtful of you I am, Titus, but I'd feel a lot better about refillin' that cup if you were to show a wee bit of silver."

Titus grimaced and dug a hand in his shirt pocket. "Think I don't have money?" he asked as he searched for a coin. "I've got money." But he couldn't find any. His frown grew darker as he fumed, "Blast it, I know I had some right here . . ."

Riley put the cork back in the neck of the jug and thumped it with the heel of his hand. "I don't mind puttin' a few drinks on your tab, but there's a limit, lad, and you've just reached it."

"Damn it, Albie—"

Riley shook his head firmly. "Come back in and pay what you owe, and it's glad I'll be to pour you another."

Cordelia. Cordelia might have some money, Titus thought. But he couldn't go ask her for it without telling her it was to pay off his bill at the tavern. And if he told her that, she wouldn't give it to him. She'd just give him a lecture instead and then run home and tell their mother all about it. Titus would never hear the end of it from either of those blasted females.

He drew himself up straight, trying to regain some of his dignity. "I'll be back," he vowed. Then he turned and marched rather unsteadily toward the door. After all, he told himself, he hadn't said *when* he would be back.

Outside on the boardwalk, he paused with one hand on a post for support and took several deep breaths. He had to clear his head. He took a plug of chewing tobacco from his pocket and bit off a piece. Let Cordelia smell that instead of the moonshine. He looked down the street toward the general store and saw Davis's clerks loading boxes of supplies into the back of the wagon. It would be time to go soon.

"Brannon."

Titus turned to see a rawboned man in tattered clothes and a ragged-brimmed black hat standing there. He recognized the man as Israel Quinn, a no-account farmer from the southern part of the county whose wife, Margery, was some sort of kin to the Fogarty bunch. Even half-drunk, Titus's muscles stiffened in response to the possible threat. Quinn had ridden with the Fogartys sometimes, and Will had been convinced the man was just as big a thief as any of the other members of the family, even if he was only related by marriage. Titus suddenly wished that he hadn't left his Sharps rifle at home, but he hadn't thought he'd need it here in town.

"What do you want, Quinn?" he asked stiffly.

Quinn rubbed his narrow, beard-stubbled jaw and inclined his head toward the door of the tavern. "I heard Riley tellin' you to pay up. Money a mite tight for you, Brannon?"

"What business is that of yours?"

"Oh, none, I reckon. It's just that I got a proposition that might interest you. A way you can lay your hands on some cash."

"What?" snapped Titus. "Robbing somebody?"

Quinn's eyes narrowed. "You sayin' I'm a thief?"

"You're related to the Fogartys, or at least your wife is."

"Fella could take offense at your tone, if he was of a mind to," Quinn said slowly. "If you ain't interested, just say so."

"I'm not interested," Titus grated. "Now get the hell away from me."

"I'm goin', I'm goin'." Quinn started to shuffle away down the boardwalk, but then he stopped and looked back at Titus. "Just you remember what I said, next time you're lookin' for a coin you ain't got."

Titus ignored him, and Quinn went on his way. Only when Quinn had rounded a corner and was out of sight did Titus draw a deep breath and lean heavily for a moment on the railing along the edge of the boardwalk.

Whatever sort of proposition Quinn had had, it was sure to have been illegal. Men such as him didn't know any other way of doing things. They would work harder to make a dishonest living than they would an honest one. Whatever had possessed Quinn to approach one of the Brannons, of all people, like that?

But what really bothered Titus was the realization, deep down, that for a second—just for a second—he had seriously considered asking Quinn just what he had in mind.

Chapter Four

I N SEPTEMBER OF 1861, Gen. Ulysses S. Grant arrived in the Mississippi River town of Cairo, Illinois, and found it already full of Yankee soldiers, headquartered in a hastily constructed compound known as Fort Defiance. Upriver, Saint Louis had been occupied by the Northern army earlier in the summer after a round of bloody clashes between Unionists and Secessionists, as had the Missouri state capital, Jefferson City. The population of Missouri was split fairly evenly between the two sides, but by September the Union had gained the upper hand militarily, under the command of Maj. Gen. John Charles Frémont. Frémont believed that control of the Mississippi River was the key to winning the struggle in the West, and to that end, he began assembling troops in Cairo, where the Ohio and the Mississippi came together. According to Frémont's plan, these troops would ultimately sweep on down the mighty river all the way to the Gulf of Mexico.

Frémont would not be part of that plan, however. A series of reverses for the Federals in western Missouri had cast doubts upon his ability, and with his political position in Washington weakened by the defeats and his own overreaching nature, Frémont suddenly found himself relieved of command by Gen. Winfield Scott. The thousands of Union troops that had been pouring into Cairo were still there, however, and needed a commander.

Brig. Gen. Ulysses S. Grant was that man.

Armed with a reputation for little more than failure from his previous stint in the army, Grant knew that he had to move quickly to establish his presence. At his order, troops from Fort Defiance marched on the town of Paducah, Kentucky, and occupied it successfully. Grant would have pushed on and attacked other nearby Confederate strongholds if the orders to do so had come. They did not, and so he waited impatiently.

But he had already sent out a message, and it traveled rapidly up and down the river: sooner or later, the Yankees were coming, and they intended to make the Mississippi their own.

CORY SHIVERED miserably. September had gone, taking with it the warm days. October brought a chill rain that turned the streets of New Madrid into a muddy, treacherous morass. The shed under which Cory huddled didn't do much to keep out the rain. It dripped steadily around him and soaked the thin blanket he was using for cover. He tried to pull the blanket more tightly around his shoulders, but that didn't do much good.

It was still afternoon, not much past four o'clock, but already the thick gray clouds were bringing on darkness. That morning, Cory had gotten a little work unloading cargo from a riverboat, but the load had been a small one and the pay not much. The coin in Cory's pocket would pay for a drink or a cup of soup, but not both, and certainly not for a place to spend the night out of the weather.

A coughing spell shook him. He was going to catch his death, staying out in the wet and the cold like this. What made his wretched condition even worse was the vivid memory of a time when he had been warm and comfortable and well-fed . . . on the *Missouri Zephyr* only a few weeks ago.

A great deal had changed in those few weeks. The river traffic had finally fallen off steeply, as everyone had predicted it would once the Yankees began taking control of the Mississippi. Cory heard enough talk to know what was going on, and he heard plenty of curses directed at some northern general called Grant. Many of the captains of the sternwheelers and sidewheelers had decided that it was too dangerous to venture this far north on the river. Once they made their runs to New Orleans, they stayed down there, coming back upriver only as far as Natchez or sometimes Memphis. Cory didn't see how they were going to make a living doing that; without Northern goods, there weren't enough cargoes to make such runs worthwhile. But he supposed the boats themselves were more important to their owners. They would try to wait out the war.

That didn't help Cory or the other dockworkers. Without cargoes to load and unload, their livelihood was gone.

Cory felt himself dozing off. His head dipped forward and his eyes closed. Maybe it would be better, he thought, if he just sat here and froze to death. Would it get cold enough for that tonight? He doubted it.

The shrill blast of a boat's whistle made his head jerk up again. He looked downriver through the gray curtains of mist and saw a big sidewheeler approaching the docks, its paddles cutting through the water. Cory couldn't make out the details at first, but then as the vessel came closer, he recognized it: the *Missouri Zephyr*, Capt. Zeke Farrell's boat.

Cory felt his heart take an unaccustomed leap. If the *Zephyr* was back in New Madrid, that meant Lucille Farrell probably was, too. Unless her father had left her back in New Orleans, Cory added to himself. But if he was lucky, she might be on the boat, and he might catch a glimpse of her. His pulse beat faster at that thought. The sight of a beautiful young woman was small consolation to a man who was soaked and cold and miserable, but it was much better than nothing.

Footsteps sounded on the dock beside the shed. Cory heard a familiar voice say, "There she is, just like I told you." The voice belonged to Mr. Vickery, the man who was in charge of the docks at New Madrid.

"And that's Farrell's boat?" The question came from another man. Cory couldn't see either him or Vickery, but he didn't like the sound of the second man's voice. It was even colder than the rain dripping around him.

"That's right. The *Missouri Zephyr*. According to my contact down in New Orleans, Farrell boasted that he'd never let the Yankees stop him from going wherever he wanted to on the river."

"We'll see about that," snarled the second man.

Cory's eyes widened. The man's words had a definite sound of menace in them, as if he intended to harm Captain Farrell and the riverboat. That would mean hurting Lucille, too. Cory started to get up. In his mind's eye, he saw himself confronting Vickery and the other man, warning them that they had better not try anything against the *Missouri Zephyr* or they would have to answer to him.

Then he shrank back into the corner of the shed and drew the blanket more tightly about him. Who was he to be threatening anyone? At best, Vickery and the other man would just laugh at him. At worst, they might put a knife in him and throw him in the river.

"Farrell will be tied up here overnight?" the second man went on.

"Yes. He's supposed to take on some cargo, but it won't be ready until in the morning. I'll see to that," Vickery promised.

The second man chuckled. It was an ugly sound. "We'll give him a warm welcome."

"Just be sure that no one knows I tipped you off, Gill. I still have to deal with these damned Rebels a while longer."

"Don't worry." The man called Gill sounded a little scornful now. "Nobody will blame you. The *Missouri Zephyr* will be just one more casualty of the war."

Cory had to bite back a groan of despair. Gill was planning to destroy the *Zephyr* somehow. He had to be a Yankee, or at least a Unionist sympathizer. There were plenty of them around, even this far south in Missouri.

Footsteps moved away. Vickery and Gill were leaving, Cory realized. He sat up straighter. Maybe this was his chance to warn Captain Farrell. The riverboat shouldn't even dock here, he thought. But it was too late to prevent that. The massive paddles had stopped revolving, and the boat was drifting to a stop next to one of the docks that extended out into the river. Several deckhands leaped off to make it fast to the mooring posts.

Cory pushed himself to his feet and stumbled out from under the protection of the shed. The cold rain lashed at his face as he started toward the *Zephyr*. He worried that Vickery was still somewhere close by and would see him and worry that he might have overheard the conversation with Gill. It was more likely, though, that even if Vickery noticed him, the man would think that Cory was just trying to beg a handout from the boat's crewmen.

He approached a deckhand who had finished wrapping a rope around one of the piers. "Is Captain Farrell on board?" Cory asked, realizing even as he spoke that it was a foolish question. Where else would the captain of the riverboat be at a time like this?

"Go on, you damned beggar," growled the crewman. "The cap'n's got no time for the likes o' you."

"No, you don't understand," Cory explained urgently. "I'm not a beggar. I work here on the docks."

"Then come back when we're ready to take on our cargo."

The man turned away, already dismissing Cory from his thoughts.

Cory darted forward and caught hold of the man's coat sleeve. "I have to talk to Captain Farrell!"

"Let go of me, you damned wharf rat!" The man jerked his arm free and swung a backhanded blow at Cory's head.

Cory saw it coming but was too slow to get out of the way. The man's knuckles cracked painfully against his cheekbone and sent him stumbling backward. His feet went out from under him and he sat down hard on the thick planks of the dock.

Stunned, Cory sat there for a moment as several members of the riverboat's crew walked past him. He gave a little shake of his head as a pair of high-topped black boots stopped beside him.

"You again?" rumbled a deep voice.

Cory lifted his face. The blow had opened a small cut on his cheek. Rain washed away the blood that oozed from it. Cory blinked, and his eyes focused on the face of the pilot, Judson.

"Figured you'd have crawled off in a hole somewheres and died by now," Judson went on.

"I have to talk to the captain," Cory croaked.

"So you can beg another meal off him? I don't think so. Times are harder now than they were a few weeks ago, and bound to get harder still." Judson bent and grasped Cory's arm, hauling him easily to his feet.

"Wh-what are you doing?"

"Makin' sure you don't bother nobody, especially the cap'n or Miss Lucille. They got enough to worry 'bout these days."

Despite the situation, Cory felt a pulse of excitement go through him. Lucille hadn't been left behind downriver. She was on the boat.

Not that her presence would do him any good, because Judson was marching him steadily away from the dock where the *Zephyr* was tied up. Cory tried to struggle out of the pilot's firm grip, but weak from malnutrition and exposure, he had no chance of getting away.

"This is far enough," Judson grunted when they had gone several blocks. He turned Cory to face him. Water dripped from the brim of Judson's cap as he glared down at Cory. He slapped a coin in Cory's hand. "There. That's all you're gettin' from anybody on the *Missouri Zephyr*. Go get drunk and don't come back. If you do, I swear I'll beat you within an inch of your life, and maybe worse'n that."

"You still don't understand," Cory muttered.

But his hand closed tightly around the coin anyway.

"I understand all I need to." Judson gave him a hard shove. "Get the hell out o' here, and stay away from the boat."

If that was what Judson wanted, Cory thought, then so be it. He had tried to warn them that trouble was waiting for the riverboat and her crew here in New Madrid. He had honestly tried. No matter what happened now, no one could blame him for it.

He stumbled away from Judson down an alley, looking back only once. When he did, the pilot raised a fist and shook it at him in warning. Cory nodded jerkily and started moving again.

He had done his best. It wasn't his fault if no one would listen to him. Besides, Red Mike's wasn't far away, and he had enough now for several drinks. As he made his way unsteadily along the alley, his thumb and forefinger slid over the surface of the coin, trying to tell exactly what it was.

A silver dollar! He was rich.

CORY HADN'T been to Red Mike's since the trouble with the Kaintuck called Strunk a few weeks earlier. Mike had told him then to get out and not come back, but tonight when the bartender saw the silver dollar Cory was holding, his attitude changed instantly. "Just don't go pickin' any fights," he warned as he set a bucket of beer on the bar in front of Cory.

"Don't worry. I'm not looking for trouble." Cory picked up the beer and took a long swallow. Almost instantly, the stuff began to warm him, weak and watery though it was.

He took the second bucket to a small table in a rear corner of the tavern. There was a potbellied stove back here, and Cory basked in the heat that radiated from it. After a few minutes, when the second bucket of beer was still half full, he put his head back and leaned it against the wall. His eyelids were incredibly heavy, and as they slid down, sleep claimed him despite the raucousness of his surroundings.

When he awoke suddenly, Cory had no idea how long he had been asleep. He sat up sharply, making the woman who had been rubbing his thigh jump back. "My, you're a touchy one, ain't you?" she commented. She wore a low-cut calico dress, and her face was heavily painted. Cory stared at her for a moment. The woman's face seemed to go away and be replaced by Lucille Farrell's. A voice as slow and soft and sweet as honey asked, "Are you all right?"

Cory gave a little shake of his head as the prostitute repeated, "Are you all right?" in a voice that wasn't nearly as sweet as the one he had just imagined belonging to Lucille. Pain throbbed behind his eyes. He pressed his hands against his temples.

"Where's my beer?" he asked as he realized the bucket was gone.

"I wouldn't know about that, darlin'," the trollop replied. "But if you go out back with me, you won't need any beer to get you through the night."

For a second, Cory thought about taking her up on the offer. But he remembered that Mike had kept his silver dollar, so he didn't have any money. Mike probably wouldn't give him any more beer, either. A bucket and a half of beer and a warm place to sleep for a while . . . that was all he was going to get out of his new-found riches.

Cory pushed to his feet. The woman caught at his arm and asked in a desperate tone, "How about it? Go out back with me?"

"I . . . I can't. There's something . . . something I have to do."

And there was, Cory realized. Something important. If he could just remember what it was . . .

The *Missouri Zephyr.* And the man called Gill.

"Oh, Lord," Cory breathed.

He couldn't believe that he had allowed Judson to run him off like that. He should have tried harder to make the pilot understand that the riverboat was in danger as long as it was tied up in New Madrid. But Judson had threatened him and then given him a dollar, and Cory had stumbled off meekly. Disgust and self-loathing filled him like a physical illness.

Maybe it wasn't too late. Maybe he could still warn Captain Farrell.

He became aware that the prostitute was still tugging on his arm. He looked down at her and asked, "What time is it?"

The question surprised the woman so much that for a moment all she could do was gape at him. "Time?" she finally said. "I don't know. What does it matter what time it is?"

Cory wasn't sure about that himself. All he knew was that he had to get back to the docks. He threw off the woman's clutching hand and turned to stumble toward the door.

No one tried to stop him, and he was glad of that. As weak as he felt and as badly as his head was hurting, he knew he wouldn't be much good in a fight. When he reached the street, he discovered that the rain had stopped. The air was still cold and heavy with moisture, though. He paused and took a few deep breaths, and that cleared his head a little.

Night had fallen, and these back alleys along the waterfront were only dimly lit. Cory had been around here long enough so that he was able to find his way even in the dark. He hurried toward the river, his pace unsteady. He stayed on the boardwalks as much as possible, because whenever he ventured off them, the quagmires that had been dirt streets slowed him down and tried to suck the boots right off his feet.

After what seemed like an hour, he saw the lamps burning on the warehouses along the river. Some of the buildings extended out over the water, and some of them actually floated on the river like gigantic barges. He stumbled past them toward the docks.

Suddenly, he heard voices and came to a stop. He listened intently. The voices and the footsteps he heard told him that a large group of men were somewhere nearby in the foggy darkness. Cory drew back into the deeper darkness of an alley mouth as they came closer.

"Got the torches?" a man's voice asked. Cory recognized it from the conversation he had overheard that afternoon. It belonged to the man called Gill.

"Right here," answered another man. "And the kegs of coal oil, too. That Rebel riverboat's going to make a mighty pretty blaze."

Cory bit back a groan. He recalled Gill's comment about giving the *Zephyr* a warm welcome. The Unionist had meant that literally, Cory realized.

They were going to burn the riverboat!

The men had paused near the mouth of the alley where Cory was hidden. He edged forward enough to get a look at them, saw there were at least a dozen of them. Outnumbered like that, how could he possibly stop them?

And as pathetic a specimen of humanity as he had become, what right did he have even to think he might be able to keep them from going through with their plan? What he should do, he told himself, was skulk away like the wharf rat he was.

That was when his shoulder brushed against a stack of crates piled against the wall of one of the buildings that formed the alley.

Without thinking about what he was doing, Cory turned and took hold of the crate on top of the stack. It was empty, and he had no trouble hefting it above his head. With a grunt of effort, he flung it out onto the boardwalk, where it crashed just behind the group of Unionists. "Damn Yankees!" Cory heard himself shouting.

Then he whirled around and broke into a run, heading deeper into the alley.

"Get him!" That was Gill, calling a low-voiced but dangerous order. "Stop that son of a bitch, whoever he is!"

Cory was trying to think coherently, but it was difficult. He had some reason for trying to distract the mob of Northern sympathizers and draw them down this alley; he knew he did. He just couldn't remember it right now.

Then instinct sent him darting to the side, squeezing into a narrow opening that most people wouldn't even notice if they didn't know it was there, especially in the dark like this. The passage led between buildings and then turned back toward the street that ran along the riverfront. As Cory made his way through it, he heard at least some of the Unionists pounding down the alley.

Cory squirted back onto the boardwalk like a seed out of a watermelon. He was between Gill's bunch and the *Zephyr* now. His intimate knowledge of the most squalid areas of the town had bought him this momentary advantage. He had to seize it. He broke into a run toward the docks.

"Up there!" Gill again. "Blast it!"

The Unionist meant that literally. Cory heard a gun crack behind him. Something whined past his ear, not too close— but not far enough away, either.

He wasn't sure where he found the speed and strength to run like that, but he was going so fast when he reached the dock that he had to grab one of the posts for support as he swung himself onto the planks. He dashed toward the gangway that connected the deck of the *Zephyr* to the dock.

A guard was on duty there, and he stepped forward to intercept Cory. "Captain Farrell!" Cory shouted as he ran up the gangway. "I've got to see Captain Farrell!"

"Get off this boat!" snapped the crewman. He grabbed Cory's arm and swung a fist at his head.

Cory ducked under the blow. Growing up, he had spent a lot of time in rough-and-tumble wrestling with his brothers, as all boys do. He threw himself forward, tackling the guard around the waist. Caught by surprise, the man went over backward and landed heavily on the riverboat's deck. Cory managed to scramble back to his feet first. "Captain Farrell!" he shouted again.

From the corner of his eye, he saw a flare of harsh light down the street. The mob was on the way, and their torches were lit now. Cory remembered the mention of coal oil. If they threw those kegs onto the boat, shattering them and splashing the oil over the deck, then tossed the torches after them, the

Zephyr would be doomed. It would burn to the waterline and be totally destroyed.

"Captain Farrell!" Cory called desperately.

"What is it?" the calm, educated voice said from behind him.

Cory spun around and saw Farrell standing there, a pistol in his hand. The guard stumbled up behind Farrell and began, "I tried to stop him, Cap'n—"

"I know this young man," Farrell cut in. "He wouldn't have invaded our boat unless it was important. I take it your visit is concerned with that large group of men coming this way with torches."

"They're . . . they're going to burn the boat!" Cory gulped. "They've got coal oil!"

"They do, do they?" Seemingly unconcerned, Farrell tucked the pistol behind his belt. "Well, we have something that will trump their hand." He turned to the crewman. "Is the cannon loaded?"

"Yes sir, just like you ordered when you decided we were comin' this far north."

"Bring it along here, would you please?"

The crewman broke into a run toward the bow of the ship. Cory watched him go, then glanced at the street. The mob of Unionists had just about reached the dock. They would be close enough to wreak their havoc in a matter of seconds.

With a rumbling of wheels, the crewman returned, pushing a small cannon in front of him. The bore of the muzzle was about three inches across, and right now that three inches looked even larger to Cory. The crewman turned the cannon so that it was pointed toward the Unionists, and Farrell stepped calmly over beside it.

"Stop where you are!" he called, his voice carrying clearly.

"Step aside, you damned Reb!" shouted a man in the forefront of the mob. "You'd better get off that boat while you've got a chance, because we're going to burn it!"

"Take one more step along that dock and you'll have a cannonball in your coat pocket, my friend," Farrell warned. He took the cannon's firing lanyard in his hand.

The Unionists hesitated. Cory had recognized the voice of the man who had threatened Farrell, and as he moved up closer to Farrell, he knew he was getting his first good look at Gill in the garish light of the torches. Gill was a tall, slender man with a lantern jaw and the fierce, deep-set eyes of a fanatic. Cory had never seen anyone who looked quite so dangerous.

More of the *Zephyr*'s crew came hurrying out of their cabins, drawn by the shouting and the general commotion. Judson, the pilot, stepped up beside Farrell and said, "I know that man, Cap'n. He's Jason Gill, the abolitionist."

"Indeed," replied Farrell. "I don't care if he's John Brown himself, come back from the grave. He's not going to do any harm to this boat."

Gill shouted, "You can't kill us all with that cannon, Reb! Before you can reload, we'll be all over you!"

"I don't intend to kill all of you with the cannon, Mr. Gill," Farrell replied, still sounding extraordinarily cool considering the circumstances. "Take a look up on the Texas deck."

From where he was, Cory couldn't see onto the Texas deck, but in the sudden silence that fell, he heard the cocking of what sounded like at least half a dozen guns.

"My riflemen are all excellent shots, Mr. Gill," Farrell went on. "Those of you who are not taken down by the cannon will be killed by my men. I offer no quarter where the safety of my boat is concerned."

Gill sneered. "You're bluffing. You can't just go around murdering people."

"Perhaps not. But I can exterminate vermin." Farrell's voice rose slightly. "You have ten seconds to throw those torches into the river and withdraw, or we shall open fire."

Gill didn't say anything, but Cory thought most of the men with him were starting to look pretty uneasy. A standoff was only a standoff as long as both sides were unwilling to start the ball. As he looked at Farrell's resolute face, Cory had no doubt the captain would give the order to fire once those ten seconds were up.

Suddenly, one of the torches arched out over the river and went into the water, where it was extinguished with a loud hiss. Another torch followed it, then another and another.

"Wait a minute!" Gill's voice rose until it was practically a howl. "We can't let this . . . this damned Rebel bluff us! We came here to burn his boat, and we're going to burn his boat!"

One of the men with him said distinctly, "You walk out the dock into the face of that cannon if you want to, Gill. Me, I'm goin' home while I still can." He turned and walked away. Several more of the men followed him.

"Stop it! Come back here! He's bluffing, I tell you!"

The other Unionists ignored Gill's ranting and continued melting away into the night.

"Mr. Judson, prepare to cast off," Farrell ordered quietly.

"Yes sir." Judson snapped commands at the other crewmen, then turned and headed for the ladder that led up to the wheelhouse. With nervous expressions on their faces, a couple of deckhands hopped across to the dock and started untying the mooring ropes under the cover of the riflemen on the Texas deck and the cannon beside which Farrell stood.

"You're leaving?" Cory asked.

"I don't believe it would be wise to remain docked here," Farrell stated. "If you'd like to disembark, my young friend, now is the time to do it."

Cory swallowed. Jason Gill was still standing at the end of the dock. Cory had never seen so much hate on a man's face. "If it's all right with you, Captain," he appealed, "I'd *really* like to go with you this time."

"I think that's the best decision under the circumstances," Farrell agreed.

Cory heard a rumble from deep in the bowels of the riverboat. That would be the boiler being stoked up, he thought. A few moments later, the paddlewheels began to revolve slowly, gradually picking up more speed. As they bit into the water, the boat backed away from the dock.

Gill stayed where he was, alone now, his followers long gone. He held a torch in his hand, one last remnant of the mob that had marched on the *Zephyr*. As he stood there, he watched the riverboat recede into the center of the mighty river. Cory could still see the flame of the torch burning in the night, and a shudder went through him as he remembered the way Gill had looked at him.

Captain Farrell inquired, "Well, Mr. Brannon—that *is* your name, isn't it?—what are we going to do with you now?"

Chapter Five

WILL BRANNON LIMPED ACROSS the muddy field toward the row of hastily erected log buildings that served as officers' quarters here at the Thirty-third Virginia's encampment near Winchester, Virginia. A few weeks earlier, during the ambush set up by Union forces, a minié ball had burned across Will's right thigh, just above the knee. That was the only injury he had suffered during the hellish few minutes before he was able to rally his men and take the fight to the Yankees.

Four of his men hadn't been so fortunate. They had died of the wounds they'd received. Only luck and the Yankees' bad aim in the dark had kept the casualties from being even worse.

Encountering more resistance than they had expected after their treacherous attack, the Union soldiers had fled into the night. Will and his men had pulled back to the Confederate camp, leaving Sgt. Darcy Bennett and a couple of troopers behind to make sure they weren't being followed. Darcy and the other two men had come back a few hours later, and Darcy had found Will in the hospital tent. Only now was Will getting his own wound tended to; before then he'd insisted that the doctors take care of the other men in the patrol who had suffered injuries.

"Them sneakin' Yanks tried to follow us, all right, Cap'n, just like you thought they might," Darcy had reported. "They sent some scouts out, but they run into us in the dark."

"They didn't make it back, did they?" Will had asked, grimacing a little as Dr. Hunter Maguire, the camp's medical director and chief surgeon, cleaned the graze on his leg with carbolic acid.

Darcy had put a hand on the hilt of the heavy-bladed hunting knife that was tucked in a leather scabbard behind his belt. "I should hope to smile they didn't."

By now, after the passage of several weeks, Will's wound had healed cleanly, leaving only a narrow white scar on his thigh. Sometimes the whole leg was still a little stiff, however, especially in wet weather—and judging from what he had seen so far of the autumn of 1861, it was never going to stop raining for more than an hour or two at a time.

Will stepped up onto the porch of the small cabin he shared with Capt. Yancy Lattimer. Yancy was sitting on a rough-hewn chair, facing the slave who had accompanied him when he enlisted in the Confederate army, a young man known as Roman. The two men were using a barrel between them as a table, and set up on top of it was a chess board. Yancy moved one of the pieces and announced triumphantly, "I believe that's check."

Roman didn't hesitate. His hand swooped down on one of his pieces and moved it a couple of spaces on the board. "And that's checkmate," he proclaimed.

Yancy stared at the board for a moment, frowning darkly, then his expression abruptly cleared and he threw his head back and laughed. "You're absolutely right, Roman. It certainly is. Damn it! When am I going to stop letting you lure me in like that?"

"One o' these days I reckon you will, Cap'n," Roman asserted with a grin. "Until then, I don't mind givin' you lessons."

Yancy glanced up at Will. "Why don't you take a crack at him, Will? See if you can beat him."

"Roman's too good for me," Will conceded with a shake of his head. "I've been watching him run you all over that chessboard for months now."

"That's what I get for teaching a nigger how to play chess, I suppose."

"I reckon," Roman agreed, still grinning.

Yancy scraped his chair back and stood up. "What's the word at headquarters?" he asked Will.

"There's a rumor 'Stonewall' is about to be promoted to major general." Will's voice contained a hint of dry humor when he referred to their commanding officer by the nickname that had become so popular following the battle of Manassas. Both Will and Yancy had been present during the battle when the late Gen. Barnard E. Bee had uttered the statement, "There stands Jackson, like a stone wall." That quote had gone through the Confederacy like wildfire, doing wonders for morale. There were some who suspected that Bee was not being complimentary and was frustrated that Jackson had not committed his troops to support the units commanded by Bee and Col. Francis S. Bartow. But facts were one thing and legends were another, and Will was already coming to understand that.

"A well-deserved promotion," Yancy said, and Will agreed with him. Regardless of Bee's opinion, Jackson's actions during the battle had proven to be correct militarily, and despite the man's personal oddities, Will had found him to be a very competent commander. Of course, he wasn't really the right one to be judging something like that, Will sometimes reminded himself, since six months earlier he himself had been a civilian, with no military experience whatsoever. He'd had to learn quickly how to function as an officer in the Confederate army.

Will leaned on the porch railing and looked out at the thin mist that had started drifting down over the field where the men drilled every day. The Confederates had acquitted themselves well at Manassas, but now they were in the process of becoming a real army. That was what they would need to be if the South was to have any hope of achieving its aims. Many people in the Confederacy, politicians, soldiers, and common citizens alike, had believed after the rout of the Yankees at Manassas that the North would immediately sue for peace. That had not happened. In fact, Abraham Lincoln had put out a call for even more troops, and Gen. George B. McClellan had been placed in charge of the Army of the Potomac, replacing Gen. Irvin McDowell. Will knew about that because he had read it in one of the Northern newspapers that circulated through the Confederate camp. Confederate sympathizers in the North bought up many of the papers, which thought nothing of detailing in their columns the military and political decisions being reached in Washington, and sent bundles of them south to serve as intelligence for the Confederacy. Will would have hoped that the Southern papers would be more discreet, but from what he had seen of the journalism coming out of Atlanta and Richmond, that wasn't the case.

The sky was growing dark with the approach of dusk. The thick clouds made darkness fall even earlier than it normally would at this time of year. Will's and Yancy's companies had gone through their usual drilling, then repaired to their tents until supper.

"I believe I'll have a drink," Yancy decided as he turned toward the door of the cabin. "How about you, Will?"

"No, thanks." Will had been raised a hardshell Baptist, his devout mother instilling in him the belief that drinking was wrong. Which wasn't to say that he didn't enjoy a beer now and then, or even a snort of whiskey, but generally he avoided the stuff.

He had gone against a lot of things his mother believed, he thought with a trace of bitterness. But the commandment he had broken that she regarded as his worst transgression was the fifth one: Thou Shalt Not Kill.

It wasn't like Joe Fogarty had given him a hell of a lot of choice. He had tried to arrest Joe peacefully there in Davis's store in Culpeper. The Fogartys had held up a group of travelers, killing a couple of them, and then had bushwhacked Will and his deputy, Luther Strawn. Luther had died in that ambush and Will had barely escaped with his life. When the chance came to bring one of the Fogartys to justice, Will wasn't going to let it pass him by.

But Joe had reached for his gun—as, deep down, Will had known he would—and Will had drawn his Navy Colt and shot him dead. That had turned the hostility between the Brannons and the Fogartys into a blood feud and ultimately led to Will's enlistment in the army so that George and Ransom Fogarty would follow him and leave the rest of his family alone.

That plan had worked, but now Will was a full-fledged officer in the Confederate army, and he knew he wouldn't be going home any time soon. He might not be going home at all . . . but there was no point in dwelling on that.

Yancy went into the cabin, leaving Will and Roman on the porch. The slave began putting away the chessboard, dropping the pieces into a soft leather pouch with a drawstring at its top. Idly, Will picked up one of the queens and looked at it, admiring the painstaking detail with which it had been carved. "Who made these?" he asked.

"My pa did," Roman said. "He was a right handy man with a whittlin' knife."

"I'd say he was," Will agreed as he handed the queen back to Roman, who dropped it in the pouch with the other pieces. "Is he still carving chess pieces?"

"Don't know." Roman cinched up the drawstring. "Ain't seen him in nigh on to eight years."

"Did he pass away?" The minute he asked the question, Will felt like a fool.

"Naw. Cap'n Yancy's pa sold him to a fella from down in the Carolinas."

Will frowned, wishing that he hadn't brought up bad memories for Roman. The Brannons had never owned slaves, like most Southerners, but also like most Southerners, they knew people who did. Many of the brutal, scandalous things the Yankees were always talking about—the beatings and the lynchings and the like—simply never happened among the slaveholders with whom Will was acquainted. Or else they happened so rarely that such an event would be a thing far out of the ordinary and would take place only under very unusual circumstances. Even Duncan Ebersole—who was a gold-plated son of a bitch as far as Will was concerned—treated the slaves on his Mountain Laurel plantation fairly well physically. As Will had gotten to know Yancy Lattimer, he had realized that Yancy's family was even more liberal in their treatment of slaves. Roman knew how to read and write, and he wasn't the only black so skilled on the Lattimer plantation.

But not beating a man wasn't the same as truly treating him like a human being, Will mused as he looked at the unreadable expression on Roman's face. He figured that Yancy's father had sold Roman's father without a second thought as to how it might affect the man's family. And Roman's father had had no choice but to go, leaving his wife and children behind forever, simply because of a whim or a financial need on the part of the elder Lattimer.

"I'm sorry, Roman," Will said awkwardly. He couldn't think of anything else to say.

Without looking up at Will, Roman closed the chessboard and placed the pouch containing the chess pieces on top of it. "Ain't your fault, Cap'n Will. That jus' the way things is."

For a moment Will felt himself warring with guilt. To one way of thinking, he was here in the Confederate army fighting to preserve the very system that callously brought such disruption and pain to families like Roman's. A system that, in his heart, Will didn't know if he believed in or not.

But at the same time, the Yankees had had no right to try to impose their will on the Southern states by force of arms. Will was absolutely dead certain of that. The states had fought for their rights politically, and when that didn't work, their only choice had been secession. The Yankees were the ones who were breaking the law by invading the South with their soldiers. After that reckless move, war was regrettable but inevitable.

None of that would have eased the pain Roman must have felt at being separated from his father, however. Will offered, "Well, I hope you see him again sometime."

"Be nice, all right," Roman said. "I just hope he still alive and he think of us sometimes."

"I'm sure he does."

But truthfully, Will realized, he wasn't sure of much of anything anymore.

THAT EVENING there was a meeting of the officers in the farmhouse that Jackson had commandeered as his headquarters. Will and Yancy were there, along with Lieutenant Colonels Preston, Ashby, and Baylor; Majors Trueheart, Harmon, and Hawks; Lieutenants Willis, Boswell, Garnett, and Pendleton, the latter functioning as General Jackson's aide-de-camp; and fellow Captains Robinson, Arney, and Trout. As they sat around the long table in the dining room of the house, Jackson confirmed the rumor Will had mentioned to Yancy earlier in the day.

"Gentlemen," Jackson began, "I have the singular honor of having been promoted to the rank of major general in the army of the Confederate States of America. I accept this humbly and with deep gratitude."

"It's well deserved, General," Lieutenant Colonel Ashby asserted.

Jackson sat at the head of the table with his right elbow extended and his forearm cocked straight up from it. Will had seldom seen the general when he did not have one arm or the other held up in the air in some fashion. Jackson claimed this habit helped keep him "in balance." Will considered it just an eccentricity, one to which Jackson was entitled.

"Not only that," Jackson continued, "but it is also my pleasure to report that the brigades under the command of Generals Carson, Meem, and Boggs will soon be joined by ample reinforcements, and two more brigades, under General Loring, are en route to join us in our noble effort."

Murmurs of approval came from the assembled officers. Their force here was growing, as it would need to in order to counter the Union forces. Each man believed in his heart that though the Confederacy might be outmanned, it would never be outfought. Still, the more even the odds were, the better.

A corporal came into the dining room, looking nervous at intruding into this gathering of his superiors, and hurried over to Lieutenant Pendleton. He bent over and spoke quietly to the aide-de-camp for a moment. Will saw Pendleton's eyes flick toward him, and he wondered if there was some sort of trouble in his company.

Pendleton nodded to the corporal, then said, "Excuse me, General, but Captain Brannon and I need to have a word in private."

"By all means," Jackson replied magnanimously.

Will rose to his feet and followed Pendleton out of the dining room into the foyer. As Pendleton quietly closed the dining room door, Will asked, "What is it, Sandy?"

"The corporal of the guard reports that there is some sort of disturbance among your men, sir. I thought you might like to deal with it yourself, rather than have it brought up among the other officers."

Pendleton was noted for his discretion. He was also, despite being only a lieutenant, respected by the senior officers of the Thirty-third because of his position as General Jackson's aide-de-camp. If there was a problem anywhere, it was Pendleton's job to sniff it out and bring it to Jackson's attention if he deemed it appropriate. He was not one to cry wolf, however, and would frequently give the company commanders an opportunity to address a thorny situation themselves before he took it to Jackson.

"Thank you, Lieutenant," Will said with a nod. "Did the corporal of the guard tell you exactly what was going on?"

"Only that it had to do with Sergeant Bennett."

Will swallowed a curse. Most of the career officers would vigorously disagree with him, but he was enough of an outsider to have realized by now that an army depended most on its noncommissioned officers to function smoothly. The generals might give the orders, but the sergeants truly ran things. And Darcy Bennett, when he was sober, was one of the best. Darcy had a fondness for the grape, though, which Will recalled all too well from their run-ins when Will was still sheriff of Culpeper County. The first time he had encountered Darcy after enlisting, in fact, a half-drunken Darcy had jumped him and tried to beat the hell out of him because of remembered grudges.

"I'll tend to it right away," Will assured Pendleton. "Thank you, and please convey my regrets to the general."

"Of course, sir. Tonight's meeting was more social than strategic, anyway."

Will took his red campaign cap from the table in the foyer where he had placed it next to the caps and hats of the other officers. He clapped it on his head and stepped out into the night. The misting had stopped, and for a change, the clouds overhead were breaking up. Will could actually see stars twinkling in the sky as he glanced up. That wouldn't last long, he thought. By tomorrow it would probably be raining again.

As he crossed the drill field toward the rows of tents that housed the enlisted men, Will heard shouting and saw a group of dark figures clustered around one of the small campfires. In weather like this, it was difficult finding enough wood that was dry enough to burn. Firewood details were kept busy scavenging. Somehow, they came up with enough planks and branches and bushes so that several fires could be built for the men each night. The troopers congregated around those blazes to swap stories or sing or simply warm themselves against the chill. Tonight, however, another sort of activity was going on.

"Kill him!" "Tear his head off!" "Stomp his guts out!"

Will heard the bloodthirsty cries coming from the men and knew that what he had feared was true: a fight had broken out, and Will would have wagered a considerable amount of his overdue captain's pay that Sgt. Darcy Bennett would be in the thick of it.

More men were hurrying over from the neighboring tents and fires and joining the group Will had spotted. As the number of spectators grew, they formed a solid ring so that he could no longer see the campfire. He shouldered into the circle of men, bulling some of them aside. He probably could have used his rank to call them to attention, but instead he attacked the problem as he would have in the days when he was the sheriff of Culpeper County.

Some of the men he roughly pushed aside started to turn angrily to confront him, but their attitudes changed immediately when they saw the officer's cap with its brass insignia in the shape of a curved bugle attached to the front above the bill, the three gold stripes on the sleeves of his gray uniform coat, and the scabbarded saber hanging from his belt. They snapped upright, and one of the men shouted, "Ten-*hutt!*"

"You no-good sons of bitches! Come on, damn you!"

That angry bellow came from the center of the knot of men. Will recognized Darcy's voice. The ring of eager spectators was parting now as more and more of them realized that an officer was in their midst. A path opened before Will, allowing him to see the campfire once more. Shapes darted around it and fists thudded against flesh as the brawl continued.

Will reached the front rank of the audience just as a man crashed to the ground in front of him. The man landed with his face in the mud and stayed that way, apparently out cold. Not wanting him to suffocate before he regained consciousness, Will reached down and grasped the collar of his coat. With a grunt of effort, he pulled the man up and rolled him over onto his back.

The fight was still going on. One large, broad-shouldered figure stood at the center of it, near the fire, as three men came at him from different directions. Darcy grabbed the shoulders of one of his opponents and flung him aside like a child tossing away a rag doll. The man rolled through the fire, scattering ashes and sparks and howling in pain.

Darcy grabbed the next man in a bear hug and concentrated on squeezing him into submission, all the while ignoring the blows being rained down on his head by the last of his attackers. The man who'd had the misfortune to be trapped in the circle of Darcy's massively muscled arms put his head back and gasped for breath that his lungs could no longer inflate to take in. His face turned dark with blood. It was a tossup which would happen first: either his ribs would splinter or he would pass out from lack of air.

Will didn't want to see either of those things happen to a Confederate soldier. It was enough that the Yankees tried to kill them without their killing each other. In a loud voice that cut through the confusion, he commanded, "Sergeant Bennett, put that man *down!*" Darcy didn't respond immediately, so Will added, "Sergeant, that's an order!"

Darcy looked at Will over the shoulder of the man he was on the verge of crushing to death. For a moment his eyes blinked in puzzlement, then understanding dawned in them. His arms opened, and the man who had narrowly escaped a grisly fate fell in a huddled heap at his feet as Darcy straightened to attention.

"Cap'n!" he said. "Beggin' your pardon, Cap'n, I didn't see you—"

"Behind you, Darcy!" Will warned as the last of the sergeant's opponents snatched up a thick branch that had been scattered from the campfire and swung it hard at Darcy's head.

Darcy turned halfway around and swung his left arm in a seemingly lazy backhand. His fist cracked into the man's jaw before the makeshift club could land its skull-crushing blow. The man flew backward, turning a complete flip in the air before landing. Darcy turned back toward Will, as seemingly unconcerned as if he had just swatted a fly.

"Thanks, Cap'n," he said. "Might've hurt a mite if that fella'd managed to clout me with that stick."

Will struggled to keep a grin from stretching across his face. It wouldn't do to let Darcy see how amused he was by that nonchalant attitude. Officers had to maintain some sort of sense of discipline, even amateur ones like Will.

"What's going on here, Sergeant?" he asked.

"You mean this?" Darcy gestured at the crumpled bodies scattered around him. "Just a friendly scuffle, sir."

"It looked to me like those men were trying to kill you."

"Well . . . they *were* a mite peeved at me."

"And why is that?"

"I reckon, sir, it was because I said the cap'n of their company don't have no more sense than God gave a boll weevil."

Will frowned. "Sergeant, not worrying for the moment about the extremely disrespectful nature of that comment— which we *will* deal with—whatever possessed you to make such an inflammatory remark?"

"Well, sir, it was probably the way they said *their* captain said you were nothin' but an ignorant farmer and didn't have no business bein' in charge of real soldiers."

Will felt his back stiffening in anger and tried to force himself to ignore the reaction. He was well aware that some of his brother officers, most of whom had attended the U.S. Military Academy at West Point and had been officers in the U.S. Army before the war, regarded him as unworthy of a captaincy because of his lack of military experience. Even those who hadn't been West Pointers were typically either plantation owners or the sons of plantation owners, so they were from a much higher social station than Will and looked down on him accordingly. Yancy Lattimer, in fact, was about the only one who didn't seem to care about Will's background and regarded him as a genuine friend.

Unfair as the attitudes of the other officers might be, that didn't give Sergeant Bennett an excuse to pound on anybody. Will asked him, "Sergeant, have you been drinking?"

"No, sir," Darcy replied crisply. "I'm stone-cold sober, sir."

Will had stepped close enough to Darcy so that he thought he would smell the liquor on the sergeant's breath if there was any there. Lacking any evidence to the contrary, he had to conclude that the brawl had been provoked solely by Darcy's defense of his captain's honor.

That was going to make it devilishly tricky to punish him, but it had to be done, regardless of Darcy's motives. Will said, "Sergeant, you'll take an extra turn on guard duty tonight and tomorrow night, and if any of these men are injured so severely that they can't perform their duties, you'll be expected to take care of those, as well."

"Yes sir!"

Turning to the troopers who had been standing around and watching the fight, Will uttered the same command he had given voice to many times during his career as a lawman: "Break it up, you men. There's nothing else to see here."

The soldiers straggled back to their tents and campfires. Will waved toward Darcy's unconscious former opponents and added, "Some of you pick up these men and see that they get where they belong."

Once they were alone, Darcy apologized quietly, "Sorry, Cap'n. I just couldn't let those fellers badmouth you like that. They didn't have no right to say them things."

"They were just repeating what they've heard, Darcy."

"But you're the best damn cap'n in the Thirty-third! Hell, maybe in the whole Confed'rate army!"

Will thought about how he'd led his men into that trap a few weeks earlier. "I appreciate the sentiment, Darcy," he replied, "but I'm afraid I've still got a lot to learn about being an officer."

He just hoped he wouldn't be responsible for the deaths of any more men before he learned everything he needed to know.

Chapter Six

FOR THE FIRST TIME in months, Cory woke up in a bed. A real bed, with clean sheets and a comforter and an oak headboard with a curved, arching top like the ceiling of a cathedral. There was no thin, filthy blanket wadded up beneath him or spread over him, no rough, splintery planks, no bugs chewing on him. The sensation was so different that for a moment he feared he was dreaming and would eventually wake up huddled under the shed on the docks back at New Madrid.

He lay there and stared up at the plaster ceiling above him for long moments, just running his hands over the sheets for the sheer joy of it. His eyelids closed, and he uttered a long sigh. As he felt himself drifting back to sleep, he snapped his eyes open. He didn't want to take any chances of this turning out to be a dream. He sat up in the bed.

It wasn't as fancy as he had thought at first. In fact, the bed was rather narrow. But it was still a bed, and that was enough to be tremendously impressive to Cory. He realized he was wearing a nightshirt instead of the ragged garments that were the only clothes he owned; the nightshirt was big and hung on him like a tent, but he didn't mind. He swung his legs out of bed and stood up.

A momentary wave of dizziness hit him, and he grasped one of the posts at the foot of the bed to steady himself. As he rested his hand on the post, he looked around the room. It was narrow, too, not much wider than the bed. The only other furnishings were a three-legged stool and a small writing desk that folded down from one wall. It was folded up now and fastened into place. The other wall had several pegs on it where clothes were hung. Cory saw a pair of pants, three shirts, and a coat.

There was no window, only a door, and like everything else in the room, it was narrow. Whoever had designed this cabin had intended that it would not take up much space.

Cory knew he was on the riverboat *Missouri Zephyr.* He remembered the night before: the dash through the streets of New Madrid, the shots fired at him in the dark, the torch-lit confrontation with the mob of Unionists led by Jason Gill. Cory remembered as well the calmness with which Captain Farrell had stood beside the cannon and forced the mob to back down.

Then, when the *Zephyr* had backed away from the dock and put New Madrid safely behind it, the captain had asked Cory what they were going to do with him now.

Thank God the answer hadn't been to put him off the boat upriver somewhere!

Captain Farrell had turned Cory over to Ike Judson, the pilot. Cory vaguely recalled being led belowdecks by Judson, who'd had some of the boat's roustabouts fill a wooden tub with water.

"If I'm goin' to loan you my bed for the night, I want to make sure you ain't got no graybacks or fleas crawlin' on you. I want you to scrub until you think you're goin' to take the hide off."

Cory had tried to utter his thanks, but Judson cut him short. "I got to be up in the wheelhouse anyway. Travelin' on the river at night ain't no easy task. The cap'n needs his best man at the wheel, and that's me."

One of the deckhands had taken over the job of making sure Cory was cleaned up, while Judson climbed to the upper deck of the riverboat and entered the wheelhouse to join Captain Farrell. As he had been instructed, Cory scrubbed vigorously, including his hair and scalp. It had felt wonderful to be clean again after so long. He'd put on the nightshirt the deckhand gave him and followed the man to Judson's cabin on the Texas deck, one level below the top of the riverboat. There he had stretched out in the bed and fallen asleep immediately, not stirring until a few minutes ago.

The sleep had done wonders for him, but he still felt the effects of the beer he'd drunk the night before plus the malnutrition, exposure, and hard labor of the past months. He felt shaky, and his head hurt. He decided that he needed something to eat and maybe some coffee, but he couldn't very well wander around the riverboat in a nightshirt, even one as voluminous as the one he was wearing. He was studying the clothes hanging on the pegs and wondering if he could roll up the legs of the trousers and the sleeves of one of the shirts enough so that he could wear them, when the door of the cabin swung back and Judson's tall, broad-shouldered figure filled the opening.

"Was wonderin' if you'd still be lyin' a-bed," the pilot commented. "Here." He tossed some clothes to Cory, who caught them and as he held them up saw that they were much closer to his own size.

"Whose are these?" he asked.

"Yours now, I reckon. The cap'n got 'em from one of the roustabouts, a scrawny little feller about like you."

"I don't want to take somebody's clothes away from them," Cory started to protest.

"Take 'em," Judson snapped. "I had one o' the firemen toss those old clothes of yours in the furnace. Best way to get rid of the varmints in 'em."

Cory felt a momentary surge of anger at the high-handedness of Judson's having his clothes burned. Then reason took over. The clothes were little more than rags, and they held no particular value to Cory, sentimental or otherwise. In fact, he was quite glad to pull on some clean, relatively new clothes.

"Here's some socks," Judson said, handing a pair to Cory. "Ain't been able to find you any boots yet, but I'm still lookin'."

"Thank you." Cory pulled up the suspenders attached to the trousers, then sat down on the edge of the bed and put on the clean, thick socks. Like everything else, they felt heavenly. "Why are you doing all this for me, Mr. Judson?"

"Because the cap'n told me to," the pilot answered curtly. Then his attitude softened a little as he added, "Besides, I reckon you helped a mite last night when them damned aboli-tionists came to burn the boat."

"I warned you they were coming," Cory noted. He thought that counted as more than just "a mite."

Judson waved a hand. "Aw, hell, the fellers on guard duty would'a seen 'em before they got here. I don't reckon a whole passel of fellers wavin' torches around could'a snuck up on the boat without somebody seein' 'em, do you?"

"Well . . ." Judson had a point. The outcome of the previous evening's events might have been the same even if Cory hadn't risked his life to reach the *Zephyr* before Gill's mob.

But he *had* risked his life. That had been *his* head those bullets had whipped past. That had to count for something, and obviously it did, because he was still on the riverboat.

"Anyway, like I said that other time, the cap'n must like you for some reason," Judson went on, "and I trust the cap'n's judgment." He added ominously, "Don't you prove him wrong."

"No, sir," Cory replied quickly. "I won't."

Judson grunted. "You want somethin' to eat?"

"That would be . . ." Cory had to stop to lick his lips. "Wonderful."

Judson jerked a thumb over his shoulder. "Come on."

They stepped out of the cabin onto a narrow deck with a railing along its edge. Cory was surprised at how high above the surface of the river they were. The *Zephyr* had three main decks, each of the top two stepped back some from the one below it so that they rose like the tiers of a wedding cake.

"This here's the hurricane deck," Judson explained. "Some folks call it the Texas deck, 'cause it's been added on like Texas was added to the Union back in '45. Next one down is the boiler deck, even though that ain't where the boilers are. They're down on the main deck, the lowest one, along with the engines and the kitchen and the cargo holds. If you been workin' on the docks for very long, you probably know all this."

Cory shook his head. "I've never been on a riverboat except to unload cargo. I rode a horse out here to Missouri from my home in Virginia."

"You got a home?" Judson sounded surprised.

"And a family," Cory said, feeling a lump in his throat as he thought about his mother and his brothers and his sister, back there on the farm in Culpeper County.

"Run you off, did they?"

"Of course not!" Cory protested. "Why would they do that?"

Judson shrugged. "Figured they must've; otherwise why would you leave?"

"Because I . . . I wanted to see the country."

Judson just looked at him, narrow-eyed, and Cory figured the pilot must think he was a fool, or crazy, or both.

They reached a set of stairs that led down to the boiler deck. Cory paused and looked behind him, lifting his gaze to the pilothouse, which was partially visible perched atop the Texas deck, and to the two towering black smokestacks that flanked it just forward of it, one for each engine. Through the big window in the front of the pilothouse, he could see the vague shape of a man standing at the wheel. The huge wheel was almost as tall as he was.

"Is that Captain Farrell?"

"Nope, that's Ned Rowley, the other pilot. Got to have two, you know. I can't be on duty twenty-four hours a day. And since I been up all night . . ."

Cory felt guilty. Judson had to be exhausted, yet he was still taking Cory under his wing, showing him around the boat, making sure he had clothes to wear and something to eat. He offered, "I really appreciate what you're doing for me."

Judson chuckled. "Don't be so sure you'll be thankin' me much longer. You'll earn your keep, boy. Count on it."

Cory suddenly wondered what Captain Farrell intended to do with him. During their first encounter, several weeks earlier,

Cory had pleaded for a job on the riverboat. Now, evidently, he had one, but he had no idea what it was. He wasn't really qualified for anything except menial labor. Maybe he would be put to work as a fireman, stoking the massive furnaces down below that powered the great paddlewheels.

He hesitated at the top of the stairs when Judson started down them. Judson paused and looked back. "Well, come on," he ordered impatiently. "Nobody's goin' to serve you breakfast in your cabin, if that's what you're waitin' for."

"No. No, of course not." Cory managed to put a smile on his face. Whatever was waiting for him, it had to be better than the miserable existence he'd led back in New Madrid. He went down the steps with Judson.

"What happened to that horse you claim you rode out here?"

"I traded him for something to eat."

"Better'n havin' to eat *him*, I suppose." Judson glanced over at Cory. "You were goin' to set the world on fire when you left home, weren't you?"

That lump was back in Cory's throat. "How . . . how did you know that?"

"Let's just say I once knew a feller who was just like you," Judson confessed.

BREAKFAST WAS a bowl of beans with chunks of salt pork floating in them and a wedge of cornpone. Cory ate hungrily, washing down the food with gulps of coffee that was heavily laced with chicory in the New Orleans style. The bald, deeply wrinkled black man who served as cook aboard the *Missouri Zephyr* watched him eat with a big grin on his face.

"Nothin' I likes better'n to see a growin' boy who 'preciates good cookin'," he observed.

"This is wonderful," Cory exclaimed between bites.

"Shadrach does a good job," Judson said. "Leastways, you don't get many complaints, do you, Shad?"

"Nary a one I 'members." Shadrach reached for the pot of beans. "Here, lemme fill up that bowl for you again, boy."

Judson held up a hand to stop him. "What are you tryin' to do, fix it so won't none of us be able to stay in the pilothouse with the boy?"

"Growin' boy needs his food," Shadrach protested.

"And the rest of us need to be able to breathe." Judson stood up as Cory wiped up the last of the bean juice with the final bite of pone. "Let's go."

Cory drained the rest of the coffee from his cup. "You said we were going up to the pilothouse?"

"Cap'n Farrell's got the idea you might make a cub. Me, I don't know." Judson sounded dubious, all right. Cory wondered what a cub was.

The rains had taken a momentary respite, although the sky was still thick with gray clouds. Cory followed Judson up the stairs from the main deck to the boiler deck to the Texas. Toward the back of the boat—the stern, Cory thought it was called—was another set of stairs that led up to the pilothouse. Cory told himself not to look down as he and Judson climbed those stairs. The height bothered him whenever he glanced down toward the river.

When they reached the top, Judson opened the door and led the way into the pilothouse. It was roomier inside than Cory had supposed it would be, looking at it from the outside. The fact that the walls were nearly all windows probably made the room seem larger than it really was. The big window on the front of the pilothouse was one single pane of glass that could be raised on hinges and latched into place as it was now, allowing a cool, almost cold, breeze to blow through the room.

The dominant feature of the pilothouse was the wheel. It was set in a recess in the floor, so that several inches of its diameter were below the level of the floor. Cory counted eighteen spokes radiating out from the hub in the middle of the wheel. They were made of polished hardwood, and each spoke ended in a brass handle that protruded outward some six inches from the wheel itself. The wheel looked heavy, and Cory thought that it probably took considerable strength to turn it.

Three high chairs with curved backs and footrests attached to their legs sat before the wheel. From one of those chairs, the pilot would have a magnificent view of the river. At the moment, however, the pilot—Ned Rowley, Judson had called him—was standing at the wheel, one hand resting lightly on it. Within easy reach were a couple of cranks and some other instruments, the functions of which Cory had no idea, and a speaking tube that connected the pilothouse to the engine room.

Ned Rowley was not the only person in the pilothouse. Standing beside him was a young man in high black boots, tight brown whipcord trousers, a loose gray linsey-woolsey shirt, and a black cap with a stiff bill. As Cory and Judson came into the pilothouse, the young man glanced back over his shoulder at them.

Cory stopped short as he realized that the young "man" was actually a young woman. Miss Lucille Farrell, to be precise, with her long, honey-colored hair tucked up underneath the cap. She looked at him with eyes so richly and beautiful that even though he was aware his jaw had dropped open, there wasn't a thing in the world he could do about it.

"Ain't many flies around this time o' year, but shut your mouth anyway," Judson hissed at him. In a louder voice, he said, "Mornin', Miss Lucille."

"Hello, Ike," she replied, and her voice was every bit as lovely as Cory had dreamed it would be. If anything, it was even more musical than it had been in his visions of her. She was still looking at Cory as she went on, "I suppose this is our wayward Galahad?"

"Uh, yeah, I reckon. He's the feller what tried to warn us about Gill and that mob o' no-good—" Judson stopped short, and Cory figured he was trying to watch his language around the captain's daughter.

Lucille turned and took a step toward Cory, extending her hand as she did so. "I'm Lucille Farrell," she offered unnecessarily. Cory knew who she was. He doubted if there was another woman as beautiful on all the Mississippi River.

"C-Cory Brannon," he managed to say as he took her hand. Her hand was cool, and her grip was surprisingly firm. "Coriolanus Brannon, actually."

Lucille's eyebrows arched. "After Mr. Shakespeare's play?"

"Yes ma'am. My father was a great reader of Mr. Shakespeare's work."

"Well, you look more like a Cory to me. Will you answer to that?"

Judson laughed before Cory could say anything. "Call this boy anything you want, just don't call him late for supper. I ain't never seen such an appetite."

"Well, he certainly hasn't been overeating lately." Lucille's eyes went up and down Cory's slender frame, and he felt himself blushing at the openness with which she regarded his body. He sort of wished he could look at her the same way, but that would have been totally improper. Just the thought of doing so made him blush even more.

"I've been working on the docks at New Madrid," he heard himself saying. "It's hard work, and we don't eat too regular."

"Yes, I know. My father has told me some things about you. I'll wager that Shadrach's cooking will fatten you up."

"Yes ma'am."

The stockily built Ned Rowley called over his shoulder, "Snag comin' up, Miss Lucille."

Eagerly, Lucille turned back so that she could lean forward and peer out the window of the pilothouse. "There to port?" she asked.

"Yep. I call that'un the Gouger, 'cause if we got too close, it'd sure gouge a hole outta our hull." Rowley moved the wheel slightly, and Cory felt the riverboat's delicate response. "You want to 'low least fifty yards to starboard of the ol' Gouger."

Lucille nodded. "I'll remember."

Judson clapped a hand on Cory's shoulder. "Well, seein' as the boy's in good hands, I reckon I'll go get some shuteye. It was a long night."

Cory's head jerked toward him. "You're leaving me up here?"

"Why not? The cap'n wants you to be a pilot's cub, and there ain't no better pair o' pilots on the river for you to learn from than me and Ned."

Cory understood now. A cub was a pilot's apprentice, learning the river so that one day he could handle the wheel of a riverboat himself. But what was Lucille Farrell doing here in the pilothouse? She was the daughter of the *Zephyr*'s captain and owner. Surely she wasn't planning to become a pilot.

Clearly, though, Cory realized, that was what Captain Farrell had in mind for *him*. He felt flattered that the captain would have that much confidence in him; he certainly hadn't done anything so far to justify it.

But he didn't want to let Farrell down. Suddenly, Cory knew that. He was willing to give almost anything a try if that was what the captain wanted.

"All right," he nodded to Judson. "And thank you . . . for everything you've done."

"Just pay attention up here, and maybe you won't turn out to be a total loss," Judson growled as he left the pilothouse.

When he was gone, Lucille laughed, and it was the prettiest sound in the world to Cory. "Don't let Ike bother you," she told him. "He likes to scowl and grumble, but he's really a good friend."

"He's the best pilot on the river," Rowley put in. Then he frowned back over his shoulder at Cory. "But don't you let him know I said that. I got a reputation of my own to protect."

Cory smiled and nodded. Lucille was standing on Rowley's right, so Cory moved up on the pilot's left and looked out the window at the broad expanse of river unfolding before them. After a moment, a question occurred to him, and even though it seemed rather stupid, he decided to go ahead and ask it anyway. "Uh, where are we?"

"On the Mississipp', of course," Rowley replied. "We're 'bout to pass the Big Oak Tree, there to port. Won't be long until we make Hickman. We got some cargo bound for Hickman. Some for Cape Girardeau, too, but we ain't goin' to make the Cape on this trip. That'd mean goin' right past Cairo, and the cap'n, he won't do that. Says they's too many Yankees up yonder, and that they might take it into their heads to grab the boat."

"This war is the worst thing to ever happen to the river," Lucille observed. "The war is going to kill it."

"Maybe not," Cory said. He had been more concerned with his own personal survival during the past months than about anything else, but he had heard plenty of talk about the war—and now he had seen firsthand some of its effects, courtesy of Jason Gill. "The Confederacy still controls it from Memphis on down to New Orleans, doesn't it?"

"For now. There's no telling how long that will last, though."

"Bluff reef comin' up," Rowley called.

Cory leaned forward, studying the surface of the river. "I don't see anything."

"There," Lucille pointed. "That dark line in the water. Do you see it?"

Cory tried to follow her finger, but he became distracted by the smooth skin on the back of her hand. With a little shake of his head, he forced his attention back onto the river. He spotted a long, dark, slanting line in the water and indicated it. "Is that it?"

"It surely is," said Rowley. "A bluff reef's a sandbar that slants sharplike on the sides, and it ain't far below the surface. It's narrow, but dangerous. When you spot one, give it a wide berth."

Cory nodded. "I understand." But he truly didn't, he thought. He had loaded and unloaded riverboats for months, but he knew nothing about how to navigate them. And evidently the river was full of dangers that had to be avoided.

Boats such as the *Missouri Zephyr* were made of fairly thin wood
so that they would be lighter and ride higher in the water, not
requiring as much draft as heavier vessels. As a result of that
construction, their hulls were easily breached. A rock, a sandbar, even a floating log could rip a huge hole in the hull and
send the boat sinking to the bottom. The more Cory thought
about it, the more he realized that being a pilot was an awe-
some responsibility. The safety of the boat, its passengers and
crew, and its cargo were all in the hands of the man who stood
at the wheel, his eyes fixed on the ever-changing surface of the
great river.

And *that* was the job Captain Farrell expected him to do?
Cory swallowed hard.

"Where are you from?"

It took Cory a moment to realize that Lucille had just
asked him a question. He said, "Ah, Virginia. Culpeper
County."

She smiled across at him. "I'm afraid I don't know where in
Virginia that is. I was raised in New Orleans. Well, on the river,
really, I suppose you could say. I've been traveling on the
Zephyr with my father ever since I was five. That was twelve
years ago."

"He brought you with him when you were five?"

"It was that or leave me with someone else to raise, and
Father wasn't going to do that."

"But what about your mother?" Too late, Cory saw the
warning glance that Ned Rowley shot toward him. The words
were already out of his mouth.

"She died," Lucille said simply.

"Oh. I . . . I'm sorry. I didn't know." Cory wished he could
think of something better to say, but that was all that came to
mind.

"Of course you didn't," Lucille said, injecting a note of
brightness in her voice again, even though Cory could tell that
it cost her an effort. "Look! There's the Big Oak Tree."

Cory looked to the left—to port, he reminded himself—and saw a towering tree on the riverbank with a huge spread of branches. It was an impressive sight, and he could understand why river pilots might use it as a landmark.

The door of the pilothouse opened behind them, and Cory glanced back to see Capt. Zeke Farrell coming into the room. The captain had no doubt been up all night after the unscheduled, hurried departure from New Madrid, but his suit was immaculate, he was freshly shaven, and he looked completely alert. Cory wondered how he managed that on little or no sleep.

"Good morning, Ned," Farrell said. He looked at Cory. "Mr. Brannon." Then he stepped up beside his daughter and placed a hand on her shoulder, squeezing gently. "Lucille."

"Good morning, Father."

"I see you've met our young Mr. Brannon."

"Yes, we've been getting along splendidly."

"You have, have you?" murmured Farrell. He looked at Cory again, raising one eyebrow as he did so. Cory swallowed and kept his gaze fixed on the river ahead of them. He wished Lucille hadn't made their conversation sound quite so . . . friendly. Not that he wanted to be unfriendly with her. He just didn't want anything to happen that might cause Captain Farrell to reconsider the generosity he had shown.

Lucille was undoubtedly the most beautiful girl Cory had ever seen in his life, and given half a chance he knew he would fall totally, madly in love with her, even though it was highly unlikely that emotion would ever be returned. But right now, as much as it went against the romantic streak in his personality, Cory wanted to continue having a decent place to sleep and good meals more than he wanted anything else.

"And do you think he might make a pilot someday?" Farrell asked his daughter.

"Of course. Not as good a one as I'll be, though. He has a bit of trouble concentrating all his attention on the river."

Ned Rowley burst out laughing.

Cory felt himself flushing again. So she *had* noticed him looking at her, even though he had tried not to. But not all the warmth flooding through him was due to embarrassment. Some of it was prompted by irritation. She had the nerve to think that she would turn out to be a better pilot than he was. They would just have to see about that. Why, she was a *girl!* Who had ever heard of a girl riverboat pilot?

"And what do you have to say for yourself, Mr. Brannon?"

Cory nodded toward the scattering of cabins and wharves he had just spotted up ahead on the riverbank. "Hickman up ahead, sir." He had never heard of Hickman before this morning, had never been there, but he remembered what Rowley had said earlier. He just hoped he wasn't guessing wrong.

"Very good, Mr. Brannon, very good."

Relief went through Cory. His hunch had been right. He leaned back a little so that he could glance over at Lucille behind her father's back.

She was sticking her tongue out at him.

Chapter Seven

"AMEN," SAID PASTOR Josiah Crosley, and the congregation of the Culpeper Baptist Church echoed, "Amen!" Pastor Crosley stepped down from the pulpit, his thick, black leather-bound Bible tucked under his arm. He went to the back of the sanctuary to shake hands with the members of the congregation, as he did after every service. With his round face wreathed in a smile, he pumped hand after hand and said, "Hello, Ed . . . Good morning to you, Mrs. Kingston . . . Nice to see you, Tom . . . How's the fishing out your way, Andy?" He had no trouble greeting the worshipers by name as they left the building. Even though the Good Book said that pride goeth before a fall, he took pride in the way he knew each member of the congregation. That was part of a pastor's job, after all: to know the needs of the Lord's flock so that he could minister to them and help them through their times of troubles and ultimately lead them into the grace of their heavenly Father.

Suddenly, Pastor Crosley's smile slipped a little as the smell of stale whiskey struck him. His hand, outstretched to shake the hand of the next person to depart from the church, dropped slightly. "Titus?" he said.

Titus Brannon shuffled past him, head down, and didn't take the offered hand. Titus's long hair hung in front of his face so that Crosley couldn't see his downcast eyes. If he had been able to see them, though, Crosley would have bet that they were bloodshot. Not that he would have actually wagered anything, of course, since gambling was a sin.

Once he was past the preacher, Titus stumbled a little on the steps leading down from the front of the church. He caught his balance before he fell and made his way toward the Brannon wagon, which was parked with dozens of others in the field beside the church.

Mac and Henry Brannon followed their brother out of the building, and behind them, arm in arm, came Abigail and Cordelia. Mac's face was set in tight, angry lines as he watched Titus's unsteady progress toward the wagon. He took Crosley's hand, shook it firmly, and gave the preacher a curt nod. "Pastor."

"Good to see you, Mac." Crosley reached across Mac to shake hands with the younger Brannon. "And you, too, Henry. How are you feeling these days?" Crosley remembered all too well how close Henry had come to dying from that bush-whacker's bullet.

"Fit as a fiddle," Henry replied with a grin. He glanced toward Titus and added roguishly, "That's more'n I can say for some people."

"I'm sorry, Pastor," Mac said quietly. "Titus was late getting home last night. I told him he ought not to come this morning—"

"Nonsense. The Lord's house is the place we should all be on the Sabbath if possible. I'm sorry that Titus is feeling, ah, a mite under the weather."

Mac's eyes narrowed. "Still, I intend to have a talk with him when we get home. A mighty good talk."

"Peacefully, Brother Brannon. Above all else, a Christian must be forgiving."

A muscle in Mac's taut jaw jumped slightly. He didn't look too forgiving at the moment. But perhaps his anger would fade during the ride back out to the farm from Culpeper. Pastor Crosley hoped so.

Mac and Henry moved on, and Crosley shook hands with Abigail. Like Mac, she looked angry, but she looked even more embarrassed. She thought that Titus's behavior reflected badly on her. Under other circumstances, Crosley might have told her that everyone had to make their own decisions, to follow their own path, whether it was one of righteousness or one of iniquity. But this was neither the time nor the place, the preacher decided, so he just shook Abigail's hand gently and patted the back of it with his other hand, saying, "So good to see you here this morning, Sister Brannon. And you, too, of course, Cordelia."

"Thank you, Pastor." Abigail's back was stiff as she tried to hang on to some of her dignity. "That was an excellent sermon. I wonder if our boys in the army ever get to hear any good preaching."

"Every company has a chaplain, I'm told," Crosley assured her, "and I'm sure they attend services whenever they have a chance."

"I hope so. I know the Lord's watching over them, but I'm sure they'd feel better if they got to go to church once in a while."

"Amen, Sister," Crosley affirmed.

"Good-bye, Pastor," Cordelia called over her shoulder as she and her mother went on down the steps. Crosley smiled at her. Cordelia Brannon had turned into quite a beauty, and she was a decent, God-fearing young woman to boot. She would make a fine wife for some young man.

That thought made a twinge of regret go through Crosley. Most of the young men from Culpeper County had gone off to fight the Yankees, and as much as he might pray that it would be otherwise, he knew that some of them would never come home. And no doubt many of the ones who did would be wounded, some so grievously that they would never be the same. If Cordelia waited until after the war to find a beau, as she might well have to, she might be out of luck, even as lovely as she was. Right now, there just weren't many men to choose from . . .

But he wasn't a matchmaker, Pastor Crosley reminded himself. In affairs of the heart, unfortunately, the young often had to find their own way.

And all their elders could do was pray that they would follow the right path.

FOR SOMETIMES as long as a half-hour, the members of the congregation lingered outside the church after services, visiting with friends and neighbors. Many of them spent the week on their farms, seldom seeing anyone outside their own family, so these informal Sunday afternoon get-togethers were important for the community. It was pleasant, standing under the trees and swapping stories and the latest news. These days, of course, the main topic of conversation was the war.

"Well, we've thrashed the Yankees twice now," Jacob Taylor observed proudly as he tucked his thumbs in the pockets of his vest. He was a thin man with muttonchop whiskers. His oldest son was already in the Confederate army, and he had two younger boys still at home, hoping that the war would last long enough for them to get into it.

He was referring to the battle of Ball's Bluff, which had taken place several days earlier near the town of Leesburg, Virginia, on the Potomac River northwest of Washington. The Confederate army controlled Leesburg, and the new Federal commander, Gen. George B. McClellan, had decided that it was unwise to allow the Rebels to sit there unmolested so close to the capital.

McClellan had been placed in charge of the Army of the Potomac, formerly the Division of the Potomac, after the debacle along the meandering stream known as Bull Run. He had immediately begun building up the Union forces: more men, more guns, more rigorous training. Instilling military discipline was uppermost, and despite the fact that the troops referred to him as "Little Mac," the Yankee soldiers came to have great respect for their new commanding officer. By late October, McClellan believed that he had his army whipped into proper fighting shape. Leesburg was to be their first real test. The Army of the Potomac was now so impressive, in McClellan's opinion, that a mere show of force would be enough to send the Rebels scurrying out of Leesburg.

To the delight of the Confederacy, things had not worked out that way.

Union troops had crossed the Potomac at Harrison's Island then ascended the steep section of riverbank known as Ball's Bluff. This geographical feature was named for the family who owned it, the family of George Washington's mother. The Federal officer commanding in the field, Brig. Gen. Charles P. Stone, could hardly have picked a worse spot to launch his attack. The Yankees reached the top of the bluff safely, but then they encountered resistance from Confederate troops under the command of Col. Nathan G. Evans, whose men had fought so fiercely during the early stages of the battle at Manassas. Evans's men fought no less fiercely here. With an open pasture full of enraged Confederates in front of them and the steep bluff leading down to the river behind them, the Union forces found themselves between a rock and a hard place, as the old saying went. Just as it had a few months earlier, their retreat turned into a bloody rout. Some soldiers had broken their necks trying to jump down the bluff, while others had drowned in the Potomac as they attempted to swim back across to safety. The fleeing soldiers had been easy targets for the Confederate sharpshooters.

"You'd think they would have learned by now," Bob Hindman responded to Taylor's comment. "Even the Yankees ought to be able to get it through their thick skulls that they can't outfight us. They just can't."

Mac stood with the men, but he wasn't really paying attention to their discussion of the war. Through slitted eyes, he watched Titus, who had climbed into the back of the wagon and sat down, slumping against one of the sideboards. Titus took his hat off and ran his fingers through his tangled hair. He looked sick, as well he ought to, thought Mac. How many jugs of whiskey had he downed the night before? Enough so that the stench still lingered around him, even though he'd washed up and put on clean clothes this morning.

"What do you hear from your brother, Mac?" one of the men asked, shaking Mac out of his disapproving glower at Titus.

He turned back to the other men and answered, "Will's still with General Jackson at Winchester. They're just waiting to see what General Johnston will have them do next."

"I'll bet Will was disappointed he wasn't at Ball's Bluff," Taylor said with a chuckle. "Will always liked a good scrape."

"He sure did," agreed Hindman.

They had changed their tune a little in the past few months, Mac thought. Though Taylor and Hindman, indeed all the Brannon family's neighbors in Culpeper County, had always been friendly, Will's scrapes with the Fogartys had caused some people to think it would be better if Will resigned as sheriff and moved on. As a matter of fact, that was exactly what had happened when the war broke out. But only after the painful morning when Abigail had disowned her oldest son and ordered him to leave so that no more violence would be visited on the rest of her children. Mac still winced a little when he thought too much about how Will had looked on that day, as their mother's angry words lashed at him.

"I'm sure Will will see his share of fighting," Mac said now. "His last letter said that he'd been wounded in a skirmish with a Yankee patrol."

"Badly wounded?" asked one of the men.

Mac shook his head. "No, just a graze on his leg. He says that he's back to normal now, except that it's stiff whenever the weather's bad."

The other men nodded in understanding. Most of them had various aches and pains that showed up whenever it happened to rain.

One of the men, a short, bearded fellow named Blayne, thumbed his bowler hat back on his head and noted with a grin, "Looks to me like Titus needs a little hair of the dog that bit him."

"Titus is all right," Mac retorted sharply, controlling with an effort the anger that tried to flare through him at Blayne's smug tone.

"Oh, I reckon he will be," Blayne agreed. "Heard tell he got tossed out of Riley's place again last night, but not before he got in a fight with a couple of gents."

"That's Titus's business." This time, Mac didn't even try to keep the anger out of his voice.

Blayne shrugged. "Maybe so, but if it was my brother strayin' from the straight and narrow like that, I'd give him a good talkin' to."

"You want to give Titus a talking to? Go right ahead."

Blayne's self-satisfied look disappeared. Like every other man here, he knew Titus's reputation as a man with a short, violent temper. "He ain't *my* brother."

"That's right. He's not." Mac looked around at the others and tugged on the brim of his hat. "Good afternoon, gentlemen," he offered as he turned to leave.

He was seething inside as he walked toward the wagon, but he didn't know if he was more angry at Titus or at Blayne. Blayne was a pompous busybody, Mac thought, but if Titus hadn't spent the past couple of months wallowing in self-pity and bad whiskey, Blayne wouldn't have had such a tempting target at which to direct his gibes.

Mac reached the wagon and tightly grasped the sideboard where Titus was slumped. "I hope you're proud of yourself," he hissed. "You've embarrassed Ma and Cordelia, not to mention me and Henry. Whatever gave you the idea you could come to church reeking of whiskey?"

Titus lifted his head slowly and blinked at Mac with bleary eyes. "You let me ride in the wagon," he said.

"You were downwind of me. I should've known better."

Titus laughed hollowly. "Hell, we all should've known better about something or other, shouldn't we, big brother?"

"What are you talking about?" asked Mac, even though he knew Titus was probably referring to his infatuation with Polly Ebersole. That was the only thing on Titus's mind these days . . . that, and getting drunk and fighting.

Titus didn't answer the question. Instead, he lifted a hand and pointed. His hand, so steady when it was gripping his Sharps rifle, trembled a little now. "Henry don't look too embarrassed to me," he said. "Fact is, he don't look like he gives a damn 'bout me and how I come to church."

"What are you talking about?" Mac snapped impatiently. He turned his head and looked where Titus was pointing, then frowned. "Who's that girl talking to Henry? She looks familiar, but I can't place her . . ."

"It's that Grange girl from Richmond," said Titus. He gave a barely muffled belch. "Katie, I think that's her name."

"Henry? henry brannon, is that you?"

When Henry heard his name called, he turned and saw a young woman coming toward him with a smile on her face. He knew her instantly, even though he hadn't seen her since the previous winter, and even then he had spoken to her only a few times and never at great length.

But many nights after that, he had gone to sleep with the memory of Katie Grange filling his senses. In his mind, he had seen the lovely face, heard the merry laugh, smelled the delicate fragrance of her cologne. Brief though their acquaintance had been, Katie Grange had made quite an impression on him.

Now she held her hands out to him, and without thinking about what he was doing, Henry took them. She was wearing gloves, but he could still feel the warmth of her fingers through them. He also felt his heart beginning to pound harder in his chest.

"I thought it was you," Katie said. "I was hoping I'd see you here in Culpeper." She was dressed for church in a sober gray dress and hat, but nothing could dim the brightness of the strawberry blonde curls that tumbled around her face.

"What . . . what are you doing here?" Henry managed to ask.

"I live here now. My father bought the hardware store."

That news was staggering to Henry. To think that Miss Katherine Grange—Katie, as she insisted on being called—was going to live right here in Culpeper, just down the road from the Brannon family farm. He could see her all the time, once or twice a week, anyway.

Suddenly, he became aware that he was still holding her hands. He let go of them abruptly. Casting about for something to say, he asked, "Why?"

"Why what?"

"Uh, why did your father buy the hardware store?"

"Because his business is selling hardware." Katie's smile wavered slightly. "And because he doesn't think it would be safe for us to live in Richmond anymore."

"Why not?"

"The war," Katie said simply.

Henry frowned. Richmond was the capital of the Confederacy. It ought to be just about the safest place in the world, he thought. Unless . . .

Lowering his voice to a whisper, he asked, "Your pa's not a Unionist, is he?"

"A what? Oh, good Lord, no, Henry!" She swatted him lightly on the arm with a gloved hand. "Shame on you for thinking such a thing."

"I'm sorry," he blurted desperately. "I didn't know—"

Katie rescued him from his misery with a casual wave of her hand. "Oh, that's all right. You never really met my father last winter, did you?"

Henry shook his head.

"He believes in the Confederacy 100 percent," she went on. "But he was in the Mexican War, and he says that sooner or later in any war, one capital or the other comes under attack, sometimes both of them. So he thinks it would be safer for me and my mama and my little brothers if we didn't live in Richmond anymore. That's why he decided to move out here to the country."

Henry had a hard time thinking of Culpeper as the country; to him it had always been town. But to somebody like Katie, who'd been raised in a big city like Richmond, he supposed the settlement here seemed pretty small.

Frequently over the years, the Brannons had traveled to Richmond for the various fairs and horse races that were held there. That was how Cordelia had come to befriend Katie Grange, and the previous winter she had introduced her friend to her brother Henry. Henry had been smitten with Katie right away, and unfortunately, he was afraid that both girls realized that, judging by the way they looked at him and whispered behind their hands and giggled. He had spent a lot of that visit to Richmond with his ears burning.

On the few occasions when he'd gotten to talk to Katie without Cordelia around, however, the two of them had gotten along well. She hadn't seemed nearly as silly then. But Henry had figured there was no chance for their budding friendship to grow into anything else, since he couldn't count on ever seeing her again.

Now here she was right in front of him, big as life and twice as pretty and telling him that she was going to be around Culpeper all the time from now on. That news left him scared and happy and somehow hollow-bellied, all at the same time.

Katie was looking at him, he realized, and it came to him that she was waiting for him to say something. "I, uh, I hope you and your folks are happy here. It's a good place to live."

"I think so," she agreed, her gaze oddly intent on him.

Now what in blazes did she mean by that?

Before Henry could ponder the matter any further, a deep male voice rumbled behind him, "Come along, Katherine. It's time to go home."

With an effort, Henry kept himself from jumping. He turned his head and saw a large, florid-faced man in a black hat and suit. He was with a plump woman who had graying hair that had once been the same brilliant shade as Katie's, and surrounding the woman were five little boys from the ages of four to twelve, all of whom glared at Henry with unabashed hostility.

"All right, Father," Katie said. "Father, you remember Henry Brannon, don't you?"

Mr. Grange grunted. "Can't say as I do."

"He comes from one of Culpeper County's finest families. His sister Cordelia is a dear friend of mine."

"Unh," Mr. Grange replied.

Henry swallowed and stuck his hand out. "I'm glad to meet you, sir. I hear you've bought the hardware store."

Grange gave him a fast, disinterested handshake. "That's right. Come on, Katherine." He turned away, and so did his wife. The boys went, too, but they cast narrow-eyed glares back at Henry.

Katie caught hold of his hands again and squeezed them. "Good-bye, Henry. I'll see you next Sunday, if not before then."

"Next Sunday. Yes. If not before."

She smiled at him again, and then she was gone. He watched as she walked alongside her parents and brothers, chatting animatedly with them. *To* them, actually, Henry noted. The rest of the family didn't seem to have much to say.

A hand fell on his shoulder. This time he couldn't keep from flinching. He looked over and saw Mac. "That was Cordelia's friend from Richmond, wasn't it?"

"Uh, yeah," Henry said. "Cordelia's friend."

"Where is Cordelia, anyway?"

"I don't know," Henry admitted, glad for the chance to change the subject. "She ought to be around somewhere." He scanned the group of churchgoers lingering outside the white-washed sanctuary without seeing his sister. "Well, that beats me. Where'd she get off to?"

"I don't know," Mac echoed, "but I reckon we ought to find out."

CORDELIA HAD walked with her mother to the wagon and helped her onto the seat. Abigail hadn't looked behind her at Titus or given any other sign that she was even aware of his existence. Cordelia was about to climb up onto the seat by her mother to keep her company until Mac and Henry were ready to leave. Then Mac would take the reins and Cordelia would step into the back with Titus and Henry.

Before Cordelia could climb up, though, she spotted a familiar figure walking along the road near the church. Nathan Hatcher was wearing a dark gray suit today, but Cordelia didn't remember seeing him in church. In fact, she couldn't recall seeing him at any of the worship services for quite a while.

"I'll be right back, Mama," she said as she turned away from the wagon.

"Where are you going, Cordelia?" Abigail called after her, but she pretended not to hear, feeling a momentary twinge of guilt as she did so. At the moment, however, curiosity was a stronger emotion.

"Hello, Nathan," she greeted him as she stepped to the edge of the road.

"Cordelia. How nice to see you." A smile touched his wide, expressive mouth. "You're not going to bump into me again, are you?"

"What—? Oh, you mean that day in Mr. Davis's store. No, I'm watching where I'm going today."

"Pity," Nathan murmured.

Cordelia felt herself reddening. "What did you say, Mr. Hatcher?"

"Nothing," he replied hastily. "Nothing at all." He glanced past her at the church. "I take it services just let out?"

"That's right. I didn't see you there."

"I, ah, haven't been attending much recently."

"Why not?" she asked with the innocence of the devout.

"Well, my work with Judge Darden keeps me extremely busy during the week, and I've been catching up on my reading on Sundays."

"Plutarch?" she asked, calling up the name from her memory.

"That's right. And on a fine day such as this, I like to take a stroll, too. You know, some people believe you can get just as close to God by communing with nature as you can by singing hymns in a church."

Cordelia gave him a skeptical look. "Nature is fine, but it can't be better than a good hymn and a fine sermon."

"I didn't say better. I said you could get just as close to God."

Nathan had started walking again, and without thinking about what she was doing, Cordelia fell in step beside him. She was caught up in the discussion, and she observed, "The church is the Lord's house."

"The whole wide world is the Lord's, isn't it?"

"Well, of course, but that's different." She waved a hand at the businesses that lined Culpeper's main street. "You might as well say that you could find God in Albie Riley's tavern."

"Why not?"

"My brother Titus seems to be looking for *something* there, that's for sure," she muttered under her breath. "Anyway, I just feel like a good Christian ought to be in church on Sunday."

"There's the problem," Nathan noted. "Maybe I'm not a good Christian."

"Of course you are! Don't say things like that, Nathan. Why, you're a fine man."

He stopped walking and turned to look at her with an unusually solemn expression on his face. "Do you really think so?"

Before Cordelia could answer, a man riding on horseback along the street suddenly veered his mount toward the two young people. "Hatcher!" he called, and Cordelia thought he sounded angry. "That you, Hatcher?"

"Go on your way, Mr. Fenton," Nathan suggested. "I don't want any trouble with you. It's the Sabbath."

The man pulled his horse to a stop, but not before the animal crowded toward Nathan and made him step back. He moved so that he was between Cordelia and the man on horseback.

"I don't give a damn what day it is," Fenton snarled. "You lawyers'd rob a man blind any day of the week!"

"It was the court that decided against you in that lawsuit, Mr. Fenton. Judge Darden simply represented your opponent. And I'm just reading for the law. I haven't passed the bar yet."

Fenton waved a big, knobby-knuckled hand. "Don't matter. I lost a whole section of good bottomland. It was flatout stole from me!"

"You never had proper title to the land in the first place," Nathan tried to explain patiently.

"I'll give you proper, you damned pipsqueak!" With no more warning than that, Fenton jerked his foot from the stirrup of his saddle and lashed out with it. The heel of his boot slammed into Nathan's chest and drove him backward into Cordelia. She let out a little scream as she started to fall.

Strong hands caught her before she could tumble to the ground. She looked up into the face of her brother Mac. He lifted her, set her on her feet, and asked, "Are you all right?"

"I . . . I'm fine," Cordelia managed to say. "But Nathan—"

He was sitting hunched over on the ground. Henry knelt beside him and said, "Nate?"

Nathan managed to lift a hand. "I'll be all right," he grated between teeth clenched against the pain. "Just let me . . . get my breath."

Furious, Cordelia glared at the man called Fenton. "How dare you kick Mr. Hatcher like that?" she demanded. "You had no right."

"I had every right," Fenton snapped. "He's a lawyer, and him and his boss stole my land right out from under me. I don't care what the damned court says about titles and such-like."

"Watch your language around my sister, Fenton," Mac warned. "And I don't appreciate the way you nearly knocked her down, either."

Henry stood up and moved over beside Mac as they faced the man on horseback. Several more men were coming down the street from the church, and for the first time, Fenton started to look a little nervous. He tugged on his hat brim and nodded to Cordelia. "I'm right sorry about that, Miss Brannon," he apologized. "I sure didn't mean for you to get hurt."

"But you meant to hurt poor Nathan!"

"Why don't you get down off that horse, Fenton?" Henry challenged.

Fenton licked his lips. "This ain't your fight, Brannon. It ain't none of y'all's fight. It's between him and me." He pointed to Nathan Hatcher, who was still sitting on the ground. Emboldened, Fenton went on, "If he wants to settle this, let him get up. Then I'll get off my horse. Be glad to."

Mac looked at Nathan. "What about it? You want us to do anything about this, Nathan?"

Lifting a hand, Nathan waved off the offer of help. "Fenton's right," he said bitterly. "The trouble is between the two of us, no one else. And I'm not going to waste a moment of my time trying to pound any sense into his head."

Fenton's lip curled in a sneer. "You're yella, you mean. You ain't goin' to fight me?"

"I fight my battles in a courtroom."

Fenton snorted in contempt. "I'm goin' back to my farm—what's left of it." The hard stare he sent at Mac and Henry was a clear challenge for them to try to stop him.

"Go on," Mac said. He turned away from Fenton, clearly dismissing the man. Taking Cordelia's arm, he went on, "Let's go back to the wagon. It's time we went home, too."

"But Nathan—" she began, looking over her shoulder.

"Nathan can take care of himself," Mac said coolly. Henry just looked at the young law clerk and shook his head.

Cordelia knew what they were thinking. Nathan's refusal to fight Fenton had sent their opinions of him plummeting. Mac was the most peaceful man Cordelia knew; Henry was more hotheaded. But to both of them, a man who wouldn't stand up and fight when he was knocked down wasn't much of a man. Probably most of the other people looking on felt the same way. And until today, Cordelia realized, she probably would have reacted in much the same fashion.

But now, as Mac led her back toward the church and the waiting wagon, she couldn't help but glance back. The crowd that had gathered so briefly was already melting away, leaving Nathan Hatcher sitting alone on the ground. Slowly, he stood up, then bent over painfully to pick up his hat. He knocked the dust off it, settled it on his head, and began to walk slowly away.

Cordelia thought that was just about the saddest sight she had ever seen in her life.

Chapter Eight

CORY HAD NEVER SEEN anything like the river. Most of the time, there was no need to put a name to it. You just said The River and people knew what you were talking about. The Mississippi. The Father of Waters—although Ike Judson had informed him one day that really wasn't an accurate translation of the Algonquin word *Mitchisipi*, which meant "great river." Some people, also erroneously, called it the Big Muddy; that name, according to Judson, was reserved for the Missouri, which flowed into the Mississippi at Saint Louis. Cory thought it would have been appropriate anyway. The Mississippi was sure enough muddy.

And big. Cory had seen plenty of rivers back in Virginia, of course: the Rappahannock, the James, the Pamunkey, and others. But none of them could hold a candle to the Mississipp'. Cory had learned to swim in the creek near the Brannon farm known as Dobie's Run. That water had been clear and cold and fast-flowing much of the time, nothing at all like the unpredictable, mile-wide behemoth on which the *Missouri Zephyr* made its way upstream and downstream. The Mississippi made long, sweeping bends between shallow banks that were sometimes little more than islands in the swamps that bordered the river. If he had been allowed to do so, Cory probably could have stood and watched the river roll past all day.

Ike Judson and Ned Rowley saw to it that he didn't have that opportunity. Cory spent most of his time in the wheelhouse with one or the other of the pilots, listening intently to them as they pointed out the landmarks along the shore and the shoals and snags and sandbars in the river. At first he had tried to write everything down, using a stub of pencil he had borrowed from Shadrach. Soon, however, he realized that when he was writing, he wasn't watching the river. He missed too many things that way. Besides, Judson didn't like that habit.

"You got to learn the river up here," he said one day, tapping a long, blunt finger against his temple. "You can't scribble it down on a piece of paper."

"I just thought it might help me remember—" Cory began.

Judson shook his head. "You can't just remember what I'm tellin' you. You got to *know* it—in your head, in your guts, in your bones." He kept one hand on the huge wheel and used the other to point. "See that ripple over yonder?"

Cory looked and nodded. "I see it." He had gotten better at spotting such things.

"Wasn't there on the last trip. It's probably a log that came floatin' down from somewhere and got wedged on somethin' under the water. You got to watch out for things like that."

Cory nodded again.

"And over there," Judson said, switching the direction in which he was pointing.

Cory studied that area of the river for a moment before frowning and admitting, "I don't see anything. The river looks like it's flowing just fine over there."

"So it is. But there was a sandbar there last time we came along here."

"What happened to it?"

"Washed away, I reckon. That means the water's flowin' faster under the surface there than it used to. Got to keep that in mind when you're steerin' through there. Sometimes what you don't see is more important than what you do see."

Cory shook his head. What he didn't see was how he could possibly learn everything he needed to know in order to be a riverboat pilot someday. Sometimes he wasn't even sure if that was what he wanted to do with his life. He certainly hadn't set out from Culpeper County, Virginia, with that goal in mind. He really hadn't had any particular objective, other that to shake the dust of home off his boots.

Those boots were long gone, along with the rest of the clothes Judson had burned after the incident with the mob in New Madrid. Now Cory wore a fairly new pair that he had bought with his own money in Vicksburg during one of the *Zephyr*'s stops there. That had felt mighty good, being able to afford to buy his own boots. He had a hat, too, a broad-brimmed straw planter's hat that Judson wouldn't allow him to wear in the wheelhouse. The pilot had taken one baleful look at it and said, "This is a riverboat, not a plantation. Get rid of that damned thing while you're up here. If you got to wear somethin' on your head, wear a riverman's cap, like mine."

So that was what Cory had on his head now, and he was proud of it, too.

The other major revelation for him, other than the Mississippi itself, had been New Orleans. Just as he had never seen a river like the Mississippi, he had never seen a city like New Orleans. Sprawling over the banks of the river as it made the huge, crescent-shaped bend that gave the city its nickname, New Orleans was by far the largest city Cory had ever visited. There were miles of docks, and beyond them, buildings as far as the eye could see. Richmond was a good-sized town, but New Orleans had it beat in every way, shape, and fashion. The first time the *Zephyr* had docked there, Cory had stood at the railing on the Texas deck and watched in awe as the multitudes went by. He saw fancy carriages with gold decorations on them, pulled by big black horses with colorful plumes attached to their heads. From those carriages alighted men in beaver hats and cutaway coats and silk vests, carrying polished hardwood canes with silver heads, and beautiful women in fancy gowns and plumed hats that reminded Cory of the plumes on the horses.

Not all the people around the docks were rich, of course. There were hundreds of dockworkers, many of them black, and Cory figured at first they were slaves. Judson set him straight on that, too. "Most of those boys are freedmen," the pilot told Cory. "'Round here, about the only slaves you'll see are the ones bein' taken off ships and sent to the market."

"There's a slave market here?"

Judson nodded. "One of the biggest. They call it the barracoon."

There were also businessmen in lightweight suits and bowler hats, and the crews of the riverboats that were docked here, and sailors from foreign ships, some of them so colorfully dressed that Cory thought they must be pirates. He saw painted women lingering around some of the docks, too, and Judson nodded toward them and said, "Best keep your distance from them, boy. A few minutes of visitin' with them'll leave you with comp'ny you'll be scratchin' a week later."

Cory felt his face warming. "I . . . I would never do anything like that."

"Don't say never. Feller with an itch in his pants'll do some damned foolish things and then wind up with another sort of itch, like I just told you."

Cory was glad Lucille Farrell wasn't anywhere around at the moment to hear such crude talk. Lucille was a lady, despite her penchant of sometimes dressing up in boys' clothing and her determination that someday she, too, would be a riverboat pilot, if not its captain.

But as Cory looked at the painted women and thought about Lucille, he had to admit that there were times when images of her that were decidedly unladylike entered his mind. He couldn't help thinking about what it would be like to kiss her and put his arms around her and touch her all over . . .

"Well, Mr. Brannon, what do you think of New Orleans?"

Captain Farrell's voice made Cory start guiltily. Farrell seemed not to notice. Cory swallowed and stammered, "It's, ah, big."

Farrell smiled. "Indeed it is. The Crescent City. I think of it as my home, even though I wasn't born here. Lucille was, of course."

Cory wished the captain hadn't mentioned Lucille. He hadn't succeeded quite fully in banishing all those indecent thoughts from his mind.

"Enjoy yourself while we're here," Farrell went on. "But be careful. New Orleans is a magnificent city, but a careless young man can get in a great deal of trouble here without meaning to."

"I don't want trouble," Cory professed fervently. "I reckon I'll just stay right here on the boat the whole time."

"Oh, I don't think you need to go quite that far. Ike, you'll watch out for the lad, won't you?"

Judson's voice was heavy with resignation as he agreed, "Sure, Cap'n. I won't let anything happen to him."

That was how it had turned out, too. Judson had taken Cory to a couple of taverns, and they had drunk some beer and then gone to a restaurant where Cory ate red beans and rice and some kind of soup with things floating in it that he didn't want to think about. After that, they'd headed back to the boat.

As the end of the year approached, Cory had made several trips up and down the lower Mississippi on the *Zephyr*, and he was beginning to feel that he knew his way around the river— the part between New Orleans and Memphis, anyway. Captain Farrell seldom ventured any farther north than that these days. All along the river, rumors were still flying fast and furious about what the Union forces under General Grant up in Cairo, Illinois, were going to do.

The *Zephyr* docked once again in New Orleans on New Year's Eve 1861. Cory watched in the wheelhouse as Ned Rowley expertly brought the boat alongside one of the massive docks that jutted into the river. As the boat was being made fast, Cory descended to the boiler deck. The main gangplank ran from that deck to the dock, though there were also ramps that connected the lower deck to the dock so that cargo could be loaded and unloaded without having to carry it up and down stairs.

Cory saw Captain Farrell and Lucille coming along the deck as he reached the gangplank. He stopped and waited for them, knowing that the captain and his daughter had the right to disembark first. As he stood there, he was startled to hear a harsh voice call, "You there! Boy!" When he glanced toward the dock, the voice went on, "Yeah, I'm talkin' to you!"

Cory's eyes widened in surprise as he saw the thick-set, bearded man who stood there glowering at him. He recognized the Kaintuck called Strunk who had wanted to gut him back in Red Mike's tavern in New Madrid. Clearly, Strunk recognized him, too, because the man lifted a hamlike fist and shook it at him. "I ain't forgot!" Strunk bellowed. "Best watch yourself, boy, 'cause one o' these nights I'll be right behind you. And when I am—"

He drew the edge of his hand across his throat in a meaningful gesture and then gave Cory an ugly, gap-toothed grin before turning away.

"I see Mr. Strunk is as charming as ever," Lucille said from behind Cory.

He turned quickly again. Captain Farrell and Lucille stood there. The captain was frowning as he said, "I would have thought that Strunk wouldn't recognize you, lad. You've put some meat on your bones since the last time he saw you, and your clothing certainly isn't as disreputable as it was then."

Cory licked his lips and said, "I'm just lucky, I reckon."

"All I can say is that you should take his advice to heart and keep a close eye behind you at all times while we're here. New Orleans is no stranger to murder."

"And neither is Mr. Strunk or anyone else from that tub the *Prometheus*," Lucille added.

"Now, my dear, there's no need to insult Captain Reese's boat."

"Why not?" she asked. "It has a crew of cutthroats, and Owen Reese himself is no better than he has to be. And to think that he thought he was going to marry me!" Lucille's chin jutted out defiantly.

"M-marry you?" Cory repeated.

"That was all a misunderstanding," Farrell explained. "I thought at first Captain Reese was proposing a business arrangement between him and me. I had no idea he was actually suggesting that he and Lucille should wed." Farrell's jaw tightened and his face flushed with anger at the memory.

"I'm glad you set him straight, Father. Why, I'd no more marry Owen Reese than I would an . . . an alligator!"

Ike Judson came up behind Cory in time to hear that statement, and he grunted in agreement before saying, "Reckon you'd be better off marryin' the 'gator, Miss Lucille."

"Wait a minute!" Cory exclaimed. "She's not going to marry an alligator, or this Captain Reese, or . . . or anybody!"

The words were out of his mouth before he could stop them, and he felt a moment of panic as he realized that Lucille, Farrell, and Judson were all staring at him. He went on quickly, "I . . . I just mean that Miss Lucille's not interested in marrying anybody right now."

A smile tugged at Lucille's mouth. "Oh, I wouldn't say that. A girl is always interested in matrimony, you know."

Cory wished the deck would just open up and swallow him whole, but he blurted out, "I . . . I think I'll go see if Shad needs any help taking on supplies while we're here."

"An excellent idea, Mr. Brannon," Farrell agreed. "I'm certain Shadrach would appreciate the assistance."

Cory tugged on the brim of his cap and turned to hurry toward the stairs that would lead him down to the main deck and the kitchen. As he went, he wondered which was the most frightening: the possibility of meeting up with a knife-wielding Strunk in a dark alley . . . or making a complete and utter fool of himself in front of Lucille.

FOLLOWING THE occupation of Paducah, Kentucky, by Union troops under Grant, the Federals' next move was to advance south along the Mississippi to the tiny settlement of Belmont, across the river from Columbus, Kentucky, which at the moment was a Confederate stronghold. The Confederates, under Gen. Leonidas Polk, had established an observation post and an artillery battery at Belmont, and Grant intended for his troops to capture this lightly manned camp. This was merely another show of force on Grant's part, but just like Ball's Bluff, the show of force quickly became the real thing as several thousand Confederate troops unexpectedly crossed the river to defend the camp and engage the Union soldiers. The advantage in the clash went back and forth until finally the Yankees withdrew, heading back north to Cairo. Both sides claimed victory in a battle that was essentially meaningless despite the blood that was spilled with more than six hundred men killed on each side.

Opposing Grant in the West was Gen. Albert Sidney Johnston, believed by many in both the North and the South to be one of Jefferson Davis's most able officers. Facing the threat of Grant's massed forces in Cairo, Johnston believed that a Yankee invasion of Tennessee was inevitable. Johnston's problems were compounded by the fact that he was short of everything: men, arms, ammunition, food, and medical supplies. There was no way to prevent the Union forces from launching an attack sooner or later, but to Johnston's way of thinking, later was definitely better. He had to delay Grant somehow, and to do that he hit upon the idea of making the Union general believe that the South's army in Tennessee was much stronger than it really was. Through a series of lightning-quick raids, in which the Rebels would strike in one place then gallop on horseback to another to hit the Yankees again, Johnston made it seem that his men were everywhere. It was a colossal bluff—but it succeeded, as Union officers begged for more men to hold off the aggressive surges of what seemed an almost limitless Southern horde.

Had that actually been true, Johnston would have had a much better chance of holding Tennessee against the enemy. As it was, all he could do was stretch a makeshift defensive line from the mountains of western Virginia to western Tennessee, where the Cumberland and Tennessee Rivers angled northward across the border into Kentucky, on their way to flow into the Ohio. That defensive line was long but thin, and to shore up the most vulnerable area, the western end, it was decided that two forts would be built, one on the Tennessee River and one on the Cumberland. The officer sent to plan and supervise the construction of these forts was Brig. Gen. Daniel S. Donelson.

Donelson was able to locate a suitable site on the Cumberland, a few miles south of the Kentucky border at a spot where some high bluffs rose steeply from the river. The Tennessee, lacking such geographic advantages along its banks, was not nearly as defensible, but Donelson had been charged with establishing a fort, so he had no choice except to do so. He settled on a site just below a bend in the river, a dozen or so miles overland from the site of the fort on the Cumberland, which by now had been designated Fort Donelson after the officer who had laid out the plans for it. The fort on the Tennessee was to be called Fort Henry.

Now all that remained was to build the forts, man them, and hold them against the inevitable Yankee onslaught.

NEWS OF these developments made its way downriver, of course. Gossip and rumors ran rampant, some of them fairly accurate, some wildly fanciful. One story had it that a quarter of a million Union soldiers were in Cairo, poised to come rampaging all the way down the Mississippi to the Gulf of Mexico. Another rumor claimed that the Federals intended to take Nashville and burn it to the ground. No one knew what the truth really was, and that uncertainty caused an air of nervousness in the Crescent City, permeating—but not halting—the New Year's celebrations.

Cory had been given a cabin of his own on the Texas deck, one that was even smaller than Judson's. On New Year's Eve, following the encounter with Strunk, Cory was in the cabin changing his shirt for what he figured would be dinner at a waterfront restaurant with Ike Judson and Ned Rowley. A knock sounded on the door.

When Cory opened it, he found Judson standing there. "I'm not quite ready to go, Mr. Judson," he began, then stopped as he noticed the clothes in Judson's hands.

Judson thrust the garments at him and said, "Put these on."

Cory took the clothing, his eyes widening as he saw that they were a fine pair of trousers, a coat, a white shirt with ruffles on the front, and a silk cravat. "What is this?" he asked in confusion. "Why am I supposed to wear this fancy stuff?"

"Cap'n's orders," Judson replied gruffly. "He sent 'em. Said he wants you to put 'em on and meet him and Miss Lucille at a place called the Golden Crab."

That surprised Cory even more, and frightened him a little as well. He knew where the Golden Crab was; he had seen it during his wanderings of the city with Judson on previous visits to New Orleans. But it was an expensive restaurant where only the finest people dined. He hardly fit into that category.

And the idea of eating with Lucille made him even more nervous. She and the captain sometimes took their meals in their cabin, and sometimes in the dining room with the passengers. They certainly didn't break bread with members of the crew.

Clearly, Judson didn't like the idea, either. He was frowning darkly as he said, "Are you gettin' dressed in them fancy duds or not?"

"I . . . I suppose so," Cory said. "If those were the captain's orders . . ."

Judson snorted. He didn't think much of Captain Farrell's orders. But he would follow them to the letter, whether he approved of them or not. As he left the cabin, he exhorted, "Better hurry up. I imagine they're waitin' for you."

Quickly, Cory dressed in the new clothes. He had trouble with the pearl studs that fastened the shirt instead of buttons, and he wished he had a mirror in his cabin so that he could see if he had gotten the cravat on straight. He licked his fingers and smoothed down his mop of curly hair as much as possible, then left the cabin to find Judson leaning on the railing outside.

"Damned if you ain't duded up to beat the band," Judson observed. He had a brown beaver hat in his hand. He held it out to Cory. "Here."

"Who paid for all these things?" Cory asked as he took the hat.

"The cap'n did, of course," Judson replied. "But he said to tell you that he'd get square with you. I reckon you won't be gettin' full wages for a while."

Cory frowned. He wished Captain Farrell hadn't done that. He'd been planning to send some money home. Not that the family needed it; the Brannon farm had always been success-ful ever since John Brannon had passed away and Will had taken over. In Cordelia's last letter, she'd written that Will had enlisted, but Cory was sure Mac and Titus and Henry would be up to the task of working the farm.

Despite Cory's misgivings about the money, this was the first time he had held something as fancy as a beaver hat in his hands. He turned it over a couple of times, then lifted it and settled it on his head. "How do I look?" he asked.

"Like a reg'lar gent," the pilot allowed. "I reckon you could pass for the son of some plantation owner. Just be on your best behavior, so's nobody'll tumble to the fact that you're just a wharf rat."

Cory tilted the hat at a more rakish angle and couldn't keep from grinning. Let Judson think whatever he wanted. Cory knew that he wasn't just a wharf rat. He suspected that by now, Judson knew that, too. The pilot was just ragging him.

Cory's step was jaunty as he went down the gangplank and started toward the Golden Crab. The restaurant was on Chartres Street, he recalled. He walked there through the cool, dank evening air, nodding to the men he passed and tipping his hat to the ladies. Several of them smiled at him.

Despite the air of cockiness he had forced upon himself, deep down he was still struggling with the nervousness he had experienced when Judson first told him he was expected to dine with Captain Farrell and Lucille. What was this all about? Why would the captain honor him in this way? He had done nothing to deserve it. His efforts to raise the alarm on board the *Missouri Zephyr* when Jason Gill and his mob were headed for the riverboat merited a good meal, perhaps even the job as pilot's cub. But not this. Not dinner with the captain and the captain's daughter.

The captain's *beautiful* daughter.

Cory couldn't stop the image of Lucille from appearing in his mind. He had seen the way she was dressed when she left the boat that afternoon, in a stylish dark blue gown suitable for day wear. She and Captain Farrell had returned to the *Zephyr* later, then departed again, and Cory hadn't seen them leave this time. He had no idea what Lucille would be wearing.

So he filled in the details with his imagination, picturing her in a beautiful white evening gown trimmed with fine lace and golden thread. The gown would swoop down low in the front, leaving most of her shoulders bare and dipping far enough so that the creamy upper swells of her breasts were visible. In his mind's eye Cory could see her sitting there at a candle-lit table with her honey blonde hair loose around her shoulders, waiting for him with an expectant look on her face, her eyes heavy-lidded from wanting him . . .

An arm went around his throat from behind and jerked back hard, forcing his chin up. As he felt the touch of cold steel on his skin, he heard Strunk rasp in his ear, "Told you to watch your back, boy. I'll bet you didn't think you'd be dyin' this soon . . ."

Chapter Nine

SHEER TERROR SHOT THROUGH Cory, and for a second he thought he was going to pass out. He hoped that he would, so he wouldn't have to feel the pain as Strunk slit his throat and let his life's blood run out onto the ground.

Strunk wasn't ready to kill him just yet, though. The Kaintuck let the tip of the blade rest against Cory's throat, pressing just hard enough on it to penetrate the skin. After a moment, Cory felt a drop of something warm and wet trickle down his neck.

That was blood, he knew. *His* blood. That knowledge petrified him.

"Too scared to even wiggle, eh?" Strunk rasped. The arm that was like a thick bar of iron jerked back again. "Come on."

Cory went. He had no choice, not with a knife at his throat. He was feeling dizzy now from lack of air, because Strunk's arm across his throat almost completely cut off his breath. His muscles were all limp, but somehow he managed to force his legs to work as Strunk hauled him off the sidewalk and into an alley.

Someone must have seen him being assaulted, Cory thought. The streets of New Orleans were busy tonight, what with all the New Year's celebrations going on. Why wasn't someone raising an outcry?

Because none of them cared, he realized bleakly. Captain Farrell had warned him that New Orleans was no stranger to murder. The people who lived here looked after themselves, and they expected everyone else to do the same.

So if anyone was going to save him from Strunk, it had to be him, Cory told himself. But Strunk was bigger and stronger and had a knife. Cory didn't have anything he could use as a weapon . . .

As the thick shadows of the alley closed in around them, Strunk unexpectedly shoved Cory away from him. Cory slammed into the wall of a building and bounced off. Before he could catch his balance, Strunk grabbed his shoulder and spun him around, then thrust him back against the wall again. Cory's head struck the bricks, knocking his beaver hat off.

Strunk crowded against him, this time resting the point of the blade just under Cory's chin. Once again it penetrated enough to draw blood. Strunk was a little shorter than Cory, so that the Kaintuck had to tip his head back slightly and come up on his toes to put his face a couple of inches from Cory's. The reek of whiskey on Strunk's breath was almost enough to make Cory gag.

"I ain't forgot what you did in New Madrid," Strunk growled. "I always pay my debts, boy."

Moving his mouth to talk made the knife jab even harder into Cory's chin, but he said, "I didn't do anything to you in New Madrid."

"Busted a bucket on my head, you did!" Strunk snarled.

"It . . . it was an accident!" Cory felt more blood dripping down his neck.

"I don't give a damn. I'm gonna open you from gullet to gizzard. Gonna watch your guts slither out of your belly like snakes." Strunk's voice was low and intense, and Cory realized to his horror that Strunk was enjoying this. The man was a little bit insane. Maybe more than a little bit.

"That . . . that's not fair!" Cory heard himself saying. This was useless. What did a man such as Strunk care about being fair?

Judging from the ugly chuckle he gave, Strunk felt the same way. He said, "Gonna take care of you, then I'm gonna go after that cap'n of yours." He turned his head to spit. "Farrell."

"C-Captain Farrell never did anything to you."

"He pointed a gun at me! That's a whole heap more'n I can forgive. He's got to die." Strunk's voice became even lower and uglier. "And when I'm done with him, I'll have me some fun with that gal of his. Yes sir, I reckon I'll enjoy that part the most."

The alley was so dark that Cory could see almost nothing. Strunk was little more than a vague shape pressing hard against him. The Kaintuck's breath hissed angrily between his teeth as he talked about what he would do to Lucille once Cory and Farrell were dead.

And as Strunk spoke, a red flame flickered into life in Cory's brain. It grew and grew, fanned by the obscene words spewing from Strunk's mouth, until it seemed to fill Cory's head. The heat and light from the fire surged outward until they had no choice but to explode.

Cory's left hand came up, seemingly of its own volition, and his wrist cracked into the wrist of the hand that held the knife. At the same instant, Cory twisted his head aside. The tip of the blade raked a line of blazing agony under his chin, but he ignored the pain as he brought his right knee up into Strunk's groin as hard as he could.

Strunk was an experienced brawler and street fighter. He reacted almost instantly to Cory's move, twisting so that Cory's knee struck his thigh rather than anything more vulnerable. With a grunt, he surged forward, intending to slam Cory against the wall once more.

Cory's right hand lashed out, finding Strunk's face. His fingers stabbed at Strunk's eyes while his thumb tore at the Kaintuck's nose. Strunk howled as one of Cory's fingers dug into his left eye. Cory felt it pop, splashing its liquid over the back of his hand.

The knife was still an immediate danger. Cory flailed for Strunk's wrist, found it and grabbed it with both hands. He lowered his shoulder and slammed it into Strunk's chest, hauling on Strunk's arm at the same time. Strunk was still bellowing about his injured eye, and he was the one who was off-balance for a change. He fell, sprawling on the debris-littered floor of the alley.

Cory let go of Strunk's wrist. For a couple of seconds, he hesitated, unsure of what he should do next. He could probably flee while Strunk was down. Cory was confident that he could outrun Strunk, especially considering that the man would have to struggle back to his feet before pursuing him and would also be hampered by the blinded eye.

But if he ran now, sooner or later he would just have to deal with Strunk again. And Cory couldn't forget the things the man had said about Lucille. Strunk wasn't just a continuing threat against Cory; he was also a very real danger to Captain Farrell and Lucille.

Cory's eyes had adjusted enough to the darkness now for him to be able to make out Strunk's hand holding the knife. Cory brought down the heel of his boot on the wrist, stamping on it as hard as he could. Strunk yelled again, but the knife came free and skittered along the alley floor. Cory dove after it.

Strunk rolled over and lunged for the weapon, too. His body hit Cory's legs and knocked them out from under him. As Cory fell, he was still reaching for the knife, and his fingers closed over the leather-wrapped hilt. He rolled over and thrust the weapon out in front of him, gripping it tightly.

He felt Strunk hit the blade, felt the steel rip through clothing and then slide into flesh. Strunk's weight came down on Cory, driving the blade deep. A whimper of surprise and pain came from Strunk's mouth, and then he went limp, pinning Cory to the floor of the alley.

Dead weight was certainly an accurate description, Cory thought a little wildly. His brain was not yet ready to comprehend that he had just killed a man. He was more concerned at the moment with getting Strunk's massive form off of him before he suffocated. Cory let go of the knife, the handle of which was digging painfully into his own chest, and got his hands on Strunk's shoulders. He heaved with all the strength he could muster.

Strunk rolled off, falling on his back with his arms flopping out loosely to each side. The knife stood up from his chest. Cory had a good view of it as he raised himself on an elbow and drew in several gasping breaths. As the desperate need for air subsided, he began to realize what had just happened. He scooted backward, trying to put some distance between himself and Strunk's body.

He had to get out of here. That thought racketed through Cory's brain. He had been defending himself, certainly; given the facts that Strunk was older, larger, and had been armed, surely no one, especially the authorities, would find fault with Cory for fighting back. And he hadn't *really* meant to kill Strunk. That had been pretty much an accident.

But he could have run, Cory reminded himself, and he hadn't. He had continued the fight, and he had deliberately gone after the knife. There was bad blood between him and Strunk, and a clever lawyer could probably even make it look as if Cory had lured Strunk into the alley with the intention of murdering him . . .

No, Cory decided, it would be much better if he was nowhere near the Kaintuck's body when it was found. He pushed himself to his feet, slapped a hand against the wall to support himself as a wave of dizziness hit him, and then waited a moment for the world to stop spinning the wrong way.

When he trusted himself to move again, he stumbled toward the mouth of the alley, leaving Strunk lying behind him. He had reached the sidewalk before he realized that he had left his new beaver hat lying back there, too. Pausing, Cory looked over his shoulder for a second, then shuddered and moved on. There was no way in the world he was going back into that stygian, death-haunted alley just to retrieve a hat.

It took him a moment to orient himself again. He had been on his way to the restaurant known as the Golden Crab to have dinner with Captain Farrell and Lucille. He couldn't let them see him like this, he thought—hat gone, clothes filthy and disheveled from rolling around in the alley, streaks of blood drying on his throat from the wounds inflicted by Strunk's knife. He turned back toward the docks and the *Missouri Zephyr.*

Again Cory hesitated after only a few steps. Ike Judson and Ned Rowley would have probably left the boat by now to have dinner themselves. Cory had thought that he could ask Judson to go to the Golden Crab and let the captain know what had happened, but that was probably impossible. Farrell and Lucille were waiting for him. What would they think of him if he just didn't show up?

But what would they think of him if he arrived at the restaurant looking like this? The questions went around and around in Cory's head, and he couldn't come up with a satisfactory answer for any of them.

Wearily, he leaned against a building and rubbed a hand over his face, then probed gently at the wounds under his chin. They weren't too bad, he decided, little more than the sort of cuts a man might get from shaving too hastily. Working by feel, he took a handkerchief from his coat pocket, spat into it, and wiped away all the blood he could. He straightened his clothes and brushed them off. There was enough light from the street lamps for him to see that the coat and trousers weren't too badly stained in the front. He couldn't tell about the back.

He took a deep breath and turned around. He had made himself as presentable as possible under the circumstances. It would have to be good enough. His steps carried him toward the Golden Crab once more.

A few minutes later, he reached Chartres Street and saw the restaurant, lights shining warmly through its window. A lamp illuminated the carved wooden sign that hung over its door and announced the establishment's name, embellished by a portrait of a crab painted in golden hues. Cory squared his shoulders, swallowed, and approached his destination.

He heard violin music as he opened the door. A tall, lean, balding man in a fancy black suit stood there, an unreadable expression on his face. "Oui, monsieur?" he murmured.

Cory recognized that as French and figured the man was asking him what he wanted. He said, "I'm supposed to meet Cap'n' Farrell and his daughter, Miss Lucille." He paused, then added, "I'm Cory Brannon."

"Oui, monsieur," the man said again, but this time it wasn't a question. His dark eyes regarded Cory suspiciously. "I was aware that Captain Farrell was having a guest for dinner, of course . . . ," the man's eyebrows arched, "but I did not expect him to look as if he had just come from a tavern brawl."

Cory felt a flash of anger. He had cleaned himself up as best he could, and anyway, it wasn't his fault that Strunk had jumped him. He had just tried to defend himself from the murderous Kaintuck.

"Why don't you just take me to the captain's table?" he snapped.

Cory's irritation didn't impress the headwaiter, or whatever he was. The man just said, "I will inform Captain Farrell that someone is asking for him. Remain here, please."

Cory started to ask what would happen if he didn't, but then he noticed two other men in black suits standing nearby. They looked a lot tougher than the headwaiter. Cory didn't want any more trouble than he'd already had tonight, so he nodded. "All right. But please hurry."

The man just gave him another supercilious look and strolled away. Cory waited just inside the door, seething with anger and impatience. He scanned the tables in the crowded room, looking for Farrell and Lucille, but he didn't see either of them.

After a few minutes, the headwaiter came back, weaving through the tables. He spoke rapidly in French to one of the black-suited men, then turned to Cory and said, "Go with Reynard."

"I don't want to go with Reynard," Cory protested angrily. "I want to see Captain Farrell."

"Reynard will take you to the captain. Please, sir, do not make a scene."

With an effort, Cory reined in his temper. He didn't completely believe that they would take him to Farrell, but he supposed it was worth a try. After surviving the run-in with Strunk, he wasn't particularly afraid of any Frenchman.

Reynard's hand closed around Cory's arm, and Cory was ushered easily out of the restaurant. Maybe he had been too quick to dismiss Reynard as a threat, he decided when he felt the strength of the man's grip. He said, "I'm not here to cause trouble," as Reynard marched him down Chartres Street.

They reached the mouth of an alley and Reynard guided Cory toward it, firmly but not roughly. Cory started to pull back. He had been pushed into one alley already tonight, and he had almost died there. He wasn't fond of the idea of venturing into another one.

"Wait a minute!" he said. "I want to see Captain Farrell—"

"Cory?" The voice came from down the alley, and it was familiar. "Cory, is that you?"

"Captain!" Cory exclaimed. "Tell this man you really know me, and that you were expecting me—"

Farrell came striding out of the darkness with a puzzled expression on his face. He gestured with one hand and said, "It's all right, Reynard, I do know the young man. Come along, Cory, there's another entrance along here."

Reynard let go of Cory's arm. Cory suppressed the impulse to rub the flesh where the Frenchman's fingers had dug in. He walked with Farrell along the alley, which was dimly lit by a lantern at the far end. There was enough light for Cory to see the door standing open to the left. He followed Farrell through it into a short hallway that led to a private room in the back of the restaurant.

This room was even more luxuriously furnished than the main room, with a crystal chandelier that hung over a table covered by a fine white linen cloth edged with lace. The walls were gleaming hardwood with brass trim, and the floor was covered by a thick carpet. The table was set with expensive china, and on the other side of it, a worried expression on her lovely face, waited Lucille Farrell. "Cory," she inquired urgently when he followed her father into the room, "are you all right?"

"I'm fine," he said. "Sorry I'm late."

"Clement said you looked as if you'd been injured," Farrell commented. He put a hand under Cory's chin and tipped it back. "Let me see."

"It's nothing," Cory insisted awkwardly. "I tried to wipe the blood off as best I could—"

"You didn't succeed." Farrell's voice was curt. "What happened, Cory?"

"I . . . I forgot your advice, Captain. I didn't watch my back close enough, I guess. Strunk jumped me while I was on my way here and put a knife to my throat. He said he was going to kill me." Cory didn't mention the other threats Strunk had made against Farrell and Lucille.

As he was speaking, he saw the way Lucille's eyes widened. He wished she hadn't had to hear this. He had intended to keep this trouble private.

"Go on," Farrell ordered. "Clearly, you got away from him."

"Yeah, I . . . I did," Cory said. He didn't want to admit that he had killed Strunk in the process. Miserably, he went on, "I'm sorry I lost the hat you bought for me, Captain, and messed up these nice new clothes."

Farrell waved a hand impatiently. "I don't care about the clothes. What about Strunk?"

"I, uh, I got away from him, like you said."

"Cory." Farrell's voice was quiet but insistent. "I've known Lydell Strunk for many years. The man is a vicious killer when provoked, and he's been mixed up in brawls and back-alley fights since before you were born. If he intended to settle a grudge with you, he wouldn't have let you just walk away."

Cory drew a deep, ragged breath. He sensed that the captain wasn't going to let go of this until he had uncovered the truth. Maybe it would be best to get things out in the open . . . but even so, Lucille didn't have to hear such a horrible tale.

Lowering his voice, Cory asked, "Could I speak to you in private, Captain?"

"No!" Lucille exclaimed before Farrell had a chance to answer. "If there's trouble, I have as much right to know about it as anyone. The *Zephyr* is my home, and her crew is my family."

So that was the way she thought of him, as just another member of the crew. Somehow, Cory felt disappointed at that realization.

Farrell shrugged. "You know how strong-willed she is, Mr. Brannon. You may as well go ahead and speak freely."

"But, sir—"

Lucille came around the table. "What happened, Cory? Please, tell us."

He gave up. As usual, nothing was going the way he intended. "All right. Strunk had a knife, and we fought over it. While we were fighting, he sort of . . . fell on the knife."

Lucille didn't gasp or put her hand to her mouth or anything like that, and Cory had to give her credit for her composure. But she did turn pale, and Captain Farrell asked, "How badly was he injured?"

"I think I . . . I killed him."

"Good Lord," Farrell murmured. "I was afraid of that."

"Are you sure you're all right, Cory?" Lucille asked.

He nodded. "Just these two little cuts on my neck. I was lucky."

"Indeed you were," Farrell agreed. "Strunk wouldn't have hesitated to kill *you.*"

"I know, sir. That's why I fought back."

"You did the right thing. A man has to defend himself."
Farrell rubbed his chin. "But Strunk's death *does* complicate matters. Had anyone found his body by the time you left the area?"

"No, but they may have by now."

"Perhaps, or perhaps not. But sooner or later, someone will find him, and Owen Reese and the other members of the crew of the *Prometheus* will be informed of his death."

Cory felt a twinge of panic. "Will they go to the law? Nobody can prove I had anything to do with—"

"I'm not worried about the law," Farrell cut in. "I'm worried about what Reese and his men will do personally. It's quite likely that they knew of Strunk's animosity toward you, and many people on the docks heard him threaten you this afternoon. When he turns up dead, you'll be blamed, no matter whether there is any proof or not."

"I didn't mean to cause trouble for you, Captain," Cory said, feeling utterly wretched.

Farrell smiled faintly. "It was my own decision to intervene, that evening in New Madrid. That was what began the trouble with Strunk." He nodded abruptly, evidently having reached a decision. He turned to Lucille and went on, "I'm sorry, my dear, but clearly this evening's dinner will have to be postponed. We'll go back to the *Zephyr* and prepare to leave New Orleans."

"All right, Father," she replied without hesitation.

"I'm so sorry," Cory said. "This is going to ruin everything—"

"Nonsense," Farrell insisted. "We were going to be departing tomorrow anyway. I'm taking on a cargo that has to be delivered upriver as soon as possible."

"Father," Lucille intervened. "I thought you weren't going to take that job."

"Now it seems a more appropriate thing to do."

"Captain . . ." Cory blurted, suddenly concerned about something else. "If we leave New Orleans in a hurry, won't that just make everybody think that I killed Strunk?"

"Owen Reese will believe that anyway, and he and his crew are the only ones who matter at the moment." He turned to Lucille again. "You and Mr. Brannon return to the boat. I'll go see Mr. Harriman and make all the arrangements to have the cargo delivered tonight. Tell Mr. Judson that we will leave New Orleans as soon as it's landed."

"If you're sure," Lucille agreed worriedly.

Farrell bent over and brushed a kiss on her forehead. "Of course I'm sure." He looked at Cory. "Are you certain you can get my daughter back to the *Zephyr* safely?"

"Yes sir," Cory declared emphatically, anxious for the chance to atone, even slightly, for the problems he had caused.

"Well, just in case . . ." Farrell reached underneath his coat and produced the pistol he had used back in New Madrid to rescue Cory from Strunk during the encounter at Red Mike's. Only a few months had passed since then, but it seemed almost like another lifetime to Cory. Farrell held out the gun. "Take this."

Cory hesitated, then reached out and closed his hand around the smooth walnut grips of the pistol. He had handled guns before, of course. Back home in Virginia, he had hunted many times with his brothers, using shotguns and rifles, and he had even fired Will's Colt Navy revolver.

He had never shot at another human being, though.

Of course, before tonight he had never shoved a knife deep in another person's chest, either . . .

He managed to nod as he tucked the pistol behind his belt. "I'll be careful this time."

"See that you are." Farrell picked up his hat from a side table and put it on, then kissed Lucille again, this time on the cheek. "I'll see you on the boat."

She nodded. "You be careful, too."

"Of course." Farrell left the room through the rear entrance.

Cory felt a wave of nervousness wash over him as he realized that he was now alone with Lucille. This wasn't the first time. The two of them had been alone in the pilothouse on the *Zephyr* on occasion, but that was different. Lucille had been dressed in boys' clothing then, not the beautiful white gown she was wearing now. It wasn't the sensuous, low-cut garment Cory had imagined her in; in fact, it was long-sleeved and high-necked and very elegant, with lace around the throat and a black velvet choker just above it. She looked stunning, though, and as always, her beauty had a strong effect on him.

"Would you help me with my jacket, Cory?" she asked.

He practically sprang to do so, picking up the dark red garment of crushed velvet and holding it so that she could slip it on. She had a shawl, too, that she wrapped around her head and shoulders, then she led the way to the alley and turned toward Chartres Street. Cory walked alongside her, letting her set the pace. It was a fast one.

"I don't know if Mr. Judson is on the boat tonight," he remarked, making conversation so the only sound wouldn't be their footsteps on the paving stones.

"Ike won't be out late," Lucille maintained confidently. "He can never bring himself to stay away from the *Zephyr* for very long."

Cory had noticed that about the pilot. Over the years, the riverboat had become Judson's home, and he simply didn't care to be anywhere else for very long at a time.

"I hope he's not too upset with me," Cory said.

"Cory." There was a touch of irritation in Lucille's crisp voice. "No one is upset with you. Lydell Strunk is a madman. No one could ever fault you for protecting yourself from him."

"What about the crew of the *Prometheus?*"

"That's different. Strunk was one of them. They won't care about the facts. They'll just want revenge."

"Then they're liable to follow us upriver," Cory asserted worriedly.

"I doubt that. Not where we're going."

"You mean the place that cargo your father mentioned is bound for?"

"That's right. You see, we're taking it to Cairo, Illinois."

Cory stopped short, stunned. Cairo, Illinois . . .

Where only Ulysses S. Grant and God knew how many Union soldiers were waiting, poised at the throat of the western Confederacy.

Chapter Ten

MAC STEPPED BACK AND looked at his handiwork. Sweat beaded on his forehead despite the chilliness of the January day. He leaned on the shovel he had used to dig a four-inch-deep trench all the way across the field.

The trench was filled in with dirt and covered up now, concealing the rope that lay inside it. The dirt was only loosely packed, so that with one good hard tug, the rope would pull up through it and become taut. One end was tied fast to a sturdy tree at the edge of the woods, about four feet above the ground. From there the rope went into the trench and was hidden until it emerged on the far side of the field, near a stout post that Mac had driven into the ground. Another buried trench crossed the field at an angle, and a rope was hidden in it as well, with the far end tied to another tree. A coiled rope lay next to the post.

The problem would be getting that rope tied between those trees in time, Mac thought. He would need help, plenty of help, if the plan that had come to him in the middle of a long, dark, sleepless night was going to work. But Henry and Cordelia had already indicated that they would be glad to assist him, even without knowing exactly what he was up to, and if Titus wasn't too drunk or hung over when the time came, he might pitch in, too.

Mac just wished he could explain what he was doing without everyone else in his family thinking he had gone stark raving mad.

Maybe he *was* mad, he thought. The mysterious silver gray stallion had preyed on his mind for so long that it was a distinct possibility.

But he didn't think it was lunacy that was compelling him to go ahead with this plan to catch the horse. In fact, it might indeed save his sanity if he could prove that the creature was really flesh and blood. Sure, Will had seen the stallion, too, and the marks left on the barn door by its unshod hooves had been plainly visible. No phantom horse could have left them. Mac knew all that, but he knew as well that he could never fully believe in the stallion until he touched it again, until he felt its strength and speed underneath him as he rode through the night with the wind in his face . . .

He turned and walked back toward the barn. The sun was going down, and Mac wondered if the horse would come to the farm tonight.

All through dinner he was distracted, eating without really thinking about it or tasting it when Cordelia placed a plate of food in front of him. He had caught her eye, and Henry's, when he came in and gave them both a brief nod, signifying that the hoped-for snare was ready. Titus was sullen and non-communicative, indicating that he was still suffering from too much whiskey the night before, so Mac didn't waste time letting him in on the plan.

Abigail didn't know about it, either, of course. If she had been aware of Mac's obsession with the silver gray stallion, she would have likely made something sinful out of it and acted like Mac was worshiping the horse, rather than just wanting to catch it.

After they had eaten and the dishes had been cleaned up, Abigail went into the parlor to read her Bible by lamplight. Mac stepped out onto the porch and began packing tobacco from a leather pouch into his old briar pipe. As he scraped a match into life and lit the pipe, he heard the front door open and close behind him.

Cordelia stepped up beside him. She had wrapped a shawl around her shoulders, but she shivered a little anyway. "It's chilly tonight," she remarked.

"Not bad for January, though," Mac commented.

"No, I suppose not. Where do you think Will is tonight?"

Mac shook his head. "No way of knowing. Still with General Jackson, wherever the Thirty-third Virginia is, I suppose." He gestured toward the Blue Ridge Mountains, looming darkly in the distance. "Over yonder somewhere in the Shenandoah Valley, if I had to guess."

"I miss him," Cordelia reflected with a sigh. "Sometimes so much I can't hardly stand it, him and Cory both."

Mac nodded, understanding what she meant. It was like the family was gradually coming apart, and there was nothing he could do to stop it. The dissolution had started when Cory rode off to find fame and fortune, and it had continued when Will enlisted and went off to war.

"I miss them, too," he echoed quietly. "But we're still here, and we have to do what we can to hold things together until they get back." He wasn't going to allow any thought that they might not come home into his head.

"Mac . . . do you think the war will come this far?"

So far the Piedmont region of Virginia had not been threatened at all. There were Yankee forces in the state, true, but they were a long way off.

Mac shook his head, but he wasn't answering in the negative. "I don't know," he said honestly. "When it all started last spring, I didn't think it would last as long as it has. I was hoping the Yankees would see that they had to leave us alone and let us work things out for ourselves. They didn't have to threaten us and go to war against us."

"They won't quit," Cordelia said, her voice hollow. "They're so . . . so damned sure that their way is the only way!"

Mac was surprised to hear such vehemence in his sister's voice. He turned toward her and put an arm around her shoulders. "We'll get through it," he promised. "One way or another, we'll—"

He stopped short as he heard the faint, ringing sound of the stallion's whinny. It was coming from the direction of the woods.

"He's here," Mac murmured, stiffening.

"Who?" Cordelia asked anxiously. She was aware of Mac's reaction, but not what had caused it.

"Don't you hear it?"

"I don't hear anything but the wind."

"Listen!" Mac hissed.

The distant, challenging cry sounded again. Beside him, Cordelia murmured, "It . . . it sounds like a horse . . ."

"Not just any horse," snapped Mac. "Get Henry and come to the woods. Hurry!" He stepped down from the porch and threw another command over his shoulder. "Don't tell Mama what we're doing."

He had to trust that Cordelia would do as she was told. He wasn't going to wait to see. He had to get out to the field and make sure with his own eyes that the stallion was there.

As he ran, he knocked the dottle from his pipe and stuck it back in his pocket. His heart was pounding heavily. All day as he had worked digging the trenches and concealing the ropes in them, something had told him that tonight might be his opportunity. That nagging voice in the back of his mind had kept him going, even when he was tired.

He circled the barn and started toward the woods. He could see the dark line of trees in the distance. His eyes searched desperately for something lighter colored moving against them. Seeing nothing, Mac stopped and listened intently.

Still nothing. Surely he hadn't imagined the stallion's cry, he thought. Cordelia had heard it, too.

And yet . . . perhaps she had just been humoring him. She knew of his preoccupation with the horse, and when he indicated that he heard something, she may have simply assumed that was what it was. She may have even convinced herself that she heard the defiant whinny.

No! Mac thought. He *had* heard the stallion. He was sure of it.

Then, suddenly, the sound came again. Mac forgot to breathe as he listened. His gaze fastened on the edge of the woods, and he saw the stallion come striding out of the shadows, a beautiful phantom emerging from the darkness.

The horse stopped at the edge of the field and tossed its head, as if daring Mac to come closer. Without his willing it, Mac's legs moved of their own volition, carrying him slowly forward. He couldn't tear his eyes off the silver gray apparition.

Footsteps pounded up behind him, but he didn't pause or turn around. "Mac?" Henry whispered uncertainly. "What's going on, Mac?"

The stallion was moving again, high-stepping out into the field, shaking its head from time to time as if it were being compelled onward just as Mac was. Mac forced his brain and his mouth to work, knowing that this might be his last chance.

"There's a rope by that post I put up," he said quietly to Henry. "Take it and circle wide around the field. Tie one end to the tree where I tied the rope on the left, and then go across to the tree where I tied the other rope. Make good knots, Henry, but hurry. We'll wait for you. When you're finished, let out a whistle."

"I understand," Henry acknowledged. He ran forward, snatched up the coiled rope Mac had left beside the post, and started along the edge of the field at a run.

Mac saw the stallion's head swing to the side as it followed Henry with its eyes. For a second, Mac feared that the horse would wheel around and gallop back into the woods before Henry had a chance to even get started. But then it looked toward him again and kept coming forward.

Was the stallion going to cooperate in its own capture? Mac wondered. After all the times the creature had practically taunted him with its speed and intelligence and seeming ability to vanish like a will-o'-the-wisp?

Mac kept going until he reached the post. He stopped beside it and rested a hand on it.

"What do you want me to do?" Cordelia asked, her voice hushed with awe so that it was little more than a whisper.

"See the rope, there by the base of the post? When I tell you, pick it up and tie it around the post, as quickly and tightly as you can, about four feet above the ground."

"All right, Mac. I'll do it."

"Be ready," he whispered. They would get only one chance.

Still, his gaze had not left the silver gray stallion as it came, inexorably but reluctantly, across the field.

Was he insane to think that mere ropes would hold the stallion? Mac asked himself. A rope corral worked fine with normal horses, but this was no normal horse. Or, at least, he had convinced himself it was not normal. Surely when the stallion realized they were trying to trap it, it would either burst through the ropes or leap over them.

But they had to try. There was a chance the plan might work, and a chance was all Mac asked.

From the corner of his eye, he saw Henry running through the field toward the woods, carrying the coiled rope. The stallion turned its head again and blew out its breath through its nose in an angry snort. It knew something was happening, something it didn't like. Yet it seemed just as powerless to turn back from the course of fate as Mac himself was. The horse paused in the center of the field, clearly torn between whatever force was urging it on and the nearly irresistible impulse to turn and flee.

"Hurry, Henry, hurry," Mac breathed.

Henry reached the edge of the woods, located the tree on the left with the rope tied to it, and quickly lashed one end of the rope he carried around it. Mac watched him run across the face of the forest, a moving shadow among shadows. Still the stallion stood in the center of the field, motionless save for a trembling that Mac sensed as much as saw.

Henry reached the tree where the other rope was tied, and Mac said, "Get ready, Cordelia."

"I'm ready," she promised, but Mac heard fear in her voice. She didn't understand this.

That was all right. Neither did he. Neither, he suspected, did the silver gray stallion.

Henry's shrill whistle cut through the night.

"Now, Cordelia!" Mac shouted. He bent and grabbed the rope on his side of the post, hauling up on it with all his strength, pulling it free of the dirt in the trench that had hidden it. On the other side of the post, Cordelia was doing the same thing. Mac whipped the end of his rope around the post and began tying it, trying to stay out of Cordelia's way as she followed suit.

In the center of the field, the stallion reared up on its back legs, pawed the air angrily with its hooves, and let out a loud sound of fury.

Mac finished tying his rope and stepped back to see what the stallion would do. Cordelia tugged hard on her knot and moved back beside him. "That's a magnificent horse, Mac," she observed breathlessly. "Is that rope enough to hold him?"

"I don't know."

The stallion wheeled around abruptly and galloped toward the woods. Mac cupped his hands around his mouth and shouted, "Henry! Get out of there!" If the stallion broke through the rope, Mac didn't want his brother getting trampled.

The huge horse stopped short of the trees, however, as if sensing the rope stretched there. It reared up again, then turned and ran to the right. The same thing happened. The stallion stopped, warned by instinct that its path was blocked.

In the moonlight, Mac could see the tautly stretched ropes that formed two sides of the makeshift triangular corral. He had debated about how high to place them. Too high and the horse might run under them or break its neck running into them. Too low and the creature would bound right over them. Mac had settled on four feet. Now that he could see the stallion in relation to the ropes, however, he was afraid they were too low. Surely the horse's powerful muscles could carry it right over the rope in a mighty leap.

Instead of trying to jump the barrier, the horse turned again and raced to the other side of the field. Once again finding its way blocked, the stallion stopped and stood there for a long moment. Mac heard the loud snort that it blew out through its nostrils. The stallion sounded disgusted, but whether that was directed at itself or at these puny humans who were trying to trap it, Mac didn't know.

The stallion turned and paced back deliberately toward the center of the field. Mac didn't hesitate. He bent over and ducked under the rope, then straightened and started walking toward the horse.

"Mac!" Cordelia exclaimed. "What are you doing?"

"What I have to," he exclaimed.

"But . . . but that horse will kill you!"

"I don't think so." A sense of unutterable calm was stealing over Mac. Destiny was what drew him on toward the center of the field, and he had no intention of flying in the face of destiny.

"Be careful!" Cordelia called after him, but Mac barely heard her. All his attention was focused on the magnificent creature waiting for him.

Cordelia heard someone coming up behind her and turned to see Titus approaching. He was carrying his Sharps rifle, and he was unsteady on his feet. "Where'd ever'body run off to?" he growled in a thick voice.

"Titus, go back to the house," Cordelia directed quickly. She wasn't sure how she knew, but she was certain that Mac wouldn't want Titus here right now. "Please, we'll be back in a few minutes."

"What're you doin' with ropes strung up all over the place? Izzat Mac out there? What's he . . . Hell, look at that horse! That brute'll trample him!" Titus started to lift his rifle.

Mac didn't hear the exchange between his sister and his next oldest brother. He began talking in a low voice to the stallion, saying, "You decided last time that you wanted to trust me, and now how do I pay you back? By penning you up. But I don't

mean you any harm; I swear I don't. I want you to know that. I
think you know this is where you're supposed to be. Otherwise
you wouldn't keep coming back here. You can trust me."

Some men who worked at gentling horses said it was important to talk to the animals. They couldn't understand what you
were saying, but they understood a low, soothing tone of voice.

Mac had always believed that animals understood a lot
more than people gave them credit for. Growing up, he'd had
dogs that he swore understood nearly everything he said to
them. Now, as he kept talking to the stallion, it blew its breath
out noisily and shifted its feet, but it didn't run. Mac came
closer and closer.

"All you have to do is give me a chance," he said. "Just give
me a chance."

At the edge of the field, Cordelia lunged at Titus, grabbing
the barrel of the rifle. She smelled whiskey on his breath as he
cursed and tried to jerk it away from her. "What's wrong with
you, gal?" he demanded. "I'm gonna shoot that wild horse
'fore it tramples Mac!"

"No!" Cordelia gasped as she hung on to the barrel of the
Sharps. "It won't hurt him, I know it won't!"

"Damn it!" Titus let go of the weapon with one hand and
swung it in a backhanded slap that cracked across Cordelia's
face and sent her stumbling backward. She had no choice but
to let go of the rifle. She lost her balance and sat down hard,
her long skirt tangled around her legs.

Titus gaped at her, as if unable to believe he had just struck
his own sister. Before he could do anything else, Henry came
out of the night, launching himself into a diving tackle that
took Titus around the waist from behind and spilled both of
them on the ground.

"You bastard!" Henry cried as he began flailing away with
his fists at Titus. "How could you do that to Cordelia?"

In the center of the field, Mac was vaguely aware of some
sort of commotion, but he didn't dare take his attention away

from the stallion. He had his hand lifted again, just like last time, and he was close enough now so that the stallion could stretch out its neck and nuzzle against Mac's hand. "That's it," Mac breathed. "I won't hurt you."

The stallion stood still, not even trembling now. Mac moved closer, rubbing the horse's nose and then moved along-side it so that he could stroke its neck and pat its shoulder. The sense of strength and power that radiated from the animal was astounding. If this was truly a ghost horse, thought Mac, then it was a ghost once more made flesh.

He dug his fingers into its mane and held on tight, thankful for his long legs. They enabled him to swing a leg over the stallion's back and pull himself up.

He waited without breathing for the horse to explode into bucking, twisting, leaping motion. Instead it sat still under him, quivering slightly. "That's it," he murmured, leaning forward a little to pat the horse's shoulder again. "That's it, boy. Nothing to worry about."

This was a wild horse, he reminded himself. He was either a fool or a crazy man to mount it like this. And yet the horse stood there calmly until Mac gently dug the heels of his boots into its flanks and said, "Let's go." Then the stallion started forward in an easy trot.

Mac lifted his head and saw several figures struggling at the edge of the field. As he came closer, he could tell that a couple of men were rolling around on the ground while Cordelia hovered above them, shouting at them and trying to pull them apart. The two men had to be Titus and Henry, Mac realized.

He brought the stallion to a halt with a tug on its mane, then called, "Stop it! Stop it, you two!"

Cordelia stepped back, looked up, and saw Mac sitting there astride the giant silver gray stallion only a few yards beyond the rope barrier. She was unable to keep from exclaiming, "Oh, my God! Mac!"

Titus threw Henry off, sending the younger man sprawling to the side. Henry scrambled up and was about to resume the attack when he, too, saw Mac and the stallion. Titus was the last one to notice, while he was groping around on the ground for his fallen rifle. He abandoned his efforts to pick up the Sharps when he saw his older brother mounted on the huge horse.

"You caught him," Henry gasped, awe in his voice. "You're riding him!"

"What's going on here?" Mac demanded. He was no longer worried about the stallion trying to buck him off or failing to obey his command. The bond between man and horse had been astonishingly quick to form, but it was strong.

Henry pointed at Titus, who was still sitting on the ground, and said, "He hit Cordelia!"

Mac looked at his sister and saw the dark mark of a bruise already forming on her cheek. Coldly he asked, "Is that true, Titus?"

Before Titus could answer, Cordelia said quickly, "He wasn't thinking straight, Mac. You know Titus wouldn't ever hurt me on purpose."

"He's probably drunk," Henry declared.

Mac looked at Titus and asked, "What about it?"

Titus waved a hand. "I'm sorry, Mac. I saw you out there with that big brute, and I figured he'd stomp you to death if I didn't shoot him."

Mac felt a wave of horror go through him at the realization of how close Titus had come to ruining everything. He wasn't sure if a bullet could even hurt the stallion, but a shot would have broken whatever force it was that had brought them together. The stallion's trust in him would have been shattered forever. He had Cordelia to thank that the tragedy hadn't occurred.

"Don't apologize to me," he directed. "It's Cordelia you should be telling you're sorry."

Titus pushed himself to his feet and brushed off his clothes. "I'm sorry, Cordelia," he said, his head drooping and his eyes downcast. If he had been drunk before, he seemed sober enough now. The sight of Mac on the stallion had probably been enough to bring that about. "I reckon I was out of my head," he went on. "I didn't know what I was doin'. I . . . I hope you'll forgive me."

"Of course I forgive you," she answered, coming to his side and giving him a brief hug. She had a generous spirit, Mac thought. Brother or no brother, he wasn't sure he would have been so quick to forgive Titus.

Obviously, Henry wouldn't have been, either, because the youngest Brannon brother protested disgustedly, "You're going to forgive him just like that, even after he slapped you?"

"He had good intentions," Cordelia said. "He just wasn't thinking straight."

"You know what the pastor says about good intentions," Mac muttered. "The road to hell is paved with 'em."

"I don't care about that," Cordelia insisted. "You caught the horse, Mac! I never dreamed you'd actually do it."

Mac patted the stallion's shoulder again. "He seems to trust me now. Why don't you untie the ropes, and I'll see if I can ride him into the barn."

Henry did that, pulling the knots loose and letting the ropes drop to the ground. Mac clucked to the stallion and heeled it forward.

The horse took off like a shot.

Mac let out a startled shout and clutched at the stallion's mane, hanging on for dear life as the ground raced past at dizzying speed. The stallion's great, galloping leaps took it around the barn. Cordelia, Titus, and Henry trailed far behind it, calling futilely for Mac to hang on.

There was nothing else Mac could do. The wind of the stallion's passage buffeted his face like a tempest. He kept his legs clamped around the horse's body and forced himself to lean forward so that he was stretched out on the stallion's neck. He could feel the smooth, efficient play of the great muscles underneath the sleek, silver gray hide. This was the ride of his life, Mac knew, and suddenly his fear faded away to be replaced by a huge exultation. Never again would he experience anything quite so thrilling as being mounted on this magnificent horse as it ran for the sheer joy of running.

The house swept past in a blur. Mac caught just a glimpse of his mother standing on the porch with a lantern in her hand. Abigail called something to him—he knew that because he saw her mouth move—but he couldn't make out the words over the roar of the wind in his ears, the thunder of the stallion's hoofbeats, and the pounding of his own heart.

He hung on tightly as the stallion swung around the house in a tight turn. They were on the lane that led down to the road running past the Brannon farm. The lane was muddy, but that didn't seem to bother the stallion. Its pace never faltered.

Suddenly, the stallion took out cross-country toward an old rock fence. Mac's eyes widened as he saw the fence approaching at dizzying speed. The stallion's muscles bunched underneath him, and Mac's wide eyes squeezed shut as the animal lifted its feet in a leap that carried it up and up and finally over the rocks.

The stallion landed lightly on the far side of the fence, its hooves striking the ground with scarcely a jar. The horse came to a stop, its body under perfect control, then began trotting down toward the point where the lane intersected the road. Mac opened his eyes again, hardly able to believe that he was still alive.

The stallion turned onto the lane and trotted toward the farmhouse as placidly as if it had just been out for a canter on a lazy Sunday afternoon.

Abigail, Cordelia, Titus, and Henry were waiting for them when Mac and the stallion came up to the house. "Dear Lord, Mac, where did you get that brute?" Abigail exclaimed. "I thought it was going to kill you."

Mac's heart was still slugging heavily in his chest, but he was beginning to catch his breath again now. He reflected, "I think he was just trying to show me what he can do."

"I'll tell you what he can do," Henry interjected excitedly. "If he can run like that, he can win every race they ever have in this part of the country!"

Horse races had been common in Virginia—before the war. Now folks had other things to worry about, and many of the best horses had gone for cavalry service, anyway.

"There won't be any horse races,," Mac announced.

"But, Mac," Titus questioned, "now that you've got him, what are you going to do with him?"

Mac looked at the stallion, and he realized suddenly that it wasn't so much a matter of what he was going to do with the horse.

It was a question of what the horse was going to do with him.

Chapter Eleven

YOU CAN'T DO IT," Cory maintained stubbornly as he stared intently at Captain Farrell. Surely the captain could see what a foolish idea it would be to try to take the *Missouri Zephyr* all the way upriver to Cairo.

Farrell stood with his hands on the railing and watched by the light of torches burning on the dock as deckhands man-handled heavy bales of cotton down the ramp from the dock to the lower deck of the riverboat. "I believe this is still my vessel," he observed dryly. "Therefore, I can do whatever I wish with it."

"But the only reason you're going to Cairo is because you think Captain Reese and the *Prometheus* won't follow us up there."

"Owen Reese has no more use for the Yankees than I do. I seriously doubt that he would risk venturing among them for no other reason than to seek revenge for the death of Lydell Strunk."

Cory still felt sick about killing Strunk, even though hours had passed since the unfortunate incident in the alley. But the guilt he felt would be compounded if Captain Farrell risked the *Zephyr* and everybody on her because of him.

"You ought to just leave me here and go on up to Natchez or Memphis for a while," he suggested. "I'll be all right."

Farrell cast a dubious look his way. "All right?" the captain repeated. "You wouldn't last a day on your own after Strunk's body is found. Reese or some of the other men from the *Prometheus* would seek you out and find you, and you'd be lucky if you were killed outright. They might take you back to their boat to make their revenge last longer."

Cory felt a shudder go through him at that thought. "I could hide," he suggested weakly. "I could go on down the delta to someplace like Barataria Bay or one of those old pirate hideouts."

"You couldn't go anywhere that Reese couldn't find you," Farrell stated firmly. "Now, I'll have no more argument about this matter. It's settled." He nodded toward the cotton being loaded. "Besides, I have a cargo to deliver in Cairo."

That cargo, Lucille had told Cory earlier in the evening as they were on their way back to the *Zephyr*, belonged to a man named Harriman. He had tried unsuccessfully to contract with Captain Farrell to carry the cotton upriver, and at that time, Farrell had refused. The only reason the captain had changed his mind, Cory knew, was because of Strunk's death. That laid the blame for whatever happened completely at his feet.

"Will the Yankees still let you put in to port there?"

"They haven't banned shipping on the river, at least as far as I know," Farrell replied. "They keep close track of it, however, using ironclad gunboats to make sure that no Confederate sympathizers in the North try to send money or guns or any vital supplies down the river. They're less concerned about goods being shipped upriver by Northern sympathizers."

"This Mr. Harriman . . ." Cory's voice was hushed and conspiratorial. "You mean he's on the side of the Yankees?"

"Good Lord, no!" Farrell exclaimed. "But he's a businessman, and he has a contract dating from before the beginning of hostilities to deliver those bales of cotton to a mill in Cairo. He intends to fulfill the contract if at all possible."

Cory just shook his head, unsure how commerce could go on in the middle of a war, but he supposed there would always be men to whom money was more important than anything else.

"Even so, I still don't think you should do it. It's too dangerous."

"The decision is out of your hands, I'm afraid," Farrell said with finality.

Cory knew it wasn't going to do any good to argue. He had known that from the start, he supposed, but he had also known that at least he had to try to dissuade Farrell from this foolishness.

At the same time, he knew the captain was right about one thing: Cory's only chance to survive the vengeance of Strunk's friends from the *Prometheus* was to get out of New Orleans quickly and go somewhere that Reese and his men wouldn't follow. Cairo seemed to fit the bill—it was a long way from New Orleans and it was in Yankee hands. And Harriman, the cotton dealer, was in such a rush to get his cargo headed north that leaving the Crescent City in a hurry wasn't going to be a problem.

Still, guilt forced Cory to play one last card. "What about Lucille?" he asked.

Farrell looked at him sharply. "What about her?"

"You'll be putting her in danger as well."

The captain's face hardened, and for a second Cory thought he had gone too far. Then Farrell asserted tightly, "Lucille is well aware of the risks posed by this voyage. She is in favor of it despite them."

Earlier, when she'd first told him they were going upriver to Cairo, Cory hadn't been able to tell if she was upset about her father's decision or not. She hadn't been willing to discuss it with him, either, telling him that he would have to talk to the captain if he had any questions or concerns. When they reached the *Zephyr,* she went straight to Ike Judson's cabin to inform the pilot they were leaving, then on to her own cabin, and she still was there as far as Cory knew.

Farrell had shown up not long after that, and behind him had come wagons loaded with the bales of cotton that were now being transferred to the deck of the riverboat.

Cory saw that he had no choice but to admit defeat. The *Zephyr* was going to Cairo whether he liked it or not. The only way he could prevent the trip was by leaving the riverboat, and even that might not work since Captain Farrell had already come to an agreement with Harriman to deliver the cotton. Farrell considered his word his bond, and he would not back out on the deal, Cory thought, even though his original motivation for doing so might have changed.

So he would be risking his life for nothing if he left the *Zephyr,* and even worse, he would be putting his friends in danger for no reason. He couldn't allow that. He hoped he wasn't just trying to rationalize away his own guilt, but it seemed there was nothing left to do but go along with Captain Farrell's decision.

"What can I do to help?" he asked.

"Go up to the pilothouse," Farrell replied without hesitation. "Mr. Judson and Mr. Rowley will be going over the charts. Do whatever you can to assist them. Traveling the river at night is sometimes difficult, you know."

Cory was well aware of that, but if anybody could guide the boat safely, it was Ike Judson. He was convinced that Judson knew the river as well as any man alive.

When he entered the pilothouse a few minutes later, Cory found Judson and Ned Rowley seated on three-legged stools at a low table that ran along one wall of the structure, below the big windows. The two pilots had several charts spread out in front of them and were studying the maps by the light of a lantern. Judson barely glanced up at Cory before he went back to what he was doing without even a grunt of acknowledgement. Rowley, on the other hand, greeted him effusively.

"Howdy, boy. Heard about what you did. It's about time somebody stuck an Arkansas toothpick in Lydell Strunk. If anybody on the river ever needed killin', it was him."

Cory winced at Rowley's blunt words. He didn't see how he could ever be happy or proud about killing a man, even a man like Strunk. "I'm sorry for all the trouble I've caused," he answered.

"You apologize too damned much," Judson said without looking up from the charts. "Come over here and write down what I tell you. It's goin' to be up to you to make sure I don't overlook nothin'."

Quickly and eagerly, Cory pulled up another stool and began writing down the landmarks and danger spots that Judson especially wanted to watch out for as they made their way upriver. He was glad to have something to do that might be of some use.

Judson charted the river's channel all the way to Natchez, even though, as he put it, "We won't make it that far tonight."

"We'll be well past it tomorrow, though," Rowley pointed out.

"I ain't worried about tomorrow. It's tonight that's got me nervous. Wouldn't be so bad if there was a moon, but the clouds got it plumb covered up."

The door of the pilothouse opened, and as Cory looked over his shoulder he saw Lucille coming into the room. She was wearing boys' clothes, as she usually did when she came into the pilothouse, and her hair was tucked up under a riverman's cap. "What can I do to help, Ike?"

Judson pushed the charts back. "Not a thing, Miss Lucille. Ned and me and the boy got ever'thing worked out."

Cory felt a flush of pride at being included in Judson's statement, even though at twenty years old he thought he was a little old to be called a boy.

Lucille stepped toward them. "But I want to help," she appealed rather plaintively.

"Then you can stay up here and give us a hand with watchin' once we pull out. We're liable to need ever' pair of eyes we got."

Lucille nodded, satisfied. "Thank you, Ike." She climbed onto one of the high chairs and sat there with her hands resting primly on her knees.

Judson put the charts back in a drawer underneath the table, then stood up. "I'm goin' to go talk to the cap'n," he announced. "Come on, Ned."

"What for?" Rowley asked.

"Just come on," Judson snapped.

Rowley looked back and forth between Cory and Lucille, then he said, "Oh," and stood up to follow Judson out of the pilothouse.

Cory felt himself growing warm with embarrassment. He knew Judson was trying to be helpful, but making a point about leaving the two of them alone like that wasn't necessarily the way to go about it. Still, he was glad for the chance to talk to Lucille privately for a few minutes.

He started to tell her how sorry he was that he had caused so much trouble, but then he remembered Judson's comment about his apologizing too much and suppressed the impulse before any of the words could leave his mouth. Instead, after a moment he commented, "Your father's determined to go through with this."

"Of course he is," Lucille answered. "Once Father makes up his mind about something, he hardly ever changes it."

"I'm not sure it's a good idea. I think you'd all be better off if I left the boat and didn't come back."

"So that Owen Reese and his band of cutthroats could cut *your* throat?" Lucille shook her head. "Father couldn't do that. You're a member of our crew. We owe you our loyalty."

Despite the fear that tightened around his chest like a band and choked the back of his throat, Cory heard himself asking, "Is that what I am to you, Lucille? Just a member of the crew?"

She looked at him for a long moment, emotions that he couldn't identify playing over her face. He noticed the way her hands pressed more tightly on her knees in the boys' trousers. Finally, she said, "Cory, you . . . you've changed so much since Father first brought you on the boat and gave you a job. I think at first he was the only one who believed in you."

Cory remembered Judson's acerbic comments at that time and said, "I know he was. But I asked about you, Lucille. How do you feel about me?"

"I think you're a . . . a fine young man. You're going to make a good pilot." She hesitated, then added, "Not as good as me, of course."

He wasn't going to let her get away with escaping into the friendly rivalry they had established. It was time for some "home truths" now. He stood up and came over to the chair where she was sitting and rested his hands on the arms so that he could lean forward, putting his face only a foot from hers. He had no idea where the audacity to do this was coming from, but now that it was begun, he knew he couldn't stop. What he was feeling now was just as inexorable as the flow of the mighty Mississippi.

"Lucille, I have to know," he began, his voice little more than a whisper. "How do you feel about me?"

"Oh, Cory, don't make me say it . . ." She drew back as far as she could in the chair, and her words had a note of desperation in them that made them almost a wail.

"I have to know."

"Oh . . . oh, all right!" Lucille leaned forward suddenly. "I think I'm falling in love with you!" Her hands came up and caught hold of his face, and her mouth pressed against his in a thunderbolt of a kiss that shook him to the very core of his being, even though it lasted only a couple of heartbeats. When Lucille pulled back, she practically spat, "There! Are you satisfied now?"

Cory had that hollow feeling inside again, and he knew there was only one way to fill it. "No. I'm not satisfied at all."

He leaned forward, his arms going around her to pull her against him, and kissed her again. For a second she resisted, but only for a second, and then she seemed to melt in his arms.

It was probably safe to say, Cory thought later, that at that precise moment neither of them gave any thought at all to the fact that they were in a well-lighted room with large windows all around them.

HEAVY FOOTSTEPS sounded on the stairs outside the pilothouse door a few minutes later. By the time the door swung open and Captain Farrell came in, followed by Ike Judson and Ned Rowley, Cory was back at the chart table and Lucille had swung her chair around so that she was looking out the large front window of the structure. "The cargo is loaded," Farrell announced. "We'll be leaving shortly."

"Good," Lucille said. "I'm ready."

"So am I," said Cory.

Farrell's eyebrows lifted, but only for a second. Cory saw the reaction and chose to ignore it. The captain probably sensed the tension between his daughter and the young apprentice pilot, but if so, Farrell was wise enough not to make an issue of it.

Judson went to the wheel. He thumbed his riverman's cap to the back of his head with one hand and rested the other on the wheel. "Ready whenever you are, cap'n," he announced.

Farrell nodded and went over to the speaking tube that connected the pilothouse to the engine room. He grasped the tube and yelled into it, "Bring up the boilers, Mr. Hovey."

"Yes sir, Cap'n." The words came back from the tube, tinny and flat, and Cory knew they were spoken by Ben Hovey, the *Zephyr*'s engineer. Three decks below, the firemen would be stoking the furnaces, getting up steam for the engines.

A few minutes later, Captain Farrell ordered, "Back one-half on the starboard! Back one-half on the larboard!"

Cory felt the faint vibrations of the steam engines through the deck under his feet as they were put into gear. The giant paddlewheels began to slowly turn in reverse, pushing the boat away from the dock. Deckhands had already cast off all the ropes holding the vessel to the dock, so the *Zephyr* began to glide unimpeded out into the river.

With a deft touch, Judson turned the wheel, adjusting the angle of the big rudder at the stern. At the same time, Farrell called into the speaking tube, "Stop the starboard! Back one-half on the larboard!"

The *Zephyr* began a sweeping turn as it continued backing away from the dock. Rowley watched behind them, alert for any unexpected obstacles. After a few moments, Judson brought the wheel back to its original position, and Farrell reached once more for the speaking tube.

"Stop the larboard! . . . Ahead one-half on the starboard! Ahead one-half on the larboard!"

The riverboat began to surge ahead, cutting small waves in the surface as the bow pushed against the flow of the Mississippi.

"Ahead three-quarters on the starboard! Ahead three-quarters on the larboard!"

Cory felt the engine vibrations increase. The *Zephyr*'s speed began to pick up. He glanced at Lucille. She was leaning forward slightly in her chair, peering intently out at the night through the large front window.

"Cory," Judson ordered, "blow out the lamps."

Cory hurried to do so, and darkness descended on the pilothouse as he blew out the last flickering flame. Now those inside could see better, although the cloud cover prevented any moonlight or starlight from penetrating to the river. Down below, on the bow, deckhands attached long iron poles that angled out ahead and away from the boat. At the end of each pole was a large basket woven of iron rods, and each basket was filled with pitch-soaked chunks of wood. Using long torches, the deckhands lit the wood, and soon a good-sized blaze was going in each of the baskets. The glare from the fires stretched out over the water in front of the riverboat, illuminating its path.

Cory had seen the torches burning on the riverboat before when it traveled at night on other occasions, but it was still an awe-inspiring sight. The water reflected the flames, so they seemed to have twins blazing in tandem with them. The circle of light cast by the torches was not large, but it was better than nothing.

It also made the *Zephyr* very visible from shore, Cory thought. If they had hoped to leave New Orleans without many people noticing, that was now impossible. Word would spread quickly along the docks that the riverboat had pulled out.

"I believe we'll leave the engines at three-quarter," Farrell directed Judson. "I'd like to put more distance between us and New Orleans, but on such a dark night, I don't believe it would be safe to run full out."

"No, sir, it wouldn't," Judson agreed, shaking his head.

Farrell turned. Cory's eyes had adjusted well enough to the darkness by now for him to be able to see that the captain was looking at Lucille. "Why don't you go on to your cabin, my dear?" he suggested. "There's really nothing you can do up here."

"I can be another pair of eyes," Lucille protested. "Ike said that might come in handy."

Farrell glanced toward Judson, who shrugged. "I trust my own eyes, Cap'n, but I don't mind havin' others watchin' out, too. The ol' Mississipp' can be mighty tricky sometimes."

"Indeed it can. Very well, Lucille, you can stay. But if you get tired, I want you to go get some sleep."

"You don't mind driving everyone else until they're exhausted," she challenged.

"Everyone else is not my daughter, and like it or not, you get special treatment sometimes. Now, don't argue with me, or you can leave now."

Lucille subsided in her chair. Captain Farrell seemed to be a bit testier than usual tonight, Cory thought, and he wondered if that was because Farrell had gone against his better judgment in deciding to make this run to Cairo.

As Cory looked out at the river, his thoughts went back to the kiss he had shared with Lucille a little while earlier. It had been incredibly exciting. His senses had been filled with the taste of her, the feel of her, the scent of her. He had kissed girls before, of course, back in Virginia, but even though he had thoroughly enjoyed those instances, none of them came close to what he had experienced with Lucille tonight.

Cory leaned on the narrow ledge that ran just under the front window, staying over to the left so that he wouldn't block the view of Captain Farrell and Ike Judson. During those moments that Lucille had been in his arms, he had undergone a definite physical reaction, the sort of reaction that had made him burn in shame at times in the past because the sins of the flesh were just that—sins. A fellow just wasn't supposed to get like that around a decent girl. It wasn't proper.

But feeling that way while he was kissing Lucille hadn't seemed sinful or shameful at all. Instead, every instinct in his body had told him that this was right, this was the way it was supposed to be. It was almost . . . innocent . . . he decided.

And he couldn't help but wonder if maybe Lucille had felt the same way.

THE LIGHTS of New Orleans fell away behind them. There was still an occasional yellow glow from the riverbank that marked an isolated cabin, or sometimes a brief scattering of lights that indicated a small settlement. The *Zephyr* was not the only boat on the river. A few other paddlewheelers, all of them similarly lit by torches, passed Captain Farrell's vessel. All the torches were set well away from the boats on the long iron poles, since the wood of which the vessels were constructed was highly flammable. An out-of-control fire was one of the worst things that could happen on a riverboat, worse even than a breach of the hull. If a hole wasn't too bad, it could be patched and the boat could be salvaged. A fire often burned a riverboat down to the waterline, totally destroying it.

Cory felt himself growing drowsy as the night passed. It seemed impossible that only twelve hours earlier, he hadn't yet encountered Struck for the second time. The third—and fatal—encounter had occurred only a few hours after that. So much had happened in such a short period of time.

A glance over at Lucille told Cory that she was getting sleepy, too. Her head drooped forward for a few seconds at a

time before she jerked it upright again. She was dozing off and
having a difficult time not falling into a deep slumber. Captain
Farrell, on the other hand, seemed as alert as ever. He stood
stiffly upright at the front window, his hands clasped together
behind his back. Judson was much the same way, only his
hands were on the wheel. Ned Rowley was yawning, though.
The long night was catching up to him, too.

Cory's eyelids were sliding shut yet again when Captain
Farrell said abruptly, "Hard starboard, Mr. Judson! *Now!*"

Judson reacted instantly, spinning the giant wheel. The
muscles of his arms and shoulders bunched as he hauled on it.

Farrell grabbed the speaking tube and shouted, "All stop!
All stop!"

Cory was jolted upright by the sudden excitement.
Vaguely, he was aware of Lucille letting out a small cry of
dismay. He looked around, blinking rapidly as he tried to
figure out what was the cause of Farrell's frantic words.

"I see it!" Judson yelled. "Lord a'mighty!"

Cory leaned forward, straining his eyes at the outer edges
of the light cast by the torches. Something was moving there,
he realized abruptly, something that was being carried toward
the riverboat by the current.

Into the speaking tube, Farrell called, "Larboard ahead
full! Pour it on, Ben!"

Neither of the paddlewheels had completely stopped turning, but they had slowed drastically. Now the one on the left
side of the *Zephyr* began to pick up speed again, the blades of
the paddles digging hard at the water. In response to that, and
to the change in the rudder, the bow of the boat began to swing
to the right.

The thing Cory had seen in the river floated closer. It was a
house. An outhouse, to be precise, Cory saw. Part of the door
with the unmistakable half-moon shape carved into it was visible above the waterline. Half the roof was caved in, leaving
jagged timbers sticking up.

"Who'd throw an outhouse into the river?" Cory wondered, and it was a moment before he realized he had spoken the words aloud. No one answered him, however.

A couple of deckhands, roused from sleep by the shouts of the mate, sprang to the edge of the main deck with long wooden poles in their hands, similar to the sort of poles that keelboatmen had employed for years to propel their craft up and down the river. In this case, though, the poles were used to fend off the dangerous object floating toward the *Zephyr.* Between the boat's change in course and the prodding of the poles, a head-on collision was averted. The outhouse merely scraped down the side of the riverboat, scarring the wooden fender but not doing any real damage.

Judson let out a big breath in relief. "Thank the Lord!" he sighed. "If we'd been sunk by one o' those things, folks would've been laughin' about it all up and down the river for years to come!"

"Not to mention the loss of the boat and the possible loss of lives," Captain Farrell added dryly.

With a sheepish smile, Judson agreed. "Yeah, that, too." He grew more serious and went on, "You've got mighty sharp eyes, Cap'n. You spotted that 'fore any of the rest of us."

"It doesn't matter who saw it first, only that we avoided the snag." Farrell glanced at Cory as he spoke, and Cory dropped his eyes toward the deck. He should have been the one to spot the floating outhouse, he thought. He was the youngest of them, except for Lucille. His eyes should have been the sharpest.

Instead, he hadn't seen the danger until several seconds after Farrell, Judson, and for all he knew, Lucille and Rowley, too, had noticed it. He kept looking down at the planks of the pilothouse deck as Farrell called into the speaking tube, "Ahead one-half starboard. Ahead one-half larboard." The *Zephyr* settled down to a more normal pace.

Gently, Judson readjusted the wheel. The riverboat angled a little to the east, following the channel of the river.

Cory took a deep breath. He lifted his head and focused his eyes on the water ahead of the boat once more. He had fallen into the trap of feeling sorry for himself, he realized. Sure, he hadn't been the one to sound the alarm this time, but maybe he would be the next time.

And if there was one thing certain about traveling on the Mississippi, it was that there *would* be a next time. The river was too full of dangers for it to be otherwise.

"Keeping your eyes open, Mr. Brannon?" Farrell asked.

"Yes sir," Cory replied. "Wide open."

Chapter Twelve

ALBERT SIDNEY JOHNSTON'S plan to make the Yankees think that he had more men at his command than was actually the case was still working, at least to an extent. So far, Union forces north of the defensive line Johnston had stretched across the Tennessee-Kentucky border had not made any direct assaults on the Confederates. There were always skirmishes between enemy patrols, of course, but during the winter of '61 and '62, the fighting was sporadic.

General Frémont had been relieved of command back in November, and instead of replacing him with one man, the secretary of war had split Frémont's responsibilities among several officers: Maj. Gen. David Hunter was placed in command of the Department of Kansas, while the Department of Missouri—which actually covered a much larger geographical area than just the state by which it was designated—was given to Maj. Gen. Henry Halleck. The Department of the Ohio, which had included much of Kentucky and previously had been under the command of Gen. William Tecumseh Sherman, was placed in the hands of Brig. Gen. Don Carlos Buell. Sherman had been unable to recognize the gigantic ruse perpetrated by Johnston, and as a result paralysis had pretty much set in along the Union front lines.

It was hoped in Washington that this infusion of fresh blood in the West would get the war moving again there, but instead the move proved divisive. None of the generals involved believed in the splitting up of Union forces; each thought that the armies should be rejoined, and each thought that he, of course, should be placed in command of the unified forces. So the troops continued to sit, the generals continued to bicker, and in Washington, President Lincoln grew more frustrated. Like everyone else, he had hoped for a short, decisive war. Instead, every effort seemed to bog down, and disheartening reports came in that indicated the South was growing stronger with the passage of time. Neither Lincoln nor any of the other Union leaders had any way of knowing that the exact opposite was actually true. A concerted attack all along the South's defensive line likely would have crumpled it, opening the heart of the Confederacy to Union occupation. Such an attack could not come, however, as long as the Yankee leaders were working at cross-purposes.

And in Cairo, Illinois, General Grant's forces had grown to number over twenty thousand men. They marched in the mud, drilled in the rain, and practiced with the cannons that had been installed at Fort Defiance to guard the junction of the Ohio and Mississippi Rivers. Many of the soldiers expected that the South was going to launch an attack any day to try to retake Cairo, while unknown to them, the Confederates downriver were just as fearful of a Yankee invasion.

So both sides sat—and waited.

THE LONG bends of the river rolled past. Natchez, with its infamous Natchez-Under-the-Hill, appeared on the eastern bank and then fell behind as the *Missouri Zephyr* steamed on without stopping. Cory was in the pilothouse with Ned Rowley as Natchez disappeared around a bend, and he heard the pilot sigh.

"What's the matter, Mr. Rowley?" Cory asked.

Rowley shook his head. "I got a gal back there in Natchez. I was hopin' to see her, but the cap'n says we ain't stoppin' until we need to take on more wood for the furnaces. That cotton's the only cargo we're carryin' this trip."

"I'm sorry," Cory said. "Maybe when we come back we'll stop in Natchez."

And maybe by then the *Prometheus* would have left New Orleans, and he would be safe from the vengeance of Capt.

Owen Reese and the other members of the crew. Reese couldn't hold a grudge forever. He had a riverboat to operate and bills to pay, or so Cory hoped would be the case.

Rowley chuckled. "Well, it ain't like Belinda's goin' to miss me all that much. She's got plenty of other beaus. Anybody with a couple of coins in his pocket, in fact."

Cory understood then that Rowley was talking about a prostitute. He was glad that Lucille wasn't in the pilothouse at the moment to hear such blunt conversation.

Cory and Rowley were alone, in fact. Captain Farrell, Lucille, and Ike Judson had all gone below to catch a few hours of sleep now that daylight had come and navigating the river was simpler. Even though the day was still gray with overcast, the snags and sandbars and other assorted menaces were much easier to see, and Rowley knew the channel just about as well as his fellow pilot Judson did. He and Cory would do fine for a while.

Lack of sleep had made Cory's eyes feel as if they had been taken out of his head, rolled around in a pan of sand, and then popped back into their sockets with a layer of grit still clinging to them. He knuckled them from time to time, shook his head and yawned, and continued to fight off his drowsiness. The boat was making this fast run up the river primarily because of him, he reminded himself, so he owed it to everyone else to pull his own weight during the voyage. If he could do even more than that, he would.

From Natchez, the Mississippi angled northeast toward the riverport city of Vicksburg. By the time the *Zephyr* passed Vicksburg, night had fallen and the torches had once more been placed on the bow and lit. Cory was asleep then, stretched out on the bunk in his tiny cabin, dead to the world with exhaustion. Captain Farrell and Ike Judson were manning the pilothouse as the night passed without incident.

The next day, the *Zephyr* made its way up the eastern border of Arkansas, traveling between flat, ugly fields on both sides of the river. This was the stretch of the trip that appealed to Cory the least, but he stood his watch dutifully, working with Ned Rowley again. Lucille spent part of the day in the pilothouse, and her mere presence was enough to brighten things up for Cory. But he couldn't talk openly to her, not with Rowley there, and both of them were frustrated by that. Cory wanted to kiss her again, but he also wanted to talk to her and find out just exactly how things stood between them. Lucille had said that she was falling in love with him, but she also had seemed terrified and even a little angered by that notion.

Cory understood the part about being scared. What he felt for Lucille was so strong, so new, so unexpected, that he was frightened, too.

Late in the afternoon, a stand of trees appeared near the western bank of the river, set back fifty yards or so from the actual bank. Between the trees and the river stood a shack with a large pile of four-foot lengths of split wood in front of it. As the *Zephyr* steamed closer, a man came out of the shack and lifted something to his mouth. Cory realized a moment later that it was a horn of some kind, because the man blew on it and a deep, resonant note floated out over the river.

"We might ought to wood up, Miss Lucille," Rowley said over his shoulder. "What do you think?"

"We're bound to be running low by now, the way Father's had the engines going full out most of the day," Lucille agreed. "Go ahead, Ned."

Rowley nodded and turned the wheel, sending the riverboat angling toward the western bank.

There were plenty of wood yards up and down the river. Anyone who had any trees on their land spent part of their time chopping and splitting cord wood for the steamboats. But Cory didn't remember stopping at this particular spot on any of the previous trips since he'd joined the crew of the *Zephyr.*

Rowley called into the speaking tube, "Stop the starboard. Stop the larboard." With the captain not in the pilothouse, the pilot had the authority to issue such commands to the engineer. The paddlewheels gradually stopped revolving, but the boat had enough momentum built up to continue gliding toward the bank. The current pushed the bow over enough so that it nosed in perfectly to a stop near the woodpile.

The mate already had the deckhands ready. They lowered a ramp from the main deck to the bank so that the wood could be loaded easily and carried into the engine room. First, though, a deal had to be negotiated, and Rowley didn't have the authority to do that. He told Lucille, "Better fetch your papa, Miss Lucille."

She had already slid down from the high chair. "I'm on my way."

Cory said, "I'll go, too."

Lucille glanced at him quickly, but she didn't tell him not to accompany her. Cory pretended not to see the grin on Rowley's face as he followed Lucille out of the pilothouse.

They went down the steep stairway to the Texas deck, Lucille first, and then on to the boiler deck. Captain Farrell was already emerging from his cabin by the time they reached it. Cory wasn't surprised. Farrell was sensitive to everything that happened on the riverboat. Even if he'd been sleeping, he would have felt the *Zephyr* coming to a stop and would have waked to find out what was going on.

"Ned and I thought we should wood up," Lucille explained to her father. "There's a wood yard right here."

Farrell looked around, studying the landscape on both sides of the river. Cory didn't see anything special about it, no real landmarks of any kind, but he had no doubt that Farrell knew exactly where they were.

Farrell confirmed that a moment later by saying, "I don't normally stop here, but I suppose it wouldn't hurt to take on some more wood. Stay here while I deal with this man."

Lucille frowned. She wasn't used to being told to stay behind. Farrell hadn't said that Cory couldn't go with him, though, so Cory followed the captain. Lucille called out quietly, "Cory?"

He turned and said to her, "I'll be right back." He couldn't explain why, but Captain Farrell seemed bothered by something, and Cory wanted to see what it was.

Farrell was halfway down the ramp by the time Cory reached the top of it. The owner of the woodyard came down to the bank to meet them. He was a tall man, sturdily built, with graying curly fair, a ruddy face, and dark circles under his eyes. He wore a big grin and said ingratiatingly, "Why, howdy, Cap'n Farrell. Been a while since I seen you."

"Yes, it has, Billy," Farrell agreed. "We need to wood up."

The man called Billy waved at the stack of cord wood. "You know me, Cap'n, always ready to deal. Have your men get started loadin', and you an' me'll work out a price."

"We'll set the price first, then load," Farrell declared firmly.

Billy shrugged. "Sure, Cap'n. Whatever you want. How's about we say . . . five dollars a cord?"

"Ridiculous," Farrell snapped. "A dollar a cord is more what I had in mind, or perhaps even fifty cents."

An exaggerated grimace appeared on Billy's face. "Four bits? Cap'n, you must be joshin' me." His voice dropped to a conspiratorial tone as he went on, "Why, if I took that little for this fine wood, the ol' lady'd take a length of it and stove my head in." He jerked a thumb toward the shack.

Cory looked in that direction and saw that a slatternly woman with lank, fair hair had appeared in the doorway. She glared at the riverboat and at her husband and cried out in a shrill voice, "Don't you let that man cheat you, Billy! You make him pay you a fair price now!"

Billy half-turned and held up a hand, saying, "I will, Mama, I will." He turned back to Farrell. "You see what I got to put up with, Cap'n? Surely you can gimme four dollars a cord?"

"A dollar and a half," Farrell said.

Cory watched as the dickering went back and forth for several more minutes, and a price of two dollars and twenty-five cents a cord was finally agreed upon. Farrell stepped back and motioned for the deckhands to get to work loading the wood.

Cory moved out of the way. Feeling eyes on him, he looked toward the bank and saw Billy watching him. The woodcutter was grinning, but the deep-set eyes above those dark circles weren't friendly. In fact, just having the man look at him made Cory feel uneasy and somehow dirty. He turned and headed for the stairs that would take him back up to the boiler deck.

Captain Farrell was waiting at the bottom of the stairs. He frowned at Cory. "I'd rather you hadn't come down here, Mr. Brannon."

"Why not?" Cory asked, surprised.

Farrell inclined his head toward the bank where the woodcutter stood. "Because that man—and I use the word generously—would sell out his own mother if it got him what he wanted. If anyone comes looking for us, Billy won't hesitate to tell them that we were here and that he saw you."

"You mean Captain Reese and the *Prometheus*, don't you?"

"That is exactly what I mean." Farrell sighed. "But I suppose Reese already knows you're on board, or else we wouldn't have left New Orleans so abruptly. Still, I'd just as soon he didn't have it confirmed for him. I should have told you to go back up to the pilothouse and stay there until we were through wooding up. Instead, I was more worried about Lucille. I didn't want her anywhere near that lecherous scum."

Cory glanced again at the woodcutter, and he agreed with Farrell's statement. He didn't want Lucille anywhere near Billy, either. Such a man wasn't fit to lay eyes on her.

Farrell fetched a bag of coins from the safe in his cabin and went back ashore to conclude the deal with the woodcutter. Cory returned to the pilothouse and found Lucille there with Ned Rowley and Ike Judson.

"We ought to be finished soon," Cory told them.

"Good," Judson said. "I know the cap'n wants to keep movin'. At this rate, we'll be in Cairo in another couple of days."

"Then what?" Cory asked.

Judson frowned and rubbed his jaw, finally admitting, "I don't rightly know."

"We can't stay there," Lucille spoke up. "The town's full of Yankees."

"We're not part of the army," Cory pointed out. "The soldiers don't have any real reason to care about us."

"Yes, but . . . the town's full of Yankees," Lucille repeated, as if she were trying to explain something obvious to a particularly backward child.

Cory shrugged. He trusted Captain Farrell to figure everything out. It was Cory's hope that they could return to the lower Mississippi and resume something like a normal life once some time had passed.

But there was no predicting what course the war would take, he realized. He had been caught up in his growing affection for Lucille and the violence that had struck so unexpectedly in New Orleans, and he hadn't thought much about the larger picture. War had a way of affecting everything, though, and Cory knew he couldn't count on anything staying the same.

Except the way he felt about Lucille, he told himself. Nothing was going to change that, not even a war.

CORY'S FIRST sight of New Madrid in a couple of months didn't prompt any nostalgic feelings in him. In fact, as he looked at the docks and warehouses lining the western bank of the river, with the rest of the settlement atop the muddy hill behind them, he seemed to have a sour taste in his mouth. He remembered the casual cruelty of Mr. Vickery and the other men he'd worked for, the long days of backbreaking labor and the even longer nights of trying to survive in miserable squalor, the cold and the rain and the sheer hopeless despair that had come so close to overpowering him . . .

"Be back in a minute," he told Judson, who was at the wheel.

"Where you goin'?" Judson asked, but Cory had already opened the pilothouse door and stepped out onto the small landing behind the structure. He spat toward New Madrid, putting some power behind it so that the gob of spittle arched well out and cleared the lower decks to land in the river. It was a foolish gesture, Cory knew, but somehow he felt better for it.

While he was standing there, he saw another steamboat come around a bend in the river just below New Madrid. Thick clouds of black smoke billowed from its twin stacks, and even at this distance, Cory could see the splashing as its twin paddlewheels churned the water. The other boat's captain was really pouring on the steam, he thought.

Suddenly, Cory's eyes widened as an unwelcome thought occurred to him. He ducked back into the pilothouse and reached for a telescope that sat on a shelf close by Judson's position at the wheel. "Let me see that spyglass," Cory said as he snatched up the instrument.

"Hey, be careful with that!" Judson exclaimed. "What's got into you, boy?"

Cory didn't waste time explaining. He hurried back outside, opened the telescope to its full extension, and lifted it to his right eye. He squinted his left eye as he peered through the spyglass.

The image he saw through it seemed to leap at him. He focused first on the bow, trying to read the letters painted there, bold red letters against the white background. His lips moved as he whispered, "P . . . r . . . o . . ."

Prometheus!

Cory took an involuntary step backward. He felt his heart begin to race faster. As he tried to force himself to remain calm, he raised the telescope higher, intending to train it on the pilothouse.

Instead, he saw two men standing at the railing at the front of the Texas deck, and as their faces sprang into clarity, Cory gasped in horror. He recognized one of the men. The bearded, belligerent face was all too familiar, as was the squat, powerfully muscled body. The only difference Cory saw in Lydell Strunk was the black patch over the Kaintuck's left eye.

Strunk was alive! How in the world was that possible? Cory had felt the blade go deep into Strunk's body, had seen Strunk lying on the filth of that alley with the hilt of the knife sticking up from his chest. Strunk should have been dead!

The other man, the man standing with Strunk, was tall and impressive-looking in a blue captain's jacket and a black cap. He had a dark, closely trimmed beard. That would be Owen Reese, Cory thought, the captain of the *Prometheus*. The man who had intended to marry Lucille.

All Cory had to do to hate him was look at him.

At the moment, both Strunk and Reese wore excited, eager expressions. They must have seen the *Zephyr* and recognized the boat. They had followed their quarry all the way from New Orleans, and they must have traveled at top speed in order to have almost caught up like this. Cory was still staring at them through the spyglass when, without warning, Reese brought up a telescope of his own and peered through it. Feeling as if the man were staring into his own eyes from a distance of mere inches, Cory nearly dropped the spyglass as he lurched backward and let out a gasp.

"Cory!" Lucille called from the bottom of the stairs that led from the Texas deck to the pilothouse. "What's wrong?"

Cory leveled an arm and pointed, knowing that Reese was probably watching his every move. "The *Prometheus*!" he said. "Go tell your father!"

Lucille didn't argue. She turned and ran for the stairs that would take her down to the boiler deck.

Cory turned and barged back into the pilothouse. From the wheel, Judson demanded, "What the hell is goin' on?"

"The . . . the *Prometheus*," Cory said shakily, waving a hand downriver. "They're right behind us."

Judson grated a curse and reached for the speaking tube. "Ben! Give 'em all you got!"

"Ike?" came back the engineer's worried reply.

"Just do it!"

A moment later, Cory felt the vibrations under his feet increase as the engines roared faster and harder, driving the *Zephyr* on against the current. The boilers had to be heated hotter and hotter to increase the power going to the paddle-wheels, and if they got hot enough they could explode. At worst, that would blow the riverboat into kindling. At best, such an explosion would start a fire that could ultimately destroy the boat as well.

Judson stood tensely at the wheel, watching the river ahead. At higher speeds, it was even more important that the pilot see every potential danger in plenty of time. Cory didn't want to distract Judson, but he couldn't keep from saying, "Strunk's alive! I saw him through the spyglass."

"What?" Judson snapped without looking around. "I thought you killed that Kaintuck son of a bitch."

"So did I." Cory swallowed hard. "But the knife must not have hit his heart, or anything else too important, because he's back there on the *Prometheus*. I saw him." An idea came to him, something hopeful for a change. "Maybe they're not chasing us after all, since I didn't really kill him."

Judson laughed harshly. "You stick a knife in Lydell Strunk's chest and think he's goin' to forget about it, whether you killed him or not? He still wants a piece of your hide, boy, take my word for it. And Reese'll pretty much go along with whatever Strunk and the rest o' them murderous bastards in his crew want."

Cory realized his hands were trembling and gripped the chart table to stop them from shaking. Of course Strunk would want revenge. The man was at least half-crazy, according to everything Cory had been told about him, and besides, he'd lost an eye during that fight in the alley and he would want vengeance for that mutilation. A boat full of men seeking to avenge Strunk's death might not be as dangerous as Strunk still alive.

Captain Farrell and Lucille came hurrying into the pilot-house. "It's the *Prometheus*, all right," Farrell confirmed. "I can recognize her even at this distance."

"That ain't the worst of it," Judson announced. "Accordin' to the boy, Strunk's still alive."

"Good Lord!" Farrell looked at Cory. "Are you sure?"

Cory took a deep breath. "I saw him plain as day through the spyglass. It was him, Captain. There was a man with him. I figure it was Captain Reese."

"Tall man, short beard, rather handsome?"

"That was him," nodded Cory. "And I think he saw me. He had a spyglass, too."

"Of course," Farrell muttered. "Bad luck continues to follow us, along with the *Prometheus*." He squared his shoulders. "Well, there's nothing we can do now except outrun them to Cairo. I still believe they won't venture that far."

"It's only about twenty miles, Cap'n," Judson put in. "You reckon we can stay in front of 'em that far?"

"Of course we can!" Lucille interjected before her father could reply to the pilot's question. "That old tub can't outrun the *Zephyr*."

Cory looked through the open door of the pilothouse. "They're not much more than half a mile behind us," he pointed out.

"Yes, but we're running at top speed now," Farrell said. "I believe we can even gain on them."

Cory watched tensely over the next few minutes as Farrell's prediction proved to be true. Not only had the *Prometheus* stopped closing the gap, it was actually falling back a bit. But then, the clouds of smoke coming from the stacks grew even thicker and darker. The pursuer surged ahead, cutting the distance between the two ships once again.

"The fool's going to blow his boilers if he keeps that up," muttered Farrell as he and Cory and Lucille watched out the back of the pilothouse.

"I hope he does!" Lucille blazed savagely. "I hope the damned boat blows up."

Farrell frowned but didn't reprimand her for either her language or her bloodthirstiness. Cory wiped the back of his hand across his mouth and kept watching.

Suddenly, white smoke bloomed on the boiler deck of the *Prometheus*. Cory heard a faint boom in the distance. Farrell grabbed his daughter and instinctively thrust her behind him. "My God!" he said incredulously. "They're firing on us!"

Cory watched, his eyes growing wider and wider, as the cannonball arched over the river toward the *Zephyr*. It fell well short, plunging into the water with a splash. The weapon boomed again, throwing out another blossom of powder smoke. Again the ball splashed into the river, but Cory thought it closer than the first.

"If they gain another two hundred yards on us, that cannon might actually be a threat," Farrell observed. Turning his face to Lucille, he said, "I want you to go to your cabin and stay there until this is over."

"No!" she protested immediately. "I won't do it, Father. I'm staying up here with you and Cory and Ike."

"Your loyalty is commendable, but I must insist—"

What Lucille did then surprised Cory more than anything else that had happened in the past few months. She stepped over to him, reached out, and took his hand in hers. "No," she quietly asserted. "I'm staying here."

Farrell looked at the two young people for a long moment. "Very well," he finally said and turned back to watch the pursuing riverboat.

Cory reveled in the warmth of Lucille's hand in his, drawing strength from it for a moment before he suggested, "You know, your father is right. You really ought to go down below—"

"Please, Cory," she pleaded, "don't ask that of me. Anything else, but don't ask me to leave you."

He looked into her blue eyes for a moment, almost losing himself in them, then nodded. "All right." Their fingers twined together and tightened.

Judson said into the speaking tube, "Is that all you can give us, Ben?"

"What the hell you want me to do, start throwin' gunpowder in the furnaces?"

Cory found himself grinning at Hovey's irascible answer, as did Lucille, Farrell, and Judson. The pilot chuckled and shouted back, "It may come to that, Ben. For now, just keep pourin' on the steam."

A riverboat's pace was supposed to be slow and stately, thought Cory, but that wasn't the case here. He had never experienced such speed except on the back of a galloping horse. The vibrations from the engines increased to the point where he began to worry about the boat literally shaking itself to pieces. A half-hour passed, and still the deadly race continued.

The speaking tube squawked. "Runnin' low on wood," Hovey announced. "We can't keep the furnaces stoked for more'n another half-hour."

Judson looked back at Farrell. "That'll put us in Cairo, Cap'n. I say we keep it up."

Farrell nodded and took the speaking tube himself. "Pour it on, Ben!"

The cannon on the *Prometheus* had fallen silent. Reese must have realized he was wasting powder and shot unless he could get closer, Cory thought. And the *Zephyr,* along with her gallant crew, was not going to allow that to happen.

Time seemed to stretch out. Cory had no idea how many minutes had ticked past when Judson suddenly exclaimed, "What the hell! Look up yonder in the river!"

Cory looked, as did Farrell and Lucille, and he saw something the likes of which he had never seen before. What appeared to be a pair of giant turtles were coming downriver toward them, trailing streamers of smoke.

"Ironclads," Captain Farrell breathed. "Union gunboats."

"Cairo dead ahead," Judson announced.

"Look!" Lucille cried excitedly. "The *Prometheus* is falling back."

That was true. The pursuing steamboat was dropping back rapidly. As Cory watched, it turned and started downriver, picking up speed. He grinned and thrust a clenched fist in the air. "They've given up!"

"They certainly have," Farrell agreed. "And in the face of that, who can blame them?"

Cory turned back toward the front of the pilothouse and tried to keep his jaw from dropping. More of the odd-looking ironclads, as Farrell had called them, had appeared.

In fact, the whole blamed Mississippi River seemed to be filled with Union gunboats.

Chapter Thirteen

T HE SITUATION WASN'T QUITE that dire, Cory realized a moment later as the approaching Union flotilla came closer. There were only four of the odd-looking ironclads, accompanied by an equal number of more conventional wooden gunboats. Lined up across the river as they were, however, the boats were very impressive. The ironclads were in the center of the formation, flanked by two of the wooden gunboats on each side.

Cory had never seen anything like the ironclads. Each of them sported twin smokestacks, just as the *Zephyr* did, but each vessel had a ring of a different color painted around its stacks, probably for identification purposes since they were otherwise identical. The paddlewheels were not visible. They had to be concealed underneath the layers of iron plating that sheathed the sloping sides of the vessels. In the bow of each boat were three ports through which the barrels of cannon protruded. Cory could see other ports down the sides of the vessels, but from the angle he was viewing them, he couldn't tell how many. Enough so that, all told, each of the gunboats could bring at least a dozen heavy cannon into play, he figured.

A large U.S. flag flew from a tall mast at the stern of each ironclad; a smaller regimental or battle flag of some sort flew from a mast at the bow. Just in front of the pilothouse was a low, circular structure with sloping sides. Cory peered at it in puzzlement for a moment before realizing that it had gun ports cut into it, too. Smaller cannon could be fired from that turret. Back of the pilothouse were several small cabins, probably used for storage. Everything was covered with iron plating. All that Cory knew about boats he had learned during his time on the *Zephyr*, but he was surprised that vessels as heavy as the ironclads had to be could even float, let alone be fast enough and maneuverable enough to function as gunboats.

At least a dozen soldiers in blue uniforms were on the decks of the ironclads and the wooden boats. Captain Farrell must have noticed that, too, because he said, "They don't look like they're spoiling for a fight. Otherwise those men would be belowdecks. Probably just a regular patrol."

Judson nodded. "Reckon you're right, Cap'n. What do we do? Steam on past 'em?"

"If they allow us to."

Cory swallowed as he looked intently at the Federal boats. They might not be looking for trouble now, but if they wanted to, they could blow the *Zephyr* right out of the water. The riverboat's single cannon likely wouldn't be able to make even a dent in the ironclads' armor.

One of the wooden gunboats advanced faster than the others and the ironclads, and after a few minutes Cory realized the boat was coming to meet them. Captain Farrell ordered through the speaking tube, "Stop the starboard. Stop the larboard." Cory could almost hear the sigh of relief Ben Hovey must have heaved at that command. The halt would give the boilers a chance to cool off a little.

Gradually the *Zephyr* came to a stop. The Union gunboat pulled alongside. An officer came to the railing on the deck and hailed the riverboat through a megaphone. "*Missouri Zephyr*, heave to!" he commanded, although the *Zephyr* had clearly come to a halt already. "I am Lt. William Gwin, in command of the United States vessel *Tyler*. What is your destination?"

Farrell took a megaphone from a shelf underneath the chart table and stepped out onto the small platform behind the pilothouse. Cory watched him anxiously from the open door of the pilothouse. "Capt. Ezekiel Farrell, master of the *Missouri Zephyr!*" Farrell called. "We're bound for Cairo!"

"Cairo is occupied by troops under the command of Gen. Ulysses S. Grant!" Gwin bellowed back.

"This is a commercial vessel, not a military one," Farrell responded. "I have no quarrel with General Grant or the United States!"

Cory had an idea what making that statement must have cost the captain. Farrell believed firmly in the Confederacy and the concept of states' rights. But under the circumstances, he couldn't very well admit that.

Lieutenant Gwin turned and conferred with several other officers on the deck of the *Tyler*. The other gunboats and iron-clads remained where they were. After a couple of minutes, Gwin picked up his megaphone again and shouted over to the *Zephyr*, "Prepare to be boarded and searched!"

"Come ahead," Farrell responded. He lowered the mega-phone and turned back to the others. "I expected as much. All the members of the crew have strict orders to cooperate with the soldiers."

Lucille frowned. "I don't like being so friendly with Yankees."

"Neither do I," Farrell sighed. "But it seems we have no other choice at the moment."

A rowboat was lowered from the *Tyler*, and several soldiers paddled it over to the steamboat. Lieutenant Gwin was in command of the group. Captain Farrell went down to the main deck to greet him, trailed by Cory. Lucille and Judson remained in the pilothouse.

The lieutenant stepped easily from the rowboat to the deck of the *Zephyr* and saluted Farrell. Farrell nodded in return and said, "Welcome to the *Zephyr*, Lieutenant."

"Sorry for the inconvenience, sir. You understand, of course, that a state of war exists between the Union and the rebel Southern states?"

"As I said before, this is a commercial vessel, not a military one. Has shipping been prohibited on the Mississippi River? If so, I knew nothing of it."

"No, sir, not officially," Gwin replied. A hint of a smile lurked around his mouth. "But you're the first Southern ship that's dared to come up here since we occupied Cairo. Are you carrying cargo?"

"Bales of cotton, bound for one of the mills here."

"Cotton," Gwin repeated, shaking his head. "You know, sir, that any cotton milled here will wind up going to the North?"

"My job is only to deliver it, Lieutenant, not to specify where it goes from here."

Gwin chuckled. "Well, I must say, that's a commendable attitude, sir, and considerably different from most of your countrymen."

Cory saw the way Farrell's shoulders stiffened. These pleasantries had to be taking a toll on the captain, Cory knew, but Farrell was doing a masterful job of keeping his natural instincts under control.

"I'd like to get on to Cairo, Lieutenant."

"Of course, sir. We'll just have to take a quick look at your cargo." Gwin hesitated then added, "I noticed another river-boat coming up behind you. Do you know anything about it?"

"Not a thing, I'm afraid."

"It's just that both vessels were going pretty fast. It appeared that you might have been racing."

"I've no more interest in racing, Lieutenant, than I do in things military."

"All right," Gwin said. "The other boat turned back south anyway. We could pursue it, but it hardly seems worthwhile." He motioned for the troopers with him to check out the bales of cotton stacked on the main deck.

Cory watched as the Union soldiers thrust the bayonets attached to the muzzles of their rifles into more than a dozen of the bales, chosen at random. When they had done that, Lieutenant Gwin, who had also been watching, lifted a hand and said, "All right, that's enough." He turned back to Farrell. "You may deliver your cargo, Captain."

"Thank you," Farrell murmured.

"But once you've done that, you'll have to receive permission from General Grant before you'll be allowed to leave Cairo. I don't know if that permission will be forthcoming or how long it will take if it is."

"Very well," Farrell said. "Thank you, Lieutenant."

Gwin sketched another salute. "Good day to you, Captain."

Cory and Farrell stayed where they were until the lieutenant and the Union soldiers had rowed back to the *Tyler*. Then Cory heaved a sigh and said, "Well, we got here. I wasn't sure we would."

"Yes," agreed Farrell, "but the question remains, now that we're here, will they let us go?"

THE *ZEPHYR* received quite a few surprised stares when it steamed up to the docks a short while later. The docks were beyond the point of land that jutted out where the Ohio and the Mississippi joined and were actually facing the Ohio. The Illinois Central Railroad paralleled the river and the docks, and beyond the tracks was the city of Cairo itself. Cory had never been here before, but although the settlement was a good-sized one, he wasn't too impressed with it. The streets were morasses of mud and had evidently been flooded recently. Most of the buildings were ugly, squat, red-brick structures. The planks of the wooden buildings were unpainted and had faded to an unappealing gray. Cory hoped they wouldn't have to stay here long, but as Captain Farrell had pointed out, that was entirely up to General Grant.

As soon as the *Zephyr* was tied up, her deckhands got busy unloading the bales of cotton. Captain Farrell told Cory and Lucille to remain on board, then he went ashore and entered the office of the dockmaster. When the man heard that Farrell was delivering a cargo of cotton bound for Avery Jimmerson's mill, he immediately sent a boy running to Jimmerson's office with the news. Within a half-hour, wagons began arriving at the docks to take on the bales.

Cory and Lucille watched the loading from the pilothouse. Lucille looked out over the drab city and shuddered. "A whole town of Yankees," she reflected. "I just can't believe it."

"They're probably not all Yankees," Cory answered. "There are bound to be some Confederate sympathizers among the townspeople. They're probably just afraid to say anything about it, what with thousands of Federal troops posted here."

"You can't blame them for that. Yankees are nothing but bloodthirsty savages."

Cory wasn't going to argue with her, but he suspected that Northerners probably thought the same thing about Confederate soldiers.

His attention wandered from the loading of the cotton bales into the wagons, and he looked instead at the people walking along the streets. There wasn't the same colorful variety in the population here that was found in New Orleans. Cory saw soldiers, farmers, businessmen, and dockworkers. There were only a few women in evidence, going in and out of the stores along Cairo's main street, and all of them wore colorless, shapeless dresses and dull bonnets. Next to those women, he thought, Lucille would shine like a bursting sun.

Idly, his gaze fell on a tall man standing on the platform at the railroad depot. The man wore a light-colored suit and a broad-brimmed planter's hat, which made him stand out from the other people on the platform. He had his thumbs hooked in the pockets of his vest and carried himself with an air of casual arrogance. Cory frowned as he looked at the man. Something about him was familiar, but it was hard to tell much about his features at this distance . . .

Suddenly, an image flashed into Cory's mind. He remembered a man who had stood at the head of a mob, a man with a torch in his hand who had threatened to burn the *Zephyr*. Cory stiffened as he realized that the man on the depot platform was Jason Gill, the abolitionist.

"Cory?" Lucille said. "What's wrong?"

"It's Gill," Cory said, gesturing. "There, at the train station."

"Who?" Lucille peered in the direction Cory indicated.

"Jason Gill. The man who led that mob back in New Madrid."

"Oh, no! What's he doing here?"

Cory shook his head. "I don't know, but I don't suppose we should be too surprised. Gill is an abolitionist, and we're right across the river from Missouri. He's probably been trying to stir up trouble over there."

"If he sees the *Zephyr*, he's bound to remember that my father has always supported the Confederacy."

Cory's mind was racing. Lucille was right: it was doubtful that Gill would have forgotten that night in New Madrid. The man's troublemaking had seldom been thwarted. He would remember a defeat, and it would sting.

With the shrill wail of a steam whistle, a train pulled into the station. Cory hoped that Gill would board the train and leave, but when it pulled out a few minutes later, Gill was still on the platform, only now he was talking to several blue-coated officers who must have gotten off the train. It came as no surprise to Cory that Gill was thick as thieves with the Yankees.

The *Zephyr* and everyone on the riverboat would be in danger as long as Gill was in Cairo. If the abolitionist told Grant about Farrell's support of the South, then the captain's charade of neutrality would be shattered. It was likely that Grant would order the confiscation of the *Zephyr*, and he might throw the ship's captain in jail.

"I have to tell your father about this," Cory said. "We have to find some way to get out of here."

"How?" asked Lucille, an edge of fear in her voice. "There are Yankee soldiers everywhere and Yankee gunboats on the river."

She was right. Not only that, but it was possible that the *Prometheus*, with Owen Reese and a vengeful Lydell Strunk on board, might be waiting downriver just in case the *Zephyr* returned.

"Talk about a rock and a hard place," Cory muttered.

"What?"

"Just something my mother always says. Stay here. I'll go talk to the captain."

"I'm getting tired of being told to stay behind, Cory," Lucille snapped, and now her voice sounded slightly ominous.

"I'll be right back," Cory cajoled. "Somebody needs to stay up here in the pilothouse, just in case." He opened the door and hurried out.

"In case of what?" Lucille called after him, but he chose to pretend he hadn't heard her.

Cory rattled down the stairs from deck to deck, searching for Captain Farrell. He finally found the captain on the main deck, where the last of the cotton bales were being man-handled off the boat and up the ramp to the dock.

"Captain," Cory began urgently.

"What is it, Mr. Brannon?"

"I just saw Jason Gill."

Farrell's head swung toward Cory. "The abolitionist?"

"The one who tried to burn the *Zephyr* back in New Madrid a few months ago, that's right."

"Where did you see him?" Farrell appeared calm, as always, but Cory knew him well enough now to see the signs of strain: the narrowed eyes, the stiffer posture, the slight forward lean of the head.

Cory inclined his own head toward the business district of Cairo. "Over there at the railroad depot. I could see it from the pilothouse. Gill was on the platform, talking to some Union officers who got off the train that just came in."

"You're certain it was Gill you saw?"

"I'm not likely to forget him, sir. And I got a good look at him that night by the light of all those torches."

"We all did," Farrell mused. "Very well, Mr. Brannon. And I believe I understand your concern as well. Lieutenant Gwin, indeed Grant himself, may not be aware of our true sympathies, but Jason Gill most certainly is."

Cory nodded. "That's what I thought. If he sees the *Zephyr*, he's liable to tell the Yankees not to let us go."

Farrell slowly rubbed his jaw and frowned in thought. "The cargo is unloaded. I suppose we could make a run for it."

"But the gunboats . . . those ironclads . . . they'd try to stop us."

"Undoubtedly. Besides, I have an appointment this evening with Avery Jimmerson, the man buying this cotton from Harriman down in New Orleans. I'd like to keep it if at all possible." Farrell looked sharply at Cory. "When you saw him, was Gill showing any interest at all in the docks?"

"Well . . . no. He was just interested in meeting those Union officers at the train station."

"He's up to some abolitionist devilment over in Missouri, I'd wager, and was asking for help from the army." Farrell nodded abruptly as he reached a decision. "Very well. We'll stand pat and take our chances. Perhaps Gill won't come near the river this evening."

"But can we count on him staying away and not seeing us until we have permission to leave?"

"We won't be waiting that long," Farrell muttered grimly.

As HE picked his way carefully on the narrow planks laid across the muddy street, Cory wondered why in the world Captain Farrell had asked him to come along tonight. It wasn't as if he had a great deal of experience at intrigues such as this. But Farrell had insisted, and Cory had come along reluctantly, donning the same suit he had worn on that fateful evening a few days earlier when he was supposed to meet Farrell and Lucille at the Golden Crab. The clothes had been cleaned and mended by the steward on the *Zephyr,* and they looked almost as good as new. That might not be the case by the time they reached their destination tonight, Cory thought. It was inevitable that at least one of them would slip and fall in the mud, and Cory was certain it would be him.

However, both he and Captain Farrell reached the other side of the street without any mishaps and with their boots only lightly splattered with mud. Farrell led the way along the boardwalk, and as the lights grew brighter and more garish and the noise more raucous, Cory realized they were entering Cairo's tenderloin. Every building along here was either a saloon, a gambling hall, or a bordello. Often all three things were combined in one establishment. Cory felt his nervousness growing. Why would a respectable businessman such as Avery Jimmerson pick such a disreputable area for a meeting?

"Here we are," Captain Farrell announced. "The Staghorn."

Indeed, a set of antlers was fastened over the doors of the building. At one time, the antlers had probably been quite impressive, but now they had a bedraggled look. Several of the tips were missing, either broken off or more likely shot off by drunks. Farrell opened the door and stepped inside, followed by Cory.

The air was thick with smoke from countless pipes and cigars, and tinny music from a banjo and a piano assaulted Cory's ears. The place was crowded. Men stood three deep at the bar that ran down the left side of the room, and all the tables were full. Cory wondered how they could make their way through the press of people, but Captain Farrell found a path to the bar. It was sort of like following the channel in the river, Cory observed.

A man with a cigar cocked in the corner of his mouth stood at the end of the bar. He was well dressed in a tweed suit and a silk brocaded vest. A gold watch chain ran from pocket to pocket across his chest. His silk cravat was held in place with a fancy stickpin. He had sleek, dark hair that stood up slightly in front and a beefy, well-fed face. At one time he had probably been a very handsome man, Cory thought, but dissipation was taking its toll.

Evidently the man knew the captain, because he took the cigar out of his mouth and greeted him warmly, "Hello, Captain Farrell. Nice to see you again."

"Hello, Kincaid." Farrell indicated Cory. "This is Cory Brannon. Mr. Brannon, Palmer Kincaid, the owner of the Staghorn."

Kincaid's eyes were a pale green, and though they swept quickly over Cory, they seemed to miss nothing. "Mr. Brannon," he acknowledged with a polite nod. Then he turned back to Farrell, "I expect you're ready to meet with Avery."

"Is he here?"

"Waiting for you in the back room."

Kincaid led Cory and Farrell to a door that opened into a narrow hallway lit only by a lamp at the far end. Cory hesitated. Something about the corridor reminded him of a dark alley where he had gotten into significant trouble recently. But Farrell didn't seem worried, and Cory followed the captain's lead. Kincaid opened another door that led off the hallway, and Cory and Farrell went through it.

The room in which they found themselves was large and luxuriously furnished. A table with a green baize cover sat in the center of the room, directly underneath a chandelier. This was probably where private poker games were held, Cory thought, but at the moment the table was empty.

The same couldn't be said of a claw-footed settee across the room. A man with a fringe of iron-gray hair around a bald head and bushy side whiskers sat there flanked by two women, both of whom were wearing low-cut, scanty gowns. One was a redhead, the other a blonde, and both had their hair piled high on their heads in elaborate arrangements of curls. Their faces were vividly painted, and their mouths were red slashes. The bald man had his arms around their bare shoulders and was laughing as Cory and Farrell came in.

"Zeke!" the man exclaimed when he noticed them. He bounded up from the settee and came across the room, his hand extended. "Zeke, you old rapscallion! It's good to see you again. I was hoping Harriman could get you to bring that cargo to me. There's nobody else I'd really trust with it."

Farrell shook hands with the man. "Hello, Avery. I see you haven't changed any."

"You mean the gals?" Avery Jimmerson threw back his head and laughed again. "Hell, I hope I never do! And so do the womenfolk!"

Cory took off his hat and tried not to stare at the two women on the settee. It was difficult not to look. They were both beautiful, and the creamy swells of their breasts threatened to spring free of the daringly low-cut gowns. Cory forced himself to focus his attention on Farrell and Jimmerson. He was in love with Lucille, he told himself, and he shouldn't even be glancing at any other woman.

"Who's this sprout?" Jimmerson asked, and Cory became aware that the man was looking at him.

"Cory Brannon," Farrell answered. "I've taken him under my wing, so to speak."

Jimmerson frowned. "Can he be trusted?"

"He wouldn't be here if I didn't trust him," Farrell replied without hesitation. "He saved the *Zephyr* from a mob led by Jason Gill down in New Madrid a few months ago."

That was stretching the truth a little, but it still felt good to hear Farrell say that, Cory thought. He was surprised that Farrell had admitted Gill's enmity, however. That was the same thing as saying he was a Confederate sympathizer.

A moment later, Cory understood why Farrell had spoken plainly. Jimmerson grimaced and said, "Gill? Somebody ought to string that abolitionist bastard up by his—"

Kincaid closed the door of the private room firmly and asked, "A drink, gentlemen?"

Cory suspected that Jimmerson had already been drinking. He also suspected that the owner of the cotton mill was really a Southern sympathizer, and Palmer Kincaid must be, too, or they wouldn't be meeting like this in the Staghorn.

Kincaid didn't wait for an answer to his question. He brought out a bottle of brandy and some widemouthed glasses. Cory had had brandy before, back in Virginia, though not often since the Baptist Church frowned on drinking and, more importantly, so did his mother. He sipped the smooth, potent liquor slowly after Kincaid handed him a snifter of it.

"Let's sit down," Jimmerson suggested. He turned and flapped a hand at the two women. "You ladies run along and come back after while when we're done talking." Jimmerson glanced at Cory. "You want one of 'em? Young buck like you probably needs all the lovin' he can get."

"Ah, no, that's all right," Cory mumbled, feeling his face growing warm. "Thank you, though."

"Well, let me know if you change your mind."

When the women were gone, Cory, Farrell, Jimmerson, and Kincaid all sat down at the poker table. Jimmerson's boisterous attitude fell away from him, and he was all business as he began, "Good job, Zeke. The guns were all right there where Harriman said they'd be."

"Guns?" Cory gasped, unable to contain his surprise.

Jimmerson looked startled, too. "The boy didn't know about 'em?" he asked.

"No one did except Harriman and me," Farrell replied.

"You mean we were carrying guns?" Cory blurted.

Farrell nodded. "Hidden in some of the bales of cotton."

"Then . . . when those gunboats stopped us and the soldiers searched the cargo . . . they could have found the guns?"

"They didn't," Farrell answered. "We were fortunate. And skilled at hiding the particular bales in question. The troops would have had to move quite a few before they ever reached the ones with the rifles hidden in them." A faint smile crossed Farrell's face. "So you see, Mr. Brannon, rescuing you from the vengeance of Lydell Strunk wasn't the only reason we came here. Although I must admit that your dilemma tipped the scales in favor of accepting Harriman's proposal."

Cory was still trying to wrap his mind around the concept of smuggling guns right into a Union stronghold. "Where are the rifles going?" he asked.

"To our people in western Missouri," Jimmerson answered. "They're desperately short of arms." He shook his head. "Of course, that's true all over the South. But all we can do is try to plug every hole we can, then move on to the next one."

"But where did they come from?"

"The South has many supporters in England," Farrell explained. "My own family is from there, you know. These rifles were brought into New Orleans on a British ship, then concealed in Harriman's bales of cotton. We have great hopes that this will be only the first shipment of many."

"Here's to that," Jimmerson toasted, raising his glass of brandy.

"Now then," Farrell resumed when they had all drunk, "we have another problem. I mentioned Jason Gill earlier. He's here in Cairo. Mr. Brannon spotted him at the depot, speaking with several Union officers."

Kincaid leaned forward, really joining the conversation for the first time. "You said that Gill tried to burn your boat. That means he knows your sympathies."

"Exactly. I told the lieutenant in command of one of the gunboats that stopped us that I had no interest in things military. Gill knows that the opposite is true, and if he realizes the *Zephyr* is here in Cairo—"

"He'll run straight to Grant and demand that your boat be seized," Jimmerson said. "Damn it, Zeke, you got to get out of here as soon as you can."

"I know," Farrell said. "I was hoping one of you gentlemen could suggest a feasible means of doing so."

"You can't go back downriver without the proper authorization," Kincaid said. "And that could take days or even weeks."

"I take it the patrol boats have the Mississippi closed off securely?"

Kincaid snorted. "Those ironclads would blow your ship to kindling wood if you tried to make a run for it."

"Palmer's right," Jimmerson noted. "Only way out is up the Ohio, and even that won't be easy. The gunboats patrol there, too, just not as often."

Kincaid leaned back in his chair and swirled the brandy that was left in his snifter. "You might be able to slip through," he suggested, "if there was something else going on to distract the Yankees."

Farrell looked at him intently. "Something that you might be able to arrange?"

Kincaid shrugged, "Maybe. For a price."

"Palmer!" protested Jimmerson. "Zeke risked his neck to get those guns through. I know you're a damned mercenary saloonkeeper, but I reckon Zeke deserves our help."

"Of course," Kincaid murmured. "I'd be glad to be of assistance, Captain."

"Thank you," Farrell said, a little stiffly. "Assuming we could escape up the Ohio, where would we go from there?"

"The Confederate army's built a couple of forts not far from here, one on the Tennessee River and one on the Cumberland. If you could make it to one of them, you'd be all right," Jimmerson suggested confidently.

"Fort Henry and Fort Donelson." Kincaid provided the names. "I've heard talk about them."

"Which one is closer?"

"Henry, on the Tennessee. But there's only about twelve miles, overland, between them."

"Fort Henry it is, then," Farrell announced decisively. "When should we be ready to leave?"

"The sooner the better, I think," Kincaid replied. "I believe I can have everything ready for a small diversion by, say, midnight."

"Very well." Farrell extended his hand to the saloon-keeper. "Thank you."

"My pleasure," Kincaid murmured. Cory's head was spinning from trying to keep up with everything that was going on around him, but he heard Kincaid's next words clearly enough. "By the way, how's that daughter of yours?"

"You mean Lucille?" Farrell asked, surprised by the question.

"Yes, indeed. I haven't seen her for a while. I expect she's turned into quite a beauty by now."

Cory didn't like the sound of that, didn't like it at all. The interest in Kincaid's voice was unmistakable.

"Lucille is fine," Farrell repled. "I'll tell her that you asked about her."

"Please do," Kincaid urged, while Cory was thinking, *No! Don't tell her anything!*

Farrell pushed back his chair. "We'd better be getting back to the boat." He looked at Kincaid. "Midnight."

Kincaid nodded.

Farrell shook hands with Jimmerson, who then turned to Cory and asked, "Sure you haven't changed your mind about those gals, son? Ain't much time left, but you could still have a go at one of 'em."

"No, sir," Cory said.

Jimmerson shook his head. "You young fellas just don't know what you're missing sometimes."

Cory knew perfectly well what he was missing. He wasn't interested in some saloon trollop. He was in love with Lucille, and that was more than enough for him.

But he might not be the only one who was attracted to Lucille, if Kincaid's words were any indication. However, before the night was over, the *Zephyr* would be leaving Cairo.

With luck, neither Lucille nor any of the rest of them would ever see Palmer Kincaid again after tonight.

Chapter Fourteen

CORY WAS FULL OF questions as he and Farrell made their way back to the docks and the *Zephyr*, but the captain didn't seem to want to answer them. It was understandable that Farrell was distracted, Cory supposed; after all, the man was about to put his boat—and his daughter—at risk by attempting to escape from Cairo.

But Cory couldn't help but wonder how Farrell knew a man like Palmer Kincaid and how well Kincaid knew Lucille.

As they walked along, Farrell muttered, "I'm not sure Fort Henry is far enough away from the Yankees. I have relatives in Nashville. Perhaps Lucille would be safer there."

"You'd send her away?" Cory asked, startled by the thought of Lucille leaving the *Zephyr*.

"If it was the safest thing for her, yes, I would."

Cory shook his head. "She'd fight you on it."

Farrell paused and looked over at him for a moment before saying, "Young man, I expect you'll find that my daughter can be argumentative about almost anything. Sometimes she has to be made to do things for her own good."

For her own good. Lucille wouldn't like that idea, Cory thought. But Farrell was right. A showdown was coming along the western rivers of the Confederacy. The Mississippi, the Tennessee, the Cumberland, all of those streams were too important for the Federals to overlook. Control of the rivers meant control of the entire region.

Besides, not even the Yankee commanders were stupid enough to leave twenty thousand troops sitting in Cairo doing nothing for very long.

When Cory and Farrell reached the riverboat, they found Ike Judson waiting on the boiler deck at the head of the gangway. "How'd it go, Cap'n?" the pilot inquired. Farrell had said earlier at the Staghorn that only he and Harriman had known about the smuggled rifles, so Judson probably wasn't aware of them. He had known that Farrell had something important to do in Cairo tonight, however.

In a low voice, Farrell replied, "We'll be leaving tonight, Mr. Judson. Are all the crew still on board?"

"Yes sir, just like you ordered." If Judson was surprised at the news of their imminent departure from Cairo, he didn't show it. "What time are we leavin'?"

"Midnight."

Judson nodded. "I'll be ready. Makin' a run for it back down the Mississipp'?"

"I'm afraid not. We'll be going up the Ohio, bound for the Tennessee River."

That bit of information finally shook Judson. The pilot's eyebrows lifted, and he repeated, "Up the Ohio?"

"That's right."

"The Yankees got a stranglehold on that river, from what I've heard."

"Perhaps they're so confident in their control of it that they'll let down their guard a bit."

"We'd better hope so," Judson warned ominously, "otherwise we'll be dodgin' Yankee gunboats all the way."

"Then dodge them we shall," Farrell retorted. "Have you seen Mr. Hovey?"

Judson pointed up with a thumb. "There's a poker game goin' on in his cabin. Reckon you'll find him there."

"I'll let him know the situation. I want us to have plenty of steam up when the time comes." Farrell slipped a watch from his vest pocket and flipped it open. In the light from a lantern hanging over the gangway, he studied the face of the watch. "Ten o'clock. We have two hours to get ready. That should be sufficient."

Cory hoped so. He didn't have any idea what sort of distraction Palmer Kincaid was going to arrange, but he knew it would provide the *Zephyr* with its only chance of slipping out of Cairo unnoticed.

Farrell started toward the stairs leading up to the Texas deck, then paused and looked back at Cory. "I expect Lucille is in her cabin," he said. "Would you be so kind as to inform her of our plans, Cory?"

"Yes sir," Cory replied, trying not to sound too eager. He turned and hurried along the main deck as Farrell and Judson went the other way.

When he reached Lucille's cabin, he paused before knocking on the door. Suddenly he felt a little trepidation. It was late enough so that Lucille had probably already prepared for bed. She might even be asleep. Cory thought about how she would look, her long, honey blonde hair tousled around her face on the pillow, her body sheathed in a thin nightdress . . . how wonderful it would be to simply lie there next to her and watch her sleeping . . .

A shiver went through him. There was a war on, he reminded himself, and they were in the middle of enemy territory. Not only that, but they had just successfully smuggled in a boatload of arms. If their part in that scheme was ever discovered, it would mean a Yankee prison or even a hangman's rope. Or did the Yankees use a firing squad on smugglers and Rebel spies?

At any rate, Cory decided, now was not the time to be indulging in romantic musings, no matter how appealing they were. Instead he rapped on the cabin door and called softly, "Miss Lucille? It's me, Cory Brannon."

The door opened almost instantly, as if Lucille had been waiting for someone to come, and Cory felt a brief, unwanted twinge of disappointment when he saw that she was fully dressed in a high-necked, cream-colored gown. "Cory, what is it?" she asked. "Is my father back, too?" She knew that the two of them had gone together into Cairo on some errand, though Farrell hadn't explained what it was.

"Yes, the captain's here," Cory answered, wanting to reassure her that nothing ill had befallen her father. "He went to find Mr. Hovey so that he could tell him to start getting some steam up."

Lucille frowned. "At this time of night?"

"We're leaving at midnight."

"Oh, dear Lord. Did the Yankees find out—"

"The Yankees don't know anything," Cory interrupted. "We just don't want to take a chance that Jason Gill will see us here. We're going up the Ohio, bound for the Tennessee River and Fort Henry." For a moment, Cory considered bringing up the possibility that Captain Farrell would send Lucille on to Nashville, but he decided against revealing that much. It wasn't his place to do so, he thought, since it was really a family matter and he wasn't family.

Yet.

That thought came unbidden into his head, but as it did, he sensed the rightness of it. He and Lucille loved each other, and it was only logical that someday, maybe when the war was over, they would be married. He knew that was what he wanted more than anything else in the world.

"How are we going to get past the Union patrols on the river?" Lucille asked. "They're bound to notice us leaving."

"There's going to some sort of distraction at midnight." Cory hesitated, then added, "Palmer Kincaid is setting it up."

"You met Uncle Palmer?"

That question took Cory by surprise. "Kincaid is your uncle?"

"Well, not really," Lucille explained. "That's just what I call him. He used to be a gambler, and he traveled some on the *Zephyr*. I haven't seen him in a couple of years, though, since he bought a saloon and settled down here in Cairo."

"That's where we went tonight." Cory didn't tell her that Kincaid had inquired about her. Cory had seen the look in the saloonkeeper's eyes, and he was convinced that Kincaid's interest was hardly avuncular, no matter how Lucille might feel about him.

"I wish Father had let me go. I've never been in a saloon."

"Well, I should hope not," Cory declared. "They're filled with wickedness."

"I wouldn't mind a little . . . wickedness."

Cory swallowed. "We'll be leaving at midnight," he repeated.

"I'll be ready," Lucille said with a nod. She put her hand on the cabin door. "Was there anything else?"

"No, I guess not."

"Then I'll see you up in the pilothouse."

As she swung the door shut, Cory started to say that he didn't know if it was a good idea for her to be in the pilothouse while they were making their escape. If the gunboats started firing on them, the pilothouse might not be safe.

Then he realized that if all those cannon on the Yankee ironclads opened up on the *Zephyr* before it was out of range, no place on the riverboat would be safe.

THE HANDS of the clock on the pilothouse wall stood at five minutes until midnight. Cory knew that even though he couldn't see them very well. All the lamps had been blown out all over the riverboat so that it would appear as if every-one on the vessel were asleep. The clouds had broken up somewhat and allowed some moonlight to shine through, cast-ing enough silvery illumination through the big windows of the pilothouse for Cory to be able to see the shapes of Cap-tain Farrell, Lucille, and Ike Judson. Judson was at the wheel, Farrell beside him at the speaking tube. Lucille stood with Cory next to the chart table.

The windows rattled slightly in their casements. A strong north wind had been responsible for the clouds parting, and it had brought a sharp chill to the air. As the four people in the

234 • *James Reasoner*

pilothouse listened to it blow, Judson observed, "Could be some snow before mornin'."

Farrell shook his head. "I don't think so. My left knee always aches just before it snows, and tonight I don't feel even a twinge."

"Well, my right big toe does the same thing, and it's hurtin' to beat the band."

"That's gout," Farrell declared.

"Hate to argue with you, Cap'n, but I reckon I know the difference 'tween gout and a snow comin' on."

Cory wanted to ask them why they were arguing over things as irrelevant as knees and toes and gout and snow, but then he realized that the two of them were just trying to relieve some of the tension they had to be feeling. Cory knew that he was nervous. He wished he could reach over and take Lucille's hand.

Farrell grasped the speaking tube and inquired, "How are the boilers, Ben?"

"Got plenty of steam, Cap'n," Hovey's voice came back. "We're r'aring to go down here." The words had a hushed quality, as if Hovey were whispering them rather than calling loudly into a speaking tube. Cory figured that anticipation was high all over the boat.

The only sign that the *Zephyr* was making ready for departure was the smoke coming from the stacks. There was no way to disguise that, and it was an unavoidable by-product of getting up steam. The furnaces had to burn. But maybe no one on shore would notice, Cory thought.

Suddenly, through the thin walls of the pilothouse, a loud but distant boom sounded. Cory jerked around sharply. The explosion had come from downstream. He peered through the larboard windows of the pilothouse and saw a large flower of flame blossoming in the night. It was far down at the other end of the docks. Beyond the docks, really, Cory decided, and on shore but near the river.

"A warehouse appears to be on fire," Farrell observed quietly.

An uproar was already spreading through town. People ran out into the streets to see what the explosion had been. Many of them were in their nightclothes, but they came anyway, fearing that the Rebels were launching an invasion. Once they saw the madly leaping flames, the citizens of Cairo streamed toward the burning warehouse, anxious to battle the blaze and keep it from spreading. Cory heard fire bells ringing.

"Back one-quarter on the larboard," Farrell called into the speaking tube. "Back one-quarter on the starboard."

Down below on the main deck, roustabouts who had been waiting for the festivities to get underway had already leaped onto the dock and cast off the ropes holding the *Zephyr.* Now as the rumble of the engines grew louder and the paddle-wheels started to turn, the men bounded back onto the river-boat. The *Zephyr* began edging away from the dock.

"Back one-half on the larboard! Back one-half on the starboard!"

By now, Cory had learned to tell how hard the engines were laboring by the vibrations he felt in the deck. His hands clamped on the edge of the chart table as the boat picked up power. Judson turned the wheel, letting the current of the Ohio do some of the work as the rear of the boat swung around.

That put the warehouse fire to the rear. "Open the door, Mr. Brannon," Farrell directed, and Cory grabbed the latch of the pilothouse door to swing it open. Judson had to keep his eyes turned forward, but the rest of them risked a look back.

The blaze was huge now. The original explosion had probably been a keg of black powder, Cory thought, and Kincaid's men must have poured more powder all around the building to cause a conflagration like that. One thing was certain: the attention of everyone in Cairo was focused on the southwest end of town, not the northeast where the *Missouri Zephyr* was now steaming away from Cairo.

"All ahead full!" Farrell ordered, and down in the engine room, Ben Hovey and his men complied. The riverboat surged forward against the current.

Cory peered intently out the open door, searching the night for some sign of the ironclads and the other Union gunboats. He spotted movement on the water, a low, dark shape gliding over the surface. That was either a giant turtle or one of the ironclads. A spout of flame suddenly split the darkness that hung over the river.

"They're firing at us!" Cory shouted. Beside him, Lucille grabbed his arm, but Cory was too intent on the situation even to notice the warm pressure of her hands. Where in blazes was that cannonball?

It went into the Ohio with a huge splash some two hundred yards behind the *Zephyr*. The fire on shore was casting a large circle of hellish light over half the river, and the black shape of the ironclad came gliding into it just as two of the forward cannon fired. Cory saw the twin explosions. Both balls fell well short again, and as Cory watched the ironclad, he could tell that it wasn't moving fast enough to catch the *Zephyr*. Not the way the riverboat was powering ahead.

A thought struck him. "Is it safe to be going this fast in the dark?" he asked.

Judson snorted. "Are you askin' if the Ohio has snags in it like the Mississipp'? It sure as blazes does, but they ain't as bad most places."

"The question is," Farrell noted dryly, "is it safe for us to go any slower? Given that one of Mr. Eads's ironclads is already pursuing us, I suspect the answer is no."

Cory didn't know who Mr. Eads was, and right now he didn't care. He just wanted the *Zephyr* to be well out of range of the guns on that floating artillery post.

Hovey continued pouring on the steam, just as in the race that afternoon to reach Cairo before the *Prometheus* caught up to them. Tonight's dash was even more fraught with danger, however. The *Prometheus* had been armed with only a single small cannon, probably no more than a 3-incher. The guns on the ironclad were much larger, probably at least 9-inchers, maybe even bigger. A ball from one of them could easily carry away a smokestack, penetrate to the boilers, or smash the pilothouse and everyone in it.

But only if the ironclad could close the gap, and it quickly became apparent that it could not. The *Zephyr* was pulling away steadily and vanishing in the darkness up the Ohio River. The Union's wooden gunboats might have been able to mount a more credible pursuit, but they were all moored at the docks, along with the other ironclads. The single ironclad that had fired the shots was the only one that had been patrolling the junction of the Ohio and Mississippi in the middle of the night.

The *Zephyr* rounded a bend, and the still-blazing warehouse was no longer visible. The low, thickly wooded banks were dark on both sides of the river. "We're well away," Captain Farrell noted. "But that doesn't mean we're out of danger. Union troops have occupied Paducah, and we'll have to get past them to reach the Tennessee."

"You reckon Grant'll let his boys know we're comin'?" inquired Judson.

"I believe we can count on that, Mr. Judson," Farrell replied. "But we'll have to deal with that when the time comes." He turned toward Cory and Lucille, and in the moonlight Cory could see that the captain was smiling. "Well, you two, how does it feel to be fugitives?"

THERE WERE two regiments of Union troops in Paducah, Kentucky, on the southern bank of the Ohio just west of the point where the Tennessee River flowed into the larger stream. These Yankee soldiers had occupied Paducah since the end of the previous summer, and in addition, several artillery batteries had been located on the northern bank of the Ohio, the Illinois side, so that they commanded the approach to the Tennessee. Col. C. F. Smith, the commander of the Federal forces in Paducah, had been told that when the time was right, he would be reinforced and could carry the fight to the Confederates. In the meantime, the only real hostilities being carried out in the region in the winter of '61–'62 were occasional forays down the Tennessee by the wooden gunboats from Cairo, which shelled Fort Henry from long distances. This was more of an annoyance and an attempt at provocation than anything else, and so far the Confederates had refused to rise to the bait.

Meanwhile, perceptive Southern officers had looked at the defensive situation at Fort Henry and declared it an unmitigated disaster. For some reason that everyone seemed at a loss to understand now, the fort had been located on bottomland next to the Tennessee River, in an area that was surrounded by swamps and prone to flooding. Higher ground to both the north and south, as well as across the river, commanded a good field of fire that could be directed at the fort. The only possible advantage the fort had was that two roads left it, one heading almost due east to Fort Donelson, twelve miles away on the western bank of the Cumberland River, and the other angling off to the southeast around an area of fallen timber that might provide some cover in the event of a running fight. Seeing how poorly the fort had been situated, the Confederates had begun to fortify one of the hills on the other side of the river, which they had named Fort Heiman after the colonel who had been put in charge of the work. The effort had barely gotten started, however, and these new fortifications were a long way from being much use to anyone.

Cory Brannon knew very little of this as he stood tensely in the darkened pilothouse while the *Zephyr* steamed toward Paducah. He checked behind the riverboat from time to time, peering back along the Ohio with the spyglass, but if the ironclads or the other gunboats from Cairo were pursuing them, the Yankees were too far back to be seen. Cory pulled his coat tighter around him and suppressed a shiver. The pilothouse had become chilly as the north wind continued to blow.

If he was this cold, then Lucille must be freezing, he thought. He looked over at her, but in the shadows of the pilot-house, he couldn't tell if she was shivering or not. He wished he could put his arm around her so that they could share whatever warmth they could muster up. If they had been alone, he would have risked it . . . but not with Captain Farrell and Judson there.

"We ought to make Paducah a little after dawn," Judson calculated. "Maybe we'll catch the Yankees sleepin'."

"I wouldn't count on that," Farrell demurred. "If their telegraph lines are intact, a message from Cairo will have already arrived there warning them to be watching for us."

"That's a pretty strong wind out there. Maybe them telegraph wires all blew down."

"We can certainly hope so," Farrell said, but he didn't sound as if he really believed that was a possibility.

Cory heard an odd, faint sound, and it took him several minutes to realize that he was listening to the clicking of Lucille's teeth against each other as they chattered from the cold. His heart went out to her, and a part of his brain said to hell with it. He lifted his arm, slipped it around her shoulders, and pulled her gently against him. At first she resisted, but only for a second. Then she leaned into him gratefully, and his arm tightened around her.

A few minutes later, Farrell glanced over his shoulder at them. In the dark, he might not be able to tell that they were embracing, but Cory really didn't care if the captain noticed or not. It felt good to have Lucille nestled against him like this. He already felt warmer, and he hoped she did, too.

Farrell turned back toward the bow of the riverboat. Cory couldn't be sure, but he thought he caught a glimpse of a smile on the man's face.

Cory waited for the approach of dawn, but the sky remained dark instead of lightening as it should have. By the time Farrell checked his watch and announced that it was seven o'clock, the sky was only marginally brighter. Cory asked, "Shouldn't it be dawn by now?"

"More clouds have blown in," Judson noted. "I reckon you must've been too busy to notice."

Cory had a hip propped on the chart table, holding himself up. Lucille was still leaning against him, and now her head rested on his shoulder. He figured she had dozed off, and he didn't want to disturb her. But he had no choice when Captain Farrell inquired, "Mr. Brannon, have you ever fired a cannon?"

"Uh, no sir, I haven't," Cory replied, and Lucille stirred sleepily in his arms. He had thought the night before about how nice it would be to watch her sleep, and here he had missed his chance. But he couldn't have seen her face very well from this angle anyway, he consoled himself.

"Well, then, I suppose it's time you learned how."

"What?" Cory blurted, his thoughts jerked from Lucille back to what Captain Farrell was saying.

"It's time you learned how to fire a cannon." Farrell added wryly, "It's a skill every young man should have in perilous times such as these."

Lucille stirred again and straightened. Cory let go of her so that she could stretch and yawn. "Are we in Paducah yet?" she murmured, and he was struck at that moment by how much she sounded like a little child.

"Soon," Farrell told her. He reached out and stroked her hair. "I want you to go to your cabin and stay there, Lucille."

She frowned. "I don't see why. It's as safe up here as anywhere else."

"From artillery fire, perhaps. But not from rifle fire. Please don't argue with me this time, Sweetheart. Just do as I say."

Lucille turned toward Cory. "What are you going to do?"

"Whatever your father tells me to do," Cory replied without hesitation, though he still didn't much like that talk about firing a cannon. "And I think you should, too."

For a second, he thought she was going to pout. Then a look of resignation appeared on her face, and Cory realized that he could *see* her face. Dawn had arrived without his even realizing it, but the sky was so clogged with thick gray clouds that it was still almost as dark as night.

"Come along, you two," Farrell said. "Ike, are you all right?"

"'Course I am," Judson grunted.

"We've all been up all night."

The pilot snorted. "I ain't sleepy, if that's what you're gettin' at. Not a bit."

"You know, neither am I," Farrell declared. Cory realized that he wasn't, either. Barging ahead right into the face of danger did wonders for waking a fellow up, he supposed.

It looked like all the crew was awake early this morning, Cory saw as he and Farrell and Lucille clattered down the stairs from the pilothouse. Or else they'd been up all night, too. Deckhands lined the rails, along with the cook and a couple of stewards and the firemen who weren't on duty at the moment down in the engine room. All of them watched Captain Farrell with what seemed to be the utmost confidence.

"We'll reach Paducah in a few minutes, gentlemen, and then proceed on down the Tennessee River," Farrell announced, raising his voice so that he could be heard by the crew. "Godspeed to us all."

"Godspeed, Cap'n!" several of them called back.

When they reached Lucille's cabin, Farrell embraced her quickly and brushed a kiss across her forehead. He was not an emotional man, Cory knew, but it was clear he was feeling something now, especially as Lucille wrapped her arms around his neck and hugged him hard. He disengaged himself as gently as possible and stepped back. Casting a glance at Cory, he said, "I'll see you on the bow in a moment, Mr. Brannon."

"Yes sir," Cory choked out.

He was almost afraid to look at Lucille, and when he did, he saw that he'd had good reason to be apprehensive. Her bottom lip was trembling, and tears shone in her eyes. "Cory . . . ," she began.

He took her in his arms. "Shhh," he murmured. "It'll be all right. You'll see."

"I don't want to lose you. Any of you."

"You won't," he assured her. "We're all going to be fine."

She came up on her toes and fiercely pressed her mouth to his for a long moment. When she took it away, she advised, "You'd damned well better be all right. I still want some wickedness in my life, Cory Brannon, and I figure you're it."

Cory didn't trust himself to speak—so he kissed her again.

His heart was pounding heavily when he joined Captain Farrell on the bow a few minutes later, and it wasn't all from fear. He was glad that Farrell was businesslike as he instructed, "Take the cannon and point it to larboard. That's where the Yankee gun emplacements are. I'm more worried about them than I am about any fire from the garrison in town."

Cory swung the 3-inch gun around, grunting with effort as he did so. Even a small cannon was heavy.

Farrell showed him how to ram the charge of gunpowder down the barrel and follow it with a cannonball. Cory grunted as he lifted the ball, too. It was heavier than it looked like it would be. Farrell put the priming charge in place and then said, "Take the lanyard."

"Me?" Cory hesitated.

"You." Farrell paused, then continued, "With this war going on, we're all going to be called upon to take part sooner or later. That means trying to kill the enemy. It's a hard thing to do, Cory. I suggest you find out if you have it in you—for my daughter's sake, if not your own."

Cory knew he was right. But that didn't make it any easier for him to reach down and take hold of the firing lanyard. His brother Will had killed men, Cory was sure, both as a lawman and since enlisting in the Confederate army as well. But he remembered his mother reading from the Bible, and he could almost hear Pastor Crosley back home in Virginia, intoning the Ten Commandments, including *Thou Shalt Not Kill.*

The Yankees had started this war, he reminded himself, and Farrell was right about something else: the safety of Lucille and countless other Southern women depended on Southern men doing what had to be done.

He gripped the lanyard firmly, "Ready, Captain."

"You know," Farrell said slowly, "I believe you are."

Something cold and wet touched Cory's face.

A second later, the sensation was repeated, then again and again. Farrell muttered as he and Cory both tipped their heads back and looked up at the gray sky, which rapidly turned white as snowflakes came spinning and whirling down from the clouds.

In a matter of moments, the banks of the river were no longer visible through the swirling clouds of snow. That meant that those ashore could no longer see the riverboat, either, and that included Yankee gunners. The thick snowfall even helped muffle the sound of the *Zephyr*'s engines.

Cory felt the vibrations lessen as the engines cut power. Ike Judson up in the pilothouse must have ordered that, and Farrell approved. "Good idea," he observed. "The Yankee artillerymen will have to aim by sound now. We'll give them as quiet a target as possible."

"Captain," Cory asked, "with all this snow, how can you even tell where we are?"

"Riverman's instinct, my boy!" Farrell laughed. "Which means, we're trusting to pure dumb luck, I suppose."

Cory didn't believe him. He knew that Farrell and Judson didn't have to be able to see to know where they were.

He heard a dull boom, then the rattle of sharper reports. "They're firing on us from both banks," Farrell said. "But they're firing blind. They know we're here, but they can't see us."

Cory lifted the lanyard. "Should I return fire, Captain?"

"Absolutely not. That would just tell them where we are."

The engines slowed even more, until the boat was barely making headway through the river. The roar of cannon and the crackle of rifle fire continued in the white snowfall. The flakes were beginning to pile up on the deck now, and they were collecting on Farrell's cap, too. Cory supposed the same thing was happening with his cap. He tried to concentrate on that, rather than the possibility that a cannonball or a minié ball from a Yankee rifle could come out of the thick whiteness at any second and smash his life out. A blind shot could kill a man just as dead as a well-aimed one.

He sensed that the riverboat was turning. "We've reached the mouth of the Tennessee," Farrell explained. "Hear the way the firing is dying away behind us."

Cory heaved a sigh of relief. "Are you sure we're in the Tennessee?"

The banks of the river began to be visible again, and Cory could tell that the stream they were now following was smaller than the Ohio. Farrell pointed out that fact and noted aloud, "We've made it, Mr. Brannon."

Cory hesitated, then said, "I would have fought, you know."

"I know that," Farrell replied quietly without looking at him. "That makes me feel considerably better about some of the decisions I've made in the past few months . . . and about some of the ones Lucille has made as well."

Cory wasn't sure if he wanted to ask the captain what he meant by that. Luckily, he didn't have to, because at that moment, Judson shouted down from the pilothouse high above them, "I told you it was goin' to snow! My big toe's always right! And it damn sure wasn't *gout!*"

Chapter Fifteen

T HE FIRST SIGHT OF Fort Henry was not impressive. Cory stood at the forward railing on the *Zephyr*'s Texas deck and looked upstream. The Tennessee widened out a bit at this point, then narrowed again beyond the fort, which consisted of a low stone-and-brick wall that had been laid out in a roughly five-sided shape with the point directed inland. The wall came down almost to the water, with only a few feet of muddy ground between its base and the river. Inlets cut into the land all around the fort, and if the river were to rise very much, Fort Henry would become a virtual island and doubtless would flood. Cory could see the tops of some tents inside the fort but not any permanent structures, although there were bound to be some. Beyond the fort, where the ground rose slightly, were more tents used to quarter the soldiers posted there. Gun emplacements were inside the fort; Cory saw the snouts of several cannon protruding where slots several feet wide and an equal distance high had been cut into the wall.

The snowfall that had been so timely at Paducah had dwindled and then finally stopped as the *Zephyr* steamed south on the Tennessee River. The day remained cold and cloudy, however. Late in the afternoon the riverboat had been forced to stop to take on more wood. By that time, Cory, Lucille, and Judson were sound asleep, exhausted from the interminable night that had followed the *Zephyr*'s escape from Cairo. Even Captain Farrell, who always seemed tireless, had snatched a nap.

That evening they stopped for the night as Farrell decided to wait until morning before proceeding to Fort Henry. "It's a calculated risk to do so," he had explained to Cory, Lucille, Judson, and Rowley as they gathered in the pilothouse. "There could still be some pursuit from Cairo. But it's less likely this far south, and I'd prefer to approach the fort by day-light, so that it's obvious we're not a Yankee vessel."

Judson grunted. "It'd be mighty bad luck to get this far and then get blown out of the water by Confederate guns."

"My sentiments exactly, Mr. Judson," Farrell had agreed. "We'll keep a close watch and hope that the Yankees have given up on us."

To improve their chances of being overlooked by the Yankees if the gunboats did indeed follow them this far, Judson found a small creek that made a sharp bend just before it entered the Tennessee. The creek was shallow but had just enough depth for the *Zephyr* to ease up about a hundred yards. That put them around the bend, but their smokestacks would still show above the brush on the low banks surrounding them. That couldn't be helped, and any hiding place was better than none, Cory supposed.

The night passed without incident, and although backing out of the creek the next morning was a tricky job, Judson was up to it. His experienced hand on the wheel guided them safely back out into the Tennessee, and they headed upstream again toward Fort Henry, reaching it about midmorning.

As the *Zephyr* drew closer, Cory saw a flag flying from a tall pole inside the fort. It was whipping around in the breeze, which was variable this morning, sometimes coming from the north, other times blowing from the south. The clouds were breaking up again, too, allowing some rays of sunlight to slant through. Some of them shone on the fort and made the bright colors of the flag stand out sharply.

Judson leaned forward and squinted toward the fort. "That ain't the Yankee flag, is it?" he asked with a hint of alarm in his voice. "They can't have taken the fort already, could they?"

Cory could see the details of the flag now. It had a circle of white stars on a blue canton and two broad horizontal red bars with a white horizontal bar between them. "No," he said with a lump in his throat. "It's the Stars and Bars."

Cory had seen the Confederate flag before but never like this, flying proudly over a fort dedicated to the defense of the South while patterns of light and dark from the shifting clouds played over it. Cory had to swallow hard, and he gripped the railing more tightly. Fort Henry might not look like much, but by God, the Yankees would get a fight if they ever tried to take it!

He was surprised to see that another riverboat was moored at the fort. Captain Farrell came up beside him, nodded toward the vessel, and noted, "Ah, there's the *DeQuincey*. I wondered what had happened to her. She traveled the Ohio regularly, and I heard that her captain was trapped up there with her when the Yankees moved into Cairo. Clearly he had the same idea we did and sought refuge here."

"You know that boat's captain?"

"Of course I do. Most of the captains know each other, all up and down the Mississippi and the Ohio. His name is Uriah Glennon. A good man."

The *Zephyr* steamed on, and when Farrell and Cory went up to the pilothouse a moment later, the captain pulled a cord to blow a loud whistle on the boat's horn. Men appeared at the top of the wall and peered over at the newcomer. Cory had a feeling more than one cannon was trained on them right now, but the Confederate soldiers would soon see that the arriving riverboat represented no threat.

It was possible to bring the *Zephyr* up almost to the bank of the river, but not quite within reach of the gangway. A rowboat had to be lowered, and Captain Farrell went ashore, accompanied by Cory, Lucille, and Judson. Lucille was dressed in a decorous dark blue gown today, with a fur-lined jacket over it, and Cory thought she looked lovely, as usual. He and Judson rowed the little boat over to a point of ground near the fort's main gate, where Judson hopped out and steadied the craft while Farrell and Lucille disembarked. Cory didn't like the fact that Lucille had to walk through some mud to reach the gate, but it was unavoidable. Mud was everywhere.

The gates were hauled up, like a portcullis on a medieval castle; Cory had seen pictures of such things in books, but never in person. A well-setup officer came out, followed by several troopers carrying shotguns and old-fashioned flintlock rifles. All of the weapons looked to be several decades old. The officer saluted Farrell and introduced himself. "Capt. Jesse Taylor, sir. Welcome to Fort Henry." A ghost of a wry smile tugged at Taylor's mouth. "It doesn't look like much, but it's all we have at the moment."

"And glad I am to see it, Captain," Farrell replied. "I'm Ezekiel Farrell, master of the *Missouri Zephyr*..." He waved a hand at the riverboat. "Late of New Orleans. But I don't know when we'll be getting back there again."

More of the formality slipped away from Taylor. "Not any time soon, I'd reckon. Come on in, Captain Farrell. I'll introduce you to the commander."

As they followed Taylor into the fort, Farrell added, "By the way, this is my daughter, Miss Lucille Farrell, and my associates, Mr. Isaac Judson and Mr. Cory Brannon."

Taylor tipped his campaign cap with its crossed cannon insignia that indicated he was an artilleryman and said to Lucille, "It's an honor, ma'am." He nodded to Cory and Judson. "Gentlemen."

At a signal from Taylor, troopers began lowering the gate once more, turning cranks that released the tension on the ropes supporting it. As if the thought had just occurred to him, Taylor glanced over his shoulder at the newcomers and asked, "You don't happen to have any Yankee gunboats hot on your heels, do you, Captain?"

"I don't believe so," Farrell said. "We came through a snowstorm up in Paducah—a minor blizzard, actually—and I believe we lost any pursuit up there."

"Glad to hear it. Those Yankees can be downright pesky, like the mosquitoes we have down here in the summer."

Half a dozen squat log buildings stood within the fort, a row of three to the right and three more to the left. A larger stone building sat by itself near the northwestern wall. Windowless and with what looked to be an extremely thick wooden door, it was probably the powder magazine, Cory figured. He hoped it was sturdy enough to withstand some cannon fire.

Captain Taylor led the party to one of the log buildings and up a couple of shallow steps to its porch. The door opened as they got there, and a man just above medium height stepped out to greet them. He wore a double-breasted gray uniform tunic with two gold stars on each side of its collar. A saber in a brass scabbard hung at his belt. His hair was dark and thick around his ears and on the back of his neck, and he sported a prominent goatee. Taylor snapped to attention and saluted him as he appeared.

"General Tilghman, sir," Taylor said, "we have guests."

"So I see," the general murmured. He extended a hand to Farrell. "Lloyd Tilghman. And you're Zeke Farrell, aren't you?"

"Yes, I am. Have we met?" Farrell asked as he shook Tilghman's hand.

"Several years ago at a social function in New Orleans."

"I remember," Farrell recalled. "At Madame Duquesne's ball. It's good to see you again, General."

"Would that it were under better circumstances," Tilghman added dryly. "I take it you're fleeing the Yankee invaders?"

"We escaped from Cairo two nights ago."

"Right out from under the Federal flotilla, eh? Mr. Glennon of the *DeQuincey* did much the same, and other steamers have sought refuge here for a time before moving on upstream." Tilghman waved a hand at the muddy compound. "Feel free to stay as long as you like, although I fear we cannot offer you much in the way of accommodations."

Farrell shook his head. "We have no need of quarters, General. There's plenty of room on the *Zephyr* for my crew."

"Very well." A shrewd look appeared on Tilghman's face. "I have a proposal for you, Captain, and while perhaps I should have invited you to dinner tonight and waited until then to issue my suggestion, I don't believe in wasting time."

"It's your fort, General," Farrell said. "Please speak freely."

"I intend to. How would you like to join forces with Captain Glennon and double the size of Fort Henry's glorious armada?"

GENERAL TILGHMAN invited them all to supper in his quarters anyway after being introduced to Cory, Lucille, and Judson. Captain Farrell begged the general's forgiveness and requested that he be given a few hours to think over Tilghman's proposition. The general agreed graciously.

Cory didn't know what to make of it, himself. Tilghman was asking if the *Zephyr*, along with Captain Glennon and the *DeQuincey*, could function as a sort of unofficial navy, patrolling downstream along the Tennessee River and alerting the fort to any new incursions by the Federal forces. It sounded like a fine idea to Cory, but the decision was up to Captain Farrell, of course.

"I'm all for it," Judson said without hesitation when they had all returned to the riverboat. "It's about time we did us some Yankee fightin'."

"General Tilghman wants us to act as scouts, not as gunboats," Farrell pointed out.

"Yeah, but I reckon we'll wind up swappin' lead with the Yankees sooner or later," Judson muttered with a shrug.

That sounded pretty likely to Cory, too. And if it happened, the *Zephyr* would definitely be outgunned. He didn't know how Captain Glennon's boat was fixed for armament, but he doubted if the *DeQuincey* carried anywhere near the same amount of firepower as the Union vessels.

Cory put on a clean shirt and trousers for the dinner at General Tilghman's. The general's quarters were in the same building in which his office was located, where Captain Taylor had taken them that morning. When the four visitors from the *Zephyr* arrived, they found that the rest of the fort's officers had been invited, too, except for those who were on duty. Captain

Taylor was there, along with Colonel Heiman, who had been supervising the work on the fortifications atop the hill across the river, and several other officers. A few minutes later a cavalry colonel named Forrest arrived, a goateed man with a high forehead, piercing dark eyes, and a face that was lean almost to the point of gauntness. He greeted the newcomers pleasantly enough, but Cory felt a bit of a chill as he looked at the man, as if Forrest had some sort of wild animal caged up inside him. A wolf, perhaps.

Capt. Uriah Glennon of the *DeQuincey* was also on hand. He was a short, broad-shouldered man with a bushy red beard and a freckled face. He pumped Farrell's hand enthusiastically, glad to see another riverman.

"I apologize for the meager fare," Tilghman said as they all sat down to a dinner of salt pork, beans, and cornbread. "Supplies are running low everywhere. I sent a hunting party out this afternoon in hopes of securing some fresh meat, but they were unsuccessful."

"Perhaps we could share some of the food from our larder with you," Farrell offered.

Tilghman shook his head. "I'd rather you kept your crew well fed, Captain, so they'll be in top shape as you patrol the river on our behalf." He chuckled. "I told you I believe in getting right to the point."

"So you did. I shall be as direct. I have decided to accept your invitation to serve the Confederacy—under certain conditions."

"And they are?" asked Tilghman.

Farrell ticked the points off on his fingers. "First of all, though we shall place ourselves under your command, neither I nor any of my crew will be compelled to officially enlist in the Confederate army."

Tilghman frowned slightly and observed, "That's a bit irregular, but I agree. Captain Glennon and his men have not enlisted, either."

"Secondly, I want another cannon for my boat. The one I have is hardly sufficient if we encounter any hostile forces."

Captain Taylor spoke up. "We don't have any cannon to spare, sir. It's been an effort simply to round up as many guns as we have now."

"You have seven lower gun emplacements along the wall facing the river, Captain," Farrell noted. "Those guns are in jeopardy of being flooded out should the Tennessee rise, as it is bound to do sooner or later. You could move two of them out now, while they're still high and dry, and give one to me and one to Captain Glennon."

"'Twould be quite a help in a pinch, General," Glennon put in.

Tilghman looked at Taylor, who was in charge of the fort's artillery. "Captain?"

The young officer hesitated, then nodded. "I suppose we could do that. Would 18-pounders be all right?"

"That would do just fine, Captain," Farrell agreed.

Tilghman nodded. "Very well, then, your second condition is accepted. Any more?"

"Just one," Farrell said. "I want a military escort to take my daughter to Nashville."

"No!" Lucille exclaimed, obviously taken by surprise. "I'm staying here with you, Father!"

Farrell turned to her. "This is neither the time nor the place for this argument, Lucille. Fort Henry is an isolated outpost in danger of being attacked by the Federals at any time. You'll be much safer in Nashville with Uncle Charles and Aunt Louise."

"I won't go," Lucille protested stubbornly. "I've always been safe on the *Zephyr*." She turned to Cory. "Cory, you have to talk to him."

Cory felt embarrassed, even though all the officers were discreetly looking down at their plates. He cleared his throat and said, "I agree with your father, Lucille. You should go to Nashville. I'll miss you, but . . . you should go."

Stricken at what she considered a betrayal, Lucille turned to Judson. "Ike," she pleaded, "surely you're on my side."

"No, ma'am," the pilot said, shaking his head. "I reckon you ought to get out of here while the gettin's good. The Yankees are comin' sooner or later. Everybody knows that."

Lucille sat back in her chair, clearly upset.

"Captain Farrell . . ." Tilghman began. "While it's not my place to interfere in a family discussion, I must point out that I agree with you. The young lady would be better off in Nashville. Unfortunately, I cannot spare an escort to take her there, and I would not recommend that she travel alone, or even with a small party. There are brigands roaming the woods at times, trying to take advantage of the countryside's unsettled conditions."

"Come, come," Farrell cajoled with a frown. "You were able to find cannon for Captain Glennon and me. Surely you can come up with a detail to escort my daughter."

Tilghman shook his head firmly. "Not at this time."

Lucille's triumphant smile took in her father, Cory, and Judson.

"But I am expecting a small number of reinforcements within the next month or six weeks," Tilghman went on, and Lucille's face fell. "I could send a party to Fort Donelson with your daughter then, and I'm certain that General Floyd, the commander there, would provide an escort thence to Nashville."

"A month or six weeks, you say?" Farrell mused. "All right, then. We are in agreement, General."

"Excellent." Tilghman lifted his glass of wine. "To the Confederacy, gentleman—and lady."

"To the Confederacy," the officers from the fort echoed him. Cory, Farrell, and Judson all lifted their glasses and drank. Only Lucille refused, a dark expression on her face.

When dinner was over, the brandy and cigars came out, and Cory leaped at the opportunity to escort Lucille back to the riverboat so that she would not have to endure the discussion of politics, military strategy, and other unfeminine matters. Not to mention the bawdy stories that would probably be told before the evening was over. Captain Farrell hugged his daughter before she left, and Cory heard her whisper to him, "You're not getting rid of me just yet."

Farrell looked pained, but he made no reply. Cory felt sympathy for him. Farrell didn't want to "get rid" of Lucille; he simply wanted her to be as safe as possible in these uncertain times. Cory understood that quite well because he felt exactly the same way.

He helped Lucille into her coat, then put his hat on and left General Tilghman's with her. As they walked carefully back across the fort toward the gate, she muttered in a low voice, "I'm very angry with you, Cory Brannon."

"Your father just has your best interests in mind," he told her. "So do I, and Mr. Judson feels the same way."

"I've always traveled with my father. Always. As far back as I can remember."

"There wasn't a war going on then."

"This awful war . . . Damn the Yankees! Why did they have to start it?"

Cory couldn't answer that. He noted, "You don't have to leave right away, you know."

"But in a month, or whenever the general gets those reinforcements, Father will send me away. You know he will."

Cory nodded, but he said, "A lot of things can happen in a month."

He couldn't help but wonder what the next few weeks would bring.

As IT turned out, very little.

January brought a considerable amount of rain to western Tennessee, and everyone at Fort Henry watched the water line of the river anxiously as it slowly rose. Most of the ground around the walls of the fort disappeared. The rain had one advantage, however: the Union gunboats stayed off the river for the most part. The *Zephyr* and the *DeQuincey* steamed up and down the Tennessee, on the alert for Federal incursions, and returned to Fort Henry with nothing to report. Only once did a gunboat slip upstream, and then it hid behind a small island about a mile downriver from the fort, where it proceeded to lob several shells that did no damage. Both of the riverboats put out from the fort, their captains hoping to get within range of the 18-pounders that had been installed on the vessels, but the gunboat turned and ran, infuriating Farrell and Glennon. Cory shared the captains' frustration to a certain extent, but he also realized that even with the new cannon, the Union vessel had still outgunned both riverboats combined.

Farrell was seething, though, and when he heard from the officers at the fort that the union boats had made a habit in the past of venturing as far upstream as the island, he began hatching a plan.

"There's a creek just beyond that island," he told Cory, Judson, and Rowley as they gathered one evening in the *Zephyr*'s pilothouse. Farrell had a map borrowed from the fort spread out on the chart table. His finger stabbed at the point he was talking about. "The *Zephyr* requires even less draft than those gunboats, so I propose that we wait up along that creek until one of the Yankees passes us, then take him from behind."

"Sounds like it'd work," Judson agreed. "You'd best send somebody to have a closer look at this creek first, though."

"That will be your job, Mr. Judson," Farrell answered with a smile. "Yours and Mr. Brannon's."

Cory suppressed a groan. That wasn't exactly what he wanted to do: row a mile downriver and back in the rain.

He didn't want to let the captain down, though, so the next morning he and Judson found themselves sculling a rowboat along the Tennessee. They stayed close to the western bank, so that they could get ashore in a hurry if they needed to. They didn't run into any Yankees, however, and the soundings that Judson took on the creek with a plumb bob told them that the little stream was indeed deep enough for the *Zephyr* to navigate it. Not only that, but the trees along the bank were probably tall enough to hide all but the very tops of the riverboat's stacks.

By the time they returned to the fort, Cory was soaked and miserable. He hadn't been this wet and cold, he decided, since he'd left New Madrid the previous autumn. But he began to feel better as soon as he saw Lucille.

She had gotten over her pique at being sent to Nashville, at least to a certain extent. Cory figured that she halfway believed it would never come about. He was hoping that it would, especially since the trap they were laying for the Union gunboat might provoke the Yankees to launch an attack. But whether that did it or not, an attack was inevitable. Even Cory, who was a far cry from a military strategist, could see that. The Yankees had been massing their forces for months now. They were a thunderstorm of blue uniforms just waiting to strike.

Unfortunately, Tilghman's hoped-for reinforcements had yet to arrive, and Cory had begun to worry that the Yankees might come before they did. In that case, he hoped that Farrell would take the *Zephyr* and head up the Tennessee River, getting out before the Union forces could overrun the fort.

Cory was not alone in the belief that Fort Henry could not be held. Farrell and Judson also agreed with him. The fort's position was simply too poor to be defended successfully, especially with the river rising and threatening the lower gun emplacements.

"What did you find out?" Lucille asked him when he came into the pilothouse of the *Zephyr*, followed by Judson. Water dripped from their clothes.

"The creek will work," Cory confirmed with a nod.

Farrell was standing by the chart table. He clenched a fist. "Tomorrow, then," he predicted. "We'll be there if one of the Yankee gunboats comes, and they'll get an unpleasant surprise."

JANUARY HAD turned into February almost without Cory noticing. He had to think about it for a while before he realized that
the date was February 5. The day was cold and gray, as usual,
although no rain was falling at the moment and hadn't all
morning. Very early, just before dawn, the *Zephyr* had steamed
downriver past the island, and then Judson had taken on the
daunting task of backing the riverboat into the mouth of the
creek. It had taken a steady hand on the wheel, plus excellent
coordination and communication between the pilothouse and
the engine room. In time, though, the chore was done, and the
Zephyr sat waiting, steam up but engines disengaged.

Of course, the gunboat might not show up today, but Farrell
was prepared to return tomorrow and as many days after that as
it took. The time had come to strike at the Yankees.

Even as tense as the situation was, Cory was bored by the
waiting. He was about to doze off, in fact, when Judson suddenly urged, "Hear that?"

Cory didn't hear anything and was about to say so, but then
a loud report sounded somewhere nearby. It was a cannon, and
it had to be on a Union gunboat. The Yankees had come back
upriver to shell Fort Henry again.

"I knew I heard engines!" Judson insisted eagerly as he took
the wheel. Farrell grabbed the speaking tube and ordered the
engines ahead one-half. The riverboat surged along the creek.

Cory leaned forward in the high chair where he was sitting.
He felt excitement gripping him. Lucille was going to be angry
that she had missed this, he thought, but she had been left
back at the fort. No amount of pouting on her part could have
ever convinced her father to bring her along on one of these
sorties downriver.

Several more shots sounded, the explosions of the cannon
little more than dull thuds in the heavy air. The *Zephyr* reached
the mouth of the creek and emerged into the river. Upstream,
no more than two hundred yards away, sat one of the Union
ironclads. Cory could even read the name painted on it—*Essex*.

The 18-pounder was loaded and ready. Even though they had been expecting one of the wooden gunboats rather than an ironclad, Captain Farrell threw up one of the windows of the pilothouse and bellowed down to the main deck, "Fire!" Flame gouted from the mouth of the cannon.

Cory's eyes widened in awe as he watched the cannonball strike the Yankee vessel. At this range, the shot was effective. Pieces of iron casemate flew high into the air as the heavy lead ball smashed into the vessel's hull. Cory couldn't tell how far it penetrated or what it struck inside, but judging from the frantic activity on the gunboat, the Yankees had been taken completely by surprise.

The 3-incher on the bow fired, its smaller explosion sounding almost like the crack of a rifle after the boom of the 18-pounder. The shot sizzled over the deck of the gunboat, scattering several of the Yankee sailors. The crew members assigned to the larger cannon were working quickly to reload it, as they had been taught by Captain Taylor at the fort. "Fire when ready!" Farrell shouted down to them, and a moment later the massive boom sounded once again. This time the ball missed, but only narrowly, passing close to the gunboat's pilothouse before splashing into the river. The gunboat swung around ponderously and started downstream angling toward the far bank in an attempt to avoid the *Zephyr.*

The rest of the riverboat's crew was lined up at the rail, sending potshots at the gunboat from an assortment of rifles, pistols, and shotguns. This small-arms fire wasn't going to do any damage to the Union vessel, but it kept the Yankees busy diving for cover.

Judson let out a whoop. "They're turnin' tail!" he shouted. "Runnin' for home!"

Both cannon on the *Zephyr* fired again, but neither shot found anything except the river. "Cease fire!" Farrell called down to the gunners. To Judson, he snapped, "Take us back to the fort, Ike."

"But, Cap'n!" Judson protested. "Ain't we goin' after 'em?"

"We were fortunate that they didn't put up a fight. One reason could be that they're trying to draw us in. I don't trust that there's not several more of those ironclads waiting around the next bend in the river."

Farrell's decision made sense, Cory supposed, but like Judson, he hated to let the Yankees go. The excitement of the moment had him firmly in its grip. This was his first real battle, the first time he hadn't been on the receiving end of the damage that was inflicted. Once again, the South had drawn first blood.

But the feeling ebbed away from Cory as the *Zephyr* steamed back toward Fort Henry. Sure, they had whipped the Yankees today, he thought.

Tomorrow might be an entirely different story.

Chapter Sixteen

THE FEDERAL FLOTILLA WAS much closer to Fort Henry than any of the Confederate defenders within its walls were aware. On the same day that the *Essex* ventured upstream within a mile of the fort, the other three Union ironclads, the *Cincinnati*, the *Carondelet*, and the *St. Louis*, along with the wooden gunboats *Tyler*, *Lexington*, and *Conestoga*, were anchored another five miles downstream under the command of Rear Adm. Andrew H. Foote. When the *Essex* rejoined them, bearing the damage inflicted by a Rebel cannonball that had breached the iron hull and smashed its way into the officers' quarters—albeit without injuring anyone—sentiment ran high for launching an immediate attack on Fort Henry. A cooler head, that of Admiral Foote, prevailed. The attack would come the next day, February 6, as planned.

The orders Grant had been waiting for had finally arrived. Thousands of Union troops were transported down the Tennessee River and put ashore on both banks early on the morning of the sixth. Their objective was to capture the high ground across the river and north and south of the fort on the eastern bank, thereby blocking any escape by the Confederates. At the same time, the ironclads and the gunboats would begin shelling the fort from the river. Grant and his officers believed that Fort Henry could not hold out for long against this double-pronged attack from land and water.

IT WASN'T raining when Cory awoke on the morning of the sixth. He noticed that right away. After enduring so much rain over the past few weeks and growing accustomed to the sound of the solid, heavy drops striking the roof of his cabin on the Texas deck, the silence seemed almost eerie to him.

When he came out on deck, he found that the air was not as chilly as usual, either. Only a light breeze was blowing. Maybe the change in the weather was an omen of better days ahead, Cory thought as he headed for the pilothouse.

He found Captain Farrell and Lucille inside, but not Judson or Rowley. The two of them were alone, and there was an air of tension in the pilothouse. Cory figured they had been arguing once again about Farrell's plan to send Lucille to Nashville. He didn't want to get in the middle of that, so he said simply, "Good morning."

"That all depends on your point of view," Farrell advised crisply. "Take a look at the river."

Cory looked and saw that the Tennessee had risen again during the night. Even though it was no longer raining here, that didn't mean it wasn't pouring upstream. The river raced by turbulently, its choppy waters dotted with branches, logs, and sometimes entire trees that had washed away from the banks upstream as the water crept upward.

Looking at Fort Henry, Cory saw the most worrisome sight of all. The riverbank alongside the wall had completely disappeared. Judging from the height of the water on the wall, it had to be flooding inside the fort as well.

"Do you think they were able to save those lower cannon?" Cory asked with a frown.

"And put them where?" Farrell shook his head. "No, I'm afraid those guns are lost, at least until the river goes back down and they can be dried out and cleaned. And that may be weeks."

"But that only leaves the fort with . . ." Cory tried to count up the remaining cannon.

"Nine guns," Farrell confirmed, saving him the calculation. "Nine guns to oppose the several dozens that the Yankees can throw at them at any time." Farrell glanced at Lucille, who had sat silently with an obstinate expression on her face since Cory entered the pilothouse. "I'm going to speak to General Tilghman again about evacuating Lucille to Fort Donelson."

"I won't go," she maintained flatly.

"You've no choice in the matter," snapped Farrell. "Come with me, Cory." He stalked out of the pilothouse.

Cory looked at Lucille, spread his hands, and shrugged. What else could he do? Captain Farrell had given him an order.

They rowed over to the fort, just the two of them, and in response to Farrell's hail, the gate was hauled open. Today they were able to row on into the fort, as two feet of water stood covering the area just inside the gate.

Colonel Tilghman was in his office in the headquarters building, looking even more harried than usual. "Gentleman, what can I do for you?" he asked as an aide showed Cory and Farrell into the room.

"Have you received word, General, concerning the reinforcements you've been awaiting?" Farrell inquired.

Tilghman shook his head solemnly. "I'm afraid not, even though I have recently wired General Johnston again, assuring him that we have a glorious chance to defeat the enemy, if only I am supplied with sufficient troops."

Cory knew that was mostly wishful thinking on Tilghman's part. As badly positioned as Henry was, it would take half the troops in the Southern army to lick the Yankees here.

"I would still like to get my daughter to Fort Donelson if at all possible, and as soon as possible—" Farrell began.

Tilghman sighed. "I know, Captain, and I sympathize with you. For the time being, though, all we can do is wait. Are you going to be taking your usual patrol down the river this morning?"

Farrell hesitated, and for a second Cory hoped the captain was considering leaving the fort for good. The situation was only going to grow worse. But then he heard Farrell say, "I supose we might as well."

"I noticed as I walked around the fort that the current is quite swift today."

"Quite swift indeed," Farrell agreed. "If the river rises much more, you may be forced to evacuate Henry entirely."

"We shall see," Tilghman concluded the conversation.

Cory and Farrell left, and even in the short time they had been in the general's office, it seemed to Cory that the river had grown a little higher. They rowed back to the *Zephyr*.

Judson was in the pilothouse when they came in, along with Lucille. "It's time for you to go over to the fort, my dear," Farrell told her. "We'll be steaming downriver shortly on patrol."

"Can't I come with you today?" she pleaded. "I have to sit with old Captain Billings, the quartermaster, and play checkers with him all day. It's as if they don't trust any of the younger officers to keep me company."

Cory thought it was more a matter of not wanting her to be in the way of their duties, but no matter the reason, he was glad she didn't associate much with the younger officers. He didn't need any competition for Lucille's affections from any of those dashing soldier boys.

"We'll be back by midday," Farrell told her. "Go on now. Find Ned and have him row you over to the fort."

Lucille rolled her eyes but left the pilothouse. Farrell said to Cory, "Watch and make sure she goes ashore, Mr. Brannon."

"Aye, sir." Cory stood by the window and watched until he had seen Ned Rowley take Lucille over in the rowboat. As Rowley started back to the *Zephyr*, Cory reported, "She's safely inside the fort, Cap'n."

"Very good. Let's go see if the Yankees are trying to sneak up on us today."

The riverboat pulled out a few minutes later, heading downstream. That didn't require much effort from the engines because the current was strong enough to do most of the work. Coming back upstream would be a different story.

A short while later, the *Zephyr* passed the island that had been the site of the battle the day before. "Battle" might not be the right word to describe it, Cory thought as he remembered the rush of emotions that had filled him as the cannon roared. The *Zephyr* was the only vessel that had fired any shots. Cory supposed that didn't really count as a battle at all.

"Cap'n," Judson spoke tentatively when they had gone a couple of miles downriver from the island, "does that look like smoke to you?"

Something about the pilot's tone told Cory that the question wasn't an idle one. He stood up straighter as Farrell stepped forward to peer out the big front window. The Tennessee made a bend up ahead, so the three men in the pilothouse couldn't see anything except about a hundred yards of the swiftly rushing stream, flanked by thickly wooded banks. Cory looked but didn't see any smoke . . .

Then he did, as a thick billow of the stuff drifted across the sky above the river.

Farrell grabbed the speaking tube and shouted, "All stop!"

Around the bend, moving slowly, came the nose of a Union ironclad. The smoke in the air thickened.

"All back full! All back full!" Farrell jerked his head toward Judson. "Get us out of here, Ike!"

Judson was already spinning the wheel as the deck shuddered from the efforts of the engines below. The Tennessee was not wide enough for the riverboat to make a full turn while still maintaining the engines in forward gear, so Judson had to back and turn. As he was doing that, the ironclad came fully into view, and another of the armored vessels began edging around the bend.

"Oh, my God," Cory breathed. They were going to be blasted out of the water. He just knew it.

Farrell threw the window open and shouted down to the gunners, "Hold your fire! Hold your fire!" He turned to the others in the pilothouse and pleaded, "Perhaps if we don't fire, they won't, either."

Judson was still manipulating the wheel. He grunted and said, "Ought to get one good shot in, anyway."

"One is all we would get," Farrell countered grimly. The *Zephyr* came around so that it was pointed upstream again. Farrell called into the speaking tube, "All ahead full! Pour it on, Ben!"

Cory opened the pilothouse door so they could watch behind them. A third ironclad came around the bend, then a fourth. "Why aren't they shooting at us?" Cory muttered.

"Perhaps they feel that we are beneath their notice," responded Farrell. "Or perhaps they are so confident of victory that they don't mind if we carry a warning to the fort."

"They've got reason to be confident," Cory admitted. Three of the faster, more maneuverable wooden gunboats had come up behind the phalanx of ironclads.

Suddenly, one of the forward guns on the leading ironclad belched flame. A second later, before Cory had time to shout a warning, water geysered up just to starboard of the *Zephyr* as the cannonball struck the river.

"Well, it appears they want to sink us after all," Farrell announced calmly.

Cory's heart was thundering in his chest. It had been thrilling the day before to fire at the Yankee ironclad, but it was an entirely different sensation now that the fire was directed at them. He was afraid, of course; only a fool would not have been. But he was also angry, he realized. He wanted to fight back.

"We can outrun them, Ike," Farrell said to the pilot. "It's only a few hundred yards to the next bend."

"Hell, they can lob shells at us whether they can see us or not, Cap'n!"

Farrell shook his head. "They won't waste too much ammunition on us. They'll be saving it for the fort."

The fort! Cory thought. Lucille was at the fort. And the Yankees were on their way to attack it right now, today. That was the only explanation for the flotilla of warships that was steaming down the Tennessee.

"We have to get back there in time to get Lucille out," he urged.

Farrell's expression was bleak as he nodded. "I wish I'd been able to get her to Nashville before now. But we'll do what we can."

Another Yankee cannon boomed, and this time the shot went into the water to the left of the riverboat. "They're gettin' the range, Cap'n," Judson warned.

Farrell turned to Cory and ordered, "Mr. Brannon, have the gunners turn the 3-incher aft and tell them to fire at will. We'll show the Yankees we have fangs!"

"Aye, sir!" Cory's chest was tight with the mixture of fear and excitement and anger as he hurried out of the pilothouse and clattered down the sets of stairs to the main deck.

The 3-inch gun could be rolled easily on its wheels by two men. Cory told the gunners assigned to it to take the weapon aft, so that they would have a clear shot at the pursuing Yankee vessels. He followed them, dragging the canvas sack that held the small, deceptively heavy cannonballs.

Another shot from the ironclad whistled overhead. Cory glanced up in time to see the ball go between the stacks and arch over the boat to plunge into the river ahead of it. He looked upriver. The bend that would give them a little protection from the shelling was nearer now, but the *Zephyr* was having a hard time of it, fighting against the strong current. The only advantage to that was that the heavier, slower ironclads were experiencing even more difficulty making headway. And with the four armored vessels stretched across the river, there was no room for the lighter wooden gunboats to go around them. The *Zephyr* was gradually pulling away.

"Ready to fire!" one of the crewmen at the cannon announced.

"Let 'em have it!" Cory heard himself shouting.

The 3-incher lurched on its carriage as the friction primer ignited the charge in its barrel and sent the cannonball whipping toward the ironclad. The gunners' aim was good. The ball slammed into the forward plating on the ironclad, but unfortunately, it glanced off, turned away by the armor. Still, the Yankees inside the vessel must have heard and felt the impact.

"Reload and fire at will!" Cory shouted. "Aim for the gun emplacements!"

He stood there with fists clenched and watched the exchange of shots. A ball from the ironclad struck the railing around the boiler deck and carried part of it away, but that was as close as the Yankees came with their fire before the *Zephyr* slid around the bend in the river and out of sight. For their part, the gunners on the riverboat had bounced a couple more balls off the ironclad's plating. All in all, the damage to both vessels was minimal.

Cory raced back up to the pilothouse, arriving in time to hear Captain Farrell ordering all the power that Ben Hovey could coax from his engines. Farrell glanced around at Cory and predicted, "We'll beat them back to Henry by a half-hour or more. Tilghman will have some warning of the attack, at least."

"He'd have that anyway, if his lookouts are any good," Judson asserted. "Those boats are puttin' out so much smoke, a blind man could see 'em comin'."

"That's true, but perhaps we can increase the odds." Farrell looked at Cory again and frowned. "Are you all right, Mr. Brannon?"

Cory's hands were shaking. He held them up and stared at them. "I stood out there on the deck with cannonballs whistling around, and I forgot to be scared," he said in awe. "I just wanted to fight. But now . . ."

"A not uncommon reaction, I'm told." Farrell clapped him on the shoulder. "Good work, lad, and don't let what you're feeling now bother you. You wouldn't be human if you could come out of a battle and feel nothing."

Cory was feeling something, all right. He seemed full to bursting with sensations and emotions. Everything seemed heightened. The wind in his face, the heavy humidity of the air, the splashing of the great paddlewheels in the river, the roar and thump of the engines . . . it all cascaded in on him and threatened to engulf him.

A shudder went through him. He drew a deep breath and forced himself to calm down.

This day, this battle, had barely begun.

IT WAS late in the morning by the time the *Zephyr* returned to Fort Henry. Farrell and Cory rowed over to the fort immediately, and as soon as they were inside, Farrell spotted Captain Taylor and reported, "I have to speak to General Tilghman right away."

"We heard what sounded like cannon fire in the distance," Taylor said as he fell in step beside the two of them. "Did you run into some Yankees?"

"Some Yankees?" Cory repeated. "We ran into an entire fleet of them!"

"Hardly that many," Farrell clarified, "but there were a significant number of vessels."

"Then they're attacking at last," Taylor concluded.

"It appears so."

The captain of artillery ushered them quickly into the general's office, where Farrell made a concise report. Tilghman's expression grew more and more worried as he heard the number of Union vessels that were approaching the fort. He ordered an aide to summon the other officers.

"We have less than four thousand men," Tilghman muttered when the room was full of gray-uniformed officers and he had informed them of the situation. Cory and Farrell remained but stepped back against the wall so that they would be out of the way. "Grant would never send the gunboats upriver unless he was planning to attack overland as well. There may be as many as twenty-five thousand Yankee troops on their way here."

274 • *James Reasoner*

"We'll make a fight of it, sir," asserted Forrest, the head of Henry's cavalry.

Tilghman shook his head and looked at Taylor. "Captain, can the artillery hold the gunboats at bay for one hour?"

"We can, sir," Taylor replied without hesitation.

"Very well, then." Tilghman looked at the other officers. "Go back to your men and be ready to move. A small force will hold the fort while the rest of you pull back to Fort Donelson."

Some of them looked as if they wanted to balk at evacuating the fort, regarding that as nothing less than running from the Yankees. But no one argued with the general's order. They were about to leave the office when Farrell stepped forward and said, "General Tilghman?"

"What is it, Captain Farrell?"

"I want my daughter out of here, as you promised would be done."

Tilghman smiled faintly. "I said that the young lady would be taken to Fort Donelson as soon as I could spare the men."

"You're sparing several thousand of them today, if I heard you correctly."

"You did indeed," Tilghman concurred with a nod.

Forrest intervened, "If it pleases the general—and the young lady's father—" He inclined his head toward Farrell. "It would be my honor to escort Miss Farrell to Fort Donelson." He turned to Farrell. "I assure you, sir, every man in my command would give his life in the young lady's service."

"Thank you, Colonel," Farrell responded sincerely. He looked at Tilghman, who nodded.

"What about yourself, Captain?" the general asked. "What will you do with your riverboat?"

Farrell squared his shoulders. "I intend to remain here and help fight the enemy, General."

Cory was disappointed, yet not surprised. And as he gauged his own reaction to Farrell's words, he realized that he was not at all unsatisfied, either. The time for running was over. They would make a stand here today.

"I must admit," mused Tilghman, "it would make the odds a bit less uneven if we had a couple of naval vessels on our side, too. Do you think Captain Glennon will go along with your decision and risk the *DeQuincey*?"

"That will be up to him. Also, I won't order any of my men to remain. They will have to make up their own minds whether to stay or go."

"The army does not have that luxury." Tilghman smiled again, wryly this time. "I can see now why you didn't want to enlist, Captain."

"That doesn't mean I'll fight any less hard."

"Naturally not." Tilghman turned to his officers. "Let's get to work, gentlemen. The Yankees will be here before we know it."

"TURN TAIL from a bunch of skalleyhootin' bluebellies?" Captain Glennon had burst out when informed of his options. "I'll be damned if I will!"

So, by a little before noon, February 6, 1862, both the *Missouri Zephyr* and the *DeQuincey* were sitting in the middle of the Tennessee River, awaiting the coming of the Union ironclads and gunboats. The 18-pounder cannon had been placed on the bow of each paddlewheeler and aimed downstream. They were charged and primed and ready to fire, as were all the cannon in Fort Henry—the ones that were not already underwater, that is.

Cory, Captain Farrell, and Ike Judson were in the pilothouse. The *Zephyr* had steam up in case any maneuvering needed to be done, but there was really nowhere to go, Cory reflected, short of turning and fleeing upstream. And Captain Farrell had made it clear that he would not be doing that.

All the members of the crew had elected to remain on the riverboat and help fight the Yankees. Cory had seen pride shining in Farrell's eyes as that decision was relayed to him by the mate and the chief engineer. Lucille was the only one not on the *Zephyr*, and that had not been her choice.

As Cory stood there in the pilothouse, he thought about his last sight of her, sitting forlornly on a wagon seat next to a red-faced corporal who flicked the reins and clucked at the team of mules pulling the vehicle. The wagon was surrounded by members of the cavalry unit commanded by Colonel Forrest. Lucille had turned her head for one last look as the wagon rolled out of the rear gate of the fort and onto the road leading east to Fort Donelson. At that moment, seeing the sadness on her face, Cory had thought his heart would break.

But she couldn't stay here; Lucille understood that.

"I'm sure the two of you will see each other again," Farrell addressed him quietly, breaking into Cory's thoughts.

"Sir?" Cory gave a small, guilty start.

"I know you were thinking about my daughter. I'd wager you lie heavy in her thoughts about now, too." Farrell looked him in the eye. "You have the makings of a fine young man, Cory. I've been pleased to have you on the *Zephyr*."

There was a finality to the captain's tone that made Cory uneasy. "We'll lick the Yankees, sir," he promised. "I'm sure of it."

"If God so wills."

Judson said, "Here they come."

The smoke from the Union vessels had been visible for several minutes. Now the ironclads themselves came into sight, steaming along the river toward the fort. The armored gunboats were lined up perfectly, four abreast.

"Steady," Farrell breathed. "They'll have to fire the first shot. They are the invaders."

Flame bloomed from the muzzle of one of the cannon on the ironclad at the far right of the formation. As if that shot had knocked open the gates of hell, the river and the fort were suddenly engulfed in noise and fire and smoke. The whistle of cannonballs was like the wailing of lost souls. The guns on board the *Zephyr* and the *DeQuincey* added to the cacophony as they opened up. Their gunners had orders to fire at will once the battle began, as it most assuredly had.

Cory put a hand on the chart table to steady himself as he watched the shelling. The remaining cannon at the fort were in action, throwing everything they had against the Union ironclads and gunboats. The Yankees seemed to be ignoring the two riverboats and were concentrating their fire on the fort instead.

Judson slammed a fist against the wheel in frustration. "We ain't nothin' but gnats to them!"

"Gnats can still bite," Farrell admonished. Below, the *Zephyr*'s cannon boomed.

Suddenly, smoke began pouring from the ironclad on the left end of the formation. "They've been hit!" Cory cried exultantly. He hoped it was a shot from the riverboat that had penetrated the Union vessel, even though he knew it had probably originated from one of the fort's heavy Columbiads. The ironclad began veering to the left, and Cory saw several figures leaping from the deck into the river, evidently fearing that the vessel's boilers were about to explode. Judging from the amount of smoke and steam billowing up, that was a distinct possibility. Even with one of the ironclads out of the fight, however, the remaining Union vessels had plenty of firepower.

"We need to be closer!" Farrell exclaimed. He snatched at the speaking tube. "Ahead one-half larboard! Ahead one-half starboard! Ike, take us at them!"

The *Zephyr* surged forward. Alongside, the *DeQuincey* did likewise as Captain Glennon followed Farrell's lead. Cory's heart thumped madly as the riverboats steamed toward the ironclads. Part of him wished he was down on the deck, yanking the lanyard that activated the primer on the cannon, striking personally at the Yankees. But the men whose job that was were better trained at it than he was, so he supposed he was better off up here.

The *Zephyr*'s larger cannon thundered, and Cory saw metal plating fly into the air on one of the ironclads. They were actually doing some damage, he thought excitedly.

But they were also forcing the Yankees to pay attention to them, he realized a moment later when a shot from an ironclad smashed into one of the *DeQuincey*'s stacks and crumpled it like paper.

"Damn them all!" Farrell exploded. Through the open window, he shouted down to his gunners, "Fire, boys, fire! For the Confederacy!"

Cory let out a whoop. He couldn't help himself. Fear remained in the back of his mind, but it was overpowered by the excitement of the moment.

"I'm going down there!" Farrell shouted as he turned toward the door. "I want to be with the cannon." He rushed out of the pilothouse.

"Cory!" Judson snapped. "Go with him. Don't let anything happen to him."

"But, Ike—"

"Go on, damn it!" Judson glared toward the Yankees. "I got the wheel."

Cory hurried out and followed Farrell down to the main deck. He found the captain standing just behind the gunners, shaking his fist at the Yankees. "Ruin the rivers, will you!" Farrell was shouting. "We'll show you how rivermen fight!"

Cory had never seen the captain like this. Farrell was caught up in the heat of the moment, he supposed. But seeing him this way, when Farrell had always been so calm and cool no matter what was going on around him made Cory temper his own enthusiasm. "Captain, be care—" he began.

A huge explosion shook the *Zephyr* and threw Cory off his feet. He landed hard, the impact knocking the breath out of him, and after a moment when he was able to push himself onto his hands and knees, all he could do was gasp for air. Then he heard Farrell crying in a stricken voice, "Oh, my God. Oh, my God."

Cory tilted his head up and saw the captain staring toward the pilothouse. Twisting his neck, Cory looked up, too, and saw that the pilothouse was gone, swept clear of the top of the Texas deck, leaving only a few scattered timbers and shards of glass behind. At least two cannonballs must have hit it at the same time to have wreaked such havoc.

"Ike!" Cory screamed. He wasn't even aware that he was scrambling to his feet. He had barely gotten upright again when another explosion jolted the riverboat and threw him down. Flame and smoke erupted from the port side of the main deck. Another shot snapped off the top half of one of the stacks before Cory's horrified eyes. The *Zephyr* leaped and shuddered like a wounded wild animal. More smoke billowed upward into the sky above the river as the fire spread.

"The boilers," Cory heard Farrell gasping in a stunned voice. "The boilers are going to go."

Cory rolled over and surged up off the deck, which was now shaking violently under his feet. He heard Ike Judson's voice in his head, telling him not to let anything happen to the captain. The excitement he had felt only moments earlier was gone, overwhelmed by fear. Cory threw himself forward, tackling Farrell around the waist, and both of them went off the deck and into the river as the *Zephyr* rose up in the middle and split in half in a gigantic explosion.

The icy waters of the Tennessee closed over them, shrouding them in frigid darkness. Something slammed into Cory like a massive fist. He felt himself sliding down, down into the water, and his feet began kicking. He had lost track of Captain Farrell. He flailed with his arms, desperate for survival but also trying to find the captain. The fingers of his left hand brushed against something. He grabbed hold and tugged on whatever it was with all his might.

Cory's head broke the surface. He shook the water out of his eyes and gasped for air. The water was so cold that he was going numb all over. He had to get out soon, or the next time he went down would be the end. Something splashed violently beside him, and Farrell's head came out of the water. The captain was still alive. Like Cory, he was trying to gulp down as much air as possible. Cory shoved him toward the closest shore, not knowing which bank of the river they were bound for. Debris fell around them, some of it still on fire as it hit the water, and Cory realized they were being pelted by the remains of the *Zephyr*, thrown high in the air by the explosion that had torn the riverboat apart.

After what seemed like an hour in the water but was probably only a couple of minutes, Cory and Farrell pulled themselves out of the river and onto a muddy bank. They rolled onto their backs and tried to catch their breath, but immediately began shivering and trembling so hard that they had to struggle to their feet and move around to keep from freezing. Cory's brain was almost as numbed as his body, but after a few moments, it began to function well enough again for him to realize that they were on the eastern bank of the Tennessee, a hundred yards or so downstream from the fort. During their time underwater, the current had swept them past the Union ironclads and gunboats. It was pure luck that they hadn't been smashed against one of the vessels. Cory shuddered even harder as he thought about all the cannonballs that had passed over their heads and crashed into the water around them. By all rights, he and Captain Farrell ought to be dead.

Everyone else who had been on the *Zephyr* most probably was. The riverboat had been completely destroyed. All that was left of it was floating debris. The *DeQuincey,* while not yet blown out of the water, was definitely out of the fight. Fires were burning out of control on the steamboat, and men were leaping off her into the river.

Farrell stared at the battle. His eyes were wide and full of horror. Cory tugged at his sodden sleeve and said, "Cap'n, we've got to go. We can't stay here. We've got to keep moving, or we'll freeze to death in these wet clothes."

"Go?" Farrell repeated hollowly. "Go where?"

There was only one answer, and it came to Cory. "Fort Donelson. Come on, Captain." He paused, then added, "Lucille's there."

"Lucille . . ." Farrell whispered. "That boat was her home. Ike was her friend."

"Mine, too," Cory said. "But, Captain, we have to go."

Farrell allowed Cory to turn him away from the river and the battle that was still going on. They faded into the woods, splashed through a bog, and a few minutes later came to the road that led to Fort Donelson. Cory kept a hand on Farrell's arm, kept him moving as they began to trudge away from the river.

Behind them, the cannon continued to roar.

TILGHMAN HAD asked for an hour's time from Captain Taylor and the artillerymen of Fort Henry. Taylor and his valiant gunners held off the Yankees for twice that long before Tilghman gave the order to strike their flag and surrender the fort. At that point, only four of the cannon inside Fort Henry were still capable of being fired. The flagpole inside the fort had been struck by cannonfire but not toppled, and Taylor himself, along with another man, climbed it to untangle the lines and lower the flag while Yankee shells were still whistling around them. Then, as the firing died away, Tilghman and several of his officers were rowed out to the Union ironclad that was serving as the flotilla's flagship to complete the surrender.

Grant's troops, having been delayed in their march on the fort, were still hours away, but they were not needed. Indeed, if the attack had been postponed a few more days, the river itself would have won the victory for the Yankees, as the fort would have been inundated by its flooding. Either way, the Union had its victory. Its first thrust into Tennessee was a smashing success. Which meant only one thing to Grant: Fort Donelson was next.

Chapter Seventeen

GRANT PROPOSED TO MOVE on to Fort Donelson and capture it the very next day after the surrender of Fort
Henry. It was not easy to move an army that quickly, however,
and besides, ten thousand more Union troops were on their
way to reinforce Grant's army. Patience was called for, and
somewhere in his makeup, Grant found it. Several days were
also required for Admiral Foote to take his gunboats back to
Cairo for repairs before they could begin their voyage down
the Cumberland River.

This respite brought with it a false promise of spring: skies
cleared and warm breezes blew from the south. The soldiers
under Grant's command celebrated. Not only had the Union
won a victory over the Confederates, but it seemed as if the
Fates themselves were smiling on the Northerners by bringing good weather.

On the Confederate side, the skies were just as balmy, but
the mood was considerably darker. At his headquarters in
Bowling Green, Kentucky, Gen. Albert Sidney Johnston conferred with P. G. T. Beauregard, one of the heroes of
Manassas, who had been sent to Tennessee to function as
Johnston's second-in-command. A lull in the fighting in Virginia had prompted Beauregard to request this move, and
once he arrived in Tennessee, he proved to be as aggressive
as ever. He suggested combining all the western armies
under Johnston's command and massing them at Fort Donelson. There they would meet Grant, Beauregard said, and
drive him back where he came from. The only other reason-
able option was to abandon the positions held by the Confederates in Kentucky and Tennessee and fall back south to

regroup in Alabama, leaving only a token force at Fort Donelson to delay Grant.

Johnston chose to do neither. He determined that most of his men would indeed retreat to Alabama, but at the same time he committed reinforcements to Fort Donelson. Privately, Beauregard must have thought this halfway measure to be mad, but Johnston was in charge.

Gen. John Floyd, the former secretary of war under President Buchanan, was in command of the garrison at Fort Donelson, and under him were Gens. Gideon J. Pillow and Simon Bolivar Buckner. Floyd and Pillow were no more than mediocre officers at best; of the three, only Buckner showed some occasional flair. With a total of seventeen thousand men, they dug in at Fort Donelson, which sat on the western bank of the Cumberland River just north of the town of Dover.

High bluffs overlooked the river at this point, and two artillery batteries had been dug in the face of the bluffs themselves. These batteries were reinforced with timbers and sandbags. More cannon were located inside the fort, which commanded a good field of fire over the river. On the western, landward side of Fort Donelson, a nearly continuous string of log-lined trenches had been dug, stretching from the swampy bogs around Hickman Creek on the north all the way around the fort and the town of Dover to the south. These trenches would serve as rifle pits, and since the approaches to them were all up rather steep hills, it was hoped that Confederate riflemen would be able to keep the Yankees from advancing on the fort from that direction.

On February 12, Grant's infantry moved up and established a line just out of range of rifle fire from the Confederate trenches. Grant's forces numbered some fifteen thousand, which meant the Rebels outnumbered them slightly. More Federals were on the way, however, an entire brigade under the command of Gen. Lew Wallace.

So as night fell, the two armies were poised to do battle. The wind changed, shifting around to the north, and a seemingly razor sharp mixture of rain, sleet, and snow began to fall on both sides.

CORY PAUSED just inside the tavern and waited for his eyes to adjust to the smoky dimness. He took off his hat and brushed snow and pieces of sleet off his shoulders and out of his hair. The wind was blowing hard outside, bringing a bone-numbing chill with it. Thank God he was wearing dry clothes tonight, he thought. If a wind like that had been blowing the day he and Captain Farrell had crawled out of the Tennessee River near Fort Henry, they would have been frozen stiff in no time.

As it was, Cory didn't like to remember that twelve-mile trudge overland between the forts six days earlier. Their sodden clothing had never really dried; it had remained miserably cold and clammy every step of the way. Only the brisk pace Cory had set had kept them even halfway warm.

Cory had been forced to take charge. Neither he nor Captain Farrell had been injured in the destruction of the *Zephyr,* but the captain could do little more than stumble along blindly. Cory worried that Farrell's mind had been unhinged by the loss of the riverboat and the death of everyone else on board. Farrell had made the decision to stay at Fort Henry and fight the Yankees, and even though he had called for volunteers to remain there with him, he must have had a pretty good idea that none of the crew would desert him. He was probably blaming himself for everything that had happened. If their positions had been reversed, Cory knew that he too would have been almost overwhelmed by guilt.

Whenever Farrell had wanted to stop during that nightmarish march, Cory had reminded him of Lucille, and that had prodded the captain into motion again. To tell the truth, thoughts of Lucille were about the only thing that had kept Cory going, too. Though he dreaded telling her of the destruction of the boat and the loss of Ike Judson and the other men, he had been anxious to see her again, to know that she was all right, to be able to hold her in his arms once more.

At this moment, as he stood just inside the two-storied log building beside the Cumberland River that housed the tavern, he was still thinking of Lucille. She had sent him here tonight to fetch her father.

He spotted Farrell sitting alone at a table across the room and started toward him. The tavern was not as busy as it had been a week earlier; only about half the tables were occupied, and there were vacant spaces at the bar. A lot of people had packed up and left Dover, afraid that the Yankees were on their way. Now that fear had proven to be accurate. From the hill where Fort Donelson was located, Cory had been able to see the fires of the Northern army where it was camped just out of rifle range.

When he reached the table, Cory pulled back one of the empty chairs and sat down. Farrell ignored him and continued staring into the glass of whiskey in front of him. The captain's cheeks were hollow and had a week's growth of beard on them. He wore no hat, and his hair was tangled. Stains dotted the front of his coat. He was a mere shadow of the man he had been before the battle at Fort Henry.

Cory leaned forward. "Captain, we have to get back to the fort," he said.

Farrell continued to ignore him, acting as if Cory hadn't even spoken. He picked up the glass, his hand shaking slightly, and lifted it to his lips. Instead of gulping down the whiskey, he merely sipped it. But he was probably drunk anyway, because he spent nearly all his time sitting in this tavern sipping whiskey.

"Lucille is leaving," Cory spoke more urgently. "She wants to see you before she goes."

As always, Lucille's name seemed to penetrate Farrell's muddled mind when nothing else would. But his reaction was not the one that Cory had hoped for.

"She doesn't need . . . need to see me," Farrell mumbled thickly. "Doesn't need to see . . . a worthless old fool."

Cory wanted to tell Farrell that he wasn't any of those things, but he knew by now that he would only be wasting his time if he argued with the captain. It was better just to be firm, tell Farrell what he had to do, and then insist upon it.

"She's waiting for you. Come on, Captain. Let's go to the fort."

Farrell turned his head and peered intently at the wall of the tavern as if he could see through the logs and out into the night. "They're out there, you know." He gestured shakily. "The Yankees. Just waiting. Waiting to kill more good Southern boys . . ."

Cory tried not to sigh in frustration. He didn't want Farrell to start crying again. That always caused an embarrassing scene. He thought of the cool-headed man who had rescued him from Lydell Strunk not once but twice, and he was ashamed of what Captain Farrell had turned into. And ashamed of himself, too, for feeling that way.

"Come on, Captain," he appealed again. This time he stood up, came around the table, and gripped Farrell's upper arm. "We have to go say good-bye to Lucille."

Putting it in words like that plunged a dagger into Cory's heart. It was the best thing, he knew, but he could hardly bear the thought of being separated from her yet again.

Of course, he could go to Nashville with her, he reminded himself. He was a civilian; he could come and go as he pleased, unlike the soldiers.

But if he stayed at Fort Donelson and pitched in to the fight, he might have a chance to make a difference. As far as he could tell with his limited military experience, Donelson was well defended, and according to the rumors he'd heard from the soldiers, the number of troops at the fort was equal to, if not superior to, the size of Grant's Union army. Fort Henry had been a lost cause from the beginning. The South might actually win here at Donelson, Cory thought, just as they had been victorious at Manassas.

"I want to stay here!" Farrell protested as Cory tugged him up out of the chair. "Don't want to go to the fort."

"It's for Lucille," Cory said.

Farrell's face contorted. "L-Lucille," he hiccupped.

"Come on," Cory cajoled, more gently this time. He picked up his captain's hat from where it had fallen on the floor beside the chair.

He was able to steer Farrell past several Confederate officers who were gathered around a big table in the corner of the room. He recognized all three of the brigadier generals from Fort Donelson—Floyd, Pillow, and Buckner. Forrest was there, too, and he gave Cory a nod as Cory and Farrell went past. Cory would always feel a debt of gratitude to Forrest, because the man had kept his promise and seen that Lucille reached Fort Donelson safely. Cory wondered if some sort of high-level strategy session was going on. He knew that the generals often met here at the tavern in Dover, rather than at the fort itself, to make their command decisions.

The precipitation outside had changed from the earlier wintry mix into mostly snow with a few pellets of sleet still intermingled in the windblown crystals of ice. Better that than rain, Cory thought as he hunched his shoulders in the thin coat. He tugged his hat down and made sure that Farrell's hat was on snugly, too. The hats had come from a merchant here in Dover when the man found out they had taken part in the futile defense of Fort Henry. The rest of the clothes were their own, all they had come away with from the *Zephyr.*

Cory and Farrell followed the road that led past the cemetery and then uphill to the fort. It was an unpleasant walk on a night such as this, and when the guards at the gate saw them, one of the troopers in butternut said in a Texas accent, "Whoo-ee, boy, you hadn't ought to be out in this weather. Y'all come on in this place."

"How do you know they're not Yankee spies?" asked one of the other guards, a man who hadn't seen Cory and Farrell before.

"'Cause I know these fellers," the Texan replied. "They're all right. Fought the damn Yanks at Fort Henry, they did."

"All right, all right," the other man muttered. "Let 'em in, so we can close the gate and get out of the wind."

Once they were inside, Cory steered Farrell toward the headquarters building. Even though the generals weren't there tonight, the place was still busy. Men had been pouring into the fort over the past few days, sent by General Johnston, but some were leaving, too, including a wagon that was departing momentarily for Nashville, carrying several wooden boxes that contained all the regimental records. Lucille was going with them.

Once the first flush of happiness at being reunited had passed, Cory had had to tell her what had happened at Fort Henry. The news of the *Zephyr*'s destruction and the deaths of all her friends, especially the two pilots, had devastated her. Having lost all that, she wouldn't hear of being parted again from all she had left in the world—her father and Cory. It had taken a considerable amount of arguing—days, in fact—to get her to agree to stick to the original plan and go on to Nashville.

Cory found Lucille in the headquarters building with Captain Morley, the fort's chief clerk and the commander of the detail that would set out tonight for Nashville. Cory wasn't sure about putting a clerk in charge of a military detail, but Morley seemed competent enough. He and Lucille were sitting at a table. He nodded to Cory and stood up as Cory and Farrell came into the room. "I'll leave the three of you alone, Mr. Brannon," he said. "Please try not to be too long, Miss Farrell. With the roads like this, there's no telling how long it will take us to reach Nashville."

"All right, Captain," Lucille answered. "Thank you." When Morley had left the room and closed the door behind him, she turned to Cory and went on, "The captain says that tonight may be the last chance to get the records out of the fort. He says the Yankees will probably lay siege to the place."

"That's the only way they'll ever get us out," Cory replied with more confidence than he felt. "This isn't Fort Henry."

"No," Lucille agreed softly. "It isn't."

"And nothing is going to happen to us."

Before Lucille could say anything else, Farrell sank down with a heavy sigh into one of the chairs. She turned to him and leaned over to slip an arm around his shoulders. "I'll stay if you want me to, Father," she whispered.

Cory was about to berate her for trying to change the plans at the last minute, but he didn't have to. Farrell straightened, and for a moment he looked more like his old self. "You're going to Nashville, and that's that," he insisted firmly.

Lucille knelt beside him and caught one of his hands in both of hers. "Why don't you come with me?" She looked over at Cory. "Both of you."

"I have to stay . . . have to fight the Yankees."

"But you've done your part already," Lucille protested.

"Done my part." The words, spoken quietly by Farrell in a hollow voice, held more pain and sorrow than Cory had ever heard before. "Gotten my friends killed and my boat blown out of the water, you mean."

"That wasn't your fault—"

"I'll not run. I should have died there with the others." Farrell cast a brief, bitter glance toward Cory. "I'll not turn tail from the Yankees. The Confederacy can use every good man it can get." The captain's hand clenched into a fist and thumped on the table. "The tide will turn here."

"I can't convince you?" Lucille looked miserably at Cory. "Either of you?"

Cory took a deep breath. "I have to stay with the captain. But we'll find you in Nashville as soon as we can get there after the battle is over."

"Yes. Of course. After the battle is over."

Lucille hugged her father fiercely, kissed his cheek, and smoothed his tangled hair. Then she stood up and came over to Cory. In a voice that was little more than a whisper, she appealed, "If you really loved me, you'd come with me."

"The captain—"

"Hit him over the head and bring him along, damn it," she hissed.

It was all Cory could do not to recoil from her. She didn't know what she was saying, he told himself. The strain had momentarily clouded her thinking. He set her straight by declaring, "He would never forgive either of us if I did that."

Lucille sighed. "No. I don't suppose he would." She moved closer to Cory, put her arms around his neck, and rested her head against his shoulder. His arms came up and encircled her, drawing her into an embrace. He felt a bit awkward, hugging her this way in front of her father, but Farrell already knew how they felt about each other. Besides, the captain's eyes were half-closed and his head was drooping forward. He was about to doze off.

Cory's arms tightened around Lucille. "We'll come to Nashville," he promised again, "as soon as the battle is over . . ."

She lifted her face to his, and he kissed her, long and hungrily, all too aware that he had to pack enough passion and tenderness into this kiss to last him perhaps the rest of his life.

However long that might be.

THE SLEET and snow were still falling on the morning of the thirteenth. It was a miserable day, especially for the Union soldiers who had thrown away their blankets and overcoats during the march from Fort Henry in warm weather. A part of Cory hoped that the Yankees would go ahead and attack, just so the defenders would have something to do besides worry about freezing to death.

The Union forces kept their distance, however, except for a foray against a fortified Confederate artillery battery on a nearby hill. Cory watched avidly from the fort, along with many of the soldiers, as withering fire from the cannon drove the Yankees back with heavy casualties, forcing them to abandon the attack. Cory had to swallow hard as he saw the blue-uniformed bodies—and pieces of bodies—that lay scattered on the frozen hillside. He had known, logically, that war was a bloody, cruel business. He was coming to understand that same fact now in his heart.

Nothing else happened that day except for a brief, harmless exchange of shots between the Confederate batteries and one of the Yankee gunboats that ventured up the Cumberland, probably on a scouting mission. In the evening, as Cory was walking across the fort, he encountered Colonel Forrest. After saying hello to the cavalryman, he asked, "Why didn't the Yankees come today, Colonel?"

Forrest shook his head. "No way of knowing. Maybe they're waiting for reinforcements, or the rest of the gunboats aren't in position yet, or Grant just wanted us to stew for a day longer. But they'll come sooner or later; never doubt that."

Cory wasn't doubting it, not for a minute. As much as he might like for it to happen, the Yankee threat wasn't going to fade away.

He found Captain Farrell in the sutler's store. Cory had asked Farrell not to go back to Dover, and the captain had agreed. Cory hadn't been sure Farrell would keep his word, however. He was afraid Farrell would head back to the tavern the first chance he got.

To his surprise, though, he found that Farrell had shaved and cleaned up. He was sitting opposite the sutler, who had set up a checkerboard on a pickle barrel between them. Farrell glanced up from the board as Cory came in and greeted him. "Good evening, Mr. Brannon. It's still a fierce night out, isn't it?"

"Yes sir," Cory said with a smile, glad to see that Farrell was looking and sounding more like his old self again. Maybe the captain had gotten over the horrible melancholy that had gripped him for the past week.

The sutler got up from his chair. "Excuse me a minute, Captain. I want to talk to our young friend here."

Farrell waved a hand. "Go right ahead. That will give me an opportunity to consider a new strategy." He stared broodingly at the checkers.

The sutler motioned for Cory to follow him. When they were on the other side of the store, out of earshot of Farrell, the man informed him, "Your cap'n's drunk as a lord, son. He's liable to pass out any minute."

Cory frowned. "But he seems so much better tonight."

"That's just the whiskey talkin'. I know, because I've watched him put away a whole jug of it. You'd better find him a place to sleep it off—too late."

Cory followed the sutler's gaze and saw that Farrell had slumped forward over the barrel, knocking the checkerboard and checkers to the puncheon floor. Cory sighed. "Can he stay here tonight?"

The sutler considered, then shrugged and nodded. "I suppose so. Help me drag him into the back room. I got a few sacks of flour left back there that'll serve as a bunk."

Once Cory had gotten Farrell settled for the night with the sutler's help, he went back out into the cold night. General Floyd had kindly allowed Cory and Farrell to stay in one of the tents with the enlisted men. It was cold and damp but better than no shelter at all. Farrell was better off tonight passed out in the back room of the sutler's store.

The weather was still snowy on the fourteenth, but during the morning the snow tapered off to flurries. Lookouts with telescopes caught an occasional glimpse of the Yankee flotilla several miles downstream, but the vessels didn't start toward the fort until midafternoon. Then, as alarm bells sounded inside Fort Donelson, four of the Yankee ironclads and two wooden gunboats steamed up the Cumberland in battle formation.

Cory was at the wall along with Farrell and Colonel Forrest as the Yankees opened fire. Cannonballs smashed into the bluffs and along the walls of the fort, but the Confederate gunners held their fire, waiting for the gunboats to get closer. Forrest watched the attack for several minutes, and then his natural impatience made him snap at his aide, a former minister, "Parson, for God's sake, pray! Nothing but God Almighty can save this fort."

Cory hoped that wasn't the case, but he sent up a few prayers of his own, figuring it wouldn't hurt. His mother had always believed in the power of prayer. Right now, so did Cory.

Finally, the Confederate batteries opened fire. The Yankees were now within range, and the cannonballs smashed into the ironclads with a great ringing noise like a giant hammer striking a massive anvil. The din of destruction was almost deafening.

And destruction it was, because the pounding by the Confederate guns took a heavy toll on the Union vessels. The ironclads that had stood up so well under the fire from Fort Henry now faced a much sterner challenge, and they began to fail. Rebel cannonballs smashed through the armored plating, destroying gun emplacements, wrecking rudders, and killing Yankee sailors. Two ironclads started to drift aimlessly, their steering ruined by the damage they had taken. Two more began taking on water and appeared to be in danger of sinking. Cheers rang out from the gunners in the Confederate batteries as the Yankee vessels turned and fled, throwing up only a weak covering fire as they hustled back downstream out of harm's way.

The soldiers inside the fort who had been watching the engagement let out whoops of their own. Cory joined in, pumping a fist in the air. Farrell just smiled. He had been badly hungover that morning, and Cory was surprised the great racket of the guns hadn't caused the captain's head to burst wide open.

Pickets on the landward side of the fort reported that Grant's infantry hadn't budged during the attack by the gunboats. Grant must have been counting on Admiral Foote's flotilla to take Fort Donelson by itself, as it had Fort Henry. But if that was the case, then the Union general had badly miscalculated, Cory thought as he listened to the talk that flew around the fort following the retreat of the ironclads and gunboats. Fort Donelson had held.

THE OPTIMISM of the men inside the fort did not extend to its triumvirate of commanders. That night, as Grant was sending a pessimistic message to Gen. Henry Halleck in Saint Louis detailing the failure of the flotilla, Generals Floyd, Pillow, and Buckner were meeting to decide what to do when—not if—Fort Donelson fell to the Yankees.

They had already been advised by General Johnston to bring their men to Nashville if at all possible. Johnston's fallback to Nashville was complete. Fort Donelson had served its purpose of occupying Grant's time. Floyd, Pillow, and Buckner decided that instead of facing a long siege, it would be better to break out of Grant's encirclement while they still could, then head for Nashville with all due speed.

But first they had to escape from Fort Donelson, which, in the minds of its commanders, had become not a stronghold but a trap.

THE WINTER storm intensified on the night of the fourteenth and early in the morning of the fifteenth. Cory huddled in a thin blanket in one of the tents and wondered if it would ever truly be summer again. He was dreaming of clear blue skies and warm breezes and a blanket spread on a wildflower-dotted hillside and Lucille there waiting for him with open arms and a welcoming smile on her face . . . when a hard hand shook him awake.

"Hey, boy, get up," a harsh voice grated. "Time to decide if you're a soldier or a damned civilian."

Cory forced himself up out of sleep to see a sergeant standing over him. Around him, the other troopers in the tent were getting up and gathering their rifles and ammunition. It was so dark in the tent that Cory knew it was not yet dawn.

"Wha . . . what's happening?" Cory asked thickly. He didn't hear any gunfire. "Are the Yankees attacking?"

"We're takin' the fight to them," the sergeant growled. "I got a rifle for you, and a box o' ca'tridges, if you want 'em. Otherwise you'll have to just sit here on your backside and hope our side wins."

Cory knew the words were intended to sting him into volunteering. The Confederates needed all the men they could get, even if not all those men were officially enlisted in the army. Cory shook his head, not in refusal but to clear it. Was this really his fight? he asked himself.

Then he thought about Ike Judson and Ned Rowley and Ben Hovey and all his other friends on the *Zephyr*. He thought about the riverboat itself, the only real home he had known since he had foolishly ridden away from the Brannon farm in Culpeper County, Virginia.

Hell, yes, it was his fight.

"I'll take the rifle and the cartridges."

"Good boy." The sergeant took hold of his shoulder and hauled him to his feet. He thrust a rifle into Cory's hands. "You're lucky. This here rifle's nearly new. Made at the armory over in Fayetteville, No'th Carolina, outta parts we captured up at Harpers Ferry. Only reason you're gettin' it is 'cause the trooper it belonged to died yesterday of the croup."

Cory looked down at the weapon with a frown, unsure just how fortunate he was to have it.

"There's coffee and pone outside," the sergeant went on. "Grab a bite to eat, then report to the south gate. That's where we're formin' up."

Forming up for what, Cory wasn't sure. But he strapped the
pouch of paper cartridges the sergeant gave him onto his belt
and went outside to get some breakfast. He wondered if he
would have time to go over to the sutler's store and fetch Captain Farrell, who had spent the previous night there as well as
the one before that, when he had passed out over the checkerboard. The sutler had taken pity on Farrell—and besides,
Farrell was just about the only man in the fort whom the sutler
could beat at checkers.

The wind was blowing and snow was falling. The coffee was
cold because it was difficult to keep a fire going for very long at a
time. Cory drank it anyway, using it to wash down a hunk of dry
corn pone. The rough meal made him feel a little better, but
weariness still gripped him. When the soldiers from his tent
began to head for the gate, he shuffled after them. He cast one
more glance at the sutler's store, then decided to let Farrell stay
where he was. The captain could use the sleep, and besides, in
his condition he wouldn't be much good in a fight, anyway.

As ranks began forming, Cory found himself beside a soldier he recognized, the lanky Texan who often stood guard
duty. The Texan glanced at him, then looked again and asked,
"What'n hell are you doin' here, boy? You ain't a soldier."

"I guess I am today," Cory replied. "One of the sergeants
asked me if I wanted to go fight the Yankees, and I said yes."

"Well, I reckon I can understand that. I like a good scrap,
too." The Texan grinned. "That's why I'm here, instead o'
back on the Brazos."

"What's the Brazos?"

"It's a river, son. Prettiest dang river you'd ever want to see.
I got a farm there, but after the war I figure to head on upriver
a ways and start a ranch, raise me some cattle and hosses.
They's miles and miles o' land there in Texas for the takin',
and I intend to get me some."

"Sounds like a good idea," Cory agreed. "I thought about
going to Texas sometime myself."

"Well, hell, when you do, come see me. Reckon by then I'll be a cattle baron, so I'll give you a job and we'll ride the range together. How's that sound?"

"Pretty good," Cory acknowledged. "Is it warm in Texas?"

"You bet. Most o' the time, anyway, when they ain't a blue norther blowin'."

"I'll be there," Cory promised. "After the war's over."

An officer with a salt-and-pepper beard rode by on horseback. The Texan nodded toward him and said, "That's Gen'ral Pillow. He's in charge, I reckon."

"Do you know where we're going?"

"Nope, not for sure. All I know is we're fixin' to go fight the Yankees."

The troops moved out a few minutes later, marching through the predawn darkness. Snow crunched on the road under their feet. They went down the hill toward Dover, where only a few lights were burning, and then skirted the town on the east side, near the Cumberland River. Beyond Dover were some thick woods, into which the Confederate troops stole quietly as the sky began to lighten. Cory stayed close to the Texan, figuring that if nothing else, the man would probably know how to fight.

The Yankees must be close by. Cory had watched them moving up and encircling the fort and the town, and the Confederate forces had come far enough now that they had to be very near the Union lines. Cory's heart was thumping quickly again, and the breakfast he'd eaten lay heavy in his belly. From time to time as he waited, he felt sick to his stomach but the food stayed down. He was cold, and he wondered what was going to happen, and when.

He suddenly smelled bacon cooking, and his stomach cramped again.

"Move up, move up."

The whispered command was passed along the line of men in the woods, and they started forward at a walk. The ground began to slope up a little, and the walk turned into a trot.

Suddenly, rifle fire crackled off to Cory's left. An instant later, more shots sounded, this time to the right and closer. "There's one of the bluebellies!" the Texan exclaimed, and he paused to throw his rifle to his shoulder and fire. The roar of the weapon was loud.

Cory saw movement ahead of them and realized he was looking at a Union soldier who had fallen to the ground and lay there flopping uncontrollably like a fish out of water. "Got him!" the Texan said as he started to reload.

Ahead of Cory, flashes of light split the early morning grayness. Those were the muzzle flashes of the rifles the Yankees were firing at them, he realized. He stopped trotting forward and brought up his rifle, pulling back the hammer as he did so. He saw a flash not too far ahead of him, aimed toward the spot where it had been, and fired. Then he dropped to one knee and reached for the pouch on his belt, fumbling out one of the paper cartridges.

As he bit the end of the cartridge and tore it open with his teeth, he sensed as much as heard something whip past him, just above his head. A feeling colder even than the Tennessee River washed through him. That was a Yankee minié ball that had just missed him, he realized. If he had not knelt down to reload, it would have caught him squarely in the chest. One of the Yankees had aimed at his muzzle flash, just as he had aimed at theirs.

His hands shook a little. He forced them to be steady as he poured the powder from the cartridge down the barrel of his rifle, then followed it with a piece of wadding and tamped it home with the ramrod. The conical bullet followed that, and Cory rammed it down as well. He came to his feet as he slid the ramrod back into its slot under the barrel of the rifle. He thumbed back the hammer and put a percussion cap on the strike plate, pressing it down so that it was well seated. The rifle was ready to fire again.

He felt like throwing it down, turning, and running.

The firing was fierce all around him. Cory looked for the Texan and saw the man's back disappearing into the gloom up ahead. Cory followed, hoping that he wouldn't run right into a Yankee bullet. The sky grew lighter with every passing moment. He saw something blue ahead of him, snapped the rifle to his shoulder, aimed for a second, then pulled the trigger. The rifle kicked heavily at his shoulder. Powder smoke drifted in front of his face and into his eyes, stinging them so that it was almost impossible to see anything. He dropped to a knee again and blinked rapidly, trying to clear his eyesight as he reloaded more by feel than anything else.

His eyes kept burning, though, because now the air was thick with smoke everywhere. From above, Cory guessed, if there had been any birds left to soar over this battleground, they probably thought the woods were on fire because of all the smoke. He finished reloading, stood up, and stumbled on ahead.

Cory didn't see the Texan anywhere. He ran down into a little gully, almost lost his balance and fell, then recovered and struggled up the far side. He took a couple more steps and then caught his foot on something. This time he did fall, sprawling facedown on the ground. He managed to hang on to the rifle, though.

As he started to push himself up on hands and knees, Cory froze. Someone was tugging at his sleeve. He looked over and almost screamed. The Texan was lying there, missing half his face. He had been hit more than once, because the front of his uniform was dark with blood. He pawed at Cory for a second, then fell back. In an instant, his remaining eye was glassy with death. He would never have that ranch on the Brazos.

Cory wasn't thinking about ranches or Texas right then. He scrambled away from the corpse in horror. He tried to get up but fell back to his knees and doubled over as the coffee and pone came back up. When the wracking spasms stopped at last, he was too weak to get up.

Someone lunged past him, going back the way the Confederate troops had come from. Cory heard a shout. "The Yankees! They're comin'!"

The Union forces were launching a counterattack. Cory was dimly aware of that. If he stayed here, he would probably be overrun and shot; either that, or the Yankees would impale him on their bayonets as if he were a pincushion. Thinking about a pincushion made an image flash through his mind: his mother, sitting in the parlor at home with her sewing spread out in her lap, the needle in her hands moving smoothly in and out of the fabric, drawing the thread behind it . . .

Cory lifted his head, saw a Union soldier running toward him, and fired from where he lay in his own vomit. The shot caught the Yankee in the chest and flipped him over backward. Cory rolled over, jackknifed to his feet, and broke into a stumbling run.

When he reached the gully, he slid down into it and paused. This was a natural rifle pit, he realized. He dug out another paper cartridge and started reloading. As long as he stayed here, he told himself, he would have some cover. If he just fled blindly through the woods, it was only a matter of time before the Yankees caught up to him and shot him in the back. He decided he would rather be facing them.

He stood up enough to peer over the edge of the gully. A handful of Union soldiers were visible about fifty yards away. They had all stopped to reload. Cory drew a bead on the one of them he could see the best and fired. The man fell back against one of his comrades and then slid down to the ground.

A couple of Confederate troopers jumped down into the gully with Cory. They fired into the knot of Yankees and sent the rest of them sprawling. One of the Southerners let out a Rebel yell.

Cory didn't feel like shouting in triumph. He was too busy reloading.

For the next hour Cory and his companions stayed there in the natural trench. They were joined by several more comrades, and together they blunted the Yankee counterattack. Cory didn't have any time to spare for thoughts of strategy, however. To him, this battle had become about nothing but survival. He loaded, he fired, he loaded again, he fired again. The Fayetteville armory rifle held up superbly under the punishment of firing shot after shot. Bullets zinged around and men cried out and died, but Cory kept fighting.

He didn't stop until Forrest's cavalry came riding through the woods, ordering the men back to Fort Donelson. Forrest himself reined in behind the gully where Cory and his companions had made their stand. "Come on, boys," he called to them. "The Yankees have all fallen back, and so will we."

It took a moment for the meaning of the words to soak into Cory's battle-stunned brain. Forrest's voice had a muffled sound, and Cory realized he was half-deaf from the firing. "What?" he said.

"Back to the fort," Forrest repeated, raising his voice. "I'd rather push on and whip some more Yankees myself, but it's orders, boys."

The guns had all fallen silent, except for an occasional pop in the distance. Cory struggled up out of the gully with the other Rebels. He wasn't sure what was going on, but he knew one thing.

He was alive. He had survived.

And it felt so damned wonderful . . . .

Chapter Eighteen

THE PLAN TO BREAK out through the Yankee lines encircling Fort Donelson had been conceived in a moment of perhaps unusual audaciousness by Generals Floyd, Pillow, and Buckner. And it had been on the verge of success when the natural timidity of Floyd and Pillow betrayed them. By pulling back to the rifle pits around the fort and the town of Dover, the Confederate leaders squandered the opening that Pillow's men had battered in the Union encirclement. Buckner bitterly opposed this, but he was the most junior of the trio and was forced to go along with Floyd and Pillow. What could have been a daring escape to Nashville was soon back to a siege, as Grant took quick advantage of the blunder.

The Union forces under Gen. Lew Wallace occupied the center of the Yankee front. Most of Wallace's men rolled right to reinforce the troops of Gen. John McClernand, who had been beaten back by Pillow's brigade. The rest of Wallace's forces pushed forward, as did the troops on the Union left, under the command of Gen. C. F. Smith. Adding to the misery of the defenders inside the fort was the fact that the Yankee gunboats had returned and were once again shelling the place.

This Union counterattack continued throughout the afternoon of February 15.

SOME OF the men with Cory were left in the rifle pits, while others were marched back to the fort itself. Cory went with that group, since he was anxious to make sure that Captain Farrell was still all right. He heard the booming of artillery and saw dirt and rock thrown high in the air as the shells struck the walls of the fort. Inside was controlled chaos—but still chaos.

Cory pushed his way past a group of soldiers who were hurrying out the gate, no doubt bound for the battlefield as reinforcements for some decimated Confederate unit. He was surprised no officer ordered him to go with them. True, he was wearing civilian clothes, but many of the troops wore only bits and pieces of uniforms and were hardly distinguishable from civilians themselves. Cory walked across the fort toward the sutler's store, stumbling occasionally from sheer exhaustion.

Farrell must have seen him coming, because the captain hurried out of the building to meet him and caught hold of his shoulders. "Cory! Are you all right?"

"Not a scratch." With a humorless grin, Cory realized that was true. After everything that had happened, after hours in the thick of the fighting, he hadn't been injured at all, not even a turned ankle or a scraped palm when he'd tripped and fallen.

"My God, when I realized you weren't in the fort, I . . . I didn't know what to think."

"I went with General Pillow's men. We took the fight to the Yankees." Strange how hollow that sounded now, he thought.

"What happened?"

Cory shook his head. "We shot Yankees, and they shot us. That's all I know."

"Come along inside. You could use a drink."

Cory's stomach lurched. Whiskey was the last thing he wanted. He didn't care if he never ate or drank again.

Farrell seemed to be sober, and Cory was glad of that. Maybe it was time they started thinking about getting out of here after all. If they could reach the river and get their hands on a boat, even a rowboat, and make it to the eastern side, they could slip away . . .

An officer striding by snapped an order in their direction, "You two men! Come with me."

Cory looked around in surprise. He recognized the handsome features and sweeping mustaches of Gen. Simon Bolivar Buckner. Buckner motioned impatiently for Cory and Farrell to follow him.

"But, sir," Cory began, "we're not actually—"

Buckner stopped and swung around to glare at him. "Are you disobeying a direct order, soldier?" he demanded. His hand rested on the butt of the pistol at his hip. The holster flap was unfastened so the officer could draw the revolver easily.

Cory opened his mouth to try to explain again that he and Farrell weren't really soldiers, but before he could say anything, Farrell's hand closed around his arm. "No sir, General," Farrell responded. "What is it you need us to do?"

"I need a couple of men to take a message to the Thirtieth Tennessee at the entrenchments. They must hold for a while longer."

"Yes sir," Farrell replied. "We can do that."

Buckner looked curiously at him. "You're a bit old to be in the army, aren't you, trooper?"

"Never too old to fight Yankees, sir," Farrell said briskly.

That brought a smile to the general's face. He took a couple of pieces of paper from inside his coat and handed one each to Cory and Farrell. "Duplicate messages, in case one of you doesn't make it. Godspeed, gentlemen."

Farrell came to attention and saluted. Cory did likewise, more to placate Buckner than anything else. He waited until the general had stridden out of earshot before turning to Farrell, "Have you gone mad, Captain? We're not soldiers!"

"You just came from a battle, didn't you?"

"Yes, but—"

"We'll perform this service for the general, then we'll see what needs to be done next." Farrell eyed the rifle Cory was still carrying. "That looks like a fine weapon. How did you get it?"

"A man died," Cory retorted shortly. Farrell might have been like a second father to him for these past few months, but that didn't mean the captain was always right. "Look, Captain," Cory tried again, "why don't we find some real soldiers to deliver these messages and then you and I—"

"You and I will do our duty to the South," Farrell insisted sternly. He started toward the gate. "Come along, Cory." He didn't look behind him to see if Cory was following.

Cory watched Farrell's back for a moment, then sighed and started after him. Two civilians with one rifle between them, venturing out onto a fiercely contested battlefield.

But if Captain Farrell was mad, then so was Cory Brannon, he supposed. He caught up with the captain and found himself striding along proudly beside the older man.

HE HAD been right earlier, Cory realized as he looked down the slope at the thick woods. They did look like they were on fire. Smoke was everywhere, and the rattle of rifle fire was constant. Cory crouched behind a tree trunk and heard minié balls thudding into the other side of it.

Farrell lay a few feet away behind an outcropping of rock. He kept his head down as bullets ricocheted over him. Amazingly, he was smiling and seemed his old calm, confident self again. The smells and sounds of battle had driven away the agonies with which he had tortured himself over the past nine days.

"Well," he called to Cory over the sound of the firing, "we found the Thirtieth Tennessee."

Indeed they had. Soldiers along the way over the half-mile or so from the fort had pointed them in the proper direction. They were on the Confederate right, facing a strong attack by the Union forces. Wave after wave of the blue-coated foes stormed up to the rifle pits, only to be driven back. But that couldn't last forever, Cory knew. From where he and Farrell had taken cover, only a short distance behind the entrenchments, he had watched as soldier after soldier in butternut brown had run out of ammunition. Soon, one of the charges was going to be successful, and then the Yankees would swarm over the rifle pits.

A saber-wielding officer ran past, and Cory shouted, "Sir!" The officer paused, and Cory extended his hand with the paper clutched in it. "Message from General Buckner, sir!" Take it, he thought. Take it so our job will be done and we can get out of here!

The officer snatched the paper out of Cory's fingers and read it in the fading gray light of the late afternoon. He crumpled it a second later and said, "Hold out? Of course we'll hold out—"

A zing, a thud, and the officer staggered back a step. He looked down at his chest, where blood was already staining his coat, and said hoarsely, "I'm killed." Then he sat down and slowly toppled over backward.

Cory's lips drew back from his teeth in a grimace and he let out a harsh, incoherent cry. He had stopped the officer to give him the message, and now the man was dead. But it wasn't his fault, Cory knew. With all the bullets flying around, no one but God Almighty could be blamed for allowing this to happen.

Instantly, Cory felt ashamed of that thought. If he had voiced such blasphemy around his mother, even at his age, she probably would have taken a switch to his backside. Right now, Cory didn't know who to blame—God, man, the Yankees, the Confederates, pure dumb luck—but he didn't care, either.

"Here they come!" someone shouted from the rifle pit.

This time the Yankees made it. They clambered over the top of the earthworks, sliding and falling down into the trenches, bayonets slashing and thrusting, guns firing at such close range that burning powder ignited uniforms. It was a flaming, screaming, dying mess inside the rifle pits. Cory brought his own rifle up, and as one of the Union soldiers hesitated just an instant too long at the top of the earthworks, Cory shot him. The Yankee toppled backward, falling into the onrushing horde of his comrades.

Then Cory was up, grabbing Farrell's shoulder and pulling the captain to his feet as well. "Come on!" Cory shouted over the pandemonium. "Come on!"

Farrell jerked away from him. The dead officer had dropped his saber on the ground, and Farrell scooped it up. "For the Confederacy!" he shouted as he charged toward the hand-to-hand fighting.

"No!" Cory screamed after him.

"For the *Missouri Zephyrrrrrr* . . . !" Farrell slammed the saber into the chest of a blue-coated infantryman who had just struggled up out of the pit. The man fell to the side, dragging the saber out of Farrell's hand.

Another Yankee was right behind the first one, and he held a pistol in his hand. It spouted flame and smoke. Farrell stumbled back, his coat smoldering from the sparks of the close-range shot. Cory saw the captain falling. Springing forward without thinking, he drove the butt of his empty rifle into the face of the Yankee soldier with the pistol. Bone crunched and the wooden stock shattered, and the man went down.

Cory dropped the gun and bent to grab Farrell's collar. He pulled with all his strength, trying to drag the captain away from the fighting, but his feet slipped on the snowy ground and went out from under him. He sprawled next to Farrell. Their faces were only inches apart, and Cory saw Farrell's lips moving. He couldn't hear anything over the screaming and yelling and gunshots.

At that moment, Cory forgot all about the battle. He wriggled closer, putting his ear next to Farrell's mouth. He understood the words then, heard Farrell rasp, "Good man . . . Cory . . . find Lucille . . . love her . . . tell her—"

Something heavy landed on Cory's back, driving his face against the ground. He felt an arm go around his neck and jerk his head up, drawing his throat tight. He was about to have his throat slashed by a Yankee, he realized.

A gun boomed and the weight fell away as the Union soldier toppled off of him, killed by a lucky shot. Cory rolled over, anxious to get away from the man. He saw Farrell staring sightlessly up at the bare branches of the trees and knew the captain was dead.

"Fall back! Fall back!" someone bellowed.

Cory scrambled to his feet and started running. He wasn't the only one. All around him, motley-colored figures ran for their lives as the last of the Confederate resistance crumbled. Cory didn't look back. There was nothing he could do for the captain now. The fact of Farrell's death hadn't really soaked in yet, and when it did, he might feel bad about leaving his friend where he had fallen, but at this moment, all Cory wanted to do was live to draw breath the next moment, and the moment after that, and the moment after that . . .

GENERAL BUCKNER'S men eventually regrouped, ending the rout, but they could not regain what they had lost. The Yankees still surrounded Fort Donelson and the town of Dover, and they were more in control of their positions than ever before. As night fell, the shelling from the river stopped, but the damage had been done there, too. Many of the fort's guns were out of action.

At the tavern in Dover, next to the Cumberland River, the generals met one last time. Neither Floyd nor Pillow had any desire to be there when the Confederate forces surrendered. Floyd was under indictment in a case stemming from his days as secretary of war under Buchanan, and he feared that the Yankees would simply hang him out of hand. Pillow wanted to be away, too, and he suggested that if each of them took only a

314 • *James Reasoner*

small force with them, they might be able to slip off unnoticed into the night.

Buckner was furious at this discussion, but not as angry as Forrest, who entered the tavern in time to hear Pillow's suggestion. He slammed a fist down on the table where the generals sat and declared, "Surrender to the Yankees? I'll not surrender, and I'll not leave my men behind! My cavalry will cut their way out, or we shall all die trying!"

"You're certainly welcome to try, Colonel," Buckner said coolly. He looked at Floyd and Pillow, who refused to meet his gaze. "It seems that command has devolved onto me. I shall be communicating with General Grant that I wish to discuss terms of surrender. Otherwise, more good men shall die for no good reason."

"No good reason but honor," Forrest grated. He turned on his heel to walk out, then stopped short as he spotted a figure sitting on the floor with his back against the wall near the doorway. The young man's head drooped forward on his chest. "Mr. Brannon?" Forrest asked.

Cory lifted his head wearily and saw the lean cavalry colonel standing before him.

"Where's Captain Farrell?"

"Dead. He was killed in the final charge against the Thirtieth Tennessee."

"A shame," Forrest said. "He was a good man. What are you going to do?"

Cory shook his head slowly. "I don't know."

"Can you ride a horse?"

"What?"

"Can you ride a horse?" Forrest repeated impatiently. "Come with me. We're leaving tonight, to fight the Yankees again another day."

Cory swallowed hard and said, "No, thank you, sir. I'm done with fighting."

For a second, Forrest didn't respond. Then he said, "I see. Good luck to you, then." He left the tavern. His words had been spoken quietly, but Cory had heard something in them. Disgust? Disappointment? Cory didn't know. All he knew was the truth of what he had just told Colonel Forrest: he was through with fighting.

And at that moment, he actually believed it.

DURING THE night Buckner sent his message to Grant, asking to discuss surrender terms. Grant's reply was swift:

Sir:

Yours of this date, proposing armistice and appointment of commissioners to settle terms of capitulation, is just received. No terms except unconditional and immediate surrender can be accepted. I propose to move immediately upon your works.

I am, sir, very respectfully, your obedient servant,

U. S. Grant

CORY WAS still sitting in the tavern early the next morning when hoofbeats sounded outside. Buckner and several junior officers were sitting at one of the tables. The general rose as a tall, dark-haired man with a thick mustache and bushy goatee came into the building, followed by several more men. All the newcomers wore the uniform of the Federal army.

"General Wallace, sir," Buckner greeted him as Cory watched. He wore a faint smile as he indicated the other Confederate officers and said, "It is not necessary to introduce you to these gentlemen; you are acquainted with them all. Would you join us for breakfast? We have corn bread and coffee."

"Thank you, General Buckner," the Union general replied. "It would be my honor." Most of the Yankees sat down with the Confederates and helped themselves from plates of corn bread and pots of coffee on the table. Some of them even took their hats off. The conversation around the table was friendly.

Cory looked on in disbelief. A few hours earlier, these men would have been doing their best to kill each other, and now they were acting like long-separated chums. He would never understand war, he decided, no matter how long he lived.

One of the Union lieutenants came over to him and nudged his foot with a boot. "Outside, Reb," he said. "Prisoners are being collected in the town square."

Cory looked up at him dumbly and repeated, "Prisoners?"

"Go on, damn you." The Yankee put his hand on his pistol. "Don't make me shoot you and ruin General Wallace's breakfast."

On the contrary, Cory thought the young lieutenant really wanted nothing more than a good excuse to shoot him. Cory stood up slowly and said, "I'm unarmed."

"Good. Saves us the trouble of disarming you."

Prodded by the officer, Cory stepped out onto the porch of the tavern. He glanced toward the river flowing nearby. General Floyd had departed that way by boat several hours earlier. General Pillow had planned to take a small detail and try to leave the area by way of a little-used road that he hoped the Yankees hadn't discovered. Cory had no idea how Forrest had planned to get out; he hadn't heard about any fighting during the night, though, so he hoped the cavalryman had made it safely. As for Floyd and Pillow, he didn't really care.

"Keep moving," the lieutenant said. To a Union private standing nearby, he added, "See that this prisoner gets to the town square."

Cory trudged on into Dover, followed by the Yankee private. He might have been able to jump the man and get hold of his rifle, he reflected, but what would be the point? There were Yankees all over the place this morning. He wouldn't get ten yards before one of them shot him down.

Several hundred Confederate prisoners had been gathered in the square in front of the courthouse. Cory joined them, hugging himself against the cold as he stood there in their dispirited ranks. The sun was shining on this Sunday morning, but it was a thin, bitter sunshine with no warmth in it.

"What do you reckon they're goin' to do with us?" asked one of the soldiers.

"Send us up north to some prison camp, is what I heard," another man replied. "Oh, Lordy, when will we ever see the South again?"

Cory didn't know. All he could think about was Lucille. She was somewhere in Nashville, waiting for him to find her.

Waiting for him—and for her father. But Captain Farrell would never come for her. And now, if he was shipped off to some godforsaken Yankee prison camp, it appeared that Cory wouldn't be able to find her, either. Someone had to listen to him, someone had to realize that he wasn't really a soldier . . .

But he had fought beside them, he realized. And more importantly, they had fought beside him, had fought and died beside him. That, more than any uniform or oath or name scrawled in a regimental record book, made him one of them for all time.

The day was a long one. The prisoners had nothing to do but mill around, and even that became difficult as their numbers grew. Cory looked at the mob of defeated Rebels and at the guards around them. There were more Confederates than Yankees, he saw, probably more than twice as many. If they jumped the guards, they could easily overpower the Union soldiers and take their guns . . .

But no one made any move to do so. The prisoners either shuffled their feet or simply stood still, looking around with dull, despairing stares. They were well and truly beaten, these men who only months earlier had been boasting about how one Rebel was worth twelve Yankees in a fight. Looking at them left a bad taste in Cory's mouth.

Only he was no better than they were, he realized bitterly. He had sat in the tavern all night, brooding about Captain Farrell's death and the defeat that the Confederacy had suffered here. He had been sunk as deeply in melancholy as any of these others. A perfect opportunity to fight again had been presented to him in the person of Nathan Bedford Forrest, and Cory had flatly refused the colonel's invitation to join the cavalry. Now, faced with the prospect of spending the rest of the war in a Yankee prison camp, he was beginning to regret that. If he had gone with Forrest, at least he could have died fighting.

Several Yankee officers rode up and looked over the mass of prisoners. Cory noticed them talking animatedly to each other for several minutes, and then one of them gestured to an aide, pointing out several sections of the town square. Once the officer seemed to be pointing directly at him, Cory thought.

An hour later more Union soldiers arrived, carrying rifles with bayonets fixed to the barrels. They moved into the mob of prisoners, splitting them into smaller sections, and anyone who didn't move quickly enough to suit the Yankees was likely to get jabbed by a bayonet. One of the troopers pushed Cory and several other prisoners toward the outer edge of the crowd, cutting them out seemingly at random. When the group was large enough, they were marched away from the square and down a road that led south out of town. They tramped across a wooden bridge over a small creek, then followed the road into an area of woods.

A horrible thought crossed Cory's mind. They were being marched out here so they could be executed, he told himself. The Yankees were going to shoot them down, drag their bodies into the woods, and leave them. He began glancing around wildly. If everyone made a break for freedom at once, there was no way the Yankees could shoot all of them. If they could just reach the trees . . .

"Halt!" the Yankee major in charge of the guards shouted. "Everyone stand right where you are!"

This was it. The shooting would start any second, Cory thought.

The major rode to the front of the group and turned his mount so that he was facing the large group of prisoners. He had bristling red mustaches and pale, freckled skin. He glared balefully at the prisoners for a moment, then said in a loud voice, "If it was up to me, I'd shoot the whole damned traitorous lot of you and be done with it!"

Cory closed his eyes and waited for the shooting to begin. He was too closely packed in with the other prisoners to do anything else.

"But General Grant has decided that as a gesture of goodwill, some of you will be paroled," the major went on. "Besides, there's not room for all you Rebels at Camp Douglas, nor train cars to take you there."

Cory swallowed and opened his eyes. What was that the major had said about some of the prisoners being paroled?

"Lift your right hands," the major ordered. He repeated it when many of the confused prisoners were slow to comply. Finally, hands began to go up, a few here, a few there, until at last all the prisoners were holding up their right hands.

"Repeat after me: I solemnly swear I will not take up arms against the United States of America for a period of one year, so help me God." Again the prisoners were slow to comply, and the major shouted savagely, "Say it, you damned Rebel dogs!"

Hoarsely, one man began swearing the oath, stumbling over the words as he tried to get them right. More joined in, then more and more, until the words no longer made sense but were just a jumble of sound.

Cory's lips moved and noises came out, but he was never sure what they were. His throat was too clogged with bitterness for him to worry about coherence.

When the oaths all died away, the major slid his saber out of its scabbard and pointed down the road. "You're free men," he proclaimed. "But if we ever see any of you with a gun in your hands, you'll be dead men! Now get the hell out of here!"

Some of the prisoners—former prisoners, they were now—began trudging down the road. Suddenly, one of the men began to trot, then broke into a full-fledged run. Others followed him, some shouting, some crying, some running in stony silence. Those men hurrying down the road were probably going home, Cory thought. They had been the recipients of a double miracle: not only had they survived the fighting, but now they had been freed and didn't even have to face the grim prospect of years in a Yankee prison camp. They were men who had somewhere to go.

So did he, Cory realized. Somewhere down that road was Nashville. Somewhere down that road was Lucille . . .

So he, too, embraced the miracle and ran with the other men into the gathering twilight.

Chapter Nineteen

NASHVILLE WAS FULL OF Yankees. Cory saw the blue-uniformed Union soldiers almost everywhere as he walked down the street. During the two days he had walked from Dover to Nashville along the Cumberland River road, he had heard rumors that the Confederate army under Albert Sidney Johnston was evacuating the Tennessee capital, but he had refused to believe it. Surely Johnston would make a stand. Surely he would not abandon Nashville to the Yankees.

But that was exactly what had happened. Cory had been able to tell that when the route he was following reached a crossroad leading into Nashville from the north. The road was full of supply wagons, ambulances, artillery caissons, and rank after rank of marching soldiers, all of them in Union blue. The Yankees were flowing into Nashville like a river.

Cory didn't join them. He turned off and found a trail that paralleled the road, but he was still close enough to see the occupying army as it moved on south. He saw an old woman, who had been sitting on the porch of her log cabin beside the road, lift a sawed-off shotgun from the folds of her dress and open fire on the soldiers, screaming curses at the Yankees as she did so. A couple of men went down from the charge of buckshot. The old woman broke open the scattergun and tried to reload, but before she could, a Yankee officer rode up and shot her through the head with a pistol. Even from where Cory was, he could see the bright red blood on her bonnet as she lay in the dirt in front of the cabin.

The sight left Cory shaken. All he wanted to do was find Lucille and take her as far away from this war as possible.

During the long walk, he had debated with himself what he would do if the opportunity to fight the Yankees arose once more. He had sworn an oath not to take up arms against them—or had he? He honestly could not remember what words had come out of his mouth. Even if he had, did an oath given to a Yankee really count for anything? Honor demanded that a man keep his word, and so did the Good Book. But duty insisted that a man defend his home against invaders, and the Yankees were nothing less than godless marauders.

The thing to do, he told himself again, was to find Lucille and leave. He had fought in two battles; that was enough. The Confederacy could ask no more of him.

The Yankees were looting Nashville when Cory got there, although he supposed they thought of it as merely commandeering supplies. Not that there was much to loot, he realized after a while. Much of the citizenry had fled on the heels of General Johnston's troops, taking with them whatever they could carry, whatever was left after Johnston's men had finished their appropriations. There were a lot of civilians left, though, and Cory hoped Lucille's aunt and uncle were among them. He knew where they lived, having been told the address several times by Captain Farrell. He arrived in Nashville in the late afternoon, and it was early evening by the time he located the place he was looking for.

The house was large but not overly fancy, a whitewashed frame structure with a porch that ran all along the front and down both sides of the house. The windows were dark and uninviting. Cory frowned as he opened the gate in the picket fence and walked up to the steps. He climbed to the porch and went to the front door. There was a brass lion's-head knocker on it, but he used his fist instead, thumping heavily on the panel. No response came from inside.

Cory knocked again, louder and harder this time. "Lucille!" he called. "Lucille, are you in there? Is anybody home?"

"Mister! Hey, mister!"

The voice came from behind Cory, not from inside the house as he had hoped. He turned and saw an elderly black man just beyond the fence. The man had been pulling a cart filled with what appeared to be scrap metal along the street.

"Ain't nobody to home there," the man said as he gestured toward the house. "Dey all done gone."

Cory went back down the walk and tightly gripped the gate. "Gone?" he repeated. "Gone where?"

The man shrugged. "I don't know, boss. Massa Charles, him an' my massa was good frien's, an' I heerd him say him an' his family was gettin' out whilst the gettin' was good, 'fore Gen'ral Buell and the Yankee army gets here."

Wearily, Cory scrubbed a hand over his face. "His family, you said. Was there a young woman with them? A girl? Really pretty, with hair the color of honey?" Cory's voice almost broke as the description called up a vivid image of Lucille in his mind's eye.

The man nodded. "Sure, I 'member her. She come to visit not long 'go. Sure, she went with 'em."

"But you don't have any idea where they went?"

"Naw, sir, I surely don't."

Cory felt desperation growing inside him. "Your master," he pressed on. "Maybe he'd know, if he was a friend of the family?"

The man threw back his head and laughed. "My massa done gone, too, boss. Long gone. Said he wasn't goin' to wait here for the Yankees to come an' kill ever'body."

"Then what are you doing still here?"

"Massa left me. Said they couldn't carry 'nough supplies to feed a worthless ol' nigger like me. So I been goin' 'round pickin' up scrap metal to sell to the Yankees so's they can melt it down an' make bullets out'n it."

Cory felt a surge of anger. "You're helping the Yankees? What's the matter with you? This is your home, too, damn it!"

The man stared at Cory for a moment, then shook his head. "Jus' tryin' to help you out, boss. I'll be movin' on now." He started tugging the cart down the street.

Cory fought down the rage that welled within him. The old man was right. In a lot of ways, this wasn't his fight, no matter how the Northerners tried to make it all sound so simple. Cory called after the man, "Thank you," which drew a glance of surprise and then a slight wave of farewell from him.

Cory went back to the house and sat down on the porch steps. Now that it was darker, he could see that there were no lights in any of the houses along this street. Everyone in the neighborhood had fled.

Soon enough the Yankees would probably take over these houses and use them to quarter troops. Nashville was firmly in Union hands. There was nothing here for him, Cory told himself, not a damned thing.

He looked up at the sky while the stars were beginning to appear. Somewhere, those same stars were looking down on Lucille. But the South was a big place, and she and her relatives could have gone anywhere. Finding them might prove next to impossible.

But he wouldn't give up, Cory vowed. Not ever.

THE BACKLASH to the loss of Fort Donelson was tremendous. Furious Southern politicians called for the ouster of Johnston, stopping just short of demanding his head on a platter. Johnston had not given up, though, and since Jefferson Davis ignored the protests of the politicians and left Johnston in charge of the Confederacy's western armies, he began making plans to strike back at the Yankees.

Beauregard, too, believed that it was important to go on the offensive once more, before the Federals had a chance to take a firm grasp on the newly captured territory. That would require more men and arms, and the South, having had its false hopes of a quick and easy victory dashed by the loss of Forts Henry and Donelson, began to respond. Subsequent events had not delivered on the early promise of Manassas, and now people understood that the war was going to be longer and harder than they had first thought. New recruits began to pour in, and the few factories the South possessed were working around the clock to produce more weapons and ammunition. The army began to grow, and Johnston and Beauregard put their heads together and debated what to do with this influx of manpower.

The Confederate army, they decided, would congregate at Corinth, in northeastern Mississippi, near the Tennessee border. It was a railroad town, an important junction controlling much of the rail traffic throughout the valley of the Tennessee River, and as such, was a tempting target for the Union men. The river itself was some twenty miles from Corinth, and there, just above the point where Tennessee, Alabama, and Mississippi all came together, was the small town of Pittsburg Landing.

Near Pittsburg Landing was a small log house of worship that was seldom used these days, but those who had built the church had given it a name from the Bible, a name that meant "place of peace."

It was called Shiloh Church.

CORY HEFTED the bag of flour and tossed it from the wagon onto the ground. The wagonload of supplies had come in earlier that afternoon, and a Yankee lieutenant had ordered him to unload it so that the cooks could get what they needed and go back to their kitchens.

Cory wiped the back of his hand across his forehead, which was beaded with sweat. The weather was warm for the middle of March, but that didn't mean anything. It might turn cold again at any time. This was a changeable season, Cory thought.

He was living proof of that. He had fought the Yankees at Henry and Donelson, and now he was working for them.

But not willingly. Like many of the other civilians left in Nashville, his services were commandeered by the Yankees whenever there was any manual labor to be done, such as unloading these sacks of flour. Half a year earlier, he had been loading and unloading cargo on the docks of New Madrid. Since then, he had become a riverman, had had dreams of someday being a pilot, maybe even the captain of his own riverboat, and had fallen in love with Lucille.

Now the *Zephyr*, what little was left of her, was on the bottom of the Tennessee River, Lucille was gone God only knew where, and he was grunting and sweating as he lifted the heavy bags of flour. He guessed there was some truth to that old saying about how the more things changed, the more they stayed the same.

He hadn't been idle during the past month since reaching Nashville. He knew that Lucille's uncle, Charles Thompson, had been a businessman, a buyer and seller of real estate. Cory had gone up and down the streets, inquiring of the owners of the few businesses that remained open if they knew Thompson. Some of them had been acquainted with him, but not well enough to say where he might have gone after leaving Nashville. He had haunted the neighborhood where Lucille's aunt and uncle had lived, hoping to meet someone who might give him a lead. Nothing had worked, and as Cory expected, the Yankees moved in and made barracks out of the houses. After that, he avoided the area. An uneasy truce existed between the soldiers and the citizens of the town. There were occasional shootings, as Tennesseans ambushed Yankees who were foolish enough to let themselves be caught alone. When the snipers were caught, they were sometimes hanged and sometimes executed by a firing squad. Sabotage and arson also took place from time to time, and the Yankees were afraid that Rebel spies were still lurking around town, as they no doubt were. So Cory didn't want to give any of the Union soldiers an excuse to be suspicious of him. A suspicious Yankee was likely to be a dangerous Yankee.

He finished unloading the flour and stacking the bags on the sidewalk. The sun was beating down hotly overhead, and the lieutenant who had given him the job was standing in the shade of an awning in front of a nearby building, talking to a woman who had been going down the street. The officer wasn't paying any attention to Cory, so he slipped underneath the wagon and leaned back against one of the wheels, glad for the chance to rest a moment in the shade himself.

He had been there for several minutes, his eyes closed, when he felt the wagon move slightly on its leather thorough-braces. Someone must have leaned on it, Cory thought as he opened his eyes. He looked over and saw two pairs of black, polished, high-topped boots on the other side of the wagon. A few inches of blue uniform trousers were visible above the top of the boots. Two Union soldiers, officers to judge by their footwear, had paused there to talk, and one of them was likely resting an elbow on the sideboard of the wagon.

". . . place called Pittsburg Landing," one of them was saying. "From there we'll move on to Corinth."

"That's where we'll catch the Rebs?"

"Yes, and maybe we'll wipe them out this time. Once General Buell's army is added to that of Grant's, we'll out-number them two to one."

"And you're sure the orders have come down?"

"I had it straight from one of Buell's aides. We'll be on the move within a day. I just thought you'd like a little advance warning. I know I always appreciate knowing when I have to have my men ready to move."

"Certainly. I appreciate it, Captain." The second officer laughed. "I hope there's some real action this time. I'm getting tired of these Rebs just running away from us all the time."

"They can run all the way to the Gulf of Mexico as far as I'm concerned."

Cory sat there silent and motionless, not wanting to betray his presence. If the Yankees knew he was under here listening to their conversation, they would surely think he was a spy, even though his eavesdropping had been entirely inadvertent.

He had heard Yankees talking over the past few weeks and knew that their confidence ran high. They wanted to smash the Confederacy and bring the war to a quick end, and many of them truly believed that was possible. Cory was vaguely familiar with the places he had just heard mentioned: Pittsburg Landing and Corinth. Grant was said to be at Pittsburg Landing with forty thousand men. Corinth was rumored to be the place where the Rebel forces were gathering, although the Yankees did not know that for certain. If what Cory had heard was true—if the troops now occupying Nashville under the command of Don Carlos Buell were to move west to Pittsburg Landing, then any Confederate forces in the vicinity of Corinth would be unable to stand against them. Cory had no idea how the war was going in the East, but if Grant and Buell were to strike the Confederate army at Corinth in a quick, combined attack, it might well be the end of the war in the West.

He stayed where he was until the officers had moved on, then slipped out from under the far side of the wagon. Trying not to look furtive, he started to walk away.

"Hey! You!"

Cory stopped, recognizing the voice of the lieutenant who had ordered him to unload the wagon in the first place. He turned slowly, fearing that the officer had noticed him listening to the other Yankees. The lieutenant was striding toward him, hands clasped behind his back.

When the Yankee was only a few feet away, he brought his hands around into sight and flipped something in the right one toward Cory. Instinctively, Cory caught the object and realized that it was a coin. A Yankee coin.

"Good job, boy," the lieutenant said. He was no older than Cory and turned away with a smirk on his lips.

Cory felt like throwing the coin and hitting the Yankee in the back of the head with it. Instead, he clenched his fist tighter around it and stood there until the officer was gone. Then he lifted his hand, opened it, and stared at the Yankee money for a moment before dropping it at his feet. Let someone else scramble for it, he thought. He was getting out of Nashville. The time had come to admit that he would never find Lucille the way he was going about it. He might never see her again. But he had another goal in mind now.

He was going to Corinth, to warn the Confederate army that General Buell was on the way.

WALKING TO Mississippi sounded a lot easier than it really was. A main road led south from Nashville into Alabama, where it intersected another road that ran west to Corinth. That was the route Cory chose, fearing that he would get lost if he took out cross-country. He didn't want to spend days blundering around the river bottoms when time might be crucial.

Getting out of Nashville to begin with meant slipping through the Union picket lines. That wasn't too hard. Most of the Yankee soldiers were convinced they had this war won; all that was left was the mopping up. Some of them dozed on sentry duty, confident that there was no danger. Once Cory figured out which ones they were, he was able to glide silently past their positions in the darkness.

General Buell sent out a few cavalry patrols to watch the roads south of Nashville, but not many. Cory avoided them with ease, taking to the underbrush whenever he heard hoofbeats coming up behind him. There were plenty of creeks to provide water, and though they were often muddy from the spring rains, at least he wouldn't die of thirst. He was hungry a lot of the time, subsisting only on what he was offered by the farmers who were still stubbornly working their land despite the war. Though many of them were on the verge of starvation themselves, they freely shared what they had once they found out Cory was a veteran of the battles at Henry and Donelson. Sometimes he slept in barns, and sometimes he found himself curled up in a thicket of brush with nothing to cover him except leaves. He was cold and hungry, tired and sore.

But he was going somewhere, and he had a reason to be doing something again. That felt good.

All told, he was on the road a little more than two weeks. He wasn't sure exactly what the date was, but he thought it was early April. Six weeks had passed since the fall of Fort Donelson, six weeks since the death of Captain Farrell. In that time, Cory had lost the weight he'd gained during his time on the *Zephyr.* He was gaunt again, little more than a walking scarecrow. His beard was ragged and untrimmed, his hair matted. When he drank from one of the rare streams that was clear enough to throw his reflection back at him, he barely recognized the hollow-eyed man he saw there.

As a matter of fact, he looked a lot like many of the Confederate soldiers he saw as he finally walked into the huge camp just outside Corinth.

He tugged on the sleeve of the first officer he saw, an infantry major with crossed rifles insignia on his campaign cap. The major turned sharply toward him and barked, "What the hell do you think you're doing, soldier? Never lay hands on an officer!"

"Not a soldier," Cory croaked. He wasn't used to talking much these days. "I've just come from Nashville. I'm looking for somebody in charge."

"Would you like to speak to General Johnston or General Beauregard?" the major sneered sarcastically. "They're both here, you know."

"You don't understand. I know what the Yankees are going to do." Cory decided to go ahead and tell this man, thinking that was probably the only way he'd be able to get an audience with Johnston or Beauregard. "General Buell is coming from Nashville with all his men. They'll outnumber you two to one."

"Yes, yes," the major scoffed impatiently. "Our scouts told us that days ago. Now, unless there's something else, I'm busy."

Cory's jaw dropped open. He had walked all the way from Nashville, worn blisters on his feet, and nearly starved to death, all to inform Johnston and Beauregard of something they already knew. In fact, from the way things were bustling around this camp, they not only knew about Buell's maneuver, they planned to do something about it.

When Cory didn't say anything else, the major stalked away on whatever errand he had been carrying out before Cory stopped him. Cory stood there, shaking his head slowly. Once more, his best efforts had been for nothing, through no real fault of his own. Despite his weariness, he began to feel angry. Was nothing in his life ever going to work out the way he wanted it to? Was he always doomed to failure?

"Cory Brannon. It is you, isn't it?"

He turned to see Nathan Bedford Forrest standing there. The colonel looked as dashing as ever in his cavalry uniform. He had a pair of gloves in one hand, and he slapped them lightly against the palm of the other hand as he went on. "I noticed you standing there but almost didn't recognize you. How did you get here from Fort Donelson?"

"Walked," Cory said simply. "First to Nashville, then here."

"I heard that the Yankees sent most of the prisoners to a camp up near Chicago. I supposed that was where you wound up after you turned down my invitation."

Cory shook his head. "They paroled me and a few others. I thought they were going to shoot us, but they let us go." He felt a quickening of his heartbeat. Oath or no oath, he felt himself gripped once again by the excitement of wanting to fight the Yankees and drive them out of the Southern homelands. "About that invitation . . ."

"I'm sorry, Cory," Forrest cut in before he could go on. "I don't have a horse for you now. So unless you have a mount of your own, I'm afraid I can't use you."

Cory's spirits sank, only to rise again as Forrest continued, "But if you can still shoot, I think I can come up with a musket you can have. I'm sure any of the infantry units here would be glad to have you as a member."

"Thank you, Colonel. I . . . I really want to fight Yankees."

"That's the spirit we need around here," Forrest smiled. "Come with me."

Cory walked beside the cavalryman across the camp, and as he did so, Forrest told him how his cavalry had taken a little-used road out of Fort Donelson, prepared to cut their way through the Yankee lines with their sabers if necessary. However, Forrest and his men had encountered no Union resistance. In fact, the biggest obstacle they'd had to overcome was a stretch of road that was underwater from the recent rains. But all of them had made it safely away from the fort and galloped to Nashville, where they found a near-riot going on as fear-crazed citizens who had heard about the Union advance on the city tried to loot the remaining military stores. General Floyd, who had taken charge in Nashville after fleeing Fort Donelson, was doing nothing to put a stop to the chaos.

Forrest had stepped in, restored order to the city, and kept the mobs at bay while his men gathered up the remainder of the military supplies. Those supplies had been brought here to Corinth, where they helped feed and arm the rapidly growing Confederate army of the West.

"Well, that's my story," Forrest concluded as they reached the area of the camp where his cavalry troops were gathered. "What about you? Did you ever find Miss Farrell?"

Cory had to shake his head. "She and her aunt and uncle had left Nashville by the time I got there. I don't have any idea where they went."

"I expect they're all right, wherever they are."

"I hope so," Cory replied.

Forrest said to one of his men, "Asa, bring me that old musket that belonged to Thaddeus." When the trooper had brought the weapon, Forrest handed it to Cory. "It's so old, it might have been carried in the first American Revolution, by one of the patriots who threw off the yoke of British oppression just as we're trying to throw off that of the North. But it's been converted to cap-and-ball, so you can use regular cartridges for it."

Cory hefted the musket, admiring the fine scrollwork on the polished stock. "What happened to the man who owned it? Another victim of the croup?"

"Actually, no. He was a scout who was killed by a Yankee patrol a few days ago. I'd thought to keep the musket myself, but I think you'll put it to better use. Fighting on horseback as I do, I'm more inclined to pistols and sabers than I am to long arms."

"Thank you," Cory said. Now that he had a weapon, it seemed that his mind was made up. He would help the Confederates fight the Yankees. After that . . .

Well, there might not be an after that, of course, but if there was, he would go back to searching for Lucille, though right now he wasn't quite sure how to go about it.

"Come along," Forrest directed. "I'll introduce you to Major Hardcastle of the Third Mississippi Infantry. I'm sure he can find a job for you."

CORY'S BELLY rumbled hungrily in the predawn gloom. He had thought that when he reached the Confederate camp, surely there would be something for him to eat, but that had not been the case. It was a line of hungry men that advanced steadily through the fields.

But that was all right, their officers had assured him. Before today, April 6, 1862, was over, they would be dining on the food left behind by fleeing Yankees.

Major Hardcastle's infantrymen were heading northeast across fields dotted with groves of trees and cut by creeks that

336 • *James Reasoner*

ran through brush-choked ravines. All the units of the Confederate army had finally finished moving into position the
night before, after Cory had found himself unofficially a
member of the Third Mississippi Infantry Battalion. He still
had not actually enlisted in the army, though he had been prepared to do so if necessary. But Colonel Forrest had simply
told Major Hardcastle that he had another man for him, and
Hardcastle had immediately put Cory to work standing guard
without even asking if Cory was a member of the army.
Forrest had waved good-bye to him, one eye drooping in a
sardonic wink.

Cory had been disappointed that there were no rations, but
by now he was used to being hungry. He'd managed to grab a
little sleep after his tour of walking a picket line was over, and
then with all the other men, he'd been awakened early this
morning and told to move up.

Now, as the sky lightened, Cory glanced up and saw that
there were only a few clouds. The day would be sunny and
warm, he thought, a perfect spring day.

"Skirmishers forward!" Major Hardcastle called softly.

Cory was in the front lines of the marching men, so he went
ahead with the others who responded to the major's order.
They came out of some trees and started across a broad, open
field. The sun poked itself up from behind another line of
trees to the east. Its rays reflected redly off something on the
other side of the field.

Bayonets and rifle barrels, Cory realized. The sun was
reflecting on bayonets and rifle barrels and the brass insignia
on campaign caps and the saber being brandished by a man
who stood there wearing a blue coat . . .

There were Yankees over there!

Cory went to a knee, bringing the old flintlock musket to his
shoulder. All along to his right and left, the other skirmishers
were also crouching and aiming. Cory saw more Union soldiers
coming toward him now, their blue-clad figures emerging from

the shadows under the trees. They came on at a steady pace, seeming not to have even noticed the Confederate skirmishers.

"Fire!" someone shouted, and Cory fired.

He had the musket aimed at one of the Yankees, but as the weapon roared and kicked back against his shoulder, the smoke that puffed from its muzzle obscured his vision. He couldn't tell if he had hit anything or not. He quickly started reloading. In the distance, someone screamed. A warm breeze swept over the field, partially clearing the smoke, and as Cory lifted the musket again, he saw that some of the Yankees were down. He fired again, aiming at the saber-wielding officer this time, but again, he was momentarily blinded and couldn't tell if his shot had found its target.

Then someone began calling, "Fall back! Skirmishers, fall back to the trees!" Cory came up on his feet, turned, and started to run toward the trees. A glance behind him told him that the Yankees were following, shouting out their hatred as they charged across the field after what they must have thought was only a handful of Rebels. But crouching in the brush at the edge of the field were hundreds of Confederate riflemen, and as Cory and his fellow skirmishers reached the brush and threw themselves down out of the line of fire, a volley roared out, the lead scything through the Yankees and cutting down many of them. Their charge was broken.

But the battle that would later be referred to as "the devil's own day" had only begun.

Chapter Twenty

THE LINES WERE FAIRLY well drawn on that beautiful spring morning. The Yankee forces under Grant were camped in a rough triangle on a plateau east of the Tennessee River. On the Union right were troops commanded by Gen. William Tecumseh Sherman, while the center was occupied by a division commanded by Gen. Benjamin M. Prentiss. On the Union left was a mixture of units, most of them from the command of Gen. Stephen A. Hurlbut, though some of Sherman's men were over there, too, as well some under the command of Gen. W. H. L. Wallace. General McClernand's troops were in the rear, while several miles away, at the junction of Snake Creek and Owl Creek, were two of Gen. Lew Wallace's regiments.

The initial clash between Major Hardcastle's skirmishers and the Union patrol was the signal for the Confederate attack to start all across the line. General Johnston had conceived a balanced attack, with the forces of Gen. Leonidas Polk taking the left wing, those of Gen. Braxton Bragg the center, and those of Gen. William J. Hardee the right. Gen. John C. Breckenridge and his men would wait in reserve and go where they were needed.

The attack did not work out exactly that way, because General Johnston, unable to resist the lure of the fighting once the guns began to sound, galloped off toward the front, leaving General Beauregard in the rear to coordinate the movements of the troops. Beauregard operated on a simple but perhaps flawed theory of battle: send more troops to wherever the firing was the loudest. So as the morning of April 6 wore on, the action began to pinch in toward the center. Many of the Union troops on the flanks had fallen back, driven into retreat by the furious charges of the Confederates, but in the center, General Prentiss's men were holding. They, too, fell back, but more slowly than the other Yankees, and when they reached an old wagon road at the edge of some woods, sunken slightly below ground level from years of use, they dug in to make a stand. The road, which had a rail fence alongside it, was also lined with brush. Prentiss's men sprawled on the road and used it for cover, and artillery was brought up and placed just behind the row of brush.

There they waited for the Confederates to catch up to them.

CORY HAD forgotten all about his hunger, though his empty belly sometimes made him feel weak and dizzy for a few moments. His thirst was incredible, though. He had breathed powder smoke all morning until his throat was raw, and his mouth tasted like it was lined with cotton. His lips were black from the powder that got on them when he tore open the paper cartridges to reload, and licking them only made his thirst worse because the powder residue was salty. His shoulder ached from the pounding it had taken from recoil after recoil of the heavy musket.

Yet despite all that, he felt strangely good. The Yankees were on the run, and he was part of it. He was driving the invaders back where they had come from.

The Third Brigade, under Brig. Gen. S. A. M. Wood, of which Major Hardcastle's infantry battalion was a part, had been slugging forward all morning. Cory had taken part in charge after charge, running forward, dropping to a knee to fire and reload, then running again, the Confederate line advancing a few yards at a time. He had lost track of how many men had been killed beside him. Once when he knelt down, he realized that the knee of his trousers was wet. He looked at the ground and saw that he was kneeling in a puddle of blood.

Artillery shells screamed overhead, coming from batteries on both sides. Some of the explosive shells burst in the air, sending shards of metal flying out that shredded anyone near them. Solid shot smashed through the ranks, decapitating men, crushing rib cages, smashing limbs to stubs of bloody pulp. Horses died as quickly and easily as men, throwing their riders or sometimes crushing them as they fell. Minié balls thudded into flesh or ricocheted with a telltale zing of sound. Bugles blew and men shouted, but none of it really meant anything. The battles at Fort Donelson had taught Cory that much. Nothing was important except what was right in front of you. The brains of the man next to you could go flying out of his head, his guts could spill out through his futilely clutching hands, his blood could fall on you like rain, and still you fired at the Yankees and reloaded and fired again until you were in amongst them and slashing right and left with your bayonet and slamming the butt of your weapon into the faces of the blue-clad figures and stumbling forward some more as they retreated and always your mouth was open and you were yelling the awful yell that froze the blood in the veins of the enemy. That was war, and Cory had thought that he knew it well.

By the end of the day, he was an expert.

THE UNION flanks continued to collapse, but along the wagon road, Prentiss's men still held, no matter how many charges the Confederates sent at them. The Rebel gunners finally found the range and poured artillery fire into the area of the road, but while the barrage killed many of the Yankees, the ones who were left fought desperately and withstood the Confederate infantry charge that followed the shelling. Hundreds died there in front of the makeshift barrier. The ground was almost invisible because of the bodies sprawled on it, and there was no way the attacking Confederate soldiers could avoid trampling on the corpses of their fallen comrades. Several times the Southerners came within yards of overrunning the road, but always they were turned back. One Rebel soldier, his uniform soaked with his own blood and the blood that had splattered on him from other men, stumbled out of the fighting and proclaimed that it was like a hornet's nest in there. It was a fitting name.

Just to the east of Prentiss's position, the Yankees moved up through a peach orchard that gave them some cover and tried to form a defensive line. Seeing that, General Johnston was determined to seize the orchard, move his men through it, and strike the Hornet's Nest from the rear. The attack went badly from the beginning, however, as the Confederate troops showed an unusual reluctance to fight. Johnston was forced to urge them into battle personally, galloping through the orchard as bullets and artillery shells whipped through the flowering trees, showering the combatants with peach blossoms. The Yankees' resistance broke, and they fled through the orchard. At the end of the charge, Johnston was flushed with triumph, but a few moments later, his enthusiasm was overcome by loss of blood. He swayed in his saddle, and when aides helped him dismount, they found his right boot full of blood. An apparently minor leg wound had cut an artery, and with no doctor nearby, Gen. Albert Sidney Johnston soon bled to death while leaning against the trunk of one of the peach trees.

The Union troops along the wagon road were still holding out, and rather than throw away more men on futile infantry charges, the Confederates resumed their shelling. This time the bombardment went on for over half an hour. When it ended, only to be followed by one more inevitable charge, the defenders could no longer stand against the onrushing Confederates. Men turned and ran, and the rout was on. Others surrendered and were taken prisoner. It was late afternoon now, April 6. Breaking through the barrier of the Hornet's Nest had taken all day.

And that had given Grant the time to pull the rest of his army back to Pittsburg Landing, hard against the Tennessee River, and regroup them there.

THE CRIES of the wounded were the most awful thing Cory had ever heard. They lay everywhere on the battlefield, some of them covered up by the bodies of dead men. Better to have been killed outright, Cory thought, than to have been badly wounded and left to die in this Gehenna.

He stumbled past a pond that was surrounded by men, some living, some dead, and thought for a moment that it was the setting sun that was turning the water red. He realized a moment later that the dull rust color came from the blood that dripped and trickled and flowed into the pond. Cory was still thirsty—but not *that* thirsty.

He limped, but not from an injury. A Yankee minié ball had torn the heel off his left boot. His trousers were slashed in several places from running through brush, and the briars had scratched the flesh underneath. His coat was in tatters. Dozens of bullets had whipped through it during the day. His hat was long gone, shot off his head in the first charge against the Hornet's Nest. And there was a six-inch long, angry red line on his right forearm, where a piece of shrapnel from an exploding artillery shell had burned a path before whining off to do more damage elsewhere to some other poor bastard. Other than that, Cory had not been hurt, though he had been in the thick of several of the infantry charges against the Yankees ranged along the wagon road.

The luck o' the Irish, John Brannon would have called it, no doubt with a devil-may-care smile. But Cory's father had never lived through anything like today's battle. Cory suspected there had never *been* a battle like this one, at least not in America. Hundreds, maybe even thousands, of men were dead. Thousands were wounded; that was certain. And for what?

Well, they had pushed the Yankees out of the area around Shiloh Church, anyway, Cory reflected.

"Brannon!"

Cory turned and saw Colonel Forrest riding out of the gathering dusk. The cavalryman was leading a riderless horse. He reined in and gave Cory a bleak, savage grin. "Tired of the infantry? I've got a horse for you now."

"I'll take it," Cory blurted. The horse was a rangy, hammer-headed dun with a strip of darker hair down its back. Cory glanced at the animal's legs and realized they were stained with blood from splashing through pools of the stuff. He swallowed and took the reins from Forrest. The strips of leather were sticky, but Cory didn't ask why. He put a foot in the stirrup and swung up. The saddle was splashed with blood, too, but he ignored it.

"I'm glad Hardcastle didn't think to swear you in," Forrest said as he and Cory rode back from the front lines. They passed the remains of a Union camp where, as the Confederate officers had promised that morning, the Southern troops were dining on food left behind by the Yankees. "I'm glad to have you in my bunch, even temporarily."

"Why?" Cory asked, and he couldn't keep the bitterness out of his voice. "I've failed at nearly everything I've tried to do."

"Ah, but you're still alive," Forrest pointed out. "You've succeeded at the most important thing of all: survival."

Cory thought about that and finally nodded. Maybe the colonel was right.

"We should have pushed ahead," Forrest went on, a note of anger coming into his voice. "We could have smashed Grant once and for all."

"Why did we stop attacking?" Cory asked, but he already knew the answer. Exhausted, half-starved, parched for water, low on ammunition, the Confederate troops had given all they had to give for one day.

"Because Beauregard's being cautious for a change," snapped Forrest. "I thought he would see what needs to be done. All he's doing now is giving Grant some breathing room. If Buell gets here tonight . . ." The colonel's voice trailed off ominously.

"I heard someone say that Buell's nowhere near Pittsburg Landing yet. That's why General Johnston and General Beauregard decided they had to go ahead and attack today."

"Johnston's dead, you know."

Cory looked at Forrest in shock. He hadn't heard about Johnston's death.

"Bled to death from a leg wound. Beauregard's running things now."

"My oldest brother was at Manassas. He spoke highly of Beauregard in his letters."

Forrest shrugged. "A general is only as good as his most recent battle. Remember that if you decide to make a career out of the army, Cory."

Cory thought about that and began to laugh, but the sound had little humor in it. After today, he didn't think he wanted to make the army his life's work. But he had luck going for him, there was no denying that. Maybe he would give it some thought—if he lived through the war.

FORREST'S MEN had found some food in a Yankee camp, salted beef and some biscuits nearly hard enough to drive nails. They tasted delicious to Cory anyway. The other cavalrymen welcomed him, though they seemed a bit suspicious of him at first. After all, he wasn't really one of them, just a civilian that Colonel Forrest had for some reason taken under his wing. What was it about him, Cory found himself wondering, that made men such as Forrest and Captain Farrell want to help him? Maybe they saw something in him that he couldn't even see in himself, he decided. He hoped that was the case. He wasn't sure he had proven worthy of

Captain Farrell; he swore to himself that he wouldn't let Colonel Forrest down.

He slept a little, and then Forrest shook him awake, along with several of the other men. The colonel had some sort of bulky garments folded over his arm. "Federal overcoats," he announced. "Put 'em on, boys. They're not too bloody." He began shrugging into one of the captured overcoats himself.

"Why are we doing this, Colonel?" asked one of the troopers.

"We're going on a little trip behind Yankee lines."

Cory hesitated, then finished pulling on the overcoat. It actually felt pretty good, because a cold rain had begun to fall. He didn't much like the idea of spying on the Yankees, but he would go along with whatever Colonel Forrest ordered.

The small group set out on horseback, then dismounted when they neared the Tennessee River below Pittsburg Landing and worked their way forward on foot. The clouds and rain made the night extremely dark. Cory followed the man in front of him by sound as much as sight.

Suddenly, someone put out an arm to stop him, and he realized they had reached the edge of the high bluff overlooking the river. Below and to the north, lights were visible. That was the settlement, Cory thought.

He saw something else he recognized: a steamboat was docked at the western bank of the river. Ramps had been lowered, and Union troops by the hundreds were marching off the steamboat. More boats were on their way from the eastern bank, and their decks were dark with men. Cory was able to tell that much in the glow from the lights that burned on the steamers.

"Buell's men," Forrest hissed. "I feared they would arrive in time to reinforce Grant." He turned away from the bluff and waved his little group of spies back. "Come on, boys, we have to warn Beauregard."

No one challenged them as they returned to the Confederate lines. The disguises had proven to be unnecessary. Cory thought about keeping the overcoat anyway, but he finally decided against that idea. Once he had thought he looked fine in the color blue, but now things were different.

BEDFORD FORREST'S foray into spying went for nothing. He couldn't locate Beauregard, and General Hardee seemed unconcerned that Buell's reinforcements were pouring into Pittsburg Landing to strengthen Grant's army. Most of the high-ranking Confederate officers were convinced that the previous day's defeat had destroyed the Yankees' will to fight.

They were surprised the next morning when the Union army began its counterattack. Grant was able to drive south with forty-five thousand men, and fully half of them were fresh troops that had been brought in during the night by General Buell. The Confederate forces numbered about twenty thousand men, and they were all still exhausted from the fight the day before.

Cory was roused from sleep early in the morning by the crackle of gunfire. He was rolled up in a borrowed blanket, and he had to struggle against it to get to his feet. Along with the dun horse, Forrest had given him a pistol belt with a holstered revolver attached to it, and Cory drew the pistol now as he looked around for the source of the shots. All around him, sleepy members of Forrest's command were doing the same thing.

An infantryman dashed past and shouted, "The Yankees are comin' back!" Bullets whipped through the leaves of the trees over his head. Forrest's men ran for their horses, snapping shots toward the advancing line of blue-clad troopers in the distance. As Forrest swung up on his mount, he roared, "By God, I told them! I told them!"

He wheeled his horse and put it to the gallop, and Cory and the other men followed. Cory hadn't ridden much for a long time, and he was almost unhorsed a time or two. He managed to hang on and even fire some shots toward the Yankees. Forrest led his men at an angle from the battle lines, skirting the Union forces so that he and his riders could rake their flanks. As far as Cory could tell, they weren't doing much good, though. There were too many Yankees, and they were coming too fast. The screams of the wounded and dying had never really stopped during the night, but now the grisly cries intensified as more men on both sides fell to the whistling bullets and exploding shells. Smoke hung thickly over fields where the battle was thought to have been over.

Outnumbered by more than two to one, the Confederates had no choice but to fall back. For the second time in less than twenty-four hours, the blood-soaked ground between Pittsburg Landing and Shiloh Church changed hands.

But when the Union counterattack reached the old log church itself, the Confederate resistance stiffened. Cory and the rest of the cavalry unit watched from a distance as members of the brigade Cory had been with the day before put up a valiant fight around the church. Cory's heart went out to them, even though he really knew none of them. They shared only the comradeship of battle—but that was enough. He found himself heeling his mount forward.

Forrest caught his arm and stopped him from galloping toward the church. "There's nothing you can do for those boys now," he advised bitterly. "This battle was lost yesterday, when Beauregard stopped us from pushing on, and last night when no one listened to what we had to tell them." Forrest shook his head. "Now all we can do is protect the inevitable retreat."

That retreat came in the middle of the afternoon. It was orderly, unlike the rout of the Yankees the day before. Unit by unit the Confederates fell back, eventually surrendering even Shiloh Church, the log walls of which were so riddled with bullet and shell holes that it looked as if a strong wind would blow it down. The Methodists would never again meet here to sing hymns and pray. The very idea of praying over ground so dark with blood seemed wrong to Cory. He knew his mother would probably disagree with him, but as he sat on his horse and surveyed the field—the bloated bodies, the pools of blood, the shell craters like ugly wounds in the earth itself, the thick palls of smoke—he thought that God had truly turned His face away from this place. The only one looking on was the devil, and Satan was probably laughing with delight.

All afternoon as the Confederates pulled back, Forrest's cavalrymen served as gnats, stinging the Yankees to keep them from closing in on the retreating Rebels. Finally the Southerners could go no farther, and they stopped wherever they were to make camp and wait for whatever was going to happen.

The Yankee pursuit had ended, though. They were nearly as spent as the Confederates, and as night fell on April 7, bringing with it more rain, an uneasy truce brought on by sheer exhaustion settled over the torn landscape.

THE GOING was slow over the road. Rain and thousands of hooves and feet had churned it into a muddy mess that threatened to suck down men and horses and wagons. But the next morning the Confederate army made its way along the road anyway, bound for Corinth.

Cory rode alongside Forrest and the other cavalrymen. They were bringing up the rear, watching for any pursuit by the Yankees, pursuit that had not come so far this morning. "Will Beauregard make a stand at Corinth?" asked Cory.

Forrest shook his head, "I don't know. I rather doubt it. We lost so much back there at Shiloh that we need more time to recover. But there'll be another fight sooner or later," he added with a confident nod. "Never you doubt that. There's always another fight."

352 • *James Reasoner*

At least as long as a man was alive, thought Cory. But there was a battle that he could never win, and that one came sooner or later, too.

"Colonel!" one of the man called urgently. "Behind us!"

Forrest, Cory, and the other riders wheeled their horses around. They had passed through an area of fallen trees a few minutes earlier, and now they saw that a line of Union skirmishers were making their way through the same fallen timbers. Forrest's saber rasped on its scabbard as he quickly pulled it free, and he shouted, "Buglers! Blow the charge!" He spurred his horse, and like a shot he was off, galloping toward the Yankees.

Cory rode after him, hoping that he wouldn't bounce completely out of the saddle. His brother Mac, now, Mac should have been a cavalryman, he thought. Mac was a born horseback fighter if ever there was one.

Forrest had his saber in one hand and his pistol in the other as he dashed among the startled Yankees. The skirmishers hadn't expected such a lightning bolt of an attack from what they thought of as a defeated, dispirited army. But they hadn't counted on Forrest and the troopers who rode after him, howling like madmen and slashing left and right with their sabers.

Cory didn't have a saber, but he emptied his pistol at the enemy. During the brief fight among the fallen trees, he caught sight of Union officers, one of whom looked like a general. Cory wondered fleetingly who he was and if he was someone important, never knowing that he had galloped within a hundred yards of William Tecumseh Sherman.

Forrest led the charge all the way, right through the line of skirmishers and up to the main body of the Union forces that were following the Confederates down the Corinth road. The other cavalrymen began falling back, seeing thousands of rifles leveled at them, but Forrest pressed on, caught up in the heat of battle and unaware of his surroundings. Cory reined in and saw what was happening, realizing that Forrest didn't know the extent of the danger surrounding him. After only a heartbeat's hesitation, Cory jabbed the heels of his boots into the dun's flanks and sent the horse leaping forward. "Colonel!" he shouted. "Colonel, look out!"

Forrest was still slashing at the Yankees with his saber. Suddenly, Cory saw him whirl his horse around. Forrest must have realized where he was, Cory thought, but that recognition might have come too late. The Yankees surrounded him like a shrieking, bloodthirsty mob—which, at the moment, was pretty much what they were.

Cory saw Forrest lurch in the saddle as a gun boomed, and his heart almost stopped as he feared that the colonel would topple off his horse and be lost. But somehow Forrest stayed upright and cut his way free of the press of soldiers all around him. He had lost his gun, which was undoubtedly empty anyway, so with his free hand he reached down and grabbed the collar of one of the Yankees, jerking the startled soldier up onto the back of the horse behind him in a display of desperate strength.

With the Yankee trooper as a makeshift shield, Forrest was able to break out of the trap and ride back toward Cory and the other cavalrymen. Cory was out in front, and having reloaded his pistol, he emptied it again toward the Yankees to give Forrest some covering fire. Forrest dashed past him, shoving the hostage off the back of his horse, and shouted over his shoulder, "Come on, Cory!" Cory wheeled the dun and galloped after him. Bullets sang through the air around him, but none of them struck him. His luck was still with him.

They rode on out of range of the Yankees, leaving them far behind before Forrest finally reined in and slid to the ground, his face pale from loss of blood. His tunic was soaked, but he waved Cory and the others off. "I'm fine," he said. "Don't worry about me."

Then he grabbed a stirrup to support himself as a wave of dizziness hit him, and Cory and the other cavalrymen closed in to help him despite his protests.

There was no more firing. The Yankee pursuit slowed to the point that it was no longer a threat. Colonel Forrest had suffered the final wound of the terrible conflict that had stretched over two days and the morning of a third.

The battle of Shiloh was over.

DAYS LATER, on a warm spring night, Cory lay on a cot in a tent on the outskirts of Corinth, where the remnants of the Confederate army had gathered. He looked up as Forrest pushed aside the entrance flap and stepped into the tent. The colonel moved stiffly from the bandages wrapped thickly around his torso. He was expected to recover from the wound he had suffered during the last clash with the Yankees, but it would be awhile before he was his dashing self again.

"I have a bit of news for you, my young friend," Forrest announced as Cory sat up and swung his legs off the bunk.

"Good news, I hope."

"I think so. Remember you told me that Miss Farrell left Nashville with her relatives before Buell got there?"

Cory looked up sharply. "You have news of Lucille?"

"Perhaps. Her uncle's name was Charles Thompson?"

"That's right."

"I saw on a preparedness report to General Beauregard that a man of that name has been appointed a captain in the Mississippi Home Guard at Vicksburg. Now, it might not be the same man," Forrest cautioned as Cory came up off the cot. "It's not an uncommon name."

"But it could be Lucille's uncle," Cory argued.

Forrest nodded. "It certainly could be." He smiled. "I take it you're going to Vicksburg, since you're not now and have never been officially under my command?"

"I have to," Cory said, his voice hoarse with emotion. "The captain told me to find her. I would have promised him I would, but . . . he died before I could."

"I think the promise was made anyway," Forrest acknowledged softly. He clapped Cory on the shoulder. "Go. Take the dun." He pointed a finger. "But don't tell anyone I gave you a horse. *And* I expect you to use it to fight the Yankees when the time comes."

Cory nodded solemnly. "I will. Thank you, Colonel." He turned toward the tent flap.

Forrest caught his arm. "There's time enough to leave in the morning. Get a good night's sleep first. You're liable to need it."

"Sleep?" Cory repeated. "I don't think I can sleep, sir."

"Try. That's an order."

He left the tent, and Cory stretched out again on the cot. Excitement prickled through him. He was sure the Home Guard captain in Vicksburg was Lucille's uncle. He would find her now; he was certain. He closed his eyes, equally certain that sleep would not come.

But it did, and as Cory lay there his mouth curved in a faint smile, and he dreamed of Lucille and of his family and his home.

Chapter Twenty-one

MAC GUIDED THE HORSE with only the slightest pressure of his knees and the gentlest of tugs on the reins. The silver gray stallion responded beautifully, turning more sharply than Mac would have thought possible and launching instantly into a full gallop that sent both horse and rider racing across the field. Mac had ridden plenty of fine horses in his life, but this stallion could do things that Mac had never dreamed a horse could do.

Cordelia clapped her hands in delight when Mac drew the stallion to a halt in front of the farmhouse a few minutes later. She and Henry had been watching from the porch as Mac put the horse through its paces. Even Abigail was standing in the doorway, and while she wasn't smiling, she wasn't frowning in disapproval, either. Of the Brannons still at home, only Titus was missing, and Mac knew where he was. He had seen Titus stumbling into the barn a little earlier in the afternoon, and he felt certain Titus was in there sleeping off another hangover.

"I've got to admit, Mac, I never thought you'd tame that beast," Henry said with a grin. "When we caught him, I thought you had yourself a devil horse."

Not a devil, Mac thought. *A ghost.* But he kept that to himself and said instead, "I knew if I worked with him, I could get him to where I could ride him."

"You do more than ride him," Cordelia said. "It's like the two of you are connected somehow, like two parts of the same thing."

Mac nodded. He knew exactly what she meant, because he had felt the same thing himself at times while he was riding the stallion. Something in him had been missing, and now it was found.

As Mac swung down from the saddle, Henry asked, "What are you going to do with him? There aren't any races to ride in now, not until after the war is over, anyway. And you sure can't make a plow horse out of an animal like that."

"No," Mac agreed, "you can't." He thought about the letters they had gotten from Will, describing life in the army and the battles and skirmishes in which he had taken part. After a long silence, they had finally gotten a letter from Cory a few days earlier, too. It hadn't said much, only that Cory was no longer in New Madrid, Missouri, and that he'd been working on a riverboat for a while before taking part in the battles of Fort Henry, Fort Donelson, and Shiloh. That his little brother had been in the thick of the fighting had come as a surprise to Mac. Cory had always been a peaceable sort. Even though he hadn't gone into detail about any of the battles, all the Brannons had read accounts of them in the Richmond newspapers that found their way to Culpeper, and they had an idea what sort of ordeal Cory must have gone through. They had prayed that the Good Lord would keep him safe.

Now, according to the letter Cory had written from Corinth, Mississippi, he was about to leave for another town in Mississippi called Vicksburg. He hadn't explained why he was going there, but Mac figured it must be something important.

What weighed heaviest on Mac's mind was the fact that he now had two brothers who were fighting the Yankees and defending the South. It had been bad enough when Will had gone off to join the army, but now to know that even happy-go-lucky Cory was part of the effort to drive back the Northern invaders . . .

"Mac, I asked you a question," Henry said, breaking into Mac's thoughts. "What are you going to do with that horse? Nobody can ride him but you."

Mac patted the silver gray shoulder with the powerful muscles under the sleek hide. He took a deep breath and said, "I was thinking he might make a pretty good cavalry horse."